SPIDER'S WEB

Agatha Christie is known throughout the world as the Queen of Crime. Her books have sold over a billion copies in English with another billion in 100 foreign languages. She is the most widely published author of all time and in any language, outsold only by the Bible and Shakespeare. She is the author of 80 crime novels and short story collections, 19 plays, and six novels written under the name of Mary Westmacott.

Agatha Christie's first novel, *The Mysterious Affair at Styles*, was written towards the end of the First World War, in which she served as a VAD. In it she created Hercule Poirot, the little Belgian detective who was destined to become the most popular detective in crime fiction since Sherlock Holmes. It was eventually published by The Bodley Head in 1920.

In 1926, after averaging a book a year, Agatha Christie wrote her masterpiece. *The Murder of Roger Ackroyd* was the first of her books to be published by Collins and marked the beginning of an author-publisher relationship which lasted for 50 years and well over 70 books. *The Murder of Roger Ackroyd* was also the first of Agatha Christie's books to be dramatized – under the name *Alibi* – and to have a successful run in London's West End. *The Mousetrap*, her most famous play of all, opened in 1952 and is the longest-running play in history.

Agatha Christie was made a Dame in 1971. She died in 1976, since when a number of books have been published posthumously: the bestselling novel *Sleeping Murder* appeared later that year, followed by her autobiography and the short story collections *Miss Marple's Final Cases*, *Problem at Pollensa Bay* and *While the Light Lasts*. In 1998 *Black Coffee* was the first of her plays to be novelized by another author, Charles Osborne.

By the same author

The ABC Murders
The Adventure of the Christmas Pudding
After the Funeral
And Then There Were None
Appointment with Death
At Bertram's Hotel
The Big Four
The Body in the Library
By the Pricking of My Thumbs
Cards on the Table
A Caribbean Mystery
Cat Among the Pigeons
The Clocks
Crooked House
Curtain: Poirot's Last Case
Dead Man's Folly
Death Comes as the End
Death in the Clouds
Death on the Nile
Destination Unknown
Dumb Witness
Elephants Can Remember
Endless Night
Evil Under the Sun
Five Little Pigs
4.50 from Paddington
Hallowe'en Party
Hercule Poirot's Christmas
Hickory Dickory Dock
The Hollow
The Hound of Death
The Labours of Hercules
The Listerdale Mystery
Lord Edgware Dies
The Man in the Brown Suit
The Mirror Crack'd from Side to Side
Miss Marple's Final Cases
The Moving Finger
Mrs McGinty's Dead
The Murder at the Vicarage
Murder in Mesopotamia
Murder in the Mews
A Murder is Announced
Murder is Easy
The Murder of Roger Ackroyd
Murder on the Links
Murder on the Orient Express
The Mysterious Affair at Styles
The Mysterious Mr Quin

The Mystery of the Blue Train
Nemesis
N or M?
One, Two, Buckle My Shoe
Ordeal by Innocence
The Pale Horse
Parker Pyne Investigates
Partners in Crime
Passenger to Frankfurt
Peril at End House
A Pocket Full of Rye
Poirot Investigates
Poirot's Early Cases
Postern of Fate
Problem at Pollensa Bay
Sad Cypress
The Secret Adversary
The Secret of Chimneys
The Seven Dials Mystery
The Sittaford Mystery
Sleeping Murder
Sparkling Cyanide
Taken at the Flood
They Came to Baghdad
They Do It With Mirrors
Third Girl
The Thirteen Problems
Three Act Tragedy
Towards Zero
While the Light Lasts
Why Didn't They Ask Evans?

*Novels under the Nom de Plume
of 'Mary Westmacott'*

Absent in the Spring
The Burden
A Daughter's A Daughter
Giant's Bread
The Rose and the Yew Tree
Unfinished Portrait

Plays novelized by Charles Osborne

Black Coffee
Spider's Web
The Unexpected Guest

Memoirs

Agatha Christie: An Autobiography
Come, Tell Me How You Live

SPIDER'S WEB

A NOVEL
ADAPTED BY CHARLES OSBORNE
FROM THE PLAY BY

Agatha Christie

HarperCollins*Publishers*

HarperCollins*Publishers*
77–85 Fulham Palace Road,
Hammersmith, London w6 8jb
www.**fire**and**water**.com

This paperback edition 2001

1 3 5 7 9 8 6 4 2

First published in Great Britain by
HarperCollins*Publishers* 2001

A catalogue record for this book is
available from the British Library

isbn 0 00 651493 6

Typeset by Palimpsest Book Production Limited,
Polmont, Stirlingshire

Printed in Great Britain by
Omnia Books Limited, Glasgow

SPIDER'S WEB

CHAPTER ONE

Copplestone Court, the elegant, eighteenth-century country home of Henry and Clarissa Hailsham-Brown, set in gently undulating hilly country in Kent, looked handsome even at the close of a rainy March afternoon. In the tastefully furnished ground-floor drawing-room, with french windows onto the garden, two men stood near a console table on which there was a tray with three glasses of port, each marked with a sticky label, one, two and three. Also on the table was a pencil and sheet of paper.

Sir Rowland Delahaye, a distinguished-looking man in his early fifties with a charming and cultivated manner, seated himself on the arm of a comfortable chair and allowed his companion to blindfold him. Hugo Birch, a man of about sixty and inclined to be somewhat irascible in manner, then placed in Sir Rowland's hand one of the glasses from the table. Sir Rowland sipped, considered for a moment, and then said, 'I should think – yes – definitely – yes, this is the Dow 'forty-two.'

Hugo replaced the glass on the table, murmuring 'Dow 'forty-two', made a note on the paper, and handed over the next glass. Again Sir Rowland sipped the wine. He paused, took another sip, and then nodded affirmatively. 'Ah, yes,' he declared with conviction. 'Now, this is a very fine port indeed.' He took another sip. 'No doubt about it. Cockburn 'twenty-seven.'

He handed the glass back to Hugo as he continued, 'Fancy Clarissa wasting a bottle of Cockburn 'twenty-seven on a silly experiment like this. It's positively sacrilegious. But then women just don't understand port at all.'

Hugo took the glass from him, noted his verdict on the piece of paper on the table, and handed him the third glass. After a quick sip, Sir Rowland's reaction was immediate and violent. 'Ugh!' he exclaimed in disgust. 'Rich Ruby port-type wine. I can't imagine why Clarissa has such a thing in the house.'

His opinion duly noted, he removed the blindfold. 'Now it's your turn,' he told Hugo.

Taking off his horn-rimmed spectacles, Hugo allowed Sir Rowland to blindfold him. 'Well, I imagine she uses the cheap port for jugged hare or for flavouring soup,' he suggested. 'I don't imagine Henry would allow her to offer it to guests.'

'There you are, Hugo,' Sir Rowland declared as he

finished tying the blindfold over his companion's eyes. 'Perhaps I ought to turn you around three times like they do in Blind Man's Buff,' he added as he led Hugo to the armchair and turned him around to sit in it.

'Here, steady on,' Hugo protested. He felt behind him for the chair.

'Got it?' asked Sir Rowland.

'Yes.'

'Then I'll swivel the glasses around instead,' Sir Rowland said as he moved the glasses on the table slightly.

'There's no need to,' Hugo told him. 'Do you think I'm likely to be influenced by what you said? I'm as good a judge of port as you are any day, Roly, my boy.'

'Don't be too sure of that. In any case, one can't be too careful,' Sir Rowland insisted.

Just as he was about to take one of the glasses across to Hugo, the third of the Hailsham-Browns' guests came in from the garden. Jeremy Warrender, an attractive young man in his twenties, was wearing a raincoat over his suit. Panting, and obviously out of breath, he headed for the sofa and was about to flop into it when he noticed what was going on. 'What on earth are you two up to?' he asked, as he removed his raincoat and jacket. 'The three-card trick with glasses?'

'What's that?' the blindfolded Hugo wanted to know. 'It sounds as though someone's brought a dog into the room.'

'It's only young Warrender,' Sir Rowland assured him. 'Behave yourself.'

'Oh, I thought it sounded like a dog that's been chasing a rabbit,' Hugo declared.

'I've been three times to the lodge gates and back, wearing a mackintosh over my clothes,' Jeremy explained as he fell heavily onto the sofa. 'Apparently the Herzoslovakian Minister did it in four minutes fifty-three seconds, weighed down by his mackintosh. I went all out, but I couldn't do any better than six minutes ten seconds. And I don't believe he did, either. Only Chris Chattaway himself could do it in that time, with or without a mackintosh.'

'Who told you that about the Herzoslovakian Minister?' Sir Rowland enquired.

'Clarissa.'

'Clarissa!' exclaimed Sir Rowland, chuckling.

'Oh, Clarissa.' Hugo snorted. 'You shouldn't pay any attention to what Clarissa tells you.'

Still chuckling, Sir Rowland continued, 'I'm afraid you don't know your hostess very well, Warrender. She's a young lady with a very vivid imagination.'

Jeremy rose to his feet. 'Do you mean she made the whole thing up?' he asked, indignantly.

'Well, I wouldn't put it past her,' Sir Rowland answered as he handed one of the three glasses to the still blind-folded Hugo. 'And it certainly sounds like her idea of a joke.'

'Does it, indeed? You just wait till I see that young woman,' Jeremy promised. 'I'll certainly have something to say to her. Gosh, I'm exhausted.' He stalked out to the hall carrying his raincoat.

[4]

'Stop puffing like a walrus,' Hugo complained. 'I'm trying to concentrate. There's a fiver at stake. Roly and I have got a bet on.'

'Oh, what is it?' Jeremy enquired, returning to perch on an arm of the sofa.

'It's to decide who's the best judge of port,' Hugo told him. 'We've got Cockburn 'twenty-seven, Dow 'forty-two, and the local grocer's special. Quiet now. This is important.' He sipped from the glass he was holding, and then murmured rather non-committally, 'Mmm-ah.'

'Well?' Sir Roland queried. 'Have you decided what the first one is?'

'Don't hustle me, Roly,' Hugo exclaimed. 'I'm not going to rush my fences. Where's the next one?'

He held on to the glass as he was handed another. He sipped and then announced, 'Yes, I'm pretty sure about those two.' He sniffed at both glasses again. 'This first one's the Dow,' he decided as he held out one glass. 'The second was the Cockburn,' he continued, handing the other glass back as Sir Rowland repeated, 'Number three glass the Dow, number one the Cockburn', writing as he spoke.

'Well, it's hardly necessary to taste the third,' Hugo declared, 'but I suppose I'd better go through with it.'

'Here you are,' said Sir Rowland, handing over the final glass.

After sipping from it, Hugo made an exclamation of extreme distaste. 'Tschah! Ugh! What unspeakable muck.'

He returned the glass to Sir Rowland, then took a handker-chief from his pocket and wiped his lips to get rid of the offending taste. 'It'll take me an hour to get the taste of that stuff out of my mouth,' he complained. 'Get me out of this, Roly.'

'Here, I'll do it,' Jeremy offered, rising and moving behind Hugo to remove his blindfold while Sir Rowland thoughtfully sipped the last of the three glasses before putting it back on the table.

'So that's what you think, Hugo, is it? Glass number two, grocer's special?' He shook his head. 'Rubbish! That's the Dow 'forty-two, not a doubt of it.'

Hugo put the blindfold in his pocket. 'Pah! You've lost your palate, Roly,' he declared.

'Let me try,' Jeremy suggested. Going to the table, he took a quick sip from each glass. He paused for a moment, sipped each of them again, and then admitted, 'Well, they all taste the same to me.'

'You young people!' Hugo admonished him. 'It's all this confounded gin you keep on drinking. Completely ruins your palate. It's not just women who don't appreciate port. Nowadays, no man under forty does, either.'

Before Jeremy had a chance to reply to this, the door leading to the library opened, and Clarissa Hailsham-Brown, a beautiful dark-haired woman in her late twen-ties, entered. 'Hello, my darlings,' she greeted Sir Rowland and Hugo. 'Have you settled it yet?'

'Yes, Clarissa,' Sir Rowland assured her. 'We're ready for you.'

'I know I'm right,' said Hugo. 'Number one's the Cockburn, number two's the port-type stuff, and three's the Dow. Right?'

'Nonsense,' Sir Rowland exclaimed before Clarissa could answer. 'Number one's the Dow, two's the Cockburn, and three's the port-type stuff. I'm right, aren't I?'

'Darlings!' was Clarissa's only immediate response. She kissed first Hugo and then Sir Rowland, and continued, 'Now one of you take the tray back to the dining-room. You'll find the decanter on the sideboard.' Smiling to herself, she selected a chocolate from a box on an occasional table.

Sir Rowland had picked up the tray with the glasses on it, and was about to leave with them. He stopped. 'The decanter?' he asked, warily.

Clarissa sat on the sofa, tucking her feet up under her. 'Yes,' she replied. 'Just one decanter.' She giggled. 'It's all the same port, you know.'

CHAPTER TWO

Clarissa's announcement produced a different reaction from each of her hearers. Jeremy burst into hoots of laughter, went across to his hostess and kissed her, while Sir Rowland stood gaping with astonishment, and Hugo seemed undecided what attitude to adopt to her having made fools of them both.

When Sir Rowland finally found words, they were, 'Clarissa, you unprincipled humbug.' But his tone was affectionate.

'Well,' Clarissa responded, 'it's been such a wet afternoon, and you weren't able to play golf. You must have some fun, and you have had fun over this, darlings, haven't you?'

'Upon my soul,' Sir Rowland exclaimed as he carried the tray to the door. 'You ought to be ashamed of yourself, showing up your elders and betters. It turns out that only young Warrender here guessed they were all the same.'

Hugo, who by now was laughing, accompanied him to the door. 'Who was it?' he asked, putting an arm around Sir Rowland's shoulder, 'Who was it who said that he'd know Cockburn 'twenty-seven anywhere?'

'Never mind, Hugo,' Sir Rowland replied resignedly, 'let's have some more of it later, whatever it is.' Talking as they went, the two men left by the door leading to the hall, Hugo closing the door behind them.

Jeremy confronted Clarissa on her sofa. 'Now then, Clarissa,' he said accusingly, 'what's all this about the Herzoslovakian Minister?'

Clarissa looked at him innocently. 'What about him?' she asked.

Pointing a finger at her, Jeremy spoke clearly and slowly. 'Did he ever run to the lodge gates and back, in a mackintosh, three times in four minutes fifty-three seconds?'

Clarissa smiled sweetly as she replied, 'The Herzo-slovakian Minister is a dear, but he's well over sixty, and I doubt very much if he's run anywhere for years.'

'So you did make the whole thing up. They told me you probably did. But why?'

'Well,' Clarissa suggested, her smile even sweeter than before, 'you'd been complaining all day about not getting enough exercise. So I thought the only friendly thing to do was to help you get some. It would have been no good ordering you to go for a brisk run through the woods, but I knew you'd respond to a challenge. So I invented someone for you to challenge.'

Jeremy gave a comical groan of exasperation. 'Clarissa,' he asked her, 'do you ever speak the truth?'

'Of course I do – sometimes,' Clarissa admitted. 'But when I am speaking the truth, nobody ever seems to believe me. It's very odd.' She thought for a moment, and then continued. 'I suppose when you're making things up, you get carried away and that makes it sound more convincing.' She drifted over to the french windows.

'I might have broken a blood vessel,' Jeremy complained. 'A fat lot you'd have cared about that.'

Clarissa laughed. Opening the window she observed, 'I do believe it's cleared up. It's going to be a lovely evening. How delicious the garden smells after rain.' She leaned out and sniffed. 'Narcissus.'

As she closed the window again, Jeremy came over to join her. 'Do you really like living down here in the country?' he asked.

'I love it.'

'But you must get bored to death,' he exclaimed. 'It's all so incongruous for you, Clarissa. You must miss the theatre terribly. I hear you were passionate about it when you were younger.'

'Yes, I was. But I manage to create my own theatre right here,' said Clarissa with a laugh.

'But you ought to be leading an exciting life in London.'

Clarissa laughed again. 'What – parties and night clubs?' she asked.

'Parties, yes. You'd make a brilliant hostess,' Jeremy told her, laughing.

She turned to face him. 'It sounds like an Edwardian novel,' she said. 'Anyway, diplomatic parties are terribly dull.'

'But it's such a waste, your being tucked away down here,' he persisted, moving close to her and attempting to take her hand.

'A waste – of me?' asked Clarissa, withdrawing her hand.

'Yes,' Jeremy responded fervently. 'Then there's Henry.'

'What about Henry?' Clarissa busied herself patting a cushion on an easy chair.

Jeremy looked at her steadily. 'I can't imagine why you ever married him,' he replied, plucking up his courage. 'He's years older than you, with a daughter who's a school-kid.' He leaned on the armchair, still observing her closely. 'He's an excellent man, I have no doubt, but really, of all the pompous stuffed shirts. Going about looking like a boiled owl.' He paused, waiting for a reaction. When none came, he continued, 'He's as dull as ditchwater.'

Still she said nothing. Jeremy tried again. 'And he has no sense of humour,' he muttered somewhat petulantly.

Clarissa looked at him, smiled, but said nothing.

'I suppose you think I oughtn't to say these things,' Jeremy exclaimed.

Clarissa sat on one end of a long stool. 'Oh, I don't mind,' she told him. 'Say anything you like.'

Jeremy went over to sit beside her. 'So you do realize that you've made a mistake?' he asked, eagerly.

'But I haven't made a mistake,' was Clarissa's softly uttered response. Then, teasingly, she added, 'Are you making immoral advances to me, Jeremy?'

'Definitely,' was his prompt reply.

'How lovely,' exclaimed Clarissa. She nudged him with her elbow. 'Do go on.'

'I think you know how I feel about you, Clarissa,' Jeremy responded somewhat moodily. 'But you're just playing with me, aren't you? Flirting. It's another one of your games. Darling, can't you be serious just for once?'

'Serious? What's so good about "serious"?' Clarissa replied. 'There's enough seriousness in the world already. I like to enjoy myself, and I like everyone around me to enjoy themselves as well.'

Jeremy smiled ruefully. 'I'd be enjoying myself a great deal more at this moment if you were serious about me,' he observed.

'Oh, come on,' she ordered him playfully. 'Of course you're enjoying yourself. Here you are, our house-guest for the weekend, along with my lovely godfather Roly. And sweet old Hugo's here for drinks this evening as well. He and Roly are so funny together. You can't say you're not enjoying yourself.'

'Of course I'm enjoying myself,' Jeremy admitted. 'But you won't let me say what I really want to say to you.'

'Don't be silly, darling,' she replied. 'You know you can say anything you like to me.'

'Really? You mean that?' he asked her.

'Of course.'

'Very well, then,' said Jeremy. He rose from the stool and turned to face her. 'I love you,' he declared.

'I'm so glad,' replied Clarissa, cheerfully.

'That's entirely the wrong answer,' Jeremy complained. 'You ought to say, "I'm so sorry" in a deep, sympathetic voice.'

'But I'm not sorry,' Clarissa insisted. 'I'm delighted. I like people to be in love with me.'

Jeremy sat down beside her again, but turned away from her. Now he seemed deeply upset. Looking at him for a moment, Clarissa asked, 'Would you do anything in the world for me?'

Turning to her, Jeremy responded eagerly. 'You know I would. Anything. Anything in the world,' he declared.

'Really?' said Clarissa. 'Supposing, for instance, that I murdered someone, would you help – no, I must stop.' She rose and walked away a few paces.

Jeremy turned to face Clarissa. 'No, go on,' he urged her.

She paused for a moment and then began to speak. 'You asked me just now if I ever got bored, down here in the country.'

'Yes.'

'Well, I suppose in a way, I do,' she admitted. 'Or, rather, I might, if it wasn't for my private hobby.'

Jeremy looked puzzled. 'Private hobby? What is that?' he asked her.

[14]

Clarissa took a deep breath. 'You see, Jeremy,' she said, 'my life has always been peaceful and happy. Nothing exciting ever happened to me, so I began to play my little game. I call it "supposing".'

Jeremy looked perplexed. 'Supposing?'

'Yes,' said Clarissa, beginning to pace about the room. 'For example, I might say to myself, "Supposing I were to come down one morning and find a dead body in the library, what should I do?" Or "Supposing a woman were to be shown in here one day and told me that she and Henry had been secretly married in Constantinople, and that our marriage was bigamous, what should I say to her?" Or "Supposing I'd followed my instincts and become a famous actress." Or "Supposing I had to choose between betraying my country and seeing Henry shot before my eyes?" Do you see what I mean?' She smiled suddenly at Jeremy. 'Or even –' She settled into the armchair. '"Supposing I were to run away with Jeremy, what would happen next?"'

Jeremy went and knelt beside her. 'I feel flattered,' he told her. 'But have you ever really imagined that particular situation?'

'Oh yes,' Clarissa replied with a smile.

'Well? What did happen?' He clasped her hand.

Again she withdrew it. 'Well, the last time I played, we were on the Riviera at Juan les Pins, and Henry came after us. He had a revolver with him.'

Jeremy looked startled. 'My God!' he exclaimed. 'Did he shoot me?'

Clarissa smiled reminiscently. 'I seem to remember,' she told Jeremy, 'that he said – ' She paused, and then, adopting a highly dramatic delivery, continued, ' "Clarissa, either you come back with me, or I kill myself." '

Jeremy rose and moved away. 'Jolly decent of him,' he said, sounding unconvinced. 'I can't imagine anything more unlike Henry. But, anyway, what did you say to that?'

Clarissa was still smiling complacently. 'Actually, I've played it both ways,' she admitted. 'On one occasion I told Henry that I was terribly sorry. I didn't really want him to kill himself, but I was very deeply in love with Jeremy, and there was nothing I could do about it. Henry flung himself at my feet, sobbing, but I was adamant. "I am fond of you, Henry," I told him, "but I can't live without Jeremy. This is goodbye." Then I rushed out of the house and into the garden where you were waiting for me. As we ran down the garden path to the front gate, we heard a shot ring out in the house, but we went on running.'

'Good heavens!' Jeremy gasped. 'Well, that was certainly telling him, wasn't it? Poor Henry.' He thought for a moment, and then continued, 'But you say you've played it both ways. What happened the other time?'

'Oh, Henry was so miserable, and pleaded so pitifully that I didn't have the heart to leave him. I decided to give you up, and devote my life to making Henry happy.'

Jeremy now looked absolutely desolate. 'Well, darling,' he declared ruefully, 'you certainly do have fun. But please, please be serious for a moment. I'm very serious when I say I love you. I've loved you for a long time. You must have realized that. Are you sure there's no hope for me? Do you really want to spend the rest of your life with boring old Henry?'

Clarissa was spared from answering by the arrival of a thin, tallish child of twelve, wearing school uniform and carrying a satchel. She called out, 'Hello, Clarissa' by way of greeting as she came into the room.

'Hullo, Pippa,' her stepmother replied. 'You're late.'

Pippa put her hat and satchel on an easy chair. 'Music lesson,' she explained, laconically.

'Oh, yes,' Clarissa remembered. 'It's your piano day, isn't it? Was it interesting?'

'No. Ghastly. Awful exercises I had to repeat and repeat. Miss Farrow said it was to improve my fingering. She wouldn't let me play the nice solo piece I'd been practising. Is there any food about? I'm starving.'

Clarissa got to her feet. 'Didn't you get the usual buns to eat in the bus?' she asked.

'Oh yes,' Pippa admitted, 'but that was half an hour ago.' She gave Clarissa a pleading look that was almost comical. 'Can't I have some cake or something to last me till supper?'

Taking her hand, Clarissa led Pippa to the hall door, laughing. 'We'll see what we can find,' she promised. As they left, Pippa asked excitedly, 'Is there any of that cake left – the one with the cherries on top?'

'No,' Clarissa told her. 'You finished that off yesterday.'

Jeremy shook his head, smiling, as he heard their voices trailing away down the hall. As soon as they were out of earshot, he moved quickly to the desk and hurriedly opened one or two of the drawers. But suddenly hearing a hearty female voice calling from the garden, 'Ahoy there!', he gave a start, and hastily closed the drawers. He turned towards the french windows in time to see a big, jolly-looking woman of about forty, in tweeds and gumboots, opening the french windows. She paused as she saw Jeremy. Standing on the window step, she asked, brusquely, 'Mrs Hailsham-Brown about?'

Jeremy moved casually away from the desk, and ambled across to the sofa as he replied, 'Yes, Miss Peake. She's just gone to the kitchen with Pippa to get her something to eat. You know what a ravenous appetite Pippa always has.'

'Children shouldn't eat between meals,' was the response, delivered in ringing, almost masculine tones.

'Will you come in, Miss Peake?' Jeremy asked.

'No, I won't come in because of my boots,' she explained, with a hearty laugh. 'I'd bring half the garden with me if I did.' Again she laughed. 'I was just going to ask her what veggies she wanted for tomorrow's lunch.'

'Well, I'm afraid I – ' Jeremy began, when Miss Peake interrupted him. 'Tell you what,' she boomed, 'I'll come back.'

She began to go, but then turned back to Jeremy. 'Oh, you will be careful of that desk, won't you, Mr Warrender?' she said, peremptorily.

'Yes, of course I will,' replied Jeremy.

'It's a valuable antique, you see,' Miss Peake explained. 'You really shouldn't wrench the drawers out like that.'

Jeremy looked bemused. 'I'm terribly sorry,' he apologized. 'I was only looking for notepaper.'

'Middle pigeon-hole,' Miss Peake barked, pointing at it as she spoke.

Jeremy turned to the desk, opened the middle pigeon-hole, and extracted a sheet of writing-paper.

'That's right,' Miss Peake continued brusquely. 'Curious how often people can't see what's right in front of their eyes.' She chortled heartily as she strode away, back to the garden. Jeremy joined in her laughter, but stopped abruptly as soon as she had gone. He was about to return to the desk when Pippa came back munching a bun.

CHAPTER THREE

'Hmm. Smashing bun,' said Pippa with her mouth full, as she closed the door behind her and wiped her sticky fingers on her skirt.

'Hello, there,' Jeremy greeted her. 'How was school today?'

'Pretty foul,' Pippa responded cheerfully as she put what was left of the bun on the table. 'It was World Affairs today.' She opened her satchel. 'Miss Wilkinson loves World Affairs. But she's terribly wet. She can't keep the class in order.'

As Pippa took a book out of her satchel, Jeremy asked her, 'What's your favourite subject?'

'Biology,' was Pippa's immediate and enthusiastic answer. 'It's heaven. Yesterday we dissected a frog's leg.' She pushed her book in his face. 'Look what I got at the second-hand bookstall. It's awfully rare, I'm sure. Over a hundred years old.'

'What is it, exactly?'

'It's a kind of recipe book,' Pippa explained. She opened the book. 'It's thrilling, absolutely thrilling.'

'But what's it all about?' Jeremy wanted to know.

Pippa was already enthralled by her book. 'What?' she murmured as she turned its pages.

'It certainly seems very absorbing,' he observed.

'What?' Pippa repeated, still engrossed in the book. To herself she murmured, 'Gosh!' as she turned another page.

'Evidently a good tuppenny-worth,' Jeremy commented, and picked up a newspaper.

Apparently puzzled by what she was reading in the book, Pippa asked him, 'What's the difference between a wax candle and a tallow candle?'

Jeremy considered for a moment before replying. 'I should imagine that a tallow candle is markedly inferior,' he said. 'But surely you can't eat it? What a strange recipe book.'

Much amused, Pippa got to her feet. '"Can you eat it?"' she declaimed. 'Sounds like "Twenty Questions".' She laughed, threw the book onto the easy chair, and fetched a pack of cards from the bookcase. 'Do you know how to play Demon Patience?' she asked.

By now Jeremy was totally occupied with his newspaper. 'Um' was his only response.

Pippa tried again to engage his attention. 'I suppose you wouldn't like to play Beggar-my-neighbour?'

'No,' Jeremy replied firmly. He replaced the newspaper on the stool, then sat at the desk and addressed an envelope.

'No, I thought you probably wouldn't,' Pippa murmured wistfully. Kneeling on the floor in the middle of the room, she spread out her cards and began to play Demon Patience. 'I wish we could have a fine day for a change,' she complained. 'It's such a waste being in the country when it's wet.'

Jeremy looked across at her. 'Do you like living in the country, Pippa?' he asked.

'Rather,' she replied enthusiastically. 'I like it much better than living in London. This is an absolutely wizard house, with a tennis court and everything. We've even got a priest's hole.'

'A priest's hole?' Jeremy queried, smiling. 'In this house?'

'Yes, we have,' said Pippa.

'I don't believe you,' Jeremy told her. 'It's the wrong period.'

'Well, I call it a priest's hole,' she insisted. 'Look, I'll show you.'

She went to the right-hand side of the bookshelves, took out a couple of books, and pulled down a small lever in the wall behind the books. A section of wall to the right of the shelves swung open, revealing itself to be a concealed door. Behind it was a good-sized recess, with another concealed door in its back wall.

'I know it isn't really a priest's hole, of course,' Pippa

admitted. 'But it's certainly a secret passage-way. Actually, that door goes through into the library.'

'Oh, does it?' said Jeremy as he went to investigate. He opened the door at the back of the recess, glanced into the library and then closed it and came back into the room. 'So it does.'

'But it's all rather secret, and you'd never guess it was there unless you knew,' Pippa said as she lifted the lever to close the panel. 'I'm using it all the time,' she continued. 'It's the sort of place that would be very convenient for putting a dead body, don't you think?'

Jeremy smiled. 'Absolutely made for it,' he agreed.

Pippa went back to her card game on the floor, as Clarissa came in.

Jeremy looked up. 'The Amazon is looking for you,' he informed her.

'Miss Peake? Oh, what a bore,' Clarissa exclaimed as she picked up Pippa's bun from the table and took a bite.

Pippa immediately got to her feet. 'Hey, that's mine!' she protested.

'Greedy thing,' Clarissa murmured as she handed over what was left of the bun. Pippa put it back on the table and returned to her game.

'First she hailed me as though I were a ship,' Jeremy told Clarissa, 'and then she ticked me off for manhandling this desk.'

'She's a terrible pest,' Clarissa admitted, leaning over one end of the sofa to peer down at Pippa's cards. 'But we're only renting the house, and she goes with it, so – '

She broke off to say to Pippa, 'Black ten on the red Jack,' before continuing, ' – so we have to keep her on. And in any case she's really a very good gardener.'

'I know,' Jeremy agreed, putting his arm around her. 'I saw her out of my bedroom window this morning. I heard these sounds of exertion, so I stuck my head out of the window, and there was the Amazon, in the garden, digging something that looked like an enormous grave.'

'That's called deep trenching,' Clarissa explained. 'I think you plant cabbages in it, or something.'

Jeremy leaned over to study the card game on the floor. 'Red three on the black four,' he advised Pippa, who responded with a furious glare.

Emerging from the library with Hugo, Sir Rowland gave Jeremy a meaningful look. He tactfully dropped his arm and moved away from Clarissa.

'The weather seems to have cleared at last,' Sir Rowland announced. 'Too late for golf, though. Only about twenty minutes of daylight left.' Looking down at Pippa's card game, he pointed with his foot. 'Look, that goes on there,' he told her. Crossing to the french windows, he failed to notice the fierce glare Pippa shot his way. 'Well,' he said, glancing out at the garden, 'I suppose we might as well go across to the club house now, if we're going to eat there.'

'I'll go and get my coat,' Hugo announced, leaning over Pippa to point out a card as he passed her. Pippa, really furious by now, leaned forward and covered the cards with her body, as Hugo turned back to address Jeremy. 'What about you, my boy?' he asked. 'Coming with us?'

'Yes,' Jeremy answered. 'I'll just go and get my jacket.' He and Hugo went out into the hall together, leaving the door open.

'You're sure you don't mind dining at the club house this evening, darling?' Clarissa asked Sir Rowland.

'Not a bit,' he assured her. 'Very sensible arrangement, since the servants are having the night off.'

The Hailsham-Browns' middle-aged butler, Elgin, came into the room from the hall and went across to Pippa. 'Your supper is ready in the schoolroom, Miss Pippa,' he told her. 'There's some milk, and fruit, and your favourite biscuits.'

'Oh, good!' Pippa shouted, springing to her feet. 'I'm ravenous.'

She darted towards the hall door but was stopped by Clarissa, who told her sharply to pick up her cards first and put them away.

'Oh, bother,' Pippa exclaimed. She went back to the cards, knelt, and slowly began to shovel them into a heap against one end of the sofa.

Elgin now addressed Clarissa. 'Excuse me, madam,' he murmured respectfully.

'Yes, Elgin, what is it?' Clarissa asked.

The butler looked uncomfortable. 'There has been a little – er – unpleasantness, over the vegetables,' he told her.

'Oh, dear,' said Clarissa. 'You mean with Miss Peake?'

'Yes, madam,' the butler continued. 'My wife finds Miss Peake most difficult, madam. She is continually coming

[26]

into the kitchen and criticizing and making remarks, and my wife doesn't like it, she doesn't like it at all. Wherever we have been, Mrs Elgin and myself have always had very pleasant relations with the garden.'

'I'm really sorry about that,' Clarissa replied, suppressing a smile. 'I'll – er – I'll try to do something about it. I'll speak to Miss Peake.'

'Thank you, madam,' said Elgin. He bowed and left the room, closing the hall door behind him.

'How tiresome they are, servants,' Clarissa observed to Sir Rowland. 'And what curious things they say. How can one have pleasant relations with the garden? It sounds improper, in a pagan kind of way.'

'I think you're lucky, however, with this couple – the Elgins,' Sir Rowland advised her. 'Where did you get them?'

'Oh, the local Registry office,' Clarissa replied.

Sir Rowland frowned. 'I hope not that what's-its-name one where they always send you crooks,' he observed.

'Cooks?' asked Pippa, looking up from the floor where she was still sorting out cards.

'No, dear. Crooks,' Sir Rowland repeated. 'Do you remember,' he continued, now addressing Clarissa, 'that agency with the Italian or Spanish name – de Botello, wasn't it? – who kept sending you people to interview, most of whom turned out to be illegal aliens? Andy Hulme was virtually cleaned out by a couple he and his wife took on. They used Andy's horsebox to move out half the house. And they've never caught up with them yet.'

'Oh, yes,' Clarissa laughed. 'I do remember. Come on, Pippa, hurry up,' she ordered the child.

Pippa picked up the cards, and got to her feet. 'There!' she exclaimed petulantly as she replaced the cards on the bookshelves. 'I wish one didn't always have to do clearing up.' She went towards the door, but was stopped by Clarissa who, picking up what was left of Pippa's bun from the table, called to her, 'Here, take your bun with you,' and handed it to her.

Pippa started to go again. 'And your satchel,' Clarissa continued.

Pippa ran to the easy chair, snatched up her satchel, and turned again towards the hall door.

'Hat!' Clarissa shouted.

Pippa put the bun on the table, picked up her hat, and ran to the hall door.

'Here!' Clarissa called her back again, picked up the piece of bun, stuffed it in Pippa's mouth, took the hat, jammed it on the child's head, and pushed her into the hall. 'And shut the door, Pippa,' she called after her.

Pippa finally made her exit, closing the door behind her. Sir Rowland laughed, and Clarissa, joining in, took a cigarette from a box on the table. Outside, the daylight was now beginning to fade, and the room was becoming a little darker.

'You know, it's wonderful!' Sir Rowland exclaimed. 'Pippa's a different child, now. You've done a remarkably good job there, Clarissa.'

Clarissa sank down on the sofa. 'I think she really likes

me now and trusts me,' she said. 'And I quite enjoy being a stepmother.'

Sir Rowland took a lighter from the occasional table by the sofa to light Clarissa's cigarette. 'Well,' he observed, 'she certainly seems a normal, happy child again.'

Clarissa nodded in agreement. 'I think living in the country has made all the difference,' she suggested. 'And she goes to a very nice school and is making lots of friends there. Yes, I think she's happy, and, as you say, normal.'

Sir Rowland frowned. 'It's a shocking thing,' he exclaimed, 'to see a kid get into the state she was in. I'd like to wring Miranda's neck. What a dreadful mother she was.'

'Yes,' Clarissa agreed. 'Pippa was absolutely terrified of her mother.'

He joined her on the sofa. 'It was a shocking business,' he murmured.

Clarissa clenched her fists and made an angry gesture. 'I feel furious every time I think of Miranda,' she said. 'What she made Henry suffer, and what she made that child go through. I still can't understand how any woman could.'

'Taking drugs is a nasty business,' Sir Rowland went on. 'It alters your whole character.'

They sat for a moment in silence, then Clarissa asked, 'What do you think started her on drugs in the first place?'

'I think it was her friend, that swine Oliver Costello,' Sir Rowland declared. 'I believe he's in on the drug racket.'

'He's a horrible man,' Clarissa agreed. 'Really evil, I always think.'

'She's married him now, hasn't she?'

'Yes, they married about a month ago.'

Sir Rowland shook his head. 'Well, there's no doubt Henry's well rid of Miranda,' he said. 'He's a nice fellow, Henry.' He repeated, emphatically, 'A really nice fellow.'

Clarissa smiled, and murmured gently, 'Do you think you need to tell me that?'

'I know he doesn't say much,' Sir Rowland went on. 'He's what you might call undemonstrative – but he's sound all the way through.' He paused, and then added, 'That young fellow, Jeremy. What do you know about him?'

Clarissa smiled again. 'Jeremy? He's very amusing,' she replied.

'Ptscha!' Sir Rowland snorted. 'That's all people seem to care about these days.' He gave Clarissa a serious look, and continued, 'You won't – you won't do anything foolish, will you?'

Clarissa laughed. 'Don't fall in love with Jeremy Warrender,' she answered him. 'That's what you mean, isn't it?'

Sir Rowland still regarded her seriously. 'Yes,' he told her, 'that's precisely what I mean. He's obviously very fond of you. Indeed, he seems unable to keep his hands off you. But you have a very happy marriage with Henry, and I wouldn't want you to do anything to put that in jeopardy.'

Clarissa gave him an affectionate smile. 'Do you really think I would do anything so foolish?' she asked, playfully.

'That would certainly be extremely foolish,' Sir Rowland advised. He paused before continuing, 'You know, Clarissa darling, I've watched you grow up. You really mean a great deal to me. If ever you're in trouble of any kind, you would come to your old guardian, wouldn't you?'

'Of course, Roly darling,' Clarissa replied. She kissed him on the cheek. 'And you needn't worry about Jeremy. Really, you needn't. I know he's very engaging, and attractive and all that. But you know me, I'm only enjoying myself. Just having fun. It's nothing serious.'

Sir Rowland was about to speak again when Miss Peake suddenly appeared at the french windows.

CHAPTER FOUR

M iss Peake had by now discarded her boots, and
was in her stockinged feet. She was carrying a
head of broccoli.

'I hope you don't mind my coming in this way, Mrs
Hailsham-Brown,' she boomed, as she strode across to
the sofa. 'I shan't make the room dirty, I've left my
boots outside. I'd just like you to look at this broccoli.'
She thrust it belligerently over the back of the sofa and
under Clarissa's nose.

'It – er – it looks very nice,' was all Clarissa could think
of by way of reply.

Miss Peake pushed the broccoli at Sir Rowland. 'Take
a look,' she ordered him.

Sir Rowland did as he was told and pronounced his
verdict. 'I can't see anything wrong with it,' he declared.

But he took the broccoli from her in order to give it a closer investigation.

'Of course there's nothing wrong with it,' Miss Peake barked at him. 'I took another one just like this into the kitchen yesterday, and that woman in the kitchen – ' She broke off to add, by way of parenthesis, 'Of course, I don't want to say anything against your servants, Mrs Hailsham-Brown, though I could say a great deal.' Returning to her main theme, she continued, 'But that Mrs Elgin actually had the nerve to tell me that it was such a poor specimen she wasn't going to cook it. She said something about, "If you can't do better than that in the kitchen garden, you'd better take up some other job." I was so angry I could have killed her.'

Clarissa began to speak, but Miss Peake ploughed on regardless. 'Now you know I never want to make trouble,' she insisted, 'but I'm not going into that kitchen to be insulted.' After a brief pause for breath, she resumed her tirade. 'In future,' she announced, 'I shall dump the vegetables outside the back door, and Mrs Elgin can leave a list there – '

Sir Rowland at this point attempted to hand the broccoli back to her, but Miss Peake ignored him, and continued, 'She can leave a list there of what is required.' She nodded her head emphatically.

Neither Clarissa nor Sir Rowland could think of anything to say in reply, and just as the gardener opened her mouth to speak again the telephone rang. 'I'll answer it,' she bellowed. She crossed to the phone and lifted the receiver. 'Hello – yes,' she barked into the mouthpiece, wiping the top of the table with a corner of her overall as she spoke. 'This is Copplestone Court – You want Mrs Brown? – Yes, she's here.'

Miss Peake held out the receiver, and Clarissa stubbed out her cigarette, went over to the phone, and took the receiver from her.

'Hello,' said Clarissa, 'This is Mrs Hailsham-Brown. – Hello – hello.' She looked at Miss Peake. 'How odd,' she exclaimed. 'They seem to have rung off.'

As Clarissa replaced the receiver, Miss Peake suddenly darted to the console table and set it back against the wall. 'Excuse me,' she boomed, 'but Mr Sellon always liked this table flat against the wall.'

Clarissa surreptitiously pulled a face at Sir Rowland, but hastened nevertheless to assist Miss Peake with the table. 'Thank you,' said the gardener. 'And,' she added, 'you will be careful about marks made with glasses on the furniture, won't you, Mrs Brown-Hailsham.' Clarissa looked anxiously at the table as the gardener corrected herself. 'I'm sorry – I mean Mrs Hailsham-Brown.' She laughed in a hearty fashion. 'Oh well, Brown-Hailsham, Hailsham-Brown,' she continued. 'It's really all the same thing, isn't it?'

'No, it's not, Miss Peake,' Sir Rowland declared, with very distinct enunciation. 'After all, a horse chestnut is hardly the same thing as a chestnut horse.'

While Miss Peake was laughing jovially at this, Hugo came into the room. 'Hello, there,' she greeted him.

'I'm getting a regular ticking off. Quite sarcastic, they're being.' Going across to Hugo, she thumped him on the back, and then turned to the others. 'Well, good night, all,' she shouted. 'I must be toddling back. Give me the broccoli.'

Sir Rowland handed it over. 'Horse chestnut – chestnut horse,' she boomed at him. 'Jolly good – I must remember that.' With another boisterous laugh she disappeared through the french windows.

Hugo watched her leave, and then turned to Clarissa and Sir Rowland. 'How on earth does Henry bear that woman?' he wondered aloud.

'He does actually find her very hard to take,' Clarissa replied. She picked up Pippa's book from the easy chair, put it on the table and collapsed into the chair as Hugo responded, 'I should think so. She's so damned arch! All that hearty schoolgirl manner.'

'A case of arrested development, I'm afraid,' Sir Rowland added, shaking his head.

Clarissa smiled. 'I agree she's maddening,' she said, 'but she's a very good gardener and, as I keep telling everyone, she goes with the house, and since the house is so wonderfully cheap – '

'Cheap? Is it?' Hugo interrupted her. 'You surprise me.'

'Marvellously cheap,' Clarissa told him. 'It was advertised. We came down and saw it a couple of months ago, and took it then and there for six months, furnished.'

'Whom does it belong to?' Sir Rowland asked.

'It used to belong to a Mr Sellon,' Clarissa replied. 'But he died. He was an antique dealer in Maidstone.'

'Ah, yes!' Hugo exclaimed. 'That's right. Sellon and Brown. I once bought a very nice Chippendale mirror from their shop in Maidstone. Sellon lived out here in the country, and used to go into Maidstone every day, but I believe he sometimes brought customers out here to see things that he kept in the house.'

'Mind you,' Clarissa told them both, 'there are one or two disadvantages about this house. Only yesterday, a man in a violent check suit drove up in a sports car and wanted to buy that desk.' She pointed to the desk. 'I told him that it wasn't ours and therefore we couldn't sell it, but he simply wouldn't believe me and kept on raising the price. He went up to five hundred pounds in the end.'

'Five hundred pounds!' exclaimed Sir Rowland, sounding really startled. He went across to the desk. 'Good Lord!' he continued. 'Why, even at the Antique Dealers' Fair I wouldn't have thought it would fetch anything near to that. It's a pleasant enough object, but surely not especially valuable.'

Hugo joined him at the desk, as Pippa came back into the room. 'I'm still hungry,' she complained.

'You can't be,' Clarissa told her firmly.

'I am,' Pippa insisted. 'Milk and chocolate biscuits and a banana aren't really filling.' She made for the armchair and flung herself into it.

Sir Rowland and Hugo were still contemplating the desk. 'It's certainly a nice desk,' Sir Rowland observed.

'Quite genuine, I imagine, but not what I'd call a collector's piece. Don't you agree, Hugo?'

'Yes, but perhaps it's got a secret drawer with a diamond necklace in it,' Hugo suggested facetiously.

'It has got a secret drawer,' Pippa chimed in.

'What?' Clarissa exclaimed.

'I found a book in the market, all about secret drawers in old furniture,' Pippa explained. 'So I tried looking at desks and things all over the house. But this is the only one that's got a secret drawer.' She got up from the armchair. 'Look,' she invited them. 'I'll show you.'

She went over to the desk and opened one of its pigeon-holes. While Clarissa came and leaned over the sofa to watch, Pippa slid her hand into the pigeon-hole. 'See,' she said as she did so, 'you slide this out, and there's a sort of little catch thing underneath.'

'Humph!' Hugo grunted. 'I don't call that very secret.'

'Ah, but that's not all,' Pippa went on. 'You press this thing underneath – and a little drawer flies out.' Again she demonstrated, and a small drawer shot out of the desk. 'See?'

Hugo took the drawer and picked a small piece of paper out of it. 'Hello,' he said, 'what's this, I wonder?' He read aloud. '"Sucks to you".'

'What!' Sir Rowland exclaimed, and Pippa went off into a gale of laughter. The others joined in, and Sir Rowland playfully shook Pippa, who pretended to punch him in return as she boasted, 'I put that there!'

'You little villain!' said Sir Rowland, ruffling her hair. 'You're getting as bad as Clarissa with your silly tricks.'

'Actually,' Pippa told them, 'there was an envelope with an autograph of Queen Victoria in it. Look, I'll show you.' She dashed to the bookshelves, while Clarissa went to the desk, replaced the drawers, and closed the pigeon-hole.

At the bookshelves, Pippa opened a small box on one of the lower shelves, took out an old envelope containing three scraps of paper, and displayed them to the assembled company.

'Do you collect autographs, Pippa?' Sir Rowland asked her.

'Not really,' replied Pippa. 'Only as a side-line.' She handed one of the pieces of paper to Hugo, who glanced at it and passed it on to Sir Rowland.

'A girl at school collects stamps, and her brother's got a smashing collection himself,' Pippa told them. 'Last autumn he thought he'd got one like the one he saw in the paper – a Swedish something or other which was worth hundreds of pounds.' As she spoke, she handed the two remaining autographs and the envelope to Hugo, who passed them on to Sir Rowland.

'My friend's brother was awfully excited,' Pippa continued, 'and he took the stamp to a dealer. But the dealer said it wasn't what he thought it was, though it was quite a good stamp. Anyway, he gave him five pounds for it.'

Sir Rowland handed two of the autographs back to Hugo, who passed them on to Pippa. 'Five pounds is pretty good, isn't it?' Pippa asked him, and Hugo grunted his agreement.

Pippa looked down at the autographs. 'How much do you think Queen Victoria's autograph would be worth?' she wondered aloud.

'About five to ten shillings, I should think,' Sir Rowland told her, as he looked at the envelope he was still holding.

'There's John Ruskin's here too, and Robert Browning's,' Pippa told them.

'They're not worth much either, I'm afraid,' said Sir Rowland, handing the remaining autograph and the envelope to Hugo, who passed them on to Pippa, murmuring sympathetically as he did so, 'Sorry, my dear. You're not doing very well, are you?'

'I wish I had Neville Duke's and Roger Bannister's,' Pippa murmured wistfully. 'These historical ones are rather mouldy, I think.' She replaced the envelope and autographs in the box, placed the box back on the shelf, and then began to back towards the hall door. 'Can I see if there are any more chocolate biscuits in the larder, Clarissa?' she asked, hopefully.

'Yes, if you like,' Clarissa told her, smiling.

'We must be off,' said Hugo, following Pippa towards the door and calling up the staircase, 'Jeremy! Hi! Jeremy!'

'Coming,' Jeremy shouted back as he hurried down the stairs carrying a golf club.

'Henry ought to be home soon,' Clarissa murmured, to herself as much as to the others.

Hugo went across to the french windows, calling to

Jeremy, 'Better go out this way. It's nearer.' He turned back to Clarissa. 'Goodnight, Clarissa dear,' he said. 'Thank you for putting up with us. I'll probably go straight home from the club, but I promise to send your weekend guests back to you in one piece.'

'Goodnight, Clarissa,' Jeremy joined in, as he followed Hugo out into the garden.

Clarissa waved them goodbye, as Sir Rowland came across and put his arm around her. 'Goodnight, my dear,' he said. 'Warrender and I will probably not be in until about midnight.'

Clarissa accompanied him to the french windows. 'It's really a lovely evening,' she observed. 'I'll come with you as far as the gate onto the golf course.'

They strolled across the garden together, making no attempt to catch up with Hugo and Jeremy. 'What time do you expect Henry home?' Sir Rowland asked.

'Oh, I'm not sure. It varies. Quite soon, I imagine. Anyway, we'll have a quiet evening together and some cold food, and we'll probably have retired to bed by the time you and Jeremy get back.'

'Yes, don't wait up for us, for heaven's sake,' Sir Rowland told her.

They walked on in companionable silence until they reached the garden gate. Then, 'All right, my dear, I'll see you later, or probably at breakfast tomorrow,' said Clarissa.

Sir Rowland gave her an affectionate peck on the cheek, and walked on briskly to catch up with his companions, while Clarissa made her way back to the house. It was a pleasant evening, and she walked slowly, stopping to enjoy the sights and smells of the garden, and allowing her thoughts to wander. She laughed to herself as the image of Miss Peake with her broccoli came into her mind, then found herself smiling when she thought of Jeremy and his clumsy attempt to make love to her. She wondered idly whether he had really been serious about it. As she approached the house, she began to contemplate with pleasure the prospect of a quiet evening at home with her husband.

CHAPTER FIVE

Clarissa and Sir Rowland had hardly been gone more than a few minutes when Elgin, the butler, entered the room from the hall, carrying a tray of drinks which he placed on a table. When the door bell rang, he went to the front door. A theatrically handsome, dark-haired man was standing outside.

'Good evening, sir,' Elgin greeted him.

'Good evening. I've come to see Mrs Brown,' the man told him, rather brusquely.

'Oh yes, sir, do come in,' said Elgin. Closing the door behind the man, he asked, 'What name, sir?'

'Mr Costello.'

'This way, sir.' Elgin led the way along the hall. He stood aside to allow the newcomer to enter the drawing-room, and then said, 'Would you wait here, sir. Madam is at home. I'll see if I can find her.' He started to go, then stopped and turned back to the man. 'Mr Costello, did you say?'

'That's right,' the stranger replied. 'Oliver Costello.'

'Very good, sir,' murmured Elgin as he left the room, closing the door behind him.

Left alone, Oliver Costello looked around the room, walked across to listen first at the library door and next at the hall door, and then approached the desk, bent over it, and looked closely at the drawers. Hearing a sound, he quickly moved away from the desk, and was standing in the centre of the room when Clarissa came in through the french windows.

Costello turned. When he saw who it was, he looked amazed.

It was Clarissa who spoke first. Sounding intensely surprised, she gasped, 'You?'

'Clarissa! What are you doing here?' exclaimed Costello. He sounded equally surprised.

'That's a rather silly question, isn't it?' Clarissa replied. 'It's my house.'

'This is your house?' His tone was one of disbelief.

'Don't pretend you don't know,' said Clarissa, sharply.

Costello stared at her without speaking for a moment or two. Then, adopting a complete change of manner, he observed, 'What a charming house this is. It used to belong to old what's-his-name, the antique dealer, didn't it? I remember he brought me out here once to show me some Louis Quinze chairs.' He took a cigarette case from his pocket. 'Cigarette?' he offered.

'No, thank you,' replied Clarissa abruptly. 'And,' she added, 'I think you'd better go. My husband will be home quite soon, and I don't think he'd be very pleased to see you.'

Costello responded with rather insolent amusement, 'But I particularly do want to see him. That's why I've come here, really, to discuss suitable arrangements.'

'Arrangements?' Clarissa asked, her tone one of puzzlement.

'Arrangements for Pippa,' Costello explained. 'Miranda's quite agreeable to Pippa's spending part of the summer holidays with Henry, and perhaps a week at Christmas. 'But otherwise –'

Clarissa interrupted him sharply. 'What do you mean?' she asked. 'Pippa's home is here.'

Costello wandered casually over to the table with the drinks on it. 'But my dear Clarissa,' he exclaimed, 'you're surely aware that the court gave Miranda the custody of the child?' He picked up a bottle of whisky. 'May I?' he asked, and without waiting for a reply poured a drink for himself. 'The case was undefended, remember?'

Clarissa faced him belligerently. 'Henry allowed Miranda to divorce him,' she declared, speaking clearly and concisely, 'only after it was agreed between them privately that Pippa should live with her father. If Miranda had not agreed to that, Henry would have divorced her.'

Costello gave a laugh which bordered on a sneer. 'You don't know Miranda very well, do you?' he asked. 'She so often changes her mind.'

Clarissa turned away from him. 'I don't believe for one moment,' she said contemptuously, 'that Miranda wants that child or even cares twopence about her.'

'But you're not a mother, my dear Clarissa,' was Costello's impertinent response. 'You don't mind my calling you Clarissa, do you?' he went on, with another unpleasant smile. 'After all, now that I'm married to Miranda, we're practically relations-in-law.'

He swallowed his drink in one gulp and put his glass down. 'Yes, I can assure you,' he continued, 'Miranda is now feeling violently maternal. She feels she must have Pippa to live with us for most of the time.'

'I don't believe it,' Clarissa snapped.

'Please yourself.' Costello made himself comfortable in the armchair. 'But there's no point in your trying to contest it. After all, there was no arrangement in writing, you know.'

'You're not going to have Pippa,' Clarissa told him firmly. 'The child was a nervous wreck when she came to us. She's much better now, and she's happy at school, and that's the way she's going to remain.'

'How will you manage that, my dear?' Costello sneered. 'The law is on our side.'

'What's behind all this?' Clarissa asked him, sounding bewildered. 'You don't care about Pippa. What do you really want?' She paused, and then struck her forehead. 'Oh! What a fool I am. Of course, it's blackmail.'

Costello was about to reply, when Elgin appeared. 'I was

looking for you, madam,' the butler told Clarissa. 'Will it be quite all right for Mrs Elgin and myself to leave now for the evening, madam?'

'Yes, quite all right, Elgin,' Clarissa replied.

'The taxi has come for us,' the butler explained. 'Supper is laid all ready in the dining-room.' He was about to go, but then turned back to Clarissa. 'Do you want me to shut up in here, madam?' he asked, keeping an eye on Costello as he spoke.

'No, I'll see to it,' Clarissa assured him. 'You and Mrs Elgin can go off for the evening now.'

'Thank you, madam,' said Elgin. He turned at the hall door to say, 'Goodnight, madam.'

'Goodnight, Elgin,' Clarissa responded.

Costello waited until the butler had closed the door behind him before he spoke again. 'Blackmail is a very ugly word, Clarissa,' he pointed out to her somewhat unoriginally. 'You should take a little more care before you accuse people wrongfully. Now, have I mentioned money at all?'

'Not yet,' replied Clarissa. 'But that's what you mean, isn't it?'

Costello shrugged his shoulders and held his hands out in an expressive gesture. 'It's true that we're not very well off,' he admitted. 'Miranda has always been very extravagant, as you no doubt know. I think she feels that Henry might be able to reinstate her allowance. After all, he's a rich man.'

Clarissa went up to Costello and faced him squarely.

'Now listen,' she ordered him. 'I don't know about Henry, but I do know about myself. You try to get Pippa away from here, and I'll fight you tooth and nail.' She paused, then added, 'And I don't care what weapons I use.'

Apparently unmoved by her outburst, Costello chuckled, but Clarissa continued, 'It shouldn't be difficult to get medical evidence proving Miranda's a drug addict. I'd even go to Scotland Yard and talk to the Narcotic Squad, and I'd suggest that they kept an eye on you as well.'

Costello gave a start at this. 'The upright Henry will hardly care for your methods,' he warned Clarissa.

'Then Henry will have to lump them,' she retorted fiercely. 'It's the child that matters. I'm not going to have Pippa bullied or frightened.'

At this point, Pippa came into the room. Seeing Costello, she stopped short, looking terrified.

'Why, hello, Pippa,' Costello greeted her. 'How you've grown.'

Pippa backed away as he moved towards her. 'I've just come to make some arrangements about you,' he told her. 'Your mother is looking forward to having you with her again. She and I are married now, and – '

'I won't come,' Pippa cried hysterically, running to Clarissa for protection. 'I won't come. Clarissa, they can't make me, can they? They wouldn't – '

'Don't worry, Pippa darling,' Clarissa said soothingly, putting her arm around the child. 'Your home is here with your father and with me, and you're not leaving it.'

'But I assure you – ' Costello began, only to be interrupted angrily by Clarissa. 'Get out of here at once,' she ordered him.

Mockingly pretending to be afraid of her, Costello put his hands above his head, and backed away.

'At once!' Clarissa repeated. She advanced upon him. 'I won't have you in my house, do you hear?'

Miss Peake appeared at the french windows, carrying a large garden-fork. 'Oh, Mrs Hailsham-Brown,' she began, 'I – '

'Miss Peake,' Clarissa interrupted her. 'Will you show Mr Costello the way through the garden to the back gate?'

Costello looked at Miss Peake, who lifted her garden-fork as she returned his gaze.

'Miss – Peake?' he queried.

'Pleased to meet you,' she replied, robustly. 'I'm the gardener here.'

'Indeed, yes,' said Costello. 'I came here once before, you may remember, to look at some antique furniture.'

'Oh, yes,' Miss Peake replied. 'In Mr Sellon's time. But you can't see him today, you know. He's dead.'

'No, I didn't come to see him,' Costello declared. 'I came to see – Mrs Brown.' He gave the name a certain emphasis.

'Oh, yes? Is that so? Well, now you've seen her,' Miss Peake told him. She seemed to realize that the visitor had outstayed his welcome.

Costello turned to Clarissa. 'Goodbye, Clarissa,' he said.

'You will hear from me, you know.' He sounded almost menacing.

'This way,' Miss Peake showed him, gesturing to the french windows. She followed him out, asking as they went, 'Do you want the bus, or did you bring your own car?'

'I left my car round by the stables,' Costello informed her as they made their way across the garden.

CHAPTER SIX

As soon as Oliver Costello had left with Miss Peake, Pippa burst into tears. 'He'll take me away from here,' she cried, sobbing bitterly as she clung to Clarissa.

'No, he won't,' Clarissa assured her, but Pippa's only response was to shout, 'I hate him. I always hated him.'

Fearing that the girl was on the verge of hysteria, Clarissa addressed her sharply, 'Pippa!'

Pippa backed away from her. 'I don't want to go back to my mother, I'd rather die,' she screamed. 'I'd much rather die. I'll kill him.'

'Pippa!' Clarissa admonished her.

Pippa now seemed completely uncontrollable. 'I'll kill myself,' she cried. 'I'll cut my wrists and bleed to death.'

Clarissa seized her by the shoulders. 'Pippa, control yourself,' she ordered the child. 'It's all right, I tell you. I'm here.'

'But I don't want to go back to Mother, and I hate Oliver,' Pippa exclaimed desperately. 'He's wicked, wicked, wicked.'

'Yes, dear, I know. I know,' Clarissa murmured soothingly.

'But you don't know.' Pippa now sounded even more desperate. 'I didn't tell you everything before – when I came to live here. I just couldn't bear to mention it. But it wasn't only Miranda being so nasty and drunk or something, all the time. One night, when she was out somewhere or other, and Oliver was at home with me – I think he'd been drinking a lot – I don't know – but – ' She stopped, and for a moment seemed unable to continue. Then, forcing herself to go on, she looked down at the floor and muttered indistinctly, 'He tried to do things to me.'

Clarissa looked aghast. 'Pippa, what do you mean?' she asked. 'What are you trying to say?'

Pippa looked desperately about her, as though seeking someone else who would say the words for her. 'He – he tried to kiss me, and when I pushed him away, he grabbed me, and started to tear my dress off. Then he – ' She stopped suddenly, and burst into a fit of sobbing.

'Oh, my poor darling,' Clarissa murmured, as she hugged the child to her. 'Try not to think about it. It's all over, and nothing like that will ever happen to you again. I'll make sure that Oliver is punished for that. The disgusting beast. He won't get away with it.'

Pippa's mood suddenly changed. Her tone now had a hopeful note, as a new thought apparently came to her. 'Perhaps he'll be struck by lightning,' she wondered aloud.

'Very likely,' Clarissa agreed. 'very likely.' Her face wore a look of grim determination. 'Now pull yourself together, Pippa,' she urged the child. 'Everything's quite all right.' She took a handkerchief from her pocket. 'Here, blow your nose.'

Pippa did as she was told, and then used the handkerchief to wipe her tears off Clarissa's dress.

Clarissa managed to summon up a laugh at this. 'Now, you go upstairs and have your bath,' she ordered, turning Pippa around to face the hall door. 'Mind you have a really good wash – your neck is absolutely filthy.'

Pippa seemed to be returning to normal. 'It always is,' she replied as she went to the door. But, as she was about to leave, she turned suddenly and ran to Clarissa. 'You won't let him take me away, will you?' she pleaded.

'Over my dead body,' Clarissa replied with determination. Then she corrected herself. 'No – over *his* dead body. There! Does that satisfy you?'

Pippa nodded, and Clarissa kissed her forehead. 'Now, run along,' she ordered.

Pippa gave her stepmother a final hug, and left. Clarissa stood for a moment in thought, and then, noticing that the room had become rather dark, switched on the concealed lighting. She went to the french windows and closed them, then sat on the sofa, staring ahead of her, apparently lost in thought.

Only a minute or two had passed when, hearing the front door of the house slam, she looked expectantly towards the hall door through which, a moment later, her husband Henry Hailsham-Brown entered. He was a quite good-looking man of about forty with a rather expressionless face, wearing horn-rimmed spectacles and carrying a briefcase.

'Hello, darling,' Henry greeted his wife, as he switched on the wall-bracket lights and put his briefcase on the armchair.

'Hello, Henry,' Clarissa replied. 'Hasn't it been an absolutely awful day?'

'Has it?' He came across to lean over the back of the sofa and kiss her.

'I hardly know where to begin,' she told him. 'Have a drink first.'

'Not just now,' Henry replied, going to the french windows and closing the curtains. 'Who's in the house?'

Slightly surprised at the question, Clarissa answered, 'Nobody. It's the Elgins' night off. Black Thursday, you know. We'll dine on cold ham, chocolate mousse, and the coffee will be really good because I shall make it.'

A questioning 'Um?' was Henry's only response to this.

Struck by his manner, Clarissa asked, 'Henry, is anything the matter?'

'Well, yes, in a way,' he told her.

'Something wrong?' she queried. 'Is it Miranda?'

'No, no, there's nothing wrong, really,' Henry assured her. 'I should say quite the contrary. Yes, quite the contrary.'

'Darling,' said Clarissa, speaking with affection and

only a very faint note of ridicule, 'do I perceive behind that impenetrable Foreign Office façade a certain human excitement?'

Henry wore an air of pleasured anticipation. 'Well,' he admitted, 'it is rather exciting in a way.' He paused, then added, 'As it happens, there's a slight fog in London.'

'Is that very exciting?' Clarissa asked.

'No, no, not the fog, of course.'

'Well?' Clarissa urged him.

Henry looked quickly around, as though to assure himself that he could not be overheard, and then went across to the sofa to sit beside Clarissa. 'You'll have to keep this to yourself,' he impressed upon her, his voice very grave.

'Yes?' Clarissa prompted him, hopefully.

'It's really very secret,' Henry reiterated. 'Nobody's supposed to know. But, actually, you'll have to know.'

'Well, come on, tell me,' she urged him.

Henry looked around again, and then turned to Clarissa. 'It's all very hush-hush,' he insisted. He paused for effect, and then announced, ' The Soviet Premier, Kalendorff, is flying to London for an important conference with the Prime Minister tomorrow.'

Clarissa was unimpressed. 'Yes, I know,' she replied.

Henry looked startled. 'What do you mean, you know?' he demanded.

'I read it in the paper last Sunday,' Clarissa informed him casually.

'I can't think why you want to read these low-class papers,' Henry expostulated. He sounded really put out.

'Anyway,' he continued, 'the papers couldn't possibly know that Kalendorff was coming over. It's top secret.'

'My poor sweet,' Clarissa murmured. Then, in a voice in which compassion was mixed with incredulity, she continued, 'But top secret? Really! The things you high-ups believe.'

Henry rose and began to stride around the room, looking distinctly worried. 'Oh dear, there must have been some leak,' he muttered.

'I should have thought,' Clarissa observed tartly, 'that by now you'd know there always is a leak. In fact I should have thought that you'd all be prepared for it.'

Henry looked somewhat affronted. 'The news was only released officially tonight,' he told her. 'Kalendorff's plane is due at Heathrow at eight-forty, but actually – ' He leaned over the sofa and looked doubtfully at his wife. 'Now, Clarissa,' he asked her very solemnly, 'can I really trust you to be discreet?'

'I'm much more discreet than any Sunday newspaper,' Clarissa protested, swinging her feet off the sofa and sitting up.

Henry sat on an arm of the sofa and leaned towards Clarissa conspiratorially. 'The conference will be at Whitehall tomorrow,' he informed her, 'but it would be a great advantage if a conversation could take place first between Sir John himself and Kalendorff. Now, naturally the reporters are all waiting at Heathrow, and the moment the plane arrives Kalendorff's movements are more or less public property.'

He looked around again, as though expecting to find gentlemen of the press peering over his shoulder, and continued, in a tone of increasing excitement, 'Fortunately, this incipient fog has played into our hands.'

'Go on,' Clarissa encouraged him. 'I'm thrilled, so far.'

'At the last moment,' Henry informed her, 'the plane will find it inadvisable to land at Heathrow. It will be diverted, as is usual on these occasions – '

'To Bindley Heath,' Clarissa interrupted him. 'That's just fifteen miles from here. I see.'

'You're always very quick, Clarissa dear,' Henry commented somewhat disapprovingly. 'But yes, I shall go off there now to the aerodrome in the car, meet Kalendorff, and bring him here. The Prime Minister is motoring down here direct from Downing Street. Half an hour will be ample for what they have to discuss, and then Kalendorff will travel up to London with Sir John.'

Henry paused. He got up and took a few paces away, before turning to say to her, disarmingly, 'You know, Clarissa, this may be of very great value to me in my career. I mean, they're reposing a lot of trust in me, having this meeting here.'

'So they should,' Clarissa replied firmly, going to her husband and flinging her arms around him. 'Henry, darling,' she exclaimed, 'I think it's all wonderful.'

'By the way,' Henry informed her solemnly, 'Kalendorff will be referred to only as Mr Jones.'

'Mr Jones?' Clarissa attempted, not altogether successfully, to keep a note of amused incredulity out of her voice.

'That's right,' Henry explained, 'one can't be too careful about using real names.'

'Yes – but – Mr Jones?' Clarissa queried. 'Couldn't they have thought of something better than that?' She shook her head doubtfully, and continued, 'Incidentally, what about me? Do I retire to the harem, as it were, or do I bring in the drinks, utter greetings to them both and then discreetly fade away?'

Henry regarded his wife somewhat uneasily as he admonished her, 'You must take this seriously, dear.'

'But Henry, darling,' Clarissa insisted, 'can't I take it seriously and still enjoy it a little?'

Henry gave her question a moment's consideration, before replying, gravely, 'I think it would be better, perhaps, Clarissa, if you didn't appear.'

Clarissa seemed not to mind this. 'All right,' she agreed, 'but what about food? Will they want something?'

'Oh no,' said Henry. 'There need be no question of a meal.'

'A few sandwiches, I think,' Clarissa suggested. She sat on an arm of the sofa, and continued, 'Ham sandwiches would be best. In a napkin to keep them moist. And hot coffee, in a Thermos jug. Yes, that'll do very well. The chocolate mousse I shall take up to my bedroom to console me for being excluded from the conference.'

'Now, Clarissa – ' Henry began, disapprovingly, only to be interrupted by his wife as she rose and flung her arms around his neck. 'Darling, I am being serious, really,' she assured him. 'Nothing will go wrong. I shan't let it.' She kissed him affectionately.

Henry gently disentangled himself from her embrace. 'What about old Roly?' he asked.

'He and Jeremy are dining at the club house with Hugo,' Clarissa told him. 'They're going to play bridge afterwards, so Roly and Jeremy won't be back here until about midnight.'

'And the Elgins are out?' Hugo asked her.

'Darling, you know they always go to the cinema on Thursdays,' Clarissa reminded him. 'They won't be back until well after eleven.'

Henry looked pleased. 'Good,' he exclaimed. 'That's all quite satisfactory. Sir John and Mr – er – '

'Jones,' Clarissa prompted him.

'Quite right, darling. Mr Jones and the Prime Minister will have left long before then.' Henry consulted his watch. 'Well, I'd better have a quick shower before I start off for Bindley Heath,' he announced.

'And I'd better go and make the ham sandwiches,' Clarissa said, dashing out of the room.

Picking up his briefcase, Henry called after her, 'You must remember about the lights, Clarissa.' He went to the door and switched off the concealed lighting. 'We're making our own electricity here, and it costs money.' He switched off the wall-brackets as well. 'It's not like London, you know.'

After a final glance around the room, which was now in darkness except for a faint glow of light from the hall door, Henry nodded and left, closing the door behind him.

CHAPTER SEVEN

At the golf club, Hugo was busily complaining about Clarissa's behaviour in making them test the port. 'Really, she ought to stop playing these games, you know,' he said as they made their way to the bar. 'Do you remember, Roly, the time I received that telegram from Whitehall telling me that I was going to be offered a knighthood in the next Honours List? It was only when I mentioned it in confidence to Henry one evening when I was dining with them both, and Henry was perplexed but Clarissa started giggling – it was only then that I discovered she'd sent the bloody thing. She can be so childish sometimes.'

Sir Rowland chuckled. 'Yes, she can indeed. And she loves play-acting. You know, she was actually a damned good actress in her school's drama club. At one time I thought she'd take it up seriously and go on the stage professionally. She's so convincing, even when she's telling the most dreadful lies. And that's what actors are, surely. Convincing liars.'

He was lost in reminiscence for a moment, and then continued, 'Clarissa's best friend at school was a girl called Jeanette Collins, whose father had been a famous footballer. And Jeanette herself was a mad football fan. Well, one day Clarissa rang Jeanette in an assumed voice, claiming to be the public relations officer for some football team or other, and told her that she'd been chosen to be the team's new mascot, but that it all depended on her dressing in a funny costume as a rabbit, and standing outside the Chelsea Stadium that afternoon as the customers were queuing up to get in. Somehow Jeanette managed to hire a costume in time, and got to the stadium dressed as a bunny rabbit, where she was laughed at by hundreds of people and photographed by Clarissa who was waiting there for her. Jeanette was furious. I don't think the friendship survived.'

'Oh, well,' Hugo growled resignedly, as he picked up a menu and began to devote his attention to the serious business of choosing what they would eat later.

Meanwhile, back in the Hailsham-Browns' drawing-room, only minutes after Henry had gone off to have his shower, Oliver Costello entered the empty room stealthily through the french windows, leaving the curtains open so that moonlight streamed in. He shone a torch carefully around the room, then went to the desk and switched on the lamp that was on it. After lifting the flap of the secret drawer, he suddenly switched off the lamp and stood motionless for a moment as though he had heard something. Apparently reassured, he switched the desk lamp on again, and opened the secret drawer.

Behind Costello, the panel beside the bookshelf slowly and quietly opened. He shut the secret drawer in the desk, switched the lamp off again, and then turned sharply as he was struck a fierce blow on the head by someone standing at the recess. Costello collapsed immediately, falling behind the sofa, and the panel closed again, this time more quickly.

The room remained in darkness for moment, until Henry Hailsham-Brown entered from the hall, switched on the wall-brackets, and shouted 'Clarissa!' Putting his spectacles on, he filled his cigarette-case from the box on a table near the sofa as Clarissa came in, calling, 'Here I am, darling. Do you want a sandwich before you go?'

'No, I think I'd better start,' Henry replied, patting his jacket nervously.

'But you'll be hours too early,' Clarissa told him. 'It can't take you more than twenty minutes to drive there.'

Henry shook his head. 'One never knows,' he declared. 'I might have a puncture, or something might go wrong with the car.'

'Don't fuss, darling,' Clarissa admonished him, straightening his tie as she spoke. 'It's all going to go very smoothly.'

'Now, what about Pippa?' Henry asked, anxiously. 'You're sure she won't come down or barge in while Sir John and Kalen – I mean, Mr Jones, are talking privately?'

'No, there's no danger of that,' Clarissa assured him. 'I'll go up to her room and we'll have a feast together. We'll toast tomorrow's breakfast sausages and share the chocolate mousse between us.'

Henry smiled affectionately at his wife. 'You're very good to Pippa, my dear,' he told her. 'It's one of the things I'm most grateful to you for.' He paused, embarrassed, then went on. 'I can never express myself very well – I – you know – so much misery – and now, everything's so different. You – ' Taking Clarissa in his arms, he kissed her.

For some moments they remained locked in a loving embrace. Then Clarissa gently broke away, but continued to hold his hands. 'You've made me very happy, Henry,' she told him. 'And Pippa is going to be fine. She's a lovely child.'

Henry smiled affectionately at her. 'Now, you go and meet your Mr Jones,' she ordered him, pushing him towards the hall door. 'Mr Jones,' she repeated. 'I still think that's a ridiculous name to have chosen.'

Henry was about to leave the room when Clarissa asked him, 'Are you going to come in by the front door? Shall I leave it unlatched?'

He paused in the doorway to consider. Then, 'No,' he said. 'I think we'll come in through the french windows.'

'You'd better put on your overcoat, Henry. It's quite chilly,' Clarissa advised, pushing him into the hall as she spoke. 'And perhaps your muffler as well.' He took his coat obediently from a rack in the hall, and she followed him to the front door with a final word of advice. 'Drive carefully, darling, won't you?'

[68]

'Yes, yes,' Henry called back. 'You know I always do.'

Clarissa shut the door behind him, and went off to the kitchen to finish making the sandwiches. As she put them on a plate, wrapping a damp napkin around it to keep them fresh, she could not help thinking of her recent unnerving encounter with Oliver Costello. She was frowning as she carried the sandwiches back to the drawing-room, where she put them on the small table.

Suddenly fearful of incurring Miss Peake's wrath for having marked the table, she snatched the plate up again, rubbed unsuccessfully at the mark it had made, and compromised by covering it with a nearby vase of flowers. She transferred the plate of sandwiches to the stool, then carefully shook the cushions on the sofa. Singing quietly to herself, she picked up Pippa's book and took it across to replace it on the bookshelves. 'Can a body meet a body, coming through the – ' She suddenly stopped singing and uttered a scream as she stumbled and nearly fell over Oliver Costello.

Bending over the body, Clarissa recognized who it was. 'Oliver!' she gasped. She stared at him in horror for what seemed an age. Then, convinced that he was dead, she straightened up quickly and ran towards the door to call Henry, but immediately realized that he had gone. She turned back to the body, and then ran to the telephone, and lifted the receiver. She began to dial, but then stopped and replaced the receiver again. She stood thinking for a moment, and looked at the panel in the wall. Making up her mind quickly, she glanced at the panel again, and then reluctantly bent down and began to drag the body across to it.

While she was engaged in doing this, the panel slowly opened and Pippa emerged from the recess, wearing a dressing-gown over her pyjamas. 'Clarissa!' she wailed, rushing to her stepmother.

Trying to stand between her and the body of Costello, Clarissa gave Pippa a little shove, in an attempt to turn her away. 'Pippa,' she begged, 'don't look, darling. Don't look.'

In a strangled voice, Pippa cried, 'I didn't mean to. Oh, really, I didn't mean to do it.'

Horrified, Clarissa seized the child by her arms. 'Pippa! Was it – you?' she gasped.

'He's dead, isn't he? He's quite dead?' Pippa asked. Sobbing hysterically, she cried, 'I didn't – mean to kill him. I didn't mean to.'

'Quiet now, quiet,' Clarissa murmured soothingly. 'It's all right. Come on, sit down.' She led Pippa to the armchair and sat her in it.

'I didn't mean to. I didn't mean to kill him,' Pippa went on crying.

Clarissa knelt beside her. 'Of course you didn't mean to,' she agreed. 'Now listen, Pippa – '

When Pippa continued to cry even more hysterically, Clarissa shouted at her. 'Pippa, listen to me. Everything's going to be all right. You've got to forget about this. Forget all about it, do you hear?'

'Yes,' Pippa sobbed, 'but – but I – '

'Pippa,' Clarissa continued more forcefully, 'you must

trust me and believe what I'm telling you. Everything is going to be all right. But you've got to be brave and do exactly what I tell you.'

Still sobbing hysterically, Pippa tried to turn away from her.

'Pippa!' Clarissa shouted. 'Will you do as I tell you?' She pulled the child around to face her. 'Will you?'

'Yes, yes, I will,' Pippa cried, putting her head on Clarissa's bosom.

'That's right.' Clarissa adopted a consoling tone as she helped Pippa out of the chair. 'Now, I want you to go upstairs and get into bed.'

'You come with me, please,' the child pleaded.

'Yes, yes,' Clarissa assured her, 'I'll come up very soon, as soon as I can, and I'll give you a nice little white tablet. Then you'll go to sleep, and in the morning everything will seem quite different.' She looked down at the body, and added, 'There may be nothing to worry about.'

'But he is dead – isn't he?' Pippa asked.

'No, no, he may not be dead,' Clarissa replied evasively. 'I'll see. Now go on, Pippa. Do as I tell you.'

Pippa, still sobbing, left the room and ran upstairs. Clarissa watched her go, and then turned back to the body on the floor. 'Supposing I were to find a dead body in the drawing-room, what should I do?' she murmured to herself. After standing for a moment in thought, she exclaimed more emphatically, 'Oh, my God, what *am* I going to do?'

CHAPTER EIGHT

Fifteen minutes later, Clarissa was still in the drawing-room and murmuring to herself. But she had been busy in the meantime. All the lights were now on, the panel in the wall was closed, and the curtains had been drawn across the open french windows. Oliver Costello's body was still behind the sofa, but Clarissa had been moving the furniture about, and had set up a folding bridge-table in the centre of the room, with cards and markers for bridge, and four upright chairs around the table.

Standing at the table, Clarissa scribbled figures on one of the markers. 'Three spades, four hearts, four no trumps, pass,' she muttered, pointing at each hand as she made its call. 'Five diamonds, pass, six spades – double – and I think they go down.' She paused for a moment, looking down at the table, and then continued, 'Let me see, doubled vulnerable, two tricks, five hundred – or shall I let them make it? No.'

She was interrupted by the arrival of Sir Rowland, Hugo, and young Jeremy, who entered through the french windows. Hugo paused a moment before coming into the room, to close one half of the windows.

Putting her pad and pencil on the bridge table, Clarissa rushed to meet them. 'Thank God you've come,' she told Sir Rowland, sounding extremely distraught.

'What is all this, my dear?' Sir Rowland asked her, with concern in his voice.

Clarissa turned to address them all. 'Darlings,' she cried, 'you've got to help me.'

Jeremy noticed the table with the playing cards spread out on it. 'Looks like a bridge party,' he observed gaily.

'You're being very melodramatic, Clarissa,' Hugo contributed. 'What are you up to, young woman?'

Clarissa clutched Sir Rowland. 'It's serious,' she insisted. 'Terribly serious. You will help me, won't you?'

'Of course we'll help you, Clarissa,' Sir Rowland assured her, 'but what's it all about?'

'Yes, come on, what is it this time?' Hugo asked, somewhat wearily.

Jeremy, too, sounded unimpressed. 'You're up to something, Clarissa,' he insisted. 'What is it? Found a body or something?'

'That's just it,' Clarissa told him. 'I have – found a body.'

'What do you mean – found a body?' Hugo asked. He sounded puzzled, but not all that interested.

'It's just as Jeremy said,' Clarissa answered him. 'I came in here, and I found a body.'

Hugo gave a cursory glance around the room. 'I don't know what you're talking about,' he complained. 'What body? Where?'

'I'm not playing games. I'm serious,' Clarissa shouted angrily. 'It's there. Go and look. Behind the sofa.' She pushed Sir Rowland towards the sofa, and moved away.

Hugo went quickly to the sofa. Jeremy followed him, and leaned over the back of it. 'My God, she's right,' Jeremy murmured.

Sir Rowland joined them. He and Hugo bent down to examine the body. 'Why, it's Oliver Costello,' Sir Rowland exclaimed.

'God almighty!' Jeremy went quickly to the french windows and drew the curtains.

'Yes,' said Clarissa. 'It's Oliver Costello.'

'What was he doing here?' Sir Rowland asked her.

'He came this evening to talk about Pippa,' Clarissa replied. 'It was just after you'd gone to the club.'

Sir Rowland looked puzzled. 'What did he want with Pippa?'

'He and Miranda were threatening to take her away,' Clarissa told him. 'But all that doesn't matter now. I'll tell you about it later. We have to hurry. We've got very little time.'

Sir Rowland held up a hand in warning. 'Just a moment,'

he instructed, coming closer to Clarissa. 'We must have the facts clear. What happened when he arrived?'

Clarissa shook her head impatiently. 'I told him that he and Miranda were not going to get Pippa, and he went away.'

'But he came back?'

'Obviously,' said Clarissa.

'How?' Sir Rowland asked her. 'When?'

'I don't know,' Clarissa answered. 'I just came into the room, as I said, and I found him – like that.' She gestured towards the sofa.

'I see,' said Sir Rowland, moving back to the body on the floor and leaning over it. 'I see. Well, he's dead all right. He's been hit over the head with something heavy and sharp.' He looked around at the others. 'I'm afraid this isn't going to be a very pleasant business,' he continued, 'but there's only one thing to be done.' He went across to the telephone as he spoke. 'We must ring up the police and – '

'No,' Clarissa exclaimed sharply.

Sir Rowland was already lifting the receiver. 'You ought to have done it at once, Clarissa,' he advised her. 'Still, I don't suppose they'll blame you much for that.'

'No, Roly, stop,' Clarissa insisted. She ran across the room, took the receiver from him, and replaced it on its rest.

'My dear child – ' Sir Rowland expostulated, but Clarissa would not let him continue. 'I could have rung up the police myself if I'd wanted to,' she admitted. 'I knew perfectly well that it was the proper thing to do. I even started dialling. Then, instead, I rang you up at the club and asked you to come back here immediately, all three of you.' She turned to Jeremy and Hugo. 'You haven't even asked me why, yet.'

'You can leave it all to us,' Sir Rowland assured her. 'We will – '

Clarissa interrupted him vehemently. 'You haven't begun to understand,' she insisted. 'I want you to help me. You said you would if I was ever in trouble.' She turned to include the other two men. 'Darlings, you've got to help me.'

Jeremy moved to position himself so that he hid the body from her sight. 'What do you want us to do, Clarissa?' he asked gently.

'Get rid of the body,' was her abrupt reply.

'My dear, don't talk nonsense,' Sir Rowland ordered her. 'This is murder.'

'That's the whole point,' Clarissa told him. 'The body mustn't be found in this house.'

Hugo gave a snort of impatience. 'You don't know what you're talking about, my dear girl,' he exclaimed. 'You've been reading too many murder mysteries. In real life you can't go monkeying about, moving dead bodies.'

'But I've already moved it,' Clarissa explained. 'I turned it over to see if he was dead, and then I started dragging it into that recess, and then I realized I was going to need help, and so I rang you up at the club, and while I was waiting for you I made a plan.'

'Including the bridge table, I assume,' Jeremy observed, gesturing towards the table.

Clarissa picked up the bridge marker. 'Yes,' she replied. 'That's going to be our alibi.'

'What on earth – ' Hugo began, but Clarissa gave him no chance to continue. 'Two and a half rubbers,' she announced. 'I've imagined all the hands, and put down the scores on this marker. You three must fill up the others in your own handwriting, of course.'

Sir Rowland stared at her in amazement. 'You're mad, Clarissa. Quite mad,' he declared.

Clarissa paid no attention to him. 'I've worked it out beautifully,' she went on. 'The body has to be taken away from here.' She looked at Jeremy. 'It will take two of you to do that,' she instructed him. 'A dead body is very difficult to manage – I've found that out already.'

'Where the hell do you expect us to take it to?' Hugo asked in exasperation.

Clarissa had already given this some thought. 'The best place, I think, would be Marsden Wood,' she advised. 'That's only two miles from here.' She gestured away to the left. 'You turn off into that side road, just a few yards after you've passed the front gate. It's a narrow road, and there's hardly ever any traffic on it.' She turned to Sir Rowland. 'Just leave the car by the side of the road when you get into the wood,' she instructed him. 'Then you walk back here.'

Jeremy looked perplexed. 'Do you mean you want us to dump the body in the wood?' he asked.

'No, you leave it in the car,' Clarissa explained. 'It's his car, don't you see? He left it here, round by the stables.'

All three men now wore puzzled expressions. 'It's really all quite easy,' Clarissa assured them. 'If anybody does happen to see you walking back, it's quite a dark night and they won't know who you are. And you've got an alibi. All four of us have been playing bridge here.' She replaced the marker on the bridge table, looking almost pleased with herself, while the men, stupefied, stared at her.

Hugo walked about in a complete circle. 'I – I – ' he spluttered, waving his hands in the air.

Clarissa went on issuing her instructions. 'You wear gloves, of course,' she told them, 'so as not to leave fingerprints on anything. I've got them here all ready for you.' Pushing past Jeremy to the sofa, she took three pairs of gloves from under one of the cushions, and laid them out on an arm of the sofa.

Sir Rowland continued to stare at Clarissa. 'Your natural talent for crime leaves me speechless,' he informed her.

Jeremy gazed at her admiringly. 'She's got it all worked out, hasn't she?' he declared.

'Yes,' Hugo admitted, 'but it's all damned foolish nonsense just the same.'

'Now, you must hurry,' Clarissa ordered them vehemently. 'At nine o'clock Henry and Mr Jones will be here.'

'Mr Jones? Who on earth is Mr Jones?' Sir Rowland asked her.

Clarissa put a hand to her head. 'Oh dear,' she exclaimed, 'I never realized what a terrible lot of explaining one has to do in a murder. I thought I'd simply ask you to help me and you would, and that is all there'd be to it.' She looked around at all three of them. 'Oh, darlings, you must.' She stroked Hugo's hair. 'Darling, darling Hugo –'

'This play-acting is all very well, my dear,' said Hugo, sounding distinctly annoyed, 'but a dead body is a nasty, serious business, and monkeying about with it could land you in a real mess. You can't go carting bodies about at dead of night.'

Clarissa went to Jeremy and placed her hand on his arm. 'Jeremy, darling, you'll help me, surely. Won't you?' she asked, with urgent appeal in her voice.

Jeremy gazed at her adoringly. 'All right, I'm game,' he replied cheerfully. 'What's a dead body or two among friends?'

'Stop, young man,' Sir Rowland ordered. 'I'm not going to allow this.' He turned to Clarissa. 'Now, you must be guided by me, Clarissa. I insist. After all, there's Henry to consider, too.'

Clarissa gave him a look of exasperation. 'But it's Henry I *am* considering,' she declared.

CHAPTER NINE

The three men greeted Clarissa's announcement in silence. Sir Rowland shook his head gravely, Hugo continued to look puzzled, while Jeremy simply shrugged his shoulders as though giving up all hope of understanding the situation.

Taking a deep breath, Clarissa addressed all three of them. 'Something terribly important is happening tonight,' she told them. 'Henry's gone to – to meet someone and bring him back here. It's very important and secret. A top political secret. No one is supposed to know about it. There was to be absolutely no publicity.'

'Henry's gone to meet a Mr Jones?' Sir Rowland queried, dubiously.

'It's a silly name, I agree,' said Clarissa, 'but that's what they're calling him. I can't tell you his real name. I can't tell you any more about it. I promised Henry I wouldn't say a word to anybody, but I have to make you see that I'm not just – ' she turned to look at Hugo as she continued, ' – not just being an idiot and play-acting as Hugo called it.'

She turned back to Sir Rowland. 'What sort of effect do you think it will have on Henry's career,' she asked him, 'if he has to walk in here with this distinguished person – and another very distinguished person travelling down from London for this meeting – only to find the police investigating a murder – the murder of a man who has just married Henry's former wife?'

'Good Lord!' Sir Rowland exclaimed. Then, looking Clarissa straight in the eye, he added, suspiciously, 'You're not making all this up now, are you? This isn't just another of your complicated games, intended to make fools of us all?'

Clarissa shook her head mournfully. 'Nobody ever believes me when I'm speaking the truth,' she protested.

'Sorry, my dear,' said Sir Rowland. 'Yes, I can see it's a more difficult problem than I thought.'

'You see?' Clarissa urged him. 'So it's absolutely vital that we get the body away from here.'

'Where's his car, did you say?' Jeremy asked.

'Round by the stables.'

'And the servants are out, I gather?'

Clarissa nodded. 'Yes.'

Jeremy picked up a pair of gloves from the sofa. 'Right,' he exclaimed decisively. 'Do I take the body to the car, or bring the car to the body?'

Sir Rowland held out a hand in a restraining gesture. 'Wait a moment,' he advised. 'We mustn't rush it
like this.'

Jeremy put the gloves down again, but Clarissa turned
to Sir Rowland, crying desperately, 'But we must hurry.'

Sir Rowland regarded her gravely. 'I'm not sure that
this plan of yours is the best one, Clarissa,' he declared.
'Now, if we could just delay finding the body until
tomorrow morning – that would meet the case, I think,
and it would be very much simpler. If, for now, we merely
moved the body to another room, for instance, I think that
might be just excusable.'

Clarissa turned to address him directly. 'It's you I've got
to convince, isn't it?' she told him. Looking at Jeremy, she
continued, 'Jeremy's ready enough.' She glanced at Hugo.
'And Hugo will grunt and shake his head, but he'd do it
all the same. It's you . . .'

She went to the library door and opened it. 'Will you
both excuse us for a short time?' she asked Jeremy and
Hugo. 'I want to speak to Roly alone.'

'Don't you let her talk you into any tomfoolery, Roly,'
Hugo warned as they left the room. Jeremy gave Clarissa
a reassuring smile and a murmured 'Good luck!'

Sir Rowland, looking grave, took a seat at the library table.

'Now!' Clarissa exclaimed, as she sat and faced him on
the other side of the table.

'My dear,' Sir Rowland warned her, 'I love you, and I
will always love you dearly. But, before you ask, in this
case the answer simply has to be no.'

Clarissa began to speak seriously and with emphasis. 'That man's body mustn't be found in this house,' she insisted. 'If he's found in Marsden Wood, I can say that he was here today for a short time, and I can also tell the police exactly when he left. Actually, Miss Peake saw him off, which turns out to be very fortunate. There need be no question of his ever having come back here.'

She took a deep breath. 'But if his body is found here,' she continued, 'then we shall all be questioned.' She paused before adding, with great deliberation, 'And Pippa won't be able to stand it.'

'Pippa?' Sir Rowland was obviously puzzled.

Clarissa's face was grim. 'Yes, Pippa. She'll break down and confess that she did it.'

'Pippa!' Sir Rowland repeated, as he slowly took in what he was hearing.

Clarissa nodded.

'My God!' Sir Rowland exclaimed.

'She was terrified when he came here today,' Clarissa told him. 'I tried to reassure her that I wouldn't let him take her away, but I don't think she believed me. You know what she's been through – the nervous breakdown she's had? Well, I don't think she could have survived being made to go back and live with Oliver and Miranda. Pippa was here when I found Oliver's body. She told me she never meant to do it, I'm sure she was telling the truth. It was sheer panic. She got hold of that stick, and struck out blindly.'

'What stick?' Sir Rowland asked.

'The one from the hall stand. It's in the recess. I left it there, I didn't touch it.'

Sir Rowland thought for a moment, and then asked sharply, 'Where is Pippa now?'

'In bed,' said Clarissa. 'I've given her a sleeping pill. She ought not to wake up till morning. Tomorrow I'll take her up to London, and my old nanny will look after her for a while.'

Sir Rowland got up and walked over to look down at Oliver Costello's body behind the sofa. Returning to Clarissa, he kissed her. 'You win, my dear,' he said. 'I apologize. That child musn't be asked to face the music. Get the others back.'

He went across to the window and closed it, while Clarissa opened the library door, calling, 'Hugo, Jeremy. Would you come back, please?'

The two men came back into the room. 'That butler of yours doesn't lock up very carefully,' Hugo announced. 'The window in the library was open. I've shut it now.'

Addressing Sir Rowland, he asked abruptly, 'Well?'

'I'm converted,' was the equally terse reply.

'Well done,' was Jeremy's comment.

'There's no time to lose,' Sir Rowland declared. 'Now, those gloves.' He picked up a pair and put them on. Jeremy picked up the others, handed one pair to Hugo, and they both put them on. Sir Rowland went over to the panel. 'How does this thing open?' he asked.

Jeremy went across to join him. 'Like this, sir,' he

said. 'Pippa showed me.' He moved the lever and opened the panel.

Sir Rowland looked into the recess, reached in, and brought out the walking stick. 'Yes, it's heavy enough,' he commented. 'Weighted in the head. All the same, I shouldn't have thought – ' He paused.

'What wouldn't you have thought?' Hugo wanted to know.

Sir Rowland shook his head. 'I should have thought,' he replied, 'that it would have to have been something with a sharper edge – metal of some kind.'

'You mean a goddam chopper,' Hugo observed bluntly.

'I don't know,' Jeremy interjected. 'That stick looks pretty murderous to me. You could easily crack a man's head open with that.'

'Evidently,' said Sir Rowland, drily. He turned to Hugo, and handed him the stick. 'Hugo, will you burn this in the kitchen stove, please,' he instructed. 'Warrender, you and I will get the body to the car.'

He and Jeremy bent down on either side of the body. As they did so, a bell suddenly rang. 'What's that?' Sir Rowland exclaimed, startled.

'It's the front doorbell,' said Clarissa, sounding bewildered. They all stood petrified for a moment. 'Who can it be?' Clarissa wondered aloud. 'It's much too early for Henry and – er – Mr Jones. It must be Sir John.'

'Sir John?' asked Sir Rowland, now sounding even more startled. 'You mean the Prime Minister is expected here this evening?'

'Yes,' Clarissa replied.

'Hm.' Sir Rowland looked momentarily undecided. Then, 'Yes,' he murmured. 'Well, we've got to do something.' The bell rang again, and he stirred into action. 'Clarissa,' he ordered, 'go and answer the door. Use whatever delaying tactics you can think of. In the meantime, we'll clear up in here.'

Clarissa went quickly out to the hall, and Sir Rowland turned to Hugo and Jeremy. 'Now then,' he explained urgently, 'this is what we do. We'll get him into that recess. Later, when everyone's in this room having their pow-wow, we can take him out through the library.'

'Good idea,' Jeremy agreed, as he helped Sir Rowland lift the body.

'Want me to give you a hand?' asked Hugo.

'No, it's all right,' Jeremy replied. He and Sir Rowland supported Costello's body under the armpits and carried it into the recess, while Hugo picked up the torch. A moment or two later, Sir Rowland emerged and pressed the lever as Jeremy hastened out behind him. Hugo quickly slipped under Jeremy's arm into the recess with the torch and stick. The panel then closed.

Sir Rowland, after examining his jacket for signs of blood, murmured, 'Gloves,' removed the gloves he was wearing, and put them under a cushion on the sofa. Jeremy removed his gloves and did likewise. Then, 'Bridge,' Sir Rowland reminded himself, as he hastened to the bridge table and sat.

Jeremy followed him and picked up his cards. 'Come

[89]

along, Hugo, make haste,' Sir Rowland urged as he picked up his own cards.

He was answered by a knock from inside the recess. Suddenly realizing that Hugo was not in the room, Sir Rowland and Jeremy looked at each other in alarm. Jeremy got up, rushed to the switch and opened the panel. 'Come along, Hugo,' Sir Rowland repeated urgently, as Hugo emerged. 'Quickly, Hugo,' Jeremy muttered impatiently, closing the panel again.

Sir Rowland took Hugo's gloves from him, and put them under the cushion. The three men took their seats quickly at the bridge table and picked up their cards, just as Clarissa came back into the room from the hall, followed by two men in uniform.

In a tone of innocent surprise, Clarissa announced, 'It's the police, Uncle Roly.'

CHAPTER TEN

The older of the two police officers, a stocky, grey-haired man, followed Clarissa into the room, while his colleague remained standing by the hall door. 'This is Inspector Lord,' Clarissa declared. 'And – ' she turned back to the younger officer, a dark-haired man in his twenties with the build of a footballer. 'I'm sorry, what did you say your name was?' she asked.

The Inspector answered for him. 'That's Constable Jones,' he announced. Addressing the three men, he continued, 'I'm sorry to intrude, gentlemen, but we have received information that a murder has been committed here.'

Clarissa and her friends all spoke simultaneously. 'What?' Hugo shouted. 'A murder!' Jeremy exclaimed. 'Good heavens,' Sir Rowland cried, as Clarissa said, 'Isn't it extraordinary?' They all sounded completely astonished.

'Yes, we had a telephone call at the station,' the Inspector told them. Nodding to Hugo, he added, 'Good evening, Mr Birch.'

'Er – good evening, Inspector,' Hugo mumbled.

'It looks as though somebody's been hoaxing you, Inspector,' Sir Rowland suggested.

'Yes,' Clarissa agreed. 'We've been playing bridge here all evening.'

The others nodded in support, and Clarissa asked, 'Who did they say had been murdered?'

'No names were mentioned,' the Inspector informed them. 'The caller just said that a man had been murdered at Copplestone Court, and would we come along immediately. They rang off before any additional information could be obtained.'

'It must have been a hoax,' Clarissa declared, adding virtuously, 'What a wicked thing to do.'

Hugo tut-tutted, and the Inspector replied, 'You'd be surprised, madam, at the potty things people do.'

He paused, glancing at each of them in turn, and then continued, addressing Clarissa. 'Well now, according to you, nothing out of the ordinary has happened here this evening?' Without waiting for an answer, he added, 'Perhaps I'd better see Mr Hailsham-Brown as well.'

'He's not here,' Clarissa told the Inspector. 'I don't expect him back until late tonight.'

'I see,' he replied. 'Who is staying in the house at present?'

'Sir Rowland Delahaye, and Mr Warrender,' said Clarissa,

indicating them in turn. She added, 'And Mr Birch, whom you already know, is here for the evening.'

Sir Rowland and Jeremy murmured acknowledgements. 'Oh, and yes,' Clarissa went on as though she had just remembered, 'my little stepdaughter.' She emphasized 'little'. 'She's in bed and asleep.'

'What about servants?' the Inspector wanted to know.

'There are two of them. A married couple. But it's their night out, and they've gone to the cinema in Maidstone.'

'I see,' said the Inspector, nodding his head gravely.

Just at that moment, Elgin came into the room from the hall, almost colliding with the Constable who was still keeping guard there. After a quick questioning look at the Inspector, Elgin addressed Clarissa. 'Would you be wanting anything, madam?' he asked.

Clarissa looked startled. 'I thought you were at the pictures, Elgin,' she exclaimed, as the Inspector gave her a sharp glance.

'We returned almost immediately, madam,' Elgin explained. 'My wife was not feeling well.' Sounding embarrassed, he added, delicately, 'Er – gastric trouble. It must have been something she ate.' Looking from the Inspector to the Constable, he asked, 'Is anything – wrong?'

'What's your name?' the Inspector asked him.

'Elgin, sir,' the butler replied. 'I'm sure I hope there's nothing – '

He was interrupted by the Inspector. 'Someone rang

up the police station and said that a murder had been committed here.'

'A murder?' Elgin gasped.

'What do you know about that?'

'Nothing. Nothing at all, sir.'

'It wasn't you who rang up, then?' the Inspector asked him.

'No, indeed not.'

'When you returned to the house, you came in by the back door – at least I suppose you did?'

'Yes, sir,' Elgin replied, nervousness now making him rather more deferential in manner.

'Did you notice anything unusual?'

The butler thought for a moment, and then replied, 'Now I come to think of it, there was a strange car standing near the stables.'

'A strange car? What do you mean?'

'I wondered at the time whose it might be,' Elgin recalled. 'It seemed a curious place to leave it.'

'Was there anybody in it?'

'Not so far as I could see, sir.'

'Go and take a look at it, Jones,' the Inspector ordered his Constable.

'Jones!' Clarissa exclaimed involuntarily, with a start.

'I beg your pardon?' said the Inspector, turning to her.

Clarissa recovered herself quickly. Smiling at him, she murmured, 'It's nothing – just – I didn't think he looked very Welsh.'

The Inspector gestured to Constable Jones and to

Elgin, indicating that they should go. They left the room together, and a silence ensued. After a moment, Jeremy moved to sit on the sofa and began to eat the sandwiches. The Inspector put his hat and gloves on the armchair, and then, taking a deep breath, addressed the assembled company.

'It seems,' he declared, speaking slowly and deliberately, 'that someone came here tonight who is unaccounted for.' He looked at Clarissa. 'You're sure you weren't expecting anyone?' he asked her.

'Oh, no – no,' Clarissa replied. 'We didn't want anyone to turn up. You see, we were just the four of us for bridge.'

'Really?' said the Inspector. 'I'm fond of a game of bridge myself.'

'Oh, are you?' Clarissa replied. 'Do you play Black-wood?'

'I just like a common-sense game,' the Inspector told her. 'Tell me, Mrs Hailsham-Brown,' he continued, 'you haven't lived here for very long, have you?'

'No,' she told him. 'About six weeks.'

The Inspector regarded her steadily. 'And there's been no funny business of any kind since you've been living here?' he asked.

Before Clarissa could answer, Sir Rowland interjected. 'What exactly do you mean by funny business, Inspector?'

The Inspector turned to address him. 'Well, it's rather a curious story, sir,' he informed Sir Rowland. 'This house used to belong to Mr Sellon, the antique dealer. He died six months ago.'

'Yes,' Clarissa remembered. 'He had some kind of accident, didn't he?'

'That's right,' said the Inspector. 'He fell downstairs, pitched on his head.' He looked around at Jeremy and Hugo, and added, 'Accidental death, they brought in. It might have been that, but it might not.'

'Do you mean,' Clarissa asked, 'that somebody might have pushed him?'

The Inspector turned to her. 'That,' he agreed, 'or else somebody hit him a crack on the head – '

He paused, and the tension among his hearers was palpable. Into the silence the Inspector went on. 'Someone could have arranged Sellon's body to look right, at the bottom of the stairs.'

'The staircase here in this house?' Clarissa asked nervously.

'No, it happened at his shop,' the Inspector informed her. 'There was no conclusive evidence, of course – but he was rather a dark horse, Mr Sellon.'

'In what way, Inspector?' Sir Rowland asked him.

'Well,' the Inspector replied, 'once or twice there were a couple of things he had to explain to us, as you might say. And the Narcotics Squad came down from London and had a word with him on one occasion . . .' He paused before continuing, 'but it was all no more than suspicion.'

'Officially, that is to say,' Sir Rowland observed.

The Inspector turned to him. 'That's right, sir,' he said meaningfully. 'Officially.'

'Whereas, unofficially – ?' Sir Rowland prompted him.

'I'm afraid we can't go into that,' the Inspector replied. He went on, 'There was, however, one rather curious circumstance. There was an unfinished letter on Mr Sellon's desk, in which he mentioned that he'd come into possession of something which he described as an unparalleled rarity, which he would – ' Here the Inspector paused, as if recollecting the exact words, ' – would guarantee wasn't a forgery, and he was asking fourteen thousand pounds for it.'

Sir Rowland looked thoughtful. 'Fourteen thousand pounds,' he murmured. In a louder voice he continued, 'Yes, that's a lot of money indeed. Now, I wonder what it could be? Jewellery, I suppose, but the word forgery suggests – I don't know, a picture, perhaps?'

Jeremy continued to munch at the sandwiches, as the Inspector replied, 'Yes, perhaps. There was nothing in the shop worth such a large sum of money. The insurance inventory made that clear. Mr Sellon's partner was a woman who has a business of her own in London, and she wrote and said she couldn't give us any help or information.'

Sir Rowland nodded his head slowly. 'So he might have been murdered, and the article, whatever it was, stolen,' he suggested.

'It's quite possible, sir,' the Inspector agreed, 'but again, the would-be thief may not have been able to find it.'

'Now, why do you think that?' Sir Rowland asked.

'Because,' the Inspector replied, 'the shop has been broken into twice since then. Broken into and ransacked.'

Clarissa looked puzzled. 'Why are you telling us all this, Inspector?' she wanted to know.

'Because, Mrs Hailsham-Brown,' said the Inspector, turning to her, 'it's occurred to me that whatever was hidden away by Mr Sellon may have been hidden here in this house, and not at his shop in Maidstone. That's why I asked you if anything peculiar had come to your notice.'

Holding up a hand as though she had suddenly remembered, Clarissa said excitedly, 'Somebody rang up only today and asked to speak to me, and when I came to the phone whoever it was had just hung up. In a way, that's rather odd, isn't it?' She turned to Jeremy, adding, 'Oh yes, of course. You know, that man who came the other day and wanted to buy things – a horsey sort of man in a check suit. He wanted to buy that desk.'

The Inspector crossed the room to look at the desk. 'This one here?' he asked.

'Yes,' Clarissa replied. 'I told him, of course, that it wasn't ours to sell, but he didn't seem to believe me. He offered me a large sum, far more than it's worth.'

'That's very interesting,' the Inspector commented as he studied the desk. 'These things often have a secret drawer, you know.'

'Yes, this one has,' Clarissa told him. 'But there was nothing very exciting in it. Only some old autographs.'

The Inspector looked interested. 'Old autographs can

be immensely valuable, I understand,' he said. 'Whose were they?'

'I can assure you, Inspector,' Sir Rowland informed him, 'that these weren't anything rare enough to be worth more than a pound or two.'

The door to the hall opened, and Constable Jones entered, carrying a small booklet and a pair of gloves.

'Yes, Jones? What is it?' the Inspector asked him.

'I've examined the car, sir,' he replied. 'Just a pair of gloves on the driving seat. But I found this registration book in the side pocket.' He handed the book to the Inspector, and Clarissa exchanged a smile with Jeremy as they heard the Constable's strong Welsh accent.

The Inspector examined the registration book. '"Oliver Costello, 27 Morgan Mansions, London SW3",' he read aloud. Then, turning to Clarissa, he asked sharply, 'Has a man called Costello been here today?'

CHAPTER ELEVEN

The four friends exchanged guiltily furtive glances. Clarissa and Sir Rowland both looked as though they were about to attempt an answer, but it was Clarissa who actually spoke. 'Yes,' she admitted. 'He was here about – ' She paused, and then, 'let me see,' she continued. 'Yes, it was about half past six.'

'Is he a friend of yours?' the Inspector asked her.

'No, I wouldn't call him a friend,' Clarissa replied. 'I had met him only once or twice.' She deliberately assumed an embarrassed look, and then said, hesitantly, 'It's – a little awkward, really – ' She looked appealingly at Sir Rowland, as though passing the ball to him.

That gentleman was quick to respond to her unspoken request. 'Perhaps, Inspector,' he said, 'it would be better if I explained the situation.'

'Please do, sir,' the Inspector responded somewhat tersely.

'Well,' Sir Rowland continued, 'it concerns the first Mrs Hailsham-Brown. She and Hailsham-Brown were divorced just over a year ago, and recently she married Mr Oliver Costello.'

'I see,' observed the Inspector. 'And Mr Costello came here today.' He turned to Clarissa. 'Why was that?' he asked. 'Did he come by appointment?'

'Oh no,' Clarissa replied glibly. 'As a matter of fact, when Miranda and my husband divorced, she took with her one or two things that weren't really hers. Oliver Costello happened to be in this part of the world, and he just looked in to return them to Henry.'

'What kind of things?' the Inspector asked quickly.

Clarissa was ready for this question. 'Nothing very important,' she said with a smile. Picking up the small silver cigarette-box from a table by the sofa, she held it out to the Inspector. 'This was one of them,' she told him. 'It belonged to my husband's mother, and he values it for sentimental reasons.'

The Inspector looked at Clarissa reflectively for a moment, before asking her, 'How long did Mr Costello remain here when he came at six-thirty?'

'Oh, a very short time,' she replied as she replaced the cigarette box on the table. 'He said he was in a hurry. About ten minutes, I should think. No longer than that.'

'And your interview was quite amicable?' the Inspector enquired.

'Oh, yes,' Clarissa assured him. 'I thought it was very kind of him to take the trouble to return the things.'

The Inspector thought for a moment, before asking, 'Did he mention where he was going when he left here?'

'No,' Clarissa replied. 'Actually, he went out by that window,' she continued, gesturing towards the french windows. 'As a matter of fact, my lady gardener, Miss Peake, was here, and she offered to show him out through the garden.'

'Your gardener – does she live on the premises?' the Inspector wanted to know.

'Well, yes. But not in the house. She lives in the cottage.'

'I think I should like a word with her,' the Inspector decided. He turned to the Constable. 'Jones, go and get her.'

'There's a telephone connection through to the cottage. Shall I call her for you, Inspector?' Clarissa offered.

'If you would be so kind, Mrs Hailsham-Brown,' the Inspector replied.

'Not at all. I don't suppose she'll have gone to bed yet,' Clarissa said, pressing a button on the telephone. She flashed a smile at the Inspector, who responded by looking bashful. Jeremy smiled to himself and took another sandwich.

Clarissa spoke into the telephone. 'Hello, Miss Peake. This is Mrs Hailsham-Brown . . . I wonder, would you mind coming over? Something rather important has happened . . . Oh yes, of course that will be all right. Thank you.'

She replaced the receiver and turned to the Inspector.

'Miss Peake has been washing her hair, but she'll get dressed and come right over.'

'Thank you,' said the Inspector. 'After all, Costello may have mentioned to her where he was going.'

'Yes, indeed, he may have,' Clarissa agreed.

The Inspector looked puzzled. 'The question that bothers me,' he announced to the room in general, 'is why Mr Costello's car is still here, and where is Mr Costello?'

Clarissa gave an involuntary glance towards the bookshelves and the panel, then walked across to the french windows to watch for Miss Peake. Jeremy, noticing her glance, sat back innocently and crossed his legs as the Inspector continued, 'Apparently this Miss Peake was the last person to see him. He left, you say, by that window. Did you lock it after him?'

'No,' Clarissa replied, standing at the window with her back to the Inspector.

'Oh?' the Inspector queried.

Something in his tone made Clarissa turn to face him. 'Well, I – I don't think so,' she said, hesitantly.

'So he might have re-entered that way,' the Inspector observed. He took a deep breath and announced importantly, 'I think, Mrs Hailsham-Brown, that, with your permission, I should like to search the house.'

'Of course,' Clarissa replied with a friendly smile. 'Well, you've seen this room. Nobody could be hidden here.' She held the window curtains open for a moment, as though awaiting Miss Peake, and then exclaimed, 'Look! Through here is the library.' Going to the library door and opening it, she suggested, 'Would you like to go in there?'

'Thank you,' said the Inspector. 'Jones!' As the two police officers went into the library, the Inspector added, 'Just see where that door leads to, Jones,' gesturing towards another door immediately inside the library.

'Very good, sir,' the Constable replied, as he went through the door indicated.

As soon as they were out of earshot, Sir Rowland went to Clarissa. 'What's on the other side?' he asked her quietly, indicating the panel.

'Bookshelves,' she replied tersely.

He nodded and strolled nonchalantly across to the sofa, as the Constable's voice was heard calling, 'Just another door through to the hall, sir.'

The two officers returned from the library. 'Right,' said the Inspector. He looked at Sir Rowland, apparently taking note of the fact that he had moved. 'Now we'll search the rest of the house,' he announced, going to the hall door.

'I'll come with you, if you don't mind,' Clarissa offered, 'in case my little stepdaughter should wake up and be frightened. Not that I think she will. It's extraordinary how deeply children can sleep. You have to practically shake them awake.'

As the Inspector opened the hall door, she asked him, 'Have you got any children, Inspector?'

'One boy and one girl,' he replied shortly, as he made his way out of the room, crossed the hall, and began to ascend the stairs.

'Isn't that nice?' Clarissa observed. She turned to the Constable. 'Mr Jones,' she invited him with a gesture to precede her. He made his way out of the room and she followed him closely.

As soon as they had gone, the three remaining occupants of the room looked at one another. Hugo wiped his hands and Jeremy mopped his forehead. 'And now what?' Jeremy asked, taking another sandwich.

Sir Rowland shook his head. 'I don't like this,' he told them. 'We're getting in very deep.'

'If you ask me,' Hugo advised him, 'there's only one thing to do. Come clean. Own up now before it's too late.'

'Damn it, we can't do that,' Jeremy exclaimed. 'It would be too unfair to Clarissa.'

'But we'll get her in a worse mess if we keep on with this,' Hugo insisted. 'How are we ever going to get the body away? The police will impound the fellow's car.'

'We could use mine,' Jeremy suggested.

'Well, I don't like it,' Hugo persisted. 'I don't like it at all. Damn it, I'm a local JP. I've got my reputation with the police here to consider.' He turned to Sir Rowland. 'What do you say, Roly? You've got a good level head.'

Sir Rowland looked grave. 'I admit I don't like it,' he replied, 'but personally I am committed to the enterprise.'

Hugo looked perplexed. 'I don't understand you,' he told his friend.

'Take it on trust, if you will, Hugo,' said Sir Rowland.

He looked gravely at both men, and continued, 'We're in a very bad jam, all of us. But if we stick together and have reasonable luck, I think there's a chance we may be able to pull it off.'

Jeremy looked as though he was about to say something, but Sir Rowland held up a hand, and went on, 'Once the police are satisfied that Costello isn't in this house, they'll go off and look elsewhere. After all, there are plenty of reasons why he might have left his car and gone off on foot.' He gestured towards them both and added, 'We're all respectable people – Hugo's a JP, as he's reminded us, and Henry Hailsham-Brown's high up in the Foreign Office – '

'Yes, yes, and you've had a blameless and even distinguished career, we know all that,' Hugo intervened. 'All right then, if you say so, we brazen it out.'

Jeremy rose to his feet and nodded towards the recess. 'Can't we do something about that straight away?' he asked.

'There's no time now,' Sir Rowland decreed, tersely. 'They'll be back any minute. He's safer where he is.'

Jeremy nodded in reluctant agreement. 'I must say Clarissa's a marvel,' he observed. 'She doesn't turn a hair. She's got that police inspector eating out of her hand.'

The front door bell rang. 'That'll be Miss Peake, I expect,' Sir Rowland announced. 'Go and let her in, Warrender, would you?'

As soon as Jeremy had left the room, Hugo beckoned to Sir Rowland.

'What's up, Roly?' he asked in an urgent whisper. 'What did Clarissa tell you when she got you to herself?'

Sir Rowland began to speak, but, hearing the voices of Jeremy and Miss Peake exchanging greetings at the front door, he made a gesture indicating 'Not now'.

'I think you'd better come in here,' Jeremy told Miss Peake as he slammed the front door shut. A moment later, the gardener preceded him into the drawing-room, looking as though she had dressed very hastily. She had a towel wrapped around her head.

'What is all this?' she wanted to know. 'Mrs Hailsham-Brown was most mysterious on the phone. Has anything happened?'

Sir Rowland addressed her with the utmost courtesy. 'I'm so sorry you've been routed out like this, Miss Peake,' he apologized. 'Do sit down.' He indicated a chair by the bridge table.

Hugo pulled the chair out for Miss Peake, who thanked him. He then seated himself in a more comfortable easy chair, while Sir Rowland informed the gardener, 'As a matter of fact, we've got the police here, and – '

'The police?' Miss Peake interrupted, looking startled. 'Has there been a burglary?'

'No, not a burglary, but – '

He stopped speaking as Clarissa, the Inspector and the Constable came back into the room. Jeremy sat on the sofa, while Sir Rowland took up a position behind it.

'Inspector,' Clarissa announced, 'this is Miss Peake.'

The Inspector went across to the gardener. His 'Good

evening, Miss Peake' was accompanied by a stiff little bow.

'Good evening, Inspector,' Miss Peake replied. 'I was just asking Sir Rowland – has there been a robbery, or what?'

The Inspector regarded her searchingly, allowed a moment or two to elapse, and then spoke. 'We received a rather peculiar telephone call which brought us out here,' he told her. 'And we think that perhaps you might be able to clear up the matter for us.'

CHAPTER TWELVE

The Inspector's announcement was greeted by Miss
Peake with a jolly laugh. 'I say, this is mysterious. I
am enjoying myself,' she exclaimed delightedly.

The Inspector frowned. 'It concerns Mr Costello,' he
explained. 'Mr Oliver Costello of 27, Morgan Mansions,
London SW3. I believe that's in the Chelsea area.'

'Never heard of him,' was Miss Peake's robustly expressed
response.

'He was here this evening, visiting Mrs Hailsham-
Brown,' the Inspector reminded her, 'and I believe you
showed him out through the garden.'

Miss Peake slapped her thigh. 'Oh, that man,' she
recalled. 'Mrs Hailsham-Brown did mention his name.'
She looked at the Inspector with a little more interest.
'Yes, what do you want to know?' she asked.

'I should like to know,' the Inspector told her, speaking

slowly and deliberately, 'exactly what happened, and when you last saw him.'

Miss Peake thought for a moment before replying. 'Let me see,' she said. 'We went out through the french window, and I told him there was a short cut if he wanted the bus, and he said no, he'd come in his car, and he'd left it round by the stables.'

She beamed at the Inspector as though she expected to be praised for her succinct recollection of what had occurred, but he merely looked thoughtful as he commented, 'Isn't that rather an odd place to leave a car?'

'That's just what I thought,' Miss Peake agreed, slapping the Inspector's arm as she spoke. He looked surprised at this, but she continued, 'You'd think he'd drive right up to the front door, wouldn't you? But people are so odd. You never know what they're going to do.' She gave a hearty guffaw.

'And then what happened?' the Inspector asked.

Miss Peake shrugged her shoulders. 'Well, he went off to his car, and I suppose he drove away,' she replied.

'You didn't see him do so?'

'No – I was putting my tools away,' was the gardener's reply.

'And that's the last you saw of him?' the Inspector asked, with emphasis.

'Yes, why?'

'Because his car is still here,' the Inspector told her. Speaking slowly and emphatically, he continued, 'A phone-call was put through to the police station at seven forty-nine, saying that a man had been murdered at Copplestone Court.'

Miss Peake looked appalled. 'Murdered?' she exclaimed. 'Here? Ridiculous!'

'That's what everybody seems to think,' the Inspector observed drily, with a significant look at Sir Rowland.

'Of course,' Miss Peake went on, 'I know there are all these maniacs about, attacking women – but you say a man was murdered – '

The Inspector cut her short. 'You didn't hear another car this evening?' he asked brusquely.

'Only Mr Hailsham-Brown's,' she replied.

'Mr Hailsham-Brown?' the Inspector queried with a raise of his eyebrows. 'I thought he wasn't expected home till late.'

His glance swung round to Clarissa, who hastened to explain. 'My husband did come home, but he had to go out again almost immediately.'

The Inspector assumed a deliberately patient expression. 'Oh, is that so?' he commented in a tone of studied politeness. 'Exactly when did he come home?'

'Let me see – ' Clarissa began to stammer. 'It must have been about – '

'It was about a quarter of an hour before I went off duty,' Miss Peake interjected. 'I work a lot of overtime, Inspector. I never stick to regulation hours,' she explained. 'Be keen on your job, that's what I say,' she continued, thumping the table as she spoke. 'Yes, it must have been about a quarter past seven when Mr Hailsham-Brown got in.'

'That would have been shortly after Mr Costello left,' the Inspector observed. He moved to the centre of the room, and his manner changed almost imperceptibly as he continued, 'He and Mr Hailsham-Brown probably passed each other.'

'You mean,' Miss Peake said thoughtfully, 'that he may have come back again to see Mr Hailsham-Brown.'

'Oliver Costello definitely didn't come back to the house,' Clarissa cut in sharply.

'But you can't be sure of that, Mrs Hailsham-Brown,' the gardener contradicted her. 'He might have got in by that window without your knowing anything about it.' She paused, and then exclaimed, 'Golly! You don't think he murdered Mr Hailsham-Brown, do you? I say, I am sorry.'

'Of course he didn't murder Henry,' Clarissa snapped irritably.

'Where did your husband go when he left here?' the Inspector asked her.

'I've no idea,' Clarissa replied shortly.

'Doesn't he usually tell you where he's going?' the Inspector persisted.

'I never ask questions,' Clarissa told him. 'I think it must be so boring for a man if his wife is always asking questions.'

Miss Peake gave a sudden squeal. 'But how stupid of me,' she shouted. 'Of course, if that man's car is still here, then he must be the one who's been murdered.' She roared with laughter.

Sir Rowland rose to his feet. 'We've no reason to believe

[116]

anyone has been murdered, Miss Peake,' he admonished her with dignity. 'In fact, the Inspector believes it was all some silly hoax.'

Miss Peake was clearly not of the same opinion. 'But the car,' she insisted. 'I do think that car still being here is very suspicious.' She got up and approached the Inspector. 'Have you looked about for the body, Inspector?' she asked him eagerly.

'The Inspector has already searched the house,' Sir Rowland answered before the police officer had a chance to speak. He was rewarded by a sharp glance from the Inspector, whom Miss Peake was now tapping on the shoulder as she continued to air her views.

'I'm sure those Elgins have something to do with it – the butler and that wife of his who calls herself a cook,' the gardener assured the Inspector confidently. 'I've had my suspicions of them for quite some time. I saw a light in their bedroom window as I came along here just now. And that in itself is suspicious. It's their night out, and they usually don't return until well after eleven.' She gripped the Inspector's arm. 'Have you searched their quarters?' she asked him urgently.

The Inspector opened his mouth to speak, but she interrupted him with another tap on the shoulder. 'Now listen,' she began. 'Suppose this Mr Costello recognized Elgin as a man with a criminal record. Costello might have decided to come back and warn Mrs Hailsham-Brown about the man, and Elgin assaulted him.'

Looking immensely pleased with herself, she flashed a

glance around the room, and continued. 'Then, of course, Elgin would have to hide the body somewhere quickly, so that he could dispose of it later in the night. Now, where would he hide it, I wonder?' she asked rhetorically, warming to her thesis. With a gesture towards the french windows, she began, 'Behind a curtain or – '

She was cut short by Clarissa who interrupted angrily. 'Oh, really, Miss Peake. There isn't anybody hidden behind any of the curtains. And I'm sure Elgin would never murder anybody. It's quite ridiculous.'

Miss Peake turned. 'You're so trusting, Mrs Hailsham-Brown,' she admonished her employer. 'When you get to my age, you'll realize how very often people are simply not quite what they seem.' She laughed heartily as she turned back to the Inspector.

When he opened his mouth to speak, she gave him yet another tap on the shoulder. 'Now then,' she continued, 'where would a man like Elgin hide the body? There's that cupboard place between here and the library. You've looked there, I suppose?'

Sir Rowland intervened hastily. 'Miss Peake, the Inspector has looked both here *and* in the library,' he insisted.

The Inspector, however, after a meaning look at Sir Rowland, turned to the gardener. 'What exactly do you mean by "that cupboard place", Miss Peake?' he enquired.

The others in the room all looked more than somewhat tense as Miss Peake replied, 'Oh, it's a wonderful place when you're playing hide-and-seek. You'd really never dream it was there. Let me show it to you.'

She walked over to the panel, followed by the Inspector. Jeremy got to his feet at the same moment that Clarissa exclaimed forcefully, 'No.'

The Inspector and Miss Peake both turned to look at her. 'There's nothing there now,' Clarissa informed them. 'I know because I went that way, through to the library, just now.'

Her voice trailed off. Miss Peake, sounding disappointed, murmured, 'Oh well, in that case, then – ' and turned away from the panel. The Inspector, however, called her back. 'Just show me all the same, Miss Peake,' he ordered. 'I'd like to see.'

Miss Peake went to the bookshelves. 'It was a door originally,' she explained. 'It matched the one over there.' She activated the lever, explaining as she did so, 'You pull this catch back, and the door comes open. See?'

The panel opened, and the body of Oliver Costello slumped down and fell forward. Miss Peake screamed.

'So,' the Inspector observed, looking grimly at Clarissa, 'You were mistaken, Mrs Hailsham-Brown. It appears that there was a murder here tonight.'

Miss Peake's scream rose to a crescendo.

CHAPTER THIRTEEN

Ten minutes later, things were somewhat quieter, for Miss Peake was no longer in the room. Nor, for that matter, were Hugo and Jeremy. The body of Oliver Costello, however, was still lying collapsed in the recess, the panel of which was open. Clarissa was stretched out on the sofa, with Sir Rowland sitting by her and holding a glass of brandy which he was attempting to make her sip. The Inspector was talking on the telephone, and Constable Jones continued to stand guard.

'Yes, yes – ' the Inspector was saying. 'What's that? – Hit and run? – Where? – Oh, I see – Yes, well, send them along as soon as you can – Yes, we'll want photographs – Yes, the whole bag of tricks.'

He replaced the receiver, and went over to the Constable. 'Everything comes at once,' he complained to his colleague. 'Weeks go by and nothing happens, and now the Divisional Surgeon's out at a bad car accident – a smash on the London road. It'll all mean quite a bit of delay. However, we'll get on as well as we can until the M.O. arrives.' He gestured towards the corpse. 'We'd better not move him until they've taken the photographs,' he suggested. 'Not that it will tell us anything. He wasn't killed there, he was put there afterwards.'

'How can you be sure, sir?' the Constable asked.

The Inspector looked down at the carpet. 'You can see where his feet have dragged,' he pointed out, crouching down behind the sofa. The Constable knelt beside him.

Sir Rowland peered over the back of the sofa, and then turned to Clarissa to ask, 'How are you feeling now?'

'Better, thanks, Roly,' she replied, faintly.

The two police officers got to their feet. 'It might be as well to close that book-case door,' the Inspector instructed his colleague. 'We don't want any more hysterics.'

'Right, sir,' the Constable replied. He closed the panel so that the body could no longer be seen. As he did so, Sir Rowland rose from the sofa to address the Inspector. 'Mrs Hailsham-Brown has had a bad shock,' he told the policeman. 'I think she ought to go to her room and lie down.'

Politely, but with a certain reserve, the Inspector replied, 'Certainly, sir, but not for a moment or two just yet. I'd like to ask her a few questions first.'

Sir Rowland tried to persist. 'She's really not fit to be questioned at present.'

'I'm all right, Roly,' Clarissa interjected, faintly. 'Really, I am.'

Sir Rowland addressed her, adopting a warning tone. 'It's very brave of you, my dear,' he said, 'but I really think it would be wiser of you to go and rest for a while.'

'Dear Uncle Roly,' Clarissa responded with a smile. To the Inspector she said, 'I sometimes call him Uncle Roly, though he's my guardian, not my uncle. But he's so sweet to me always.'

'Yes, I can see that,' was the dry response.

'Do ask me anything you want to, Inspector,' Clarissa continued graciously. 'Though actually I don't think I can help you very much, I'm afraid, because I just don't know anything at all about any of this.'

Sir Rowland sighed, shook his head slightly, and turned away.

'We shan't worry you for long, madam,' the Inspector assured her. Going to the library door, he held it open, and turned to address Sir Rowland. 'Will you join the other gentlemen in the library, sir?' he suggested.

'I think I'd better remain here, in case – ' Sir Rowland began, only to be interrupted by the Inspector whose tone had now become firmer. 'I'll call you if it should be necessary, sir. In the library, please.'

After a short duel of eyes, Sir Rowland conceded defeat and went into the library. The Inspector closed the door after him, and indicated silently to the Constable that he should sit and take notes. Clarissa swung her feet off the sofa and sat up, as Jones got out his notebook and pencil.

'Now, Mrs Hailsham-Brown,' the Inspector began, 'if

you're ready, let's make a start.' He picked up the cigarette box from the table by the sofa, turned it over, opened it, and looked at the cigarettes in it.

'Dear Uncle Roly, he always wants to spare me everything,' Clarissa told the Inspector with an enchanting smile. Then, seeing him handling the cigarette box, she became anxious. 'This isn't going to be the third degree or anything, is it?' she asked, trying to make her question sound like a joke.

'Nothing of that kind, madam, I assure you,' said the Inspector. 'Just a few simple questions.' He turned to the Constable. 'Are you ready, Jones?' he asked, as he pulled out a chair from the bridge table, turned it around, and sat facing Clarissa.

'All ready, sir,' Constable Jones replied.

'Good. Now, Mrs Hailsham-Brown,' the Inspector began. 'Do you say that you had no idea there was a body concealed in that recess?'

The Constable began his note-taking as Clarissa answered, wide-eyed, 'No, of course not. It's horrible.' She shivered. 'Quite horrible.'

The Inspector looked at her enquiringly. 'When we were searching this room,' he asked, 'why didn't you call our attention to that recess?'

Clarissa met his gaze with a look of wide-eyed innocence. 'Do you know,' she said, 'the thought never struck me. You see, we never use the recess, so it just didn't come into my head.'

The Inspector pounced. 'But you said,' he reminded

her, 'that you had just been through there into the library.'

'Oh no,' Clarissa exclaimed quickly. 'You must have misunderstood me.' She pointed to the library door. 'What I meant was that we had gone through that door into the library.'

'Yes, I certainly must have misunderstood you,' the Inspector observed grimly. 'Now, let me at least be clear about this. You say you have no idea when Mr Costello came back to this house, or what he might have come for?'

'No, I simply can't imagine,' Clarissa replied, her voice dripping with innocent candour.

'But the fact remains that he did come back,' the Inspector persisted.

'Yes, of course. We know that now.'

'Well, he must have had some reason,' the Inspector pointed out.

'I suppose so,' Clarissa agreed. 'But I've no idea what it could have been.'

The Inspector thought for a moment, and then tried another line of approach. 'Do you think that perhaps he wanted to see your husband?' he suggested.

'Oh, no,' Clarissa replied quickly, 'I'm quite sure he didn't. Henry and he never liked each other.'

'Oh!' the Inspector exclaimed. 'They never liked each other. I didn't realize that. Had there been a quarrel between them?'

Again Clarissa spoke quickly to forestall a new and

potentially dangerous line of enquiry. 'Oh no,' she assured the Inspector, 'no, they hadn't quarrelled. Henry just thought he wore the wrong shoes.' She smiled engagingly. 'You know how odd men can be.'

The Inspector's look suggested that this was something of which he was personally ignorant. 'You're absolutely certain that Costello wouldn't have come back here to see you?' he asked again.

'Me?' Clarissa echoed innocently. 'Oh no, I'm sure he didn't. What reason could he possibly have?'

The Inspector took a deep breath. Then, speaking slowly and deliberately, he asked her, 'Is there anybody else in the house he might have wanted to see? Now please think carefully before you answer.'

Again, Clarissa gave him her look of bland innocence. 'I can't think who,' she insisted. 'I mean, who else is there?'

The Inspector rose, turned his chair around and put it back against the bridge table. Then, pacing slowly about the room, he began to muse. 'Mr Costello comes here,' he began slowly, 'and returns the articles which the first Mrs Hailsham-Brown had taken from your husband by mistake. Then he says good-bye. But then he comes back to the house.'

He went across to the french windows. 'Presumably he effects an entrance through these windows,' he continued, gesturing at them. 'He is killed – and his body is pushed into that recess – all in a space of about ten to twenty minutes.'

He turned back to face Clarissa. 'And nobody hears anything?' he ended, on a rising inflection. 'I find that very difficult to believe.'

'I know,' Clarissa agreed. 'I find it just as difficult to believe. It's really extraordinary, isn't it?'

'It certainly is,' the Inspector agreed, his tone distinctly ironical. He tried one last time. 'Mrs Hailsham-Brown, are you absolutely sure that you didn't hear anything?' he asked her pointedly.

'I heard nothing at all,' she answered. 'It really is fantastic.'

'Almost too fantastic,' the Inspector commented grimly. He paused, then went over to the hall door and held it open. 'Well, that's all for the present, Mrs Hailsham-Brown.'

Clarissa rose and walked rather quickly towards the library door, only to be intercepted by the Inspector. 'Not that way, please,' he instructed her, and led her over to the hall door.

'But I think, really, I'd rather join the others,' she protested.

'Later, if you don't mind,' said the Inspector tersely.

Very reluctantly, Clarissa went out through the hall door.

CHAPTER FOURTEEN

The Inspector closed the hall door behind Clarissa, then went over to Constable Jones who was still writing in his notebook. 'Where's the other woman? The gardener. Miss – er – Peake?' the Inspector asked.

'I put her on the bed in the spare room,' the Constable told his superior. 'After she came out of the hysterics, that is. A terrible time I had with her, laughing and crying something terrible, she was.'

'It doesn't matter if Mrs Hailsham-Brown goes and talks to her,' the Inspector told him. 'But she's not to talk to those three men. We'll have no comparing of stories, and no prompting. I hope you locked the door from the library to the hall?'

'Yes, sir,' the Constable assured him. 'I've got the key here.'

'I don't know what to make of them at all,' the Inspector

confessed to his colleague. 'They're all highly respectable people. Hailsham-Brown's a Foreign Office diplomat, Hugo Birch is a JP whom we know, and Hailsham-Brown's other two guests seem decent upper-class types – well, you know what I mean . . . But there's something funny going on. None of them are being straightforward with us – and that includes Mrs Hailsham-Brown. They're hiding something, and I'm determined to find out what it is, whether it's got anything to do with this murder or not.'

He stretched his arms above his head as though seeking inspiration from on high, and then addressed the Constable again. 'Well, we'd better get on with it,' he said. 'Let's take them one at a time.'

As the Constable got to his feet, the Inspector changed his mind. 'No. Just a moment. First I'll have a word with that butler chap,' he decided.

'Elgin?'

'Yes, Elgin. Call him in. I've got an idea he knows something.'

'Certainly, sir,' the Constable replied.

Leaving the room, he found Elgin hovering near the sitting-room door. The butler made a tentative pretence of heading for the stairs, but stopped when the Constable called him and came into the room rather nervously.

The Constable closed the hall door and resumed his place for note-taking, while the Inspector indicated the chair near the bridge table.

Elgin sat down, and the Inspector began his interrogation.

'Now, you started off for the pictures this evening,' he reminded the butler, 'but you came back. Why was that?'

'I've told you, sir,' Elgin replied. 'My wife wasn't feeling well.'

The Inspector regarded him steadily. 'It was you who let Mr Costello into the house when he called here this evening, was it not?' he asked.

'Yes, sir.'

The Inspector took a few paces away from Elgin, and then turned back suddenly. 'Why didn't you tell us at once that it was Mr Costello's car outside?' he asked.

'I didn't know whose car it was, sir. Mr Costello didn't drive up to the front door. I didn't even know he'd come in a car.'

'Wasn't that rather peculiar? Leaving his car around by the stables?' the Inspector suggested.

'Well, yes, sir, I suppose it was,' the butler replied. 'But I expect he had his reasons.'

'Just what do you mean by that?' the Inspector asked quickly.

'Nothing, sir,' Elgin answered. He sounded almost smug. 'Nothing at all.'

'Had you ever seen Mr Costello before?' The Inspector's voice was sharp as he asked this.

'Never, sir,' Elgin assured him.

The Inspector adopted a meaning tone to enquire, 'It wasn't because of Mr Costello that you came back this evening?'

'I've told you, sir,' said Elgin. 'My wife – '

'I don't want to hear any more about your wife,' the Inspector interrupted. Moving away from Elgin, he continued, 'How long have you been with Mrs Hailsham-Brown?'

'Six weeks, sir,' was the reply.

The Inspector turned back to face Elgin. 'And before that?'

'I'd – I'd been having a little rest,' the butler replied uneasily.

'A rest?' the Inspector echoed, in a tone of suspicion. He paused and then added, 'You do realize that, in a case like this, your references will have to be looked into very carefully.'

Elgin began to get to his feet. 'Will that be all – ' he started to say, and then stopped and resumed his seat. 'I – I wouldn't wish to deceive you, sir,' he continued. 'It wasn't anything really wrong. What I mean is – the original reference having got torn – I couldn't quite remember the wording – '

'So you wrote your own references,' the Inspector interrupted. 'That's what it comes to, doesn't it?'

'I didn't mean any harm,' Elgin protested. 'I've got my living to earn – '

The Inspector interrupted him again. 'At the moment, I'm not interested in fake references,' he told the butler. 'I want to know what happened here tonight, and what you know about Mr Costello.'

'I'd never set eyes on him before,' Elgin insisted.

Looking around at the hall door, he continued, 'But I've got a good idea of why he came here.'

'Oh, and what is that?' the Inspector wanted to know.

'Blackmail,' Elgin told him. 'He had something on her.'

'By "her",' said the Inspector, 'I assume you mean Mrs Hailsham-Brown.'

'Yes,' Elgin continued eagerly. 'I came in to ask if there was anything more she wanted, and I heard them talking.'

'What did you hear exactly?'

'I heard her say "But that's blackmail. I won't submit to it".' Elgin adopted a highly dramatic tone as he quoted Clarissa's words.

'Hm!' the Inspector responded a little doubtfully. 'Anything more?'

'No,' Elgin admitted. 'They stopped when I came in, and when I went out they dropped their voices.'

'I see,' the Inspector commented. He looked intently at the butler, waiting for him to speak again.

Elgin got up from his chair. His voice was almost a whine as he pleaded, 'You won't be hard on me, sir, will you? I've had a lot of trouble one way and another.'

The Inspector regarded him for a moment longer, and then said dismissively, 'Oh, that will do. Get out.'

'Yes, sir. Thank you, sir,' Elgin responded quickly as he made a hasty exit into the hall.

The Inspector watched him go, and then turned to the Constable. 'Blackmail, eh?' he murmured, exchanging glances with his colleague.

'And Mrs Hailsham-Brown such a nice seeming lady,' Constable Jones observed with a somewhat prim look.

'Yes, well one never can tell,' the Inspector observed. He paused, and then ordered curtly, 'I'll see Mr Birch now.' The Constable went to the library door. 'Mr Birch, please.'

Hugo came through the library door, looking dogged and rather defiant. The Constable closed the door behind him and took a seat at the table, while the Inspector greeted Hugo pleasantly. 'Come in, Mr Birch,' he invited. 'Sit down here, please.'

Hugo sat, and the Inspector continued, 'This is a very unpleasant business, I'm afraid, sir. What have you to tell us about it?'

Slapping his spectacle case on the table, Hugo replied defiantly, 'Absolutely nothing.'

'Nothing?' queried the Inspector, sounding surprised.

'What do you expect me to say?' Hugo expostulated. 'The blinking woman snaps open the blinking cupboard, and out falls a blinking corpse.' He gave a snort of impatience. 'Took my breath away,' he declared. 'I've not got over it yet.' He glared at the Inspector. 'It's no good asking me anything,' he said firmly, 'because I don't know anything about it.'

The Inspector regarded Hugo steadily for a moment before asking, 'That's your statement, is it? Just that you know nothing at all about it?'

'I'm telling you,' Hugo repeated. 'I didn't kill the fellow.' Again he glared defiantly. 'I didn't even know him.'

'You didn't know him,' the Inspector repeated. 'Very

well. I'm not suggesting that you did know him. I'm certainly not suggesting that you murdered him. But I can't believe that you "know nothing", as you put it. So let's collaborate to find out what you do know. To begin with, you'd heard of him, hadn't you?'

'Yes,' snapped Hugo, 'and I'd heard he was a nasty bit of goods.'

'In what way?' the Inspector asked calmly.

'Oh, I don't know,' Hugo blustered. 'He was the sort of fellow that women liked and men had no use for. That sort of thing.'

The Inspector paused before asking carefully, 'You've no idea why he should come back to this house a second time this evening?'

'Not a clue,' replied Hugo dismissively.

The Inspector took a few steps around the room, then turned abruptly to face Hugo. 'Was there anything between him and the present Mrs Hailsham-Brown, do you think?' he asked.

Hugo looked shocked. 'Clarissa? Good Lord, no! Nice girl, Clarissa. Got a lot of sense. She wouldn't look twice at a fellow like that.'

The Inspector paused again, and then said, finally, 'So you can't help us.'

'Sorry. But there it is,' replied Hugo with an attempt at nonchalance.

Making one last effort to extract at least a crumb of information from Hugo, the Inspector asked, 'Had you really no idea that the body was in that recess?

'Of course not,' replied Hugo, now sounding offended.

'Thank you, sir,' said the Inspector, turning away from him.

'What?' queried Hugo vaguely.

'That's all, thank you, sir,' the Inspector repeated. He went to the desk and picked up a red book that lay on it.

Hugo rose, picked up his spectacle case, and was about to go across to the library door when the Constable got up and barred his way. Hugo then turned towards the french windows, but the Constable said, 'This way, Mr Birch, please,' and opened the hall door. Giving up, Hugo went out and the policeman closed the door behind him.

The Inspector carried his huge red book over to the bridge table, and sat consulting it, as Constable Jones commented satirically, 'Mr Birch was a mine of information, wasn't he? Mind you, it's not very nice for a JP to be mixed up in a murder.'

The Inspector began to read aloud. '"Delahaye, Sir Rowland Edward Mark, KCB, MVO – "'

'What have you got there?' the Constable asked. He peered over the Inspector's shoulder. 'Oh, *Who's Who*.'

The Inspector went on reading. '"Educated Eton – Trinity College – " Um! "Attached Foreign Office – second Secretary – Madrid – Plenipotentiary".'

'Ooh!' the Constable exclaimed at this last word.

The Inspector gave him an exasperated look, and continued, '"Constantinople, Foreign Office – special commission rendered – Clubs – Boodles – Whites".'

'Do you want him next, sir?' the Constable asked.

The Inspector thought for a moment. 'No,' he decided. 'He's the most interesting of the lot, so I'll leave him till the last. Let's have young Warrender in now.'

CHAPTER FIFTEEN

Constable Jones, standing at the library door, called, 'Mr Warrender, please.'

Jeremy came in, attempting rather unsuccessfully to look completely at his ease. The Constable closed the door and resumed his seat at the table, while the Inspector half rose and pulled out a chair from the bridge table for Jeremy.

'Sit down,' he ordered somewhat brusquely as he resumed his seat. Jeremy sat, and the Inspector asked formally, 'Your name?'

'Jeremy Warrender.'

'Address?'

'Three hundred and forty, Broad Street, and thirty-four Grosvenor Square,' Jeremy told him, trying to sound non-chalant. He glanced across at the Constable who was writing all this down, and added, 'Country address, Hepplestone, Wiltshire.'

'That sounds as though you're a gentleman of independent means,' the Inspector commented.

'I'm afraid not,' Jeremy admitted, with a smile. 'I'm private secretary to Sir Kenneth Thomson, the Chairman of Saxon-Arabian Oil. Those are his addresses.'

The Inspector nodded. 'I see. How long have you been with him?'

'About a year. Before that, I was personal assistant to Mr Scott Agius for four years.'

'Ah, yes,' said the Inspector. 'He's that wealthy businessman in the City, isn't he?' He thought for a moment before going on to ask, 'Did you know this man, Oliver Costello?'

'No, I'd never heard of him till tonight,' Jeremy told him.

'And you didn't see him when he came to the house earlier this evening?' the Inspector continued.

'No,' Jeremy replied. 'I'd gone over to the golf club with the others. We were dining there, you see. It was the servants' night out, and Mr Birch had asked us to dine with him at the club.'

The Inspector nodded his head. After a pause, he asked, 'Was Mrs Hailsham-Brown invited, too?'

'No, she wasn't,' said Jeremy.

The Inspector raised his eyebrows, and Jeremy hurried on. 'That is,' he explained, 'she could have come if she'd liked.'

'Do you mean,' the Inspector asked him, 'that she was asked, then? And she refused?'

'No, no,' Jeremy replied hurriedly, sounding as though

he was getting rattled. 'What I mean is – well, Hailsham-Brown is usually quite tired by the time he gets down here, and Clarissa said they'd just have a scratch meal here, as usual.'

The Inspector looked confused. 'Let me get this clear,' he said rather snappily. 'Mrs Hailsham-Brown expected her husband to dine here? She didn't expect him to go out again as soon as he came in?'

Jeremy was now quite definitely flustered. 'I – er – well – er – really, I don't know,' he stammered. 'No – Now that you mention it, I believe she did say he was going to be out this evening.'

The Inspector rose and took a few paces away from Jeremy. 'It seems odd, then,' he observed, 'that Mrs Hailsham-Brown should not have come out to the club with the three of you, instead of remaining here to dine all by herself.'

Jeremy turned on his chair to face the Inspector. 'Well – er – well –' he began, and then, gaining confidence, continued quickly, 'I mean, it was the kid – Pippa, you know. Clarissa wouldn't have liked to go out and leave the kid all by herself in the house.'

'Or perhaps,' the Inspector suggested, speaking with heavy significance, 'perhaps she was making plans to receive a visitor of her own?'

Jeremy rose to his feet. 'I say, that's a rotten thing to suggest,' he exclaimed hotly. 'And it isn't true. I'm sure she never planned anything of the kind.'

'Yet Oliver Costello came here to meet someone,' the

[141]

Inspector pointed out. 'The two servants had the night off. Miss Peake has her own cottage. There was really no one he could have come to the house to meet except Mrs Hailsham-Brown.'

'All I can say is –' Jeremy began. Then, turning away, he added limply, 'Well, you'd better ask her.'

'I have asked her,' the Inspector informed him.

'What did she say?' asked Jeremy, turning back to face the police officer.

'Just what you say,' the Inspector replied suavely.

Jeremy sat down again at the bridge table. 'There you are, then,' he observed.

The Inspector took a few steps around the room, his eyes on the floor as though deep in thought. Then he turned back to face Jeremy. 'Now tell me,' he queried, 'just how you all happened to come back here from the club. Was that your original plan?'

'Yes,' Jeremy replied, but then quickly changed his answer. 'I mean, no.'

'Which do you mean, sir?' the Inspector queried smoothly.

Jeremy took a deep breath. 'Well,' he began, 'it was like this. We all went over to the club. Sir Rowland and old Hugo went straight into the dining-room and I came in a bit later. It's all a cold buffet, you know. I'd been knocking balls about until it got dark, and then – well, somebody said "Bridge, anyone?", and I said, "Well, why don't we go back to the Hailsham-Browns' where it's more cosy, and play there?" So we did.'

'I see,' observed the Inspector. 'So it was your idea?'

Jeremy shrugged his shoulders. 'I really don't remember who suggested it first,' he admitted. 'It may have been Hugo Birch, I think.'

'And you arrived back here – when?'

Jeremy thought for a moment, and then shook his head. 'I can't say exactly,' he murmured. 'We probably left the club house just a bit before eight.'

'And it's – what?' the Inspector wondered. 'Five minutes' walk?'

'Yes, just about that. The golf course adjoins this garden,' Jeremy answered, glancing out of the window.

The Inspector went across to the bridge table, and looked down at its surface. 'And then you played bridge?'

'Yes,' Jeremy confirmed.

The Inspector nodded his head slowly. 'That must have been about twenty minutes before my arrival here,' he calculated. He began to walk slowly around the table. 'Surely you didn't have time to complete two rubbers and start – ' he held up Clarissa's marker so that Jeremy could see it – 'a third?'

'What?' Jeremy looked confused for a moment, but then said quickly, 'Oh, no. No. That first rubber must have been yesterday's score.'

Indicating the other markers, the Inspector remarked thoughtfully, 'Only one person seems to have scored.'

'Yes,' Jeremy agreed. 'I'm afraid we're all a bit lazy about scoring. We left it to Clarissa.'

The Inspector walked across to the sofa. 'Did you know

about the passage-way between this room and the library?' he asked.

'You mean the place where the body was found?'

'That's what I mean.'

'No. No, I'd no idea,' Jeremy asserted. 'Wonderful bit of camouflage, isn't it? You'd never guess it was there.'

The Inspector sat on an arm of the sofa, leaning back and dislodging a cushion. He noticed the gloves that had been lying under the cushion. His face wore a serious expression as he said quietly, 'Consequently, Mr Warrender, you couldn't know there was a body in that passage-way. Could you?'

Jeremy turned away. 'You could have knocked me over with a feather, as the saying goes,' he replied. 'Absolute blood and thunder melodrama. Couldn't believe my eyes.'

While Jeremy was speaking, the Inspector had been sorting out the gloves on the sofa. He now held up one pair of them, rather in the manner of a conjuror. 'By the way, are these your gloves, Mr Warrender?' he asked, trying to sound off-handed.

Jeremy turned back to him. 'No. I mean, yes,' he replied confusedly.

'Again, which do you mean, sir?'

'Yes, they are mine, I think.'

'Were you wearing them when you came back here from the golf club?'

'Yes,' Jeremy recalled. 'I remember now. Yes, I was wearing them. There's a bit of a nip in the air this evening.'

The Inspector got up from the arm of the sofa, and approached Jeremy. 'I think you're mistaken, sir.' Indicating the initials in the gloves, he pointed out, 'These have Mr Hailsham-Brown's initials inside them.'

Returning his gaze calmly, Jeremy replied, 'Oh, that's funny. I've got a pair just the same.'

The Inspector returned to the sofa, sat on the arm again and, leaning over, produced the second pair of gloves. 'Perhaps these are yours?' he suggested.

Jeremy laughed. 'You don't catch me a second time,' he replied. 'After all, one pair of gloves looks exactly like another.'

The Inspector produced the third pair of gloves. 'Three pairs of gloves,' he murmured, examining them. 'All with Hailsham-Brown's initials inside. Curious.'

'Well, it is his house, after all,' Jeremy pointed out. 'Why shouldn't he have three pairs of gloves lying about?'

'The only interesting thing,' the Inspector replied, 'is that you thought one of them might have been yours. And I think that your gloves are just sticking out of your pocket, now.'

Jeremy put his hand in his right-hand pocket. 'No, the other one,' the Inspector told him.

Removing the gloves from his left-hand pocket, Jeremy exclaimed, 'Oh yes. Yes, so they are.'

'They're not really very like these. Are they?' the Inspector asked, pointedly.

'Actually, these are my golfing gloves,' Jeremy replied with a smile.

'Thank you, Mr Warrender,' the Inspector said abruptly and dismissively, patting the cushion back into place on the sofa. 'That will be all for now.'

Jeremy rose, looking upset. 'Look here,' he exclaimed, 'you don't think – ' He paused.

'I don't think what, sir?' asked the Inspector.

'Nothing,' Jeremy replied uncertainly. He paused, and then made for the library door, only to be intercepted by the Constable. Turning back to the Inspector, Jeremy pointed mutely and enquiringly at the hall door. The Inspector nodded, and Jeremy made his way out of the room, closing the hall door behind him.

Leaving the gloves on the sofa, the Inspector went across to the bridge table, sat, and consulted *Who's Who* again. 'Here we are,' he murmured, and began to read aloud, '"Thomson, Sir Kenneth. Chairman of Saxon-Arabian Oil Company, Gulf Petroleum Company." Hmm! Impressive. "Recreations: Philately, golf, fishing. Address, three hundred and forty Broad Street, thirty-four Grosvenor Square".'

While the Inspector was reading, Constable Jones went across to the table by the sofa and began to sharpen his pencil into the ashtray. Stooping to pick up some shavings from the floor, he saw a playing-card lying there and brought it to the bridge table, throwing it down in front of his superior.

'What have you got there?' the Inspector asked.

'Just a card, sir. Found it over there, under the sofa.'

The Inspector picked up the card. 'The ace of spades,'

he noted. 'A very interesting card. Here, wait a minute.' He turned the card over. 'Red. It's the same pack.' He picked up the red pack of cards from the table, and spread them out.

The Constable helped him sort through the cards. 'Well, well, no ace of spades,' the Inspector exclaimed. He rose from his chair. 'Now, that's very remarkable, don't you think, Jones?' he asked, putting the card in his pocket and going across to the sofa. 'They managed to play bridge without missing the ace of spades.'

'Very remarkable indeed, sir,' Constable Jones agreed, as he tidied the cards on the table.

The Inspector collected the three pairs of gloves from the sofa. 'Now I think we'll have Sir Rowland Delahaye,' he instructed the Constable, as he took the gloves to the bridge table and spread them out in pairs.

CHAPTER SIXTEEN

T he Constable opened the library door, calling, 'Sir
     Rowland Delahaye.'
     As Sir Rowland paused in the doorway, the Inspec-
tor called, 'Do come in, sir, and sit down here, please.'

Sir Rowland approached the bridge table, paused for a
moment as he noticed the gloves spread out on it, and
then sat.

'You are Sir Rowland Delahaye?' the Inspector asked
him formally. Receiving a grave, affirmative nod, he next
asked, 'What is your address?'

'Long Paddock, Littlewich Green, Lincolnshire,' Sir
Rowland replied. Tapping a finger on the copy of *Who's
Who*, he added, 'Couldn't you find it, Inspector?'

The Inspector chose to ignore this. 'Now, if you please,'
he said, 'I'd like your account of the evening, after you left
here shortly before seven.'

Sir Rowland had obviously already given some thought to this. 'It had been raining all day,' he began smoothly, 'and then it suddenly cleared up. We had already arranged to go to the golf club for dinner, as it is the servants' night out. So we did that.' He glanced across at the Constable, as though to make sure he was keeping up, then continued, 'As we were finishing dinner, Mrs Hailsham-Brown rang up and suggested that, as her husband had unexpectedly had to go out, we three should return here and make up a four for bridge. We did so. About twenty minutes after we'd started playing, you arrived, Inspector. The rest – you know.'

The Inspector looked thoughtful. 'That's not quite Mr Warrender's account of the matter,' he observed.

'Indeed?' said Sir Rowland. 'And how did he put it?'

'He said that the suggestion to come back here and play bridge came from one of you. But he thought it was probably Mr Birch.'

'Ah,' replied Sir Rowland easily, 'but you see Warrender came into the dining-room at the club rather late. He did not realize that Mrs Hailsham-Brown had rung up.'

Sir Rowland and the Inspector looked at each other, as though trying to stare each other out. Then Sir Rowland continued, 'You must know better than I do, Inspector, how very rarely two people's accounts of the same thing agree. In fact, if the three of us were to agree exactly, I should regard it as suspicious. Very suspicious indeed.'

The Inspector chose not to comment on this observation. Drawing a chair up close to Sir Rowland, he sat down.

'I'd like to discuss the case with you, sir, if I may,' he suggested.

'How very agreeable of you, Inspector,' Sir Rowland replied.

After looking thoughtfully at the table-top for a few seconds, the Inspector began the discussion. 'The dead man, Mr Oliver Costello, came to this house with some particular object in view.' He paused. 'Do you agree that that is what must have happened, sir?'

'My understanding is that he came to return to Henry Hailsham-Brown certain objects which Mrs Miranda Hailsham-Brown, as she then was, had taken away in error,' Sir Rowland replied.

'That may have been his excuse, sir,' the Inspector pointed out, 'though I'm not even sure of that. But I'm certain it wasn't the real reason that brought him here.'

Sir Rowland shrugged his shoulders. 'You may be right,' he observed. 'I can't say.'

The Inspector pressed on. 'He came, perhaps, to see a particular person. It may have been you, it may have been Mr Warrender, or it may have been Mr Birch.'

'If he had wanted to see Mr Birch, who lives locally,' Sir Rowland pointed out, 'he would have gone to his house. He wouldn't have come here.'

'That is probably so,' the Inspector agreed. 'Therefore that leaves us with the choice of four people. You, Mr Warrender, Mr Hailsham-Brown and Mrs Hailsham-Brown.' He paused and gave Sir Rowland a searching glance before asking, 'Now, sir, how well did you know Oliver Costello?'

'Hardly at all. I've met him once or twice, that's all.'

'Where did you meet him?' asked the Inspector.

Sir Rowland reflected. 'Twice at the Hailsham-Browns' in London, over a year ago, and once in a restaurant, I believe.'

'But you had no reason for wishing to murder him?'

'Is that an accusation, Inspector?' Sir Rowland asked with a smile.

The Inspector shook his head. 'No, Sir Rowland,' he replied. 'I should call it more an elimination. I don't think you have any motive for doing away with Oliver Costello. So that leaves just three people.'

'This is beginning to sound like a variant of "Ten Little Indians",' Sir Rowland observed with a smile.

The Inspector smiled back. 'We'll take Mr Warrender next,' he proposed. 'Now, how well do you know him?'

'I met him here for the first time two days ago,' Sir Rowland replied. 'He appears to be an agreeable young man, well bred, and well educated. He's a friend of Clarissa's. I know nothing about him, but I should say he's an unlikely murderer.'

'So much for Mr Warrender,' the Inspector noted. 'That brings me to my next question.'

Anticipating him, Sir Rowland nodded. 'How well do I know Henry Hailsham-Brown, and how well do I know Mrs Hailsham-Brown? That's what you want to know, isn't it?' he asked. 'Actually, I know Henry Hailsham-Brown very well indeed. He is an old friend. As for Clarissa, I know all there is to know about her. She is my ward, and inexpressibly dear to me.'

'Yes, sir,' said the Inspector. 'I think that answer makes certain things very clear.'

'Does it, indeed?'

The Inspector rose and took a few paces about the room before turning back to face Sir Rowland. 'Why did you three change your plans this evening?' he asked. 'Why did you come back here and pretend to play bridge?'

'Pretend?' Sir Rowland exclaimed sharply.

The Inspector took the playing card from his pocket. 'This card,' he said, 'was found on the other side of the room under the sofa. I can hardly believe that you would have played two rubbers of bridge and started a third with a pack of fifty-one cards, and the ace of spades missing.'

Sir Rowland took the card from the Inspector, looked at the back of it, and then returned it. 'Yes,' he admitted. 'Perhaps that is a little difficult to believe.'

The Inspector cast his eyes despairingly upwards before adding, 'I also think that three pairs of Mr Hailsham-Brown's gloves need a certain amount of explanation.'

After a moment's pause, Sir Rowland replied, 'I'm afraid, Inspector, you won't get any explanation from me.'

'No, sir,' the Inspector agreed. 'I take it that you are out to do your best for a certain lady. But it's not a bit of good, sir. The truth will out.'

'I wonder if it will,' was Sir Rowland's only response to this observation.

The Inspector went across to the panel. 'Mrs Hailsham-Brown knew that Costello's body was in the recess,' he

[153]

insisted. 'Whether she dragged it there herself, or whether you helped her, I don't know. But I'm convinced that she knew.' He came back to face Sir Rowland. 'I suggest,' he continued, 'that Oliver Costello came here to see Mrs Hailsham-Brown and to obtain money from her by threats.'

'Threats?' Sir Rowland asked. 'Threats of what?'

'That will all come out in due course, I have no doubt,' the Inspector assured him. 'Mrs Hailsham-Brown is young and attractive. This Mr Costello was a great man for the ladies, they say. Now, Mrs Hailsham-Brown is newly married and – '

'Stop!' Sir Rowland interrupted peremptorily. 'I must put you right on certain matters. You can confirm what I tell you easily enough. Henry Hailsham-Brown's first marriage was unfortunate. His wife, Miranda, was a beautiful woman, but unbalanced and neurotic. Her health and disposition had degenerated to such an alarming state that her little daughter had to be removed to a nursing home.'

He paused in reflection. Then, 'Yes, a really shocking state of affairs,' he continued. 'It seemed that Miranda had become a drug addict. How she obtained these drugs was not found out, but it was a very fair guess that she had been supplied with them by this man, Oliver Costello. She was infatuated with him, and finally ran away with him.'

After another pause and a glance across at the Constable, to see if he was keeping up, Sir Rowland resumed his story. 'Henry Hailsham-Brown, who is old-fashioned in his views, allowed Miranda to divorce him,' he explained. 'Henry has now found happiness and peace in his marriage with Clarissa, and I can assure you, Inspector, that there are no guilty secrets in Clarissa's life. There is nothing, I can swear, with which Costello could possibly threaten her.'

The Inspector said nothing, but merely looked thoughtful.

Sir Rowland stood up, tucked his chair under the table, and walked over to the sofa. Then, turning to address the police officer again, he suggested, 'Don't you think, Inspector, that you're on the wrong track altogether? Why should you be so certain that it was a person Costello came here to see? Why couldn't it have been a place?'

The Inspector now looked perplexed. 'What do you mean, sir?' he asked.

'When you were talking to us about the late Mr Sellon,' Sir Rowland reminded him, 'you mentioned that the Narcotics Squad took an interest in him. Isn't there a possible link there? Drugs – Sellon – Sellon's house?'

He paused but, receiving no reaction from the Inspector, continued, 'Costello has been here once before, I understand, ostensibly to look at Sellon's antiques. Supposing Oliver Costello wanted something in this house. In that desk, perhaps.'

The Inspector glanced at the desk, and Sir Rowland expanded on his theory. 'There is the curious incident of a man who came here and offered an exorbitant price for that desk. Supposing it was that desk that Oliver

Costello wanted to examine – wanted to search, if you like. Supposing that he was followed here by someone. And that that someone struck him down, there by the desk.'

The Inspector did not seem impressed. 'There's a good deal of supposition – ' he began, only to be interrupted by Sir Rowland who insisted, 'It's a very reasonable hypothesis.'

'The hypothesis being,' the Inspector queried, 'that this somebody put the body in the recess?'

'Exactly.'

'That would have to be somebody who knew about the recess,' the Inspector observed.

'It could be someone who knew the house in Sellon's time,' Sir Rowland pointed out.

'Yes, that's all very well, sir,' the Inspector replied impatiently, 'but it still doesn't explain one thing – '

'What is that?' asked Sir Rowland.

The Inspector looked at him steadily. 'Mrs Hailsham-Brown knew the body was in that recess. She tried to prevent us looking there.'

Sir Rowland opened his mouth to speak, but the Inspector held up a hand and continued, 'It's no good trying to convince me otherwise. She knew.'

For a few moments, a tense silence prevailed. Then Sir Rowland said, 'Inspector, will you allow me to speak to my ward?'

'Only in my presence, sir,' was the prompt reply.

'That will do.'

The Inspector nodded. 'Jones!' The Constable, under-standing what was required, left the room.

'We are very much in your hands, Inspector,' Sir Rowland told the police officer. 'I will ask you to make what allowances you can.'

'My one concern is to get at the truth, sir, and to find out who killed Oliver Costello,' the Inspector replied.

CHAPTER SEVENTEEN

The Constable came back into the room, holding the door open for Clarissa.

'Come in here, please, Mrs Hailsham-Brown,' the Inspector called. As Clarissa entered, Sir Rowland went over to her. He spoke very solemnly. 'Clarissa, my dear,' he said. 'Will you do what I ask you? I want you to tell the Inspector the truth.'

'The truth?' Clarissa echoed, sounding very doubtful.

'The truth,' Sir Rowland repeated with emphasis. 'It's the only thing to do. I mean it. Seriously.' He looked at her steadily and indeed seriously for a moment, and then left the room. The Constable closed the door after him and resumed his seat for note-taking.

'Do sit down, Mrs Hailsham-Brown,' the Inspector invited her, this time indicating the sofa.

Clarissa smiled at him, but the look he returned was a

stern one. She moved slowly to the sofa, sat, and waited for a moment before speaking. Then, 'I'm sorry,' she told him. 'I'm terribly sorry I told you all those lies. I didn't mean to.' She did indeed sound rueful as she continued, 'One gets into things, if you know what I mean?'

'I can't say that I do know,' the Inspector replied coldly. 'Now, please just give me the facts.'

'Well, it's really all quite simple,' she explained, ticking off the facts on her fingers as she spoke. 'First, Oliver Costello left. Then, Henry came home. Then, I saw him off again in the car. Then, I came in here with the sandwiches.'

'Sandwiches?' the Inspector queried.

'Yes. You see, my husband is bringing home a very important delegate from abroad.'

The Inspector looked interested. 'Oh, who is this delegate?'

'A Mr Jones,' Clarissa told him.

'I beg your pardon?' said the Inspector, with a look at Constable Jones.

'Mr Jones. That's not his real name, but that's what we have to call him. It's all very hush-hush.' Clarissa went on speaking. 'They were going to have the sandwiches while they talked, and I was going to have mousse in the schoolroom.'

The Inspector was looking perplexed. 'Mousse in the — yes, I see,' he murmured, sounding as though he did not see at all.

'I put the sandwiches down there,' Clarissa told him,

pointing to the stool, 'and then I began tidying up, and I went to put a book back on the bookshelf and – then – and then I practically fell over it.'

'You fell over the body?' the Inspector asked.

'Yes. It was here, behind the sofa. And I looked to see if it – if he was dead, and he was. It was Oliver Costello, and I didn't know what to do. In the end, I rang up the golf club, and I asked Sir Rowland, Mr Birch and Jeremy Warrender to come back right away.'

Leaning over the sofa, the Inspector asked coldly, 'It didn't occur to you to ring up the police?'

'Well, it occurred to me, yes,' Clarissa answered, 'but then – well – ' She smiled at him again. 'Well, I didn't.'

'You didn't,' the Inspector murmured to himself. He walked away, looked at the Constable, lifted his hands despairingly, and then turned back to face Clarissa. 'Why didn't you ring the police?' he asked her.

Clarissa was prepared for this. 'Well, I didn't think it would be nice for my husband,' she replied. 'I don't know whether you know many people in the Foreign Office, Inspector, but they're frightfully unassuming. They like everything very quiet, not noticeable. You must admit that murders are rather noticeable.'

'Quite so,' was all that the Inspector could think of in response to this.

'I'm so glad you understand,' Clarissa told him warmly and almost gushingly. She went on with her story, but her delivery became more and more unconvincing as she began to feel that she was not making headway. 'I mean,' she said, 'he was quite dead, because I felt his pulse, so we couldn't do anything for him.'

The Inspector walked about, without replying. Following him with her eyes, Clarissa continued, 'What I mean is, he might just as well be dead in Marsden Wood as in our drawing-room.'

The Inspector turned sharply to face her. 'Marsden Wood?' he asked abruptly. 'How does Marsden Wood come into it?'

'That's where I was thinking of putting him,' Clarissa replied.

The Inspector put a hand to the back of his head, and looked at the floor as though seeking inspiration there. Then, shaking his head to clear it, he said firmly, 'Mrs Hailsham-Brown, have you never heard that a dead body, if there's any suggestion of foul play, should never be moved?'

'Of course I know that,' Clarissa retorted. 'It says so in all the detective stories. But, you see, this is real life.'

The Inspector lifted his hands in despair.

'I mean,' she continued, 'real life's quite different.'

The Inspector looked at Clarissa in incredulous silence for a moment, before asking her, 'Do you realize the seriousness of what you're saying?'

'Of course I do,' she replied, 'and I'm telling you the truth. So, you see, in the end, I rang up the club and they all came back here.'

'And you persuaded them to hide the body in that recess.'

'No,' Clarissa corrected him. 'That came later. My plan, as I told you, was that they should take Oliver's body away in his car and leave the car in Marsden Wood.'

'And they agreed?' The Inspector's tone was distinctly unbelieving.

'Yes, they agreed,' said Clarissa, smiling at him.

'Frankly, Mrs Hailsham-Brown,' the Inspector told her brusquely, 'I don't believe a word of it. I don't believe that three responsible men would agree to obstruct the course of justice in such a manner for such a paltry cause.'

Clarissa rose to her feet. Walking away from the Inspector, she said more to herself than to him, 'I knew you wouldn't believe me if I told you the truth.' She turned to face him. 'What *do* you believe, then?' she asked him.

Watching Clarissa closely as he spoke, the Inspector replied, 'I can see only one reason why those three men should agree to lie.'

'Oh? What do you mean? What other reason would they have?'

'They would agree to lie,' the Inspector continued, 'if they believed, or, even more so, if they actually knew – that you had killed him.'

Clarissa stared at him. 'But I had no *reason* for killing him,' she protested. 'Absolutely no reason.' She flung away from him. 'Oh, I knew you'd react like this,' she exclaimed. 'That's why – '

She broke off suddenly, and the Inspector turned to her. 'That's why what?' he asked abruptly.

Clarissa stood thinking. Some moments passed, and

then her manner appeared to change. She began to speak more convincingly. 'All right, then,' she announced, with the air of one who is making a clean breast of things. 'I'll tell you why.'

'I think that would be wiser,' the Inspector said.

'Yes,' she agreed, turning to face him squarely. 'I suppose I'd better tell you the *truth*.' She emphasized the word.

The Inspector smiled. 'I can assure you,' he advised her, 'that telling the police a pack of lies will do you very little good, Mrs Hailsham-Brown. You'd better tell me the real story. And from the beginning.'

'I will,' Clarissa promised. She sat down in a chair by the bridge table. 'Oh dear,' she sighed, 'I thought I was being so clever.'

'It's much better not to try to be clever,' the Inspector told her. He seated himself facing Clarissa. 'Now then,' he asked, 'what really did happen this evening?'

CHAPTER EIGHTEEN

Clarissa was silent for a few moments. Then, looking the Inspector steadily in the eye, she began to speak. 'It all started as I've already explained to you. I said good-bye to Oliver Costello, and he'd gone off with Miss Peake. I had no idea he would come back again, and I still can't understand why he did.'

She paused, and seemed to be trying to recall what had happened next. 'Oh, yes,' she continued. 'Then my husband came home, explaining that he would have to go out again immediately. He went off in the car, and it was just after I had shut the front door, and made sure that it was latched and bolted, that I suddenly began to feel nervous.'

'Nervous?' asked the Inspector, looking puzzled. 'Why?'

'Well, I'm not usually nervous,' she told him, speaking with great feeling, 'but it occurred to me that I'd never been alone in the house at night.'

She paused. 'Yes, go on,' the Inspector encouraged her.

'I told myself not to be so silly. I said to myself, "You've got the phone, haven't you? You can always ring for help." I said to myself, "Burglars don't come at this time of the evening. They come in the middle of the night." But I still kept thinking I heard a door shutting somewhere, or footsteps up in my bedroom. So I thought I'd better do something.'

She paused again, and again the Inspector prompted her. 'Yes?'

'I went into the kitchen,' Clarissa said, 'and made the sandwiches for Henry and Mr Jones to have when they got back. I got them all ready on a plate, with a napkin around them to keep them soft, and I was just coming across the hall to put them in here, when – ' she paused dramatically – 'I really heard something.'

'Where?' the Inspector asked.

'In this room,' she told him. 'I knew that, this time, I wasn't imagining it. I heard drawers being pulled open and shut, and then I suddenly remembered that the french windows in here weren't locked. We never do lock them. Somebody had come in that way.'

Again she paused. 'Go on, Mrs Hailsham-Brown,' said the Inspector impassively.

Clarissa made a gesture of helplessness. 'I didn't know what to do. I was petrified. Then I thought, "What if I'm just being a fool? What if it's Henry come back for something – or even Sir Rowland or one of the others? A

[168]

nice fool you'll look if you go upstairs and ring the police on the extension." So then I thought of a plan.'

She paused once more, and the Inspector's 'Yes?' this time sounded a trifle impatient.

'I went to the hall stand,' Clarissa said slowly, 'and I took the heaviest stick I could find. Then I went into the library. I didn't turn the light on. I felt my way across the room to that recess. I opened it very gently and slipped inside. I thought I could ease the door into here and see who it was.' She pointed to the panel. 'Unless anyone knew about it, you'd never dream there was a door just there.'

'No,' the Inspector agreed, 'you certainly wouldn't.'

Clarissa seemed now to be almost enjoying her narrative. 'I eased the catch open,' she continued, 'and then my fingers slipped, and the door swung right open and hit against a chair. A man who was standing by the desk straightened up. I saw something bright and shining in his hand. I thought it was a revolver. I was terrified. I thought he was going to shoot me. I hit out at him with the stick with all my might, and he fell.'

She collapsed and leant on the table with her face in her hands. 'Could I – could I have a little brandy, please?' she asked the Inspector.

'Yes, of course.' The Inspector got to his feet. 'Jones!' he called. The Constable poured some brandy into a glass and handed it to the Inspector. Clarissa had lifted her face, but quickly covered it with her hands again and held out her hand as the Inspector brought her the brandy.

She drank, coughed, and returned the glass. Constable Jones replaced it on a table and resumed his seat and his note-taking.

The Inspector looked at Clarissa. 'Do you feel able to continue, Mrs Hailsham-Brown?' he asked sympathetically.

'Yes,' Clarissa replied, glancing up at him. 'You're very kind.' She took a breath and continued her story. 'The man just lay there. He didn't move. I switched on the light and I saw then that it was Oliver Costello. He was dead. It was terrible. I – I couldn't understand it.'

She gestured towards the desk. 'I couldn't understand what he was doing there, tampering with the desk. It was all like some ghastly nightmare. I was so frightened that I rang the golf club. I wanted my guardian to be with me. They all came over. I begged them to help me, to take the body away – somewhere.'

The Inspector stared at her intently. 'But why?' he asked.

Clarissa turned away from him. 'Because I was a coward,' she said. 'A miserable coward. I was frightened of the publicity, of having to go to a police court. And it would be so bad for my husband and for his career.'

She turned back to the Inspector. 'If it had really been a burglar, perhaps I could have gone through with it, but being someone we actually knew, someone who is married to Henry's first wife – Oh, I just felt I couldn't go through with it.'

'Perhaps,' the Inspector suggested, 'because the dead man had, a short while before, attempted to blackmail you?'

'Blackmail me? Oh, that's nonsense!' Clarissa replied with complete confidence. 'That's just silly. There's nothing anyone could blackmail me about.'

'Elgin, your butler, overheard a mention of blackmail,' the Inspector told her.

'I don't believe he heard anything of the kind,' replied Clarissa. 'He couldn't. If you ask me, he's making the whole thing up.'

'Come now, Mrs Hailsham-Brown,' the Inspector insisted, 'are you deliberately telling me that the word blackmail was never mentioned? Why would your butler make it up?'

'I swear there was no mention of blackmail,' Clarissa exclaimed, banging the table with her hand. 'I assure you —' Her hand stopped in mid-air, and she suddenly laughed. 'Oh, how silly. Of course. That was it.'

'You've remembered?' the Inspector asked calmly.

'It was nothing, really,' Clarissa assured him. 'It was just that Oliver was saying something about the rent of furnished houses being absurdly high, and I said we'd been amazingly lucky and were only paying four guineas a week for this. And he said, "I can hardly believe it, Clarissa. What's your pull? It must be blackmail." And I laughed and said, "That's it. Blackmail."'

She laughed now, apparently recalling the exchange. 'Just a silly, joking way of talking. Why, I didn't even remember it.'

'I'm sorry, Mrs Hailsham-Brown,' said the Inspector, 'but I really can't believe that.'

Clarissa looked astonished. 'Can't believe what?'

'That you're only paying four guineas a week for this house, furnished.'

'Honestly! You really are the most unbelieving man I've ever met,' Clarissa told him as she rose and went to the desk. 'You don't seem to believe a single thing I've said to you this evening. Most things I can't prove, but this one I can. And this time I'm going to show you.'

She opened a drawer of the desk and searched through the papers in it. 'Here it is,' she exclaimed. 'No, it isn't. Ah! Here we are.' She took a document from the drawer and showed it to the Inspector. 'Here's the agreement for our tenancy of this house, furnished. It's made out by a firm of solicitors acting for the executors and, look – four guineas per week.'

The Inspector looked jolted. 'Well, I'm blessed! It's extraordinary. Quite extraordinary. I'd have thought it was worth much more than that.'

Clarissa gave him one of her most charming smiles. 'Don't you think, Inspector, that you ought to beg my pardon?' she suggested.

The Inspector injected a certain amount of charm into his voice as he responded. 'I do apologize, Mrs Hailsham-Brown,' he said, 'but it really is extremely odd, you know.'

'Why? What do you mean?' Clarissa asked, as she replaced the document in the drawer.

'Well, it so happens,' the Inspector replied, 'that a lady and a gentleman were down in this area with orders to view this house, and the lady happened to lose a very valuable brooch somewhere in the vicinity. She called in at the police station to give particulars, and she happened to mention this house. She said the owners were asking an absurd price. She thought eighteen guineas a week for a house out in the country and miles from anywhere was ridiculous. I thought so too.'

'Yes, that is extraordinary, very extraordinary,' Clarissa agreed, with a friendly smile. 'I understand why you were sceptical. But perhaps now you'll believe some of the other things I said.'

'I'm not doubting your final story, Mrs Hailsham-Brown,' the Inspector assured her. 'We usually know the truth when we hear it. I knew, too, that there would have to be some serious reason for those three gentlemen to cook up this harebrained scheme of concealment.'

'You mustn't blame them too much, Inspector,' Clarissa pleaded. 'It was my fault. I went on and on at them.'

All too aware of her charm, the Inspector replied, 'Ah, I've no doubt you did. But what I still don't understand is, who telephoned the police in the first place and reported the murder?'

'Yes, that is extraordinary!' said Clarissa, sounding startled. 'I'd completely forgotten that.'

'It clearly wasn't you,' the Inspector pointed out, 'and it wouldn't have been any of the three gentlemen – '

Clarissa shook her head. 'Could it have been Elgin?' she wondered. 'Or perhaps Miss Peake?'

'I don't think it could possibly have been Miss Peake,' said the Inspector. 'She clearly didn't know Costello's body was there.'

'I wonder if that's so,' said Clarissa thoughtfully.

'After all, when the body was discovered, she had hysterics,' the Inspector reminded her.

'Oh, that's nothing. Anyone can have hysterics,' Clarissa remarked incautiously. The Inspector shot her a suspicious glance, at which she felt it expedient to give him as innocent a smile as she could manage.

'Anyway, Miss Peake doesn't live in the house,' the Inspector observed. 'She has her own cottage in the grounds.'

'But she could have been in the house,' said Clarissa. 'You know, she has keys to all the doors.'

The Inspector shook his head. 'No, it looks to me more like Elgin who must have called us,' he said.

Clarissa moved closer to him, and flashed him a somewhat anxious smile. 'You're not going to send me to prison, are you?' she asked. 'Uncle Roly said he was sure you wouldn't.'

The Inspector gave her an austere look. 'It's a good thing you changed your story in time, and told us the truth, madam,' he advised her sternly. 'But, if I may say so, Mrs Hailsham-Brown, I think you should get in touch with your solicitor as soon as possible and give him all the relevant facts. In the meantime, I'll get your statement typed out and read over to you, and perhaps you will be good enough to sign it.'

Clarissa was about to reply when the hall door opened and Sir Rowland entered. 'I couldn't keep away any longer,' he explained. 'Is it all right now, Inspector? Do you understand what our dilemma was?'

Clarissa went across to her guardian before he could say any more. 'Roly, darling,' she greeted him, taking his hand. 'I've made a statement, and the police – or rather Mr Jones here – is going to type it out. Then I've got to sign it, and I've told them everything.'

The Inspector went over to confer with the Constable, and Clarissa continued speaking quietly to Sir Rowland. 'I told them how I thought it was a burglar,' she said with emphasis, 'and hit him on the head – '

When Sir Rowland looked at her in alarm and opened his mouth to speak, she quickly covered his mouth with her hands so that he could not get the words out. She continued hurriedly, 'Then I told them how it turned out to be Oliver Costello, and how I got in a terrible flap and rang you, and how I begged and begged and at last you all gave in. I see now how wrong of me it was – '

The Inspector turned back to them, and Clarissa removed her hand from Sir Rowland's mouth just in time. 'But when it happened,' she was saying, 'I was just scared stiff, and I thought it would be cosier for everybody – me, Henry and even Miranda – if Oliver was found in Marsden Wood.'

Sir Rowland looked aghast. 'Clarissa! What on earth have you been saying?' he gasped.

'Mrs Hailsham-Brown has made a very full statement, sir,' the Inspector said complacently.

Recovering himself somewhat, Sir Rowland replied drily, 'So it seems.'

'It's the best thing to do,' said Clarissa. 'In fact, it was the only thing to do. The Inspector made me see that. And I'm truly sorry to have told all those silly lies.'

'It will lead to far less trouble in the end,' the Inspector assured her. 'Now, Mrs Hailsham-Brown,' he went on, 'I shan't ask you to go into the recess while the body is still there, but I'd like you to show me exactly where the man was standing when you came through that way into this room.'

'Oh – yes – well – he was – ' Clarissa began hesitantly. She went across to the desk. 'No,' she continued, 'I remember now. He was standing here like this.' She stood at one end of the desk, and leaned over it.

'Be ready to open the panel when I give you the word, Jones,' said the Inspector, motioning to the Constable, who rose and put his hand on the panel switch.

'I see,' the Inspector said to Clarissa. 'That's where he was standing. And then the door opened and you came out. All right, I don't want you to have to look in there at the body now, so just stand in front of the panel when it opens. Now – Jones.'

The Constable activated the switch, and the panel opened. The recess was empty except for a small piece of paper on the floor which Constable Jones retrieved, while the Inspector looked accusingly at Clarissa and Sir Rowland.

The Constable read out what was on the slip of paper. 'Sucks to you!' As the Inspector snatched the paper from him, Clarissa and Sir Rowland looked at each other in astonishment.

A loud ring from the front-door bell broke the silence.

CHAPTER NINETEEN

A few moments later Elgin came into the drawing-room to announce that the Divisional Surgeon Surgeon had arrived. The Inspector and Constable Jones immediately accompanied the butler to the front door, where the Inspector had the unenviable task of confessing to the Divisional Surgeon that, as it turned out, there was at present no body to examine.

'Really, Inspector Lord,' the Divisional Surgeon said irritably, 'Do you realize how infuriating it is to have brought me all this way on a wild-goose chase?'

'But I assure you, Doctor,' the Inspector attempted to explain, 'we did have a body.'

'The Inspector's right, Doctor,' Constable Jones added his voice. 'We certainly did have a body. It just happens to have disappeared.'

The sound of their voices had brought Hugo and

Jeremy out from the dining-room on the other side of the hall. They could not refrain from making unhelpful comments. 'I can't think how you policemen ever get anything done – losing bodies indeed,' Hugo expostulated, while Jeremy exclaimed, 'I don't understand why a guard wasn't put on the body.'

'Well, whatever has happened, if there's no body for me to examine, I'm not wasting any more time here,' the Divisional Surgeon snapped at the Inspector. 'I can assure you that you'll hear more about this, Inspector Lord.'

'Yes, Doctor. I've no doubt of that. Goodnight, Doctor,' the Inspector replied wearily.

The Divisional Surgeon left, slamming the front door behind him, and the Inspector turned to Elgin, who forestalled him by saying quickly, 'I know nothing about it, I assure you, sir, nothing at all.'

Meanwhile, in the drawing-room, Clarissa and Sir Rowland were enjoying overhearing the discomfiture of the police officers. 'Rather a bad moment for the police reinforcements to arrive,' Sir Rowland chuckled. 'The Divisional Surgeon seems very annoyed at finding no corpse to examine.'

Clarissa giggled. 'But who can have spirited it away?' she asked. 'Do you think Jeremy managed it somehow?'

'I don't see how he could have done,' Sir Rowland replied. 'They didn't let anyone back into the library, and the door from the library to the hall was locked. Pippa's "Sucks to you" was the last straw.'

Clarissa laughed, and Sir Rowland continued, 'Still,

it shows us one thing. Costello had managed to open the secret drawer.' He paused, and his manner changed. 'Clarissa,' he said in a serious tone, 'why on earth didn't you tell the truth to the Inspector when I begged you to?'

'I did,' Clarissa protested, 'except for the part about Pippa. But he just didn't believe me.'

'But, for Heaven's sake, why did you have to stuff him with all that nonsense?' Sir Rowland insisted on knowing.

'Well,' Clarissa replied with a helpless gesture, 'it seemed to me the most likely thing he would believe. And,' she ended triumphantly, 'he does believe me now.'

'And a nice mess you're in as a result,' Sir Rowland pointed out. 'You'll be up on a charge of manslaughter, for all you know.'

'I shall claim it was self-defence,' Clarissa said confidently.

Before Sir Rowland had a chance to reply, Hugo and Jeremy entered from the hall, and Hugo walked over to the bridge table, grumbling. 'Wretched police, pushing us around here and there. Now it seems they've gone and lost the body.'

Jeremy closed the door behind him, then went over to the stool and took a sandwich. 'Damn peculiar, I call it,' he announced.

'It's fantastic,' said Clarissa. 'The whole thing's fantastic. The body's gone, and we still don't know who rang up the police in the first place and said there'd been a murder here.'

'Well, that was Elgin, surely,' Jeremy suggested, as he sat on an arm of the sofa and began to eat his sandwich.

'No, no,' Hugo disagreed. 'I'd say it was that Peake woman.'

'But why?' Clarissa asked. 'Why would either of them do that, and not tell us? It doesn't make sense.'

Miss Peake put her head in at the hall door and looked around with a conspiratorial air. 'Hello, is the coast clear?' she asked. Closing the door, she strode confidently into the room. 'No bobbies about? They seem to be swarming all over the place.'

'They're busy searching the house and grounds now,' Sir Rowland informed her.

'What for?' asked Miss Peake.

'The body,' Sir Rowland replied. 'It's gone.'

Miss Peake gave her usual hearty laugh. 'What a lark!' she boomed. 'The disappearing body, eh?'

Hugo sat at the bridge table. Looking around the room, he observed to no one in particular, 'It's a nightmare. The whole thing's a damn nightmare.'

'Quite like the movies, eh, Mrs Hailsham-Brown?' Miss Peake suggested with another hoot of laughter.

Sir Rowland smiled at the gardener. 'I hope you are feeling better now, Miss Peake?' he asked her courteously.

'Oh, I'm all right,' she replied. 'I'm pretty tough really,

you know. I was just a bit bowled over by opening that door and finding a corpse. Turned me up for the moment, I must admit.'

'I wondered, perhaps,' said Clarissa quietly, 'if you already knew it was there.'

The gardener stared at her. 'Who? Me?'

'Yes. You.'

Again seeming to be addressing the entire universe, Hugo said, 'It doesn't make sense. Why take the body away? We all know there is a body. We know his identity and everything. No point in it. Why not leave the wretched thing where it was?'

'Oh, I wouldn't say there was no point in it, Mr Birch,' Miss Peake corrected Hugo, leaning across the bridge table to address him. 'You've got to have a body, you know. Habeas corpus and all that. Remember? You've got to have a body before you can bring a charge of murder against anybody.' She turned around to Clarissa. 'So don't you worry, Mrs Hailsham-Brown,' she assured her. 'Everything's going to be all right.'

Clarissa stared at her. 'What do you mean?'

'I've kept my ears open this evening,' the gardener told her. 'I haven't spent all my time lying on the bed in the spare room.' She looked around at everyone. 'I never liked that man Elgin, or his wife,' she continued. 'Listening at doors, and running to the police with stories about blackmail.'

'So you heard that?' Clarissa asked, wonderingly.

'What I always say is, stand by your own sex,' Miss

[183]

Peake declared. She looked at Hugo. 'Men!' she snorted. 'I don't hold with them.' She sat down next to Clarissa on the sofa. 'If they can't find the body, my dear,' she explained, 'they can't bring a charge against you. And what I say is, if that brute was blackmailing you, you did quite right to crack him over the head and good riddance.'

'But I didn't – ' Clarissa began faintly, only to be interrupted by Miss Peake.

'I heard you tell that Inspector all about it,' the gardener informed her. 'And if it wasn't for that eaves-dropping skulking fellow Elgin, your story would sound quite all right. Perfectly believable.'

'Which story do you mean?' Clarissa wondered aloud.

'About mistaking him for a burglar. It's the blackmail angle that puts a different complexion on it all. So I thought there was only one thing to do,' the gardener continued. 'Get rid of the body and let the police chase their tails looking for it.'

Sir Rowland took a few steps backward, staggering in disbelief, as Miss Peake looked complacently around the room. 'Pretty smart work, even if I do say so myself,' she boasted.

Jeremy rose, fascinated. 'Do you mean to say that it was you who moved the body?' he asked, incredulously.

Everyone was now staring at Miss Peake. 'We're all friends here, aren't we?' she asked, looking around at them. 'So I may as well spill the beans. Yes,' she admitted, 'I moved the body.' She tapped her pocket. 'And I locked the door. I've got keys to all the doors in this house, so that was no problem.'

Open-mouthed, Clarissa gazed at her in wonderment. 'But how? Where – where did you put the body?' she gasped.

Miss Peake leaned forward and spoke in a conspiratorial whisper. 'The bed in the spare room. You know, that big four-poster. Right across the head of the bed, under the bolster. Then I remade the bed and lay down on top of it.'

Sir Rowland, flabbergasted, sat down at the bridge table.

'But how did you get the body up to the spare room?' Clarissa asked. 'You couldn't manage it all by yourself.'

'You'd be surprised,' said Miss Peake jovially. 'Good old fireman's lift. Slung it over my shoulder.' With a gesture, she demonstrated how it was done.

'But what if you had met someone on the stairs?' Sir Rowland asked her.

'Ah, but I didn't,' replied Miss Peake. 'The police were in here with Mrs Hailsham-Brown. You three chaps were being kept in the dining-room by then. So I grabbed my chance, and of course grabbed the body too, took it through the hall, locked the library door again, and carried it up the stairs to the spare room.'

'Well, upon my soul!' Sir Rowland gasped.

Clarissa got to her feet. 'But he can't stay under the bolster for ever,' she pointed out.

Miss Peake turned to her. 'No, not for ever, of course, Mrs Hailsham-Brown,' she admitted. 'But he'll be all right for twenty-four hours. By that time, the police will have finished with the house and grounds. They'll be searching further afield.'

She looked around at her enthralled audience. 'Now, I've been thinking about how to get rid of him,' she went on. 'I happened to dig out a nice deep trench in the garden this morning – for the sweet peas. Well, we'll bury the body there and plant a nice double row of sweet peas all along it.'

Completely at a loss for words, Clarissa collapsed onto the sofa.

'I'm afraid, Miss Peake,' said Sir Rowland, 'grave-digging is no longer a matter for private enterprise.'

The gardener laughed merrily at this. 'Oh, you men!' she exclaimed, wagging her finger at Sir Rowland. 'Always such sticklers for propriety. We women have got more common sense.' She turned to address Clarissa. 'We can even take murder in our stride. Eh, Mrs Hailsham-Brown?'

Hugo suddenly leapt to his feet. 'This is absurd!' he shouted. 'Clarissa didn't kill him. I don't believe a word of it.'

'Well, if she didn't kill him,' Miss Peake asked breezily, 'who did?'

At that moment, Pippa entered the room from the

hall, wearing a dressing-gown, walking in a very sleepy manner, yawning, and carrying a glass dish containing chocolate mousse with a teaspoon in it. Everyone turned and looked at her.

CHAPTER TWENTY

Startled, Clarissa jumped to her feet. 'Pippa!' she cried. 'What are you doing out of bed?'

'I woke up, so I came down,' said Pippa between yawns.

Clarissa led her to the sofa. 'I'm so frightfully hungry,' Pippa complained, yawning again. She sat, then looked up at Clarissa and said, reproachfully, 'You said you'd bring this up to me.'

Clarissa took the dish of chocolate mousse from Pippa, placed it on the stool, and then sat on the sofa next to the child. 'I thought you were still asleep, Pippa,' she explained.

'I was asleep,' Pippa told her, with another enormous yawn. 'Then I thought a policeman came in and looked at me. I'd been having an awful dream, and then I half woke up. Then I was hungry, so I thought I'd come down.'

She shivered, looked around at everyone, and continued, 'Besides, I thought it might be true.'

Sir Rowland came and sat on the sofa on Pippa's other side. 'What might be true, Pippa?' he asked her.

'That horrible dream I had about Oliver,' Pippa replied, shuddering as she recollected it.

'What was your dream about Oliver, Pippa?' Sir Rowland asked quietly. 'Tell me.'

Pippa looked nervous as she took a small piece of moulded wax from a pocket of her dressing-gown. 'I made this earlier tonight,' she said. 'I melted down a wax candle, then I made a pin red hot, and I stuck the pin through it.'

As she handed the small wax figure to Sir Rowland, Jeremy suddenly gave a startled exclamation of 'Good Lord!' He leapt up and began to look around the room, searching for the book Pippa had tried to show him earlier.

'I said the right words and everything,' Pippa was explaining to Sir Rowland, 'but I couldn't do it quite the way the book said.'

'What book?' Clarissa asked. 'I don't understand.'

Jeremy, who had been looking along the bookshelves, now found what he was seeking. 'Here it is,' he exclaimed, handing the book to Clarissa over the back of the sofa. 'Pippa got it in the market today. She called it a recipe book.'

Pippa suddenly laughed. 'And you said to me, "Can you eat it?"' she reminded Jeremy.

Clarissa examined the book. '*A Hundred Well-tried and Trusty Spells*,' she read on the cover. She opened the book, and read on. ' "How to cure warts. How to get your heart's desire. How to destroy your enemy." Oh, Pippa – is that what you did?'

Pippa looked at her stepmother solemnly. 'Yes,' she answered.

As Clarissa handed the book back to Jeremy, Pippa looked at the wax figure Sir Rowland was still holding. 'It isn't very like Oliver,' she admitted, 'and I couldn't get any clippings of his hair. But it was as much like him as I could make it – and then – then – I dreamed, I thought – ' She pushed her hair back from her face as she spoke. 'I thought I came down here and he was there.' She pointed behind the sofa. 'And it was all true.'

Sir Rowland put the wax figure down on the stool quietly, as Pippa continued, 'He was there, dead. I had killed him.' She looked around at them all, and began to shake. 'Is it true?' she asked. 'Did I kill him?'

'No, darling. No,' said Clarissa tearfully, putting an arm around Pippa.

'But he was there,' Pippa insisted.

'I know, Pippa,' Sir Rowland told her. 'But you didn't kill him. When you stuck the pin through that wax figure, it was your hate and your fear of him that you killed in that way. You're not afraid of him and you don't hate him any longer. Isn't that true?'

Pippa turned to him. 'Yes, it's true,' she admitted. 'But I did see him.' She glanced over the back of the sofa. 'I came down here and I saw him lying there, dead.' She leaned her head on Sir Rowland's chest. 'I did see him, Uncle Roly.'

'Yes, dear, you did see him,' Sir Rowland told her gently. 'But it wasn't you who killed him.' She looked up at him anxiously, and he continued, 'Now, listen to me, Pippa. Somebody hit him over the head with a big stick. You didn't do that, did you?'

'Oh, no,' said Pippa, shaking her head vigorously. 'No, not a stick.' She turned to Clarissa. 'You mean a golf stick like Jeremy had?'

Jeremy laughed. 'No, not a golf club, Pippa,' he explained. 'Something like that big stick that's kept in the hall stand.'

'You mean the one that used to belong to Mr Sellon, the one Miss Peake calls a knobkerry?' Pippa asked.

Jeremy nodded.

'Oh, no,' Pippa told him. 'I wouldn't do anything like that. I couldn't.' She turned back to Sir Rowland. 'Oh, Uncle Roly, I wouldn't have killed him really.'

'Of course you wouldn't,' Clarissa intervened in a voice of calm common-sense. 'Now come along, darling, you eat up your chocolate mousse and forget all about it.' She picked up the dish and offered it, but Pippa refused with a shake of her head, and Clarissa replaced the dish on the stool. She and Sir Rowland helped Pippa to lie down on the sofa, Clarissa took Pippa's hand, and Sir Rowland stroked the child's hair affectionately.

'I don't understand a word of all this,' Miss Peake

announced. 'What is that book, anyway?' she asked Jeremy who was now glancing through it.

'"How to bring a murrain on your neighbour's cattle." Does that attract you, Miss Peake?' he replied. 'I daresay with a little adjusting you could bring black spot to your neighbour's roses.'

'I don't know what you're talking about,' the gardener said brusquely.

'Black magic,' Jeremy explained.

'I'm not superstitious, thank goodness,' she snorted dismissively, moving away from him.

Hugo, who had been attempting to follow the train of events, now confessed, 'I'm in a complete fog.'

'Me, too,' Miss Peake agreed, tapping him on the shoulder. 'So I'll just have a peep and see how the boys in blue are getting on.' With another of her boisterous laughs, she went out into the hall.

Sir Rowland looked around at Clarissa, Hugo and Jeremy. 'Now where does that leave us?' he wondered aloud.

Clarissa was still recovering from the revelations of the previous few minutes.

'What a fool I've been,' she exclaimed, confusedly. 'I should have known Pippa couldn't possibly – I didn't know anything about this book. Pippa said she killed him and I – I thought it was true.'

Hugo got to his feet. 'Oh, you mean that you thought Pippa – '

'Yes, darling,' Clarissa interrupted him urgently and

emphatically to stop him from saying any more. But Pippa, fortunately, was now sleeping peacefully on the sofa.

'Oh, I see,' said Hugo. 'That explains it. Good God!'

'Well, we'd better go to the police now, and tell them the truth at last,' Jeremy suggested.

Sir Rowland shook his head thoughtfully. 'I don't know,' he murmured. 'Clarissa has already told them three different stories – '

'No. Wait,' Clarissa interrupted suddenly. 'I've just had an idea. Hugo, what was the name of Mr Sellon's shop?'

'It was just an antique shop,' Hugo replied, vaguely.

'Yes, I know that,' Clarissa exclaimed impatiently. 'But what was it called?'

'What do you mean – "what was it called"?'

'Oh, dear, you are being difficult,' Clarissa told him. 'You said it earlier, and I want you to say it again. But I don't want to tell you to say it, or say it for you.'

Hugo, Jeremy and Sir Rowland all looked at one another. 'Do you know what the blazes the girl is getting at, Roly?' Hugo asked plaintively.

'I've no idea,' replied Sir Rowland. 'Try us again, Clarissa.'

Clarissa looked exasperated. 'It's perfectly simple,' she insisted. 'What was the name of the antique shop in Maidstone?'

'It hadn't got a name,' Hugo replied. 'I mean, antique shops aren't called "Seaview" or anything.'

'Heaven give me patience,' Clarissa muttered between clenched teeth. Speaking slowly and distinctly, and pausing after each word, she asked him again, 'What – was – written – up – over – the – door?'

'Written up? Nothing,' said Hugo. 'What should be written up? Only the names of the owners, "Sellon and Brown", of course.'

'At last,' Clarissa cried jubilantly. 'I thought that was what you said before, but I wasn't sure. Sellon and Brown. My name is Hailsham-Brown.' She looked at the three men in turn, but they merely stared back at her with total incomprehension written on their faces.

'We got this house dirt cheap,' Clarissa continued. 'Other people who came to see it before us were asked such an exorbitant rent that they went away in disgust. Now have you got it?'

Hugo looked at her blankly before replying, 'No.'

Jeremy shook his head. 'Not yet, my love.'

Sir Rowland looked at her keenly. 'In a glass darkly,' he said thoughtfully.

Clarissa's face wore a look of intense excitement. 'Mr Sellon's partner who lives in London is a woman,' she explained to her friends. 'Today, someone rang up here and asked to speak to Mrs Brown. Not Mrs Hailsham-Brown, just Mrs Brown.'

'I see what you're getting at,' Sir Rowland said, nodding his head slowly.

Hugo shook his head. 'I don't,' he admitted.

Clarissa looked at him. 'A horse chestnut or a chestnut

horse – one of them makes all the difference,' she observed inscrutably.

'You're not delirious or anything, are you, Clarissa?' Hugo asked her anxiously.

'Somebody killed Oliver,' Clarissa reminded them. 'It wasn't any of you three. It wasn't me or Henry.' She paused, before continuing, 'And it wasn't Pippa, thank God. Then who was it?'

'Surely it's as I said to the Inspector,' Sir Rowland suggested. 'An outside job. Someone followed Oliver here.'

'Yes, but why did they?' Clarissa asked meaningfully. Getting no reply from anyone, she continued with her speculation. 'When I left you all at the gate today,' she reminded her three friends, 'I came back in through the french windows, and Oliver was standing here. He was very surprised to see me. He said, "What are you doing here, Clarissa?" I just thought it was an elaborate way of annoying me. But suppose it was just what it seemed?'

Her hearers looked attentive, but said nothing. Clarissa continued, 'Just suppose that he was surprised to see me. He thought the house belonged to someone else. He thought the person he'd find here would be the Mrs Brown who was Mr Sellon's partner.'

Sir Rowland shook his head. 'Wouldn't he know that you and Henry had this house?' he asked her. 'Wouldn't Miranda know?'

'When Miranda has to communicate, she always does it through her lawyers. Neither she nor Oliver necessarily knew that we lived in this house,' Clarissa explained. 'I tell you, I'm sure Oliver Costello had no idea he was going to see me. Oh, he recovered pretty quickly and made the excuse that he'd come to talk about Pippa. Then he pretended to go away, but he came back because – '

She broke off as Miss Peake came in through the hall door. 'The hunt's still on,' the gardener announced briskly. 'They've looked under all the beds, I gather, and now they're out in the grounds.' She gave her familiar hearty laugh.

Clarissa looked at her keenly. Then, 'Miss Peake,' she said, 'do you remember what Mr Costello said just before he left? Do you?'

Miss Peake looked blank. 'Haven't the foggiest idea,' she admitted.

'He said, didn't he, "I came to see Mrs Brown"?' Clarissa reminded her.

Miss Peake thought for a moment, and then answered, 'I believe he did. Yes. Why?'

'But it wasn't me he came to see,' Clarissa insisted.

'Well, if it wasn't you, then I don't know who it could have been,' Miss Peake replied with another of her jovial laughs.

Clarissa spoke with emphasis. 'It was you,' she said to the gardener. '*You* are Mrs Brown, aren't you?'

CHAPTER TWENTY-ONE

Miss Peake, looking extremely startled at Clarissa's accusation, seemed for a moment unsure how to act. When she did reply, her manner had changed. Dropping her usual jolly, hearty tone, she spoke gravely. 'That's very bright of you,' she said. 'Yes, I'm Mrs Brown.'

Clarissa had been doing some quick thinking. 'You're Mr Sellon's partner,' she said. 'You own this house. You inherited it from Sellon with the business. For some reason, you had the idea of finding a tenant for it whose name was Brown. In fact, you were determined to have a Mrs Brown in residence here. You thought that wouldn't be too difficult, since it's such a common name. But in the end you had to compromise on Hailsham-Brown. I don't know exactly why you wanted me to be in the limelight whilst you watched. I don't understand the ins and outs – '

Mrs Brown, alias Miss Peake, interrupted her. 'Charles Sellon was murdered,' she told Clarissa. 'There's no doubt of that. He'd got hold of something that was very valuable. I don't know how – I don't even know what it was. He wasn't always very – ' she hesitated ' – scrupulous.'

'So we have heard,' Sir Rowland observed drily.

'Whatever it was,' Mrs Brown continued, 'he was killed for it. And whoever killed him didn't find the thing. That was probably because it wasn't in the shop, it was here. I thought that whoever it was who killed him would come here sooner or later, looking for it. I wanted to be on the watch, therefore I needed a dummy Mrs Brown. A substitute.'

Sir Rowland made an exclamation of annoyance. 'It didn't worry you,' he asked the gardener, speaking with feeling, 'that Mrs Hailsham-Brown, a perfectly innocent woman who had done you no harm, would be in danger?'

'I've kept an eye on her, haven't I?' Mrs Brown replied defensively. 'So much so that it annoyed you all sometimes. The other day, when a man came along and offered her a ridiculous price for that desk, I was sure I was on the right track. Yet I'll swear there was nothing in that desk that meant anything at all.'

'Did you examine the secret drawer?' Sir Rowland asked her.

Mrs Brown looked surprised. 'A secret drawer, is there?' she exclaimed, moving towards the desk.

Clarissa intercepted her. 'There's nothing there now,' she assured her. 'Pippa found the drawer, but there were only some old autographs in it.'

'Clarissa, I'd rather like to see those autographs again,' Sir Rowland requested.

Clarissa went to the sofa. 'Pippa,' she called, 'where did you put – ? Oh, she's asleep.'

Mrs Brown moved to the sofa and looked down at the child. 'Fast asleep,' she confirmed. 'It's all the excitement that's done that.' She looked at Clarissa. 'I'll tell you what,' she said, 'I'll carry her up and dump her on her bed.'

'No,' said Sir Rowland, sharply.

Everyone looked at him. 'She's no weight at all,' Mrs Brown pointed out. 'Not a quarter as heavy as the late Mr Costello.'

'All the same,' Sir Rowland insisted, 'I think she'll be safer here.'

The others now all looked at Miss Peake/Mrs Brown, who took a step backwards, looked around her, and exclaimed indignantly, 'Safer?'

'That's what I said,' Sir Rowland told her. He glanced around the room, and continued, 'That child said a very significant thing just now.'

He sat down at the bridge table, watched by all. There was a pause, and then Hugo, moving to sit opposite Sir Rowland at the bridge table, asked, 'What did she say, Roly?'

'If you all think back,' Sir Rowland suggested, 'perhaps you'll realize what it was.'

His hearers looked at one another, while Sir Rowland picked up the copy of *Who's Who* and began to consult it.

'I don't get it,' Hugo admitted, shaking his head.

'What did Pippa say?' Jeremy wondered aloud.

'I can't imagine,' said Clarissa. She tried to cast her mind back. 'Something about the policeman? Or dreaming? Coming down here? Half awake?'

'Come on, Roly,' Hugo urged his friend. 'Don't be so damned mysterious. What's this all about?'

Sir Rowland looked up. 'What?' he asked, absent-mindedly. 'Oh, yes. Those autographs. Where are they?'

Hugo snapped his fingers. 'I believe I remember Pippa putting them in that shell box over there,' he recalled.

Jeremy went over to the bookshelves. 'Up here?' he asked. Locating the shell box, he took out the envelope. 'Yes, quite right. Here we are,' he confirmed as he took the autographs from the envelope and handed them to Sir Rowland, who had now closed *Who's Who*. Jeremy put the empty envelope in his pocket while Sir Rowland examined the autographs with his eyeglass.

'Victoria Regina, God bless her,' murmured Sir Rowland, looking at the first of the autographs. 'Queen Victoria. Faded brown ink. Now, what's this one? John Ruskin – yes, that's authentic, I should say. And this one? Robert Browning – Hm – the paper's not as old as it ought to be.'

'Roly! What do you mean?' Clarissa asked excitedly.

'I had some experience of invisible inks and that sort

of thing, during the war,' Sir Rowland explained. 'If you wanted to make a secret note of something, it wouldn't be a bad idea to write it in invisible ink on a sheet of paper, and then fake an autograph. Put that autograph with other genuine autographs and nobody would notice it or look at it twice, probably. Any more than we did.'

Mrs Brown looked puzzled. 'But what could Charles Sellon have written which would be worth fourteen thousand pounds?' she wanted to know.

'Nothing at all, dear lady,' Sir Rowland replied. 'But it occurs to me, you know, that it might have been a question of safety.'

'Safety?' Mrs Brown queried.

'Oliver Costello,' Sir Rowland explained, 'is suspected of supplying drugs. Sellon, so the Inspector tells us, was questioned once or twice by the Narcotics Squad. There's a connection there, don't you think?'

When Mrs Brown merely looked blank, he continued, 'Of course, it might be just a foolish idea of mine.' He looked down at the autograph he was holding. 'I don't think it would be anything elaborate on Sellon's part. Lemon juice, perhaps, or a solution of barium chloride. Gentle heat might do the trick. We can always try iodine vapour later. Yes, let's try a little gentle heat first.'

He rose to his feet. 'Shall we attempt the experiment?'

'There's an electric fire in the library,' Clarissa remembered. 'Jeremy, will you get it?'

Hugo rose and tucked in his chair, while Jeremy went off to the library.

'We can plug it in here,' Clarissa pointed out, indicating a socket in the skirting-board running around the drawing-room.

'The whole thing's ridiculous,' Mrs Brown snorted. 'It's too far-fetched for words.'

Clarissa disagreed. 'No, it isn't. I think it's a wonderful idea,' she declared, as Jeremy returned from the library carrying a small electric radiator. 'Got it?' she asked him.

'Here it is,' he replied. 'Where's the plug?'

'Down there,' Clarissa told him, pointing. She held the radiator while Jeremy plugged its lead into the socket, and then she put it down on the floor.

Sir Rowland took the Robert Browning autograph and stood close to the radiator. Jeremy knelt by it, and the others stood as close as possible to observe the result.

'We mustn't hope for too much,' Sir Rowland warned them. 'After all, it's only an idea of mine, but there must have been some very good reason why Sellon kept these bits of paper in such a secret place.'

'This takes me back years,' Hugo recalled. 'I remember writing secret messages with lemon juice when I was a kid.'

'Which one shall we start with?' Jeremy asked enthusiastically.

'I say Queen Victoria,' said Clarissa.

'No, six to one on Ruskin,' was Jeremy's guess.

'Well, I'm putting my money on Robert Browning,' Sir Rowland decided, bending over and holding the paper in front of the radiator.

'Ruskin? Most obscure chap. I never could understand

[204]

a word of his poetry,' Hugo felt moved to comment.

'Exactly,' Sir Rowland agreed. 'It's full of hidden meaning.'

They all craned over Sir Rowland. 'I can't bear it if nothing happens,' Clarissa exclaimed.

'I believe – yes, there's something there,' Sir Rowland murmured.

'Yes, there is something coming up,' Jeremy noticed.

'Is there? Let me see,' said Clarissa excitedly.

Hugo pushed between Clarissa and Jeremy. 'Out of the way, young man.'

'Steady,' Sir Rowland complained. 'Don't joggle me – yes – there is writing.' He paused for a moment, and then straightened up with a cry of, 'We've got it!'

'What have you got?' Mrs Brown wanted to know.

'A list of six names and addresses,' Sir Rowland told them. 'Distributors in the drug racket, I should say. And one of those names is Oliver Costello.'

There were exclamations all around. 'Oliver!' said Clarissa. 'So that's why he came, and someone must have followed him and – Oh, Uncle Roly, we must tell the police. Come along, Hugo.'

Clarissa rushed to the hall door followed by Hugo who, as he went, was muttering, 'Most extraordinary thing I ever heard of.' Sir Rowland picked up the other autographs, while Jeremy unplugged the radiator and took it back into the library.

About to follow Clarissa and Hugo out, Sir Rowland paused in the doorway. 'Coming, Miss Peake?' he asked.

[205]

'You don't need me, do you?'

'I think we do. You were Sellon's partner.'

'I've never had anything to do with the drug business,' Mrs Brown insisted. 'I just ran the antique side. I did all the London buying and selling.'

'I see,' Sir Rowland replied non-committally as he held the hall door open for her.

Jeremy returned from the library, closing the door carefully behind him. He went over to the hall door and listened for a moment. After a glance at Pippa, he went over to the easy chair, picked up the cushion from it, and moved slowly back towards the sofa where Pippa lay sleeping.

Pippa stirred in her sleep. Jeremy stood frozen for a moment, but when he was certain she was still asleep, he continued towards the sofa until he stood behind Pippa's head. Then, slowly, he began to lower the cushion over her face.

At that moment, Clarissa re-entered the room from the hall. Hearing the door, Jeremy carefully placed the cushion over Pippa's feet. 'I remembered what Sir Rowland said,' he explained to Clarissa, 'so I thought perhaps we oughtn't to leave Pippa all alone. Her feet seemed a bit cold, so I was just covering them up.'

Clarissa went across to the stool. 'All this excitement has made me feel terribly hungry,' she declared. She looked down at the plate of sandwiches, and then continued in a tone of great disappointment, 'Oh, Jeremy, you've eaten them all.'

'Sorry, but I was starving,' he said, sounding not at all sorry.

'I don't see why you should be,' she reprimanded him. 'You've had dinner. I haven't.'

Jeremy perched on the back of the sofa. 'No, I haven't had any dinner either,' he told her. 'I was practising approach shots. I only came into the dining-room just after your telephone call came.'

'Oh, I see,' Clarissa replied nonchalantly. She bent over the back of the sofa to pat the cushion. Suddenly her eyes widened. In a deeply moved voice she repeated, 'I see. You – it was you.'

'What do you mean?'

'You!' Clarissa repeated, almost to herself.

'What do you mean?'

Clarissa looked him in the eye. 'What were you doing with that cushion when I came into the room?' she asked.

He laughed. 'I told you. I was covering up Pippa's feet. They were cold.'

'Were you? Is that really what you were going to do? Or were you going to put that cushion over her mouth?'

'Clarissa!' he exclaimed indignantly. 'What a ridiculous thing to say!'

'I was certain that none of us could have killed Oliver Costello. I said so to everyone,' Clarissa recalled. 'But one of us could have killed him. You. You were out on the golf course alone. You could have come back to the house, got in through the library window which you'd left open, and you had your golf club still in your hand. Of course. That's what Pippa saw. That's what she meant when she said, "A golf stick like Jeremy had". She saw you.'

'That's absolute nonsense, Clarissa,' Jeremy objected, with a poor attempt at a laugh.

'No, it isn't,' she insisted. 'Then, after you'd killed Oliver you went back to the club and rang the police so that they would come here, find the body, and think it was Henry or I who had killed him.'

Jeremy leaped to his feet. 'What bloody rubbish!' he declared.

'It's not rubbish. It's true. I know it's true,' Clarissa exclaimed. 'But why? That's what I don't understand. Why?'

They stood facing each other in tense silence for a few moments. Then Jeremy gave a deep sigh. He took from his pocket the envelope that had contained the autographs. He held it out to Clarissa, but did not let her take it. 'This is what it's all about,' he told her.

Clarissa glanced at it. 'That's the envelope the autographs were kept in,' she said.

'There's a stamp on it,' Jeremy explained quietly. 'It's what's known as an error stamp. Printed in the wrong colour. One from Sweden sold last year for fourteen thousand three hundred pounds.'

'So that's it,' Clarissa gasped, stepping backwards.

'This stamp came into Sellon's possession,' Jeremy continued. 'He wrote to my boss Sir Kenneth about it. But it was I who opened the letter. I came down here and visited Sellon – '

He paused, and Clarissa completed his sentence for him: ' – and killed him.'

Jeremy nodded without saying anything.

'But you couldn't find the stamp,' Clarissa guessed aloud, backing away from him.

'You're right again,' Jeremy admitted. 'It wasn't in the shop, so I felt sure it must be here, in his house.'

He began to move towards Clarissa, as she continued to back away. 'Tonight I thought Costello had beaten me to it.'

'And so you killed him, too,' said Clarissa.

Jeremy nodded again.

'And just now, you would have killed Pippa?' she gasped.

'Why not?' he replied blandly.

'I can't believe it,' Clarissa told him.

'My dear Clarissa, fourteen thousand pounds is a great deal of money,' he observed with a smile that contrived to be both apologetic and sinister.

'But why are you telling me this?' she asked, sounding both perplexed and anxious. 'Do you imagine for one moment that I shan't go to the police?'

'You've told them so many lies, they'll never believe you,' he replied off-handedly.

'Oh yes, they will.'

'Besides,' Jeremy continued, advancing upon her, 'you're not going to get the chance. Do you think that when I've killed two people I shall worry about killing a third?'

He gripped Clarissa by the throat, and she screamed.

CHAPTER TWENTY-TWO

Clarissa's scream was answered immediately. Sir
Rowland came in swiftly from the hall, switching
on the wall-brackets as he did so, while Constable
Jones rushed into the room through the french windows,
and the Inspector hurried in from the library.

The Inspector grabbed Jeremy. 'All right, Warrender.
We've heard it all, thank you,' he announced. 'And that's
just the evidence we need,' he added. 'Give me that
envelope.'

Clarissa backed behind the sofa, holding her throat, and
Jeremy handed the envelope to the Inspector, observing
coolly, 'So it was a trap, was it? Very clever.'

'Jeremy Warrender,' said the Inspector, 'I arrest you
for the murder of Oliver Costello, and I must warn you
that anything you say may be taken down and given in
evidence.'

'You can save your breath, Inspector,' was Jeremy's smoothly uttered reply. 'I'm not saying anything. It was a good gamble, but it just didn't work.'

'Take him away,' the Inspector instructed Constable Jones, who took Jeremy by the arm.

'What's the matter, Mr Jones? Forgotten your handcuffs?' Jeremy asked coldly as his right arm was twisted behind his back and he was marched off through the french windows.

Shaking his head sadly, Sir Rowland watched him go, and then turned to Clarissa. 'Are you all right, my dear?' he asked her anxiously.

'Yes, yes, I'm all right,' Clarissa replied somewhat breathlessly.

'I never meant to expose you to this,' Sir Rowland said apologetically.

She looked at him shrewdly. 'You knew it was Jeremy, didn't you?' she asked.

The Inspector added his voice. 'But what made you think of the stamp, sir?'

Sir Rowland approached Inspector Lord and took the envelope from him. 'Well, Inspector,' he began, 'it rang a bell when Pippa gave me the envelope this evening. Then, when I found from *Who's Who* that young Warrender's employer, Sir Kenneth Thomson, was a stamp collector, my suspicion developed, and just now, when he had the impertinence to pocket the envelope under my nose, I felt it was a certainty.'

He returned the envelope to the Inspector. 'Take great

care of this, Inspector. You'll probably find it's extremely valuable, besides being evidence.'

'It's evidence, all right,' replied the Inspector. 'A particularly vicious young criminal is going to get his deserts.' Walking across to the hall door, he continued, 'However, we've still got to find the body.'

'Oh, that's easy, Inspector,' Clarissa assured him. 'Look in the bed in the spare room.'

The Inspector turned and regarded her disapprovingly. 'Now, really, Mrs Hailsham-Brown – ' he began.

He was interrupted by Clarissa. 'Why does nobody ever believe me?' she cried plaintively. 'It is in the spare room bed. You go and look, Inspector. Across the bed, under the bolster. Miss Peake put it there, trying to be kind.'

'Trying to be – ?' The Inspector broke off, clearly at a loss for words. He went to the door, turned, and said reproachfully, 'You know, Mrs Hailsham-Brown, you haven't made things easier for us tonight, telling us all these tall stories. I suppose you thought your husband had done it, and were lying to cover up for him. But you shouldn't do it, madam. You really shouldn't do it.' With a final shake of his head, he left the room.

'Well!' Clarissa exclaimed indignantly. She turned towards the sofa. 'Oh, Pippa – ' she remembered.

'Better get her up to bed,' Sir Rowland advised. 'She'll be safe now.'

Gently shaking the child, Clarissa said softly, 'Come on, Pippa. Ups-a-daisy. Time you were in bed.'

Pippa got up, waveringly. 'I'm hungry,' she murmured.

'Yes, yes, I'm sure you are,' Clarissa assured her as she led her to the hall door. 'Come on, we'll see what we can find.'

'Good night, Pippa,' Sir Rowland called to her, and was rewarded with a yawned 'Goo' night' as Clarissa and Pippa left the room. He sat down at the bridge table and had begun to put the playing cards in their boxes when Hugo came in from the hall.

'God bless my soul,' Hugo exclaimed. 'I'd never have believed it. Young Warrender, of all people. He seemed a decent enough young fellow. Been to a good school. Knew all the right people.'

'But was quite willing to commit murder for the sake of fourteen thousand pounds,' Sir Rowland observed suavely. 'It happens now and then, Hugo, in every class of society. An attractive personality, and no moral sense.'

Mrs Brown, the erstwhile Miss Peake, stuck her head around the hall door. 'I thought I'd just tell you, Sir Rowland,' she announced, reverting to her familiar booming voice, 'I've got to go along to the police station. They want me to make a statement. They're not too pleased at the trick I played on them. I'm in for a wigging, I'm afraid.' She roared with laughter, withdrew, and slammed the door shut.

Hugo watched her go, then went over to join Sir Rowland at the bridge table. 'You know, Roly, I still don't quite get it,' he admitted. 'Was Miss Peake Mrs Sellon, or was Mr Sellon Mr Brown? Or the other way round?'

Sir Rowland was saved from having to reply by the return of the Inspector who came into the room to pick up his cap and gloves. 'We're removing the body now, gentlemen,' he informed them both. He paused momentarily before adding, 'Sir Rowland, would you mind advising Mrs Hailsham-Brown that, if she tells these fancy stories to the police, one day she'll get into real trouble.'

'She did actually tell you the truth once, you know, Inspector,' Sir Rowland reminded him gently, 'but on that occasion you simply wouldn't believe her.'

The Inspector looked a trifle embarrassed. 'Yes – hmmm – well,' he began. Then, pulling himself together, he said, 'Frankly, sir, it was a bit difficult to swallow, you'll admit.'

'Oh, I admit that, certainly,' Sir Rowland assured him.

'Not that I blame you, sir,' the Inspector went on in a confidential tone. 'Mrs Hailsham-Brown is a lady who has a very taking way with her.' He shook his head reflectively, then, 'Well, good night, sir,' he said.

'Good night, Inspector,' Sir Rowland replied amiably.

'Good night, Mr Birch,' the Inspector called, backing towards the hall door.

'Good night, Inspector, and well done,' Hugo responded, coming over to him and shaking hands.

'Thank you, sir,' said the Inspector.

He left, and Hugo yawned. 'Oh, well, I suppose I'd better be going home to bed,' he announced to Sir Rowland. 'Some evening, eh?'

'As you say, Hugo, some evening,' Sir Rowland replied, tidying the bridge table as he spoke. 'Good night.'

'Good night,' Hugo responded, and made his way out into the hall.

Sir Rowland left the cards and markers in a neat pile on the table, then picked up *Who's Who* and replaced it on the bookshelves. Clarissa came in from the hall, went over to him and put her hands on his arms. 'Darling Roly,' she addressed him. 'What would we have done without you? You are so clever.'

'And you are a very lucky young woman,' he told her. 'It's a good thing you didn't lose your heart to that young villain, Warrender.'

Clarissa shuddered. 'There was no danger of that,' she replied. Then, smiling tenderly, 'If I lost my heart to anybody, darling, it would be to you,' she assured him.

'Now, now, none of your tricks with me,' Sir Rowland warned her, laughing. 'If you – '

He stopped short as Henry Hailsham-Brown came in through the french windows, and Clarissa gave a startled exclamation. 'Henry!'

'Hello, Roly,' Henry greeted his friend. 'I thought you were going to the club tonight.'

'Well – er – I thought I'd turn in early,' was all that Sir Rowland felt capable of saying at that moment. 'It's been rather a strenuous evening.'

Henry looked at the bridge table. 'What? Strenuous bridge?' he inquired playfully.

Sir Rowland smiled. 'Bridge and – er – other things,' he replied as he went to the hall door. 'Good night, all.'

Clarissa blew him a kiss and he blew one to her in

return as he left the room. Then Clarissa turned to Henry. 'Where's Kalendorff – I mean, where's Mr Jones?' she asked urgently.

Henry put his briefcase on the sofa. In a voice of weary frustration he muttered, 'It's absolutely infuriating. He didn't come.'

'What?' Clarissa could hardly believe her ears.

'The plane arrived with nothing but a half-baked aide-de-camp in it,' Henry told her, unbuttoning his overcoat as he spoke.

Clarissa helped him off with the coat, and Henry continued, 'The first thing he did was to turn round and fly back again where he'd come from.'

'What on earth for?'

'How do I know?' Understandably, Henry sounded somewhat on edge. 'He was suspicious, it seems. Suspicious of what? Who knows?'

'But what about Sir John?' Clarissa asked as she removed Henry's hat from his head.

'That's the worst of it,' he groaned. 'I was too late to stop him, and he'll be arriving down here any minute now, I expect.' Henry consulted his watch. 'Of course, I rang up Downing Street at once from the aerodrome, but he'd already started out. Oh, the whole thing's a most ghastly fiasco.'

Henry sank on to the sofa with an exhausted sigh, and as he did so the telephone rang. 'I'll answer it,' Clarissa said, crossing the room to do so. 'It may be the police.' She lifted the receiver.

Henry looked at her questioningly. 'The police?'

'Yes, this is Copplestone Court,' Clarissa was saying into the telephone. 'Yes – yes, he's here.' She looked across at Henry. 'It's for you, darling,' she told him. 'It's Bindley Heath aerodrome.'

Henry rose and began to rush across to the phone, but stopped half-way and proceeded at a dignified walk. 'Hello,' he said into the receiver.

Clarissa took Henry's hat and coat to the hall but returned immediately and stood behind him.

'Yes – speaking,' Henry announced. 'What? – Ten minutes later? – Shall I? – Yes – Yes, yes – No – No, no – You have? – I see – Yes – Right.'

He replaced the receiver, shouted 'Clarissa!', and then turned to find that she was right behind him. 'Oh! There you are. Apparently another plane came in just ten minutes after the first, and Kalendorff was on it.'

'Mr Jones, you mean,' Clarissa reminded him.

'Quite right, darling. One can't be too careful,' he acknowledged. 'Yes, it seems that the first plane was a kind of security precaution. Really, one can't fathom how these people's minds work. Well, anyway, they're sending – er – Mr Jones over here now with an escort. He'll be here in about a quarter of an hour. Now then, is everything all right? Everything in order?' He looked at the bridge table. 'Do get rid of those cards, will you, darling?'

Clarissa hurriedly collected the cards and markers and put them out of sight, while Henry went to the stool and picked up the sandwich plate and mousse dish with an air of great surprise. 'What's on earth's this?' he wanted to know.

Rushing over to him, Clarissa seized the plate and dish. 'Pippa was eating it,' she explained. 'I'll take it away. And I'd better go and make some more ham sandwiches.'

'Not yet – these chairs are all over the place.' Henry's tone was slightly reproachful. 'I thought you were going to have everything ready, Clarissa.'

He began to fold the legs of the bridge table. 'What have you been doing all the evening?' he asked her as he carried the bridge table off to the library.

Clarissa was now busy pushing chairs around. 'Oh, Henry,' she exclaimed, 'it's been the most terribly exciting evening. You see, I came in here with some sandwiches soon after you left, and the first thing that happened was I fell over a body. There.' She pointed. 'Behind the sofa.'

'Yes, yes, darling,' Henry muttered absent-mindedly, as he helped her push the easy chair into its usual position. 'Your stories are always enchanting, but really there isn't time now.'

'But, Henry, it's true,' she insisted. 'And that's only the beginning. The police came, and it was just one thing after another.' She was beginning to babble. 'There was a narcotic ring, and Miss Peake isn't Miss Peake, she's really Mrs Brown, and Jeremy turned out to be the murderer and he was trying to steal a stamp worth fourteen thousand pounds.'

'Hmm! Must have been a second Swedish yellow,'

Henry commented. His tone was indulgent, but he was not really listening.

'I believe that's just what it was!' Clarissa exclaimed delightedly.

'Really, the things you imagine, Clarissa,' said Henry affectionately. He moved the small table, set it between the armchair and the easy chair, and flicked the crumbs off it with his handkerchief.

'But, darling, I didn't imagine it,' Clarissa went on. 'I couldn't have imagined half as much.'

Henry put his briefcase behind a cushion on the sofa, plumped up another cushion, then made his way with a third cushion to the easy chair. Meanwhile, Clarissa continued her attempts to engage his attention. 'How extraordinary it is,' she observed. 'All my life nothing has really happened to me, and tonight I've had the lot. Murder, police, drug addicts, invisible ink, secret writing, almost arrested for manslaughter, and very nearly murdered.' She paused and looked at Henry. 'You know, darling, in a way it's almost too much all in one evening.'

'Do go and make that coffee, darling,' Henry replied. 'You can tell me all your lovely rigmarole tomorrow.'

Clarissa looked exasperated. 'But don't you realize, Henry,' she asked him, 'that I was nearly murdered this evening?'

Henry looked at his watch. 'Either Sir John or Mr Jones might arrive at any minute,' he said anxiously.

'What I've been through this evening,' Clarissa continued. 'Oh dear, it reminds me of Sir Walter Scott.'

'What does?' Henry asked vaguely as he looked around the room to make sure that everything was now in its proper place.

'My aunt made me learn it by heart,' Clarissa recalled.

Henry looked at her questioningly, and she recited, 'O what a tangled web we weave, when first we practise to deceive.'

Suddenly conscious of her, Henry leaned over the armchair and put his arms around her. 'My adorable spider!' he said.

Clarissa put her arms around his shoulders. 'Do you know the facts of life about spiders?' she asked him. 'They eat their husbands.' She scratched his neck with her fingers.

'I'm more likely to eat you,' Henry replied passionately, as he kissed her.

The front door bell suddenly rang. 'Sir John!' gasped Clarissa, starting away from Henry who exclaimed at the same time, 'Mr Jones!'

Clarissa pushed Henry towards the hall door. 'You go out and answer the front door,' she ordered. 'I'll put coffee and sandwiches in the hall, and you can bring them in here when you're ready for them. High level talks will now begin.' She kissed her hand, then put it to his mouth. 'Good luck, darling.'

'Good luck,' Henry replied. He turned away, then turned back again. 'I mean, thanks. I wonder which one of them has got here first.' Hastily buttoning his jacket and straightening his tie, he rushed off to the front door.

Clarissa picked up the plate and dish, began to go to the hall door, but stopped when she heard Henry's voice saying heartily, 'Good evening, Sir John.' She hesitated briefly, then quickly went over to the bookshelves and activated the panel switch. The panel opened, and she backed into it. 'Exit Clarissa mysteriously,' she declaimed in a dramatic stage whisper as she disappeared into the recess, a split second before Henry ushered the Prime Minister into the drawing-room.

The Plays of Agatha Christie

Alibi, the earliest Agatha Christie play to reach the stage, opening at the Prince of Wales Theatre, London, in May 1928, was not written by Christie herself. It was an adaptation by Michael Morton of her 1926 crime novel, *The Murder of Roger Ackroyd*, and Hercule Poirot was played by Charles Laughton. Christie disliked both the play and Laughton's performance. It was largely because of her dissatisfaction with *Alibi* that she decided to put Poirot on the stage in a play of her own. The result was *Black Coffee*, which ran for several months at St Martin's Theatre, London, in 1930.

Seven years passed before Agatha Christie wrote her next play, *Akhnaton*. It was not a murder mystery but the story of the ancient Pharaoh who attempted to persuade a polytheistic Egypt to turn to the worship of one deity, the sun-god Aton. *Akhnaton* failed to reach the stage in

1937, and lay forgotten for thirty-five years until, in the course of spring cleaning, its author found the typescript again and had it published.

Although she had disliked *Alibi* in 1928, Agatha Christie gave her permission, over the years, for five more of her works to be adapted for the stage by other hands. The earliest of these was *Love From a Stranger* (1936), which Frank Vosper, a popular leading man in British theatre in the twenties and thirties, adapted from the short story 'Philomel Cottage', writing the leading male role for himself to play. The 1932 Hercule Poirot novel, *Peril at End House*, became a play of the same title in 1940, adapted by Arnold Ridley, who was well known as the author of *The Ghost Train*, a popular play of the time. With *Murder at the Vicarage*, a 1949 dramatization by Moie Charles and Barbara Toy of a 1940 novel of the same title, Agatha Christie's other popular investigator, Miss Marple, made her stage debut.

Disillusioned with one or two of these stage adaptations by other writers, in 1945 Agatha Christie had herself begun to adapt some of her already published novels for the theatre. The 1939 murder mystery *Ten Little Niggers* (a title later changed, for obvious reasons, to *And Then There Were None*) was staged very successfully both in London in 1943 and in New York the following year.

Christie's adaptation of *Appointment with Death*, a crime novel published in 1928, was staged in 1945, and two other novels which she subsequently turned into plays were *Death on the Nile* (1937), performed in 1945 as *Murder on the Nile*, and *The Hollow*, published in 1946 and staged in 1951. These three novels all featured Hercule Poirot as the investigator, but in adapting them for the stage, Christie removed Poirot. 'I had got used to having Poirot in my books,' she said of one of them, 'and so naturally he had come into this one, but he was all wrong there. He did his stuff all right, but how much better, I kept thinking, would the book have been without him. So when I came to sketch out the play, out went Poirot.'

For her next play after *The Hollow*, Agatha Christie turned not to a novel, but to her short story 'Three Blind Mice', which had itself been based on a radio play she wrote in 1947 for one of her greatest fans, Queen Mary, widow of the British monarch George V. The Queen, who was celebrating her eightieth birthday that year, had asked the BBC to commission a radio play from Agatha Christie, and 'Three Blind Mice' was the result. For its transmogrification into a stage play, a new title was found, lifted from Shakespeare's *Hamlet*. During the performance which Hamlet causes to be staged before Claudius and Gertrude, the King asks, 'What do you call the play?' to which Hamlet replies, 'The Mousetrap'. *The Mousetrap* opened in London in November 1952, and its producer, Peter Saunders, told Christie that he had hopes for a long run of a year or even fourteen months. 'It won't run that long,' the playwright replied. 'Eight months, perhaps.' Forty-eight years later, *The Mousetrap* is still running, and may well go on for ever.

A few weeks into the run of *The Mousetrap*, Saunders suggested to Agatha Christie that she should adapt for the stage another of her short stories, 'Witness for the Prosecution'. But she thought this would prove too difficult, and told Saunders to try it himself. This he proceeded to do, and in due course he delivered the first draft of a play to her. When she had read it, Christie told him she did not think his version good enough, but that he had certainly shown her how it could be done. Six weeks later, she had completed the play that she later considered one of her best. On its first night in October 1953 at the Winter Garden Theatre in Drury Lane, the audience sat spellbound by the ingenuity of the surprise ending. *Witness for the Prosecution* played for 468 performances, and enjoyed an even longer run of 646 performances in New York.

Shortly after *Witness for the Prosecution* was launched, Agatha Christie agreed to write a play for the British film star, Margaret Lockwood, who wanted a role that would exploit her talent for comedy. The result was an enjoyable comedy-thriller, *Spider's Web*, which made satirical use of that creaky old device, the secret passage. In December 1954, it opened at the Savoy Theatre, where it stayed for 774 performances, joining *The Mousetrap* and *Witness for the Prosecution*. Agatha Christie had three successful plays running simultaneously in London.

For the next theatre venture, Christie collaborated with Gerald Verner to adapt *Towards Zero*, a murder mystery she had written ten years previously. Opening at St James's Theatre in September 1956, it had a respectable run of six months. The author was now in her late sixties, but still producing at least one novel a year and several short stories, as well as working on her autobiography. She was to write five more plays, all but one of them original works for the stage and not adaptations of novels. The exception was *Go Back for Murder*, a stage version of her 1943 Hercule Poirot murder mystery, *Five Little Pigs*, and once again she banished Poirot from the plot, making the investigator a personable young solicitor. The play opened at the Duchess Theatre in March 1960, but closed after only thirty-one performances.

Her four remaining plays, all original stage works, were *Verdict*, *The Unexpected Guest* (both first staged in 1958), *Rule of Three* (1962), and *Fiddlers Three* (1972). *Rule of Three* is actually three unconnected one-act plays, the last of which, 'The Patient', is an excellent mystery thriller with an unbeatable final line. However, audiences stayed away from this evening of three separate plays, and *Rule of Three* closed at the Duchess Theatre after ten weeks.

Christie's final work for the theatre, *Fiddlers Three*, did not even reach London. It toured the English provinces in

1971 as *Fiddlers Five*, was withdrawn to be rewritten, and reopened at the Yvonne Arnaud Theatre, Guildford, in August 1972. After touring quite successfully for several weeks, it failed to find a suitable London theatre and closed out-of-town.

Verdict, which opened at London's Strand Theatre in May 1958, is unusual in that, although a murder does occur in the play, there is no mystery attached to it, for it is committed in full view of the audience. It closed after a month, but its resilient author murmured, 'At least I am glad *The Times* liked it,' immediately set to work to write another play, and completed it within four weeks. This was *The Unexpected Guest*, which, after a week in Bristol, moved to the Duchess Theatre, London, where it opened in August 1958 and had a satisfactory run of eighteen months. One of the best of Agatha Christie's plays, its dialogue is taut and effective, and its plot full of surprises, despite being economical and not over-complex. Reviews were uniformly enthusiastic, and now, more than forty years later, it has begun a new lease of life as a novel.

A few months before her death in 1976, Agatha Christie gave her consent for a stage adaptation to be made by Leslie Darbon of her 1950 novel, *A Murder is Announced*, which featured Miss Marple. When the play reached the stage posthumously in 1977, the critic of *The Financial Times* predicted that it would run as long as *The Mousetrap*. It did not.

In 1981, Leslie Darbon adapted one more Christie novel, *Cards on the Table*, a Poirot murder mystery published forty-five years earlier. Taking a leaf from the author's book where Hercule Poirot was concerned, Darbon removed him from the cast of characters. To date, there have been no more stage adaptations of Agatha Christie novels. With *Black Coffee*, *The Unexpected Guest*, and now *Spider's Web*, I have started a trend in the opposite direction.

CHARLES OSBORNE

The Agatha Christie Society

The Agatha Christie Society was launched in 1993 under the guidance of Mathew Prichard, Christie's grandson, to offer fun and fellowship to Dame Agatha's readers around the world. David Suchet, star of the *Poirot* television series, and the distinguished novelist and critic H.R.F. Keating are Society Vice Presidents.

The quarterly *Christie Chronicle* offers a column from Mathew Prichard, entertaining articles, information on new books, films and television productions, quizzes and competitions, special offers, information for collectors, an events calendar, and a lively letters section. New members receive several gifts: a Society pin (enamel badge), collectable bookmarks, bookplates, postcards, reading lists and a special Keepsake Edition of the *Chronicle*.

The Society arranges events on both sides of the Atlantic including: an annual outing to see *The Mousetrap* in London, Gatherings at Christie-related sites in England, and activities at mystery conventions. We hope that you will become our partner in crime!

If you wish to apply for membership of the Society, please write with your name, address, telephone number and E-mail address (if applicable) to:

THE AGATHA CHRISTIE SOCIETY
PB Box 1896, Radio City Station
New York, NY 10101-1896, USA
E-mail: Society@AgathaChristie.com *or*
AgathaUS@aol.com
Web: www.AgathaChristie.com/Society

YEARLY FEES
U.K.: £12.50   U.S.: $24
Canada: $30CAN or $24US   Elsewhere:$24US or £15
Cheques accepted in British pounds, Canadian dollars & U.S. dollars

THE AGATHA CHRISTIE SOCIETY IS RUN BY AGATHA CHRISTIE LTD., A COMPANY REGISTERED IN ENGLAND, NUMBER 550864

The Life and Crimes of Agatha Christie

Agatha Christie was the author of over 100 plays, short
story collections and novels which have been translated
into 103 languages; she is outsold only by the Bible and
Shakespeare. Many have tried to copy her but none has
succeeded. Attempts to capture her personality on paper, to
discover her motivations or the reasons for her popularity,
have usually failed. Charles Osborne, a lifelong student of
Agatha Christie, has approached this most private of people
above all through her books, and the result is a fascinating
companion to her life and work.

This 'professional life' of Agatha Christie provides auth-
oritative information on each book's provenance, on the
work itself and on its contemporary critical reception set
against the background of the major events in the author's
life. Illustrated with many rare photographs, this compre-
hensive guide to the world of Agatha Christie has been fully
updated to include details of all the publications, films and
TV adaptations in the 25 years since her death.

'A delightful bedside companion.' *The Tablet*

PUFFIN BOOKS

A DOG SO SMALL

Ben longed for a dog, but he lived in London in a back street, far from any open spaces for exercise and adventure.

His grandfather had promised him a dog for his birthday, but the promise was kept twistily; Ben found himself with what seemed a foolish woolwork picture of the smallest dog of the smallest breed in the world. That started something in Ben's mind. What about *a dog so small you could see it only with your eyes shut?*

So begin the strange adventures that end with Ben's finding his own, true dog and also the green spaces, even in London, where they can roam together.

This story, told by Philippa Pearce and illustrated by Antony Maitland, will be claimed by every child who has ever sought for a companion in adventure.

Philippa Pearce was born and brought up in the Cambridge-shire village where she now lives. Between then and now were twenty-five years, spent mostly in London. There she worked as a scriptwriter and producer in radio, for the Schools Broadcasting service of the BBC, and then as the children's editor of André Deutsch Ltd. Her novels for older children include *Tom's Midnight Garden*, which was awarded the Carnegie Medal.

Other books by Philippa Pearce

PHILIPPA PEARCE

A DOG SO SMALL

Illustrated by Antony Maitland

PUFFIN BOOKS

PUFFIN BOOKS

Published by the Penguin Group
Penguin Books Ltd, 27 Wrights Lane, London W8 5TZ, England
Penguin Books USA Inc., 375 Hudson Street, New York, New York 10014, USA
Penguin Books Australia Ltd, Ringwood, Victoria, Australia
Penguin Books Canada Ltd, 10 Alcorn Avenue, Toronto, Ontario, Canada M4V 3B2
Penguin Books (NZ) Ltd, 182–190 Wairau Road, Auckland 10, New Zealand

Penguin Books Ltd, Registered Offices: Harmondsworth, Middlesex, England

First published by Constable 1962
Published in Puffin Books 1964
25 27 29 30 28 26 24

Printed in England by Clays Ltd, St Ives plc
Set in Linotype Pilgrim

CONTENTS

ACKNOWLEDGEMENTS

The quotations on page 69 and page 73 are respec-
tively from *The Dog Owner's Guide*, by Eric Fitch
Daglish, *Dogs in Britain* by Clifton Hubbard, and
About Our Dogs by H. Croxton Smith. The author
also acknowledges indebtedness to
Cordelia Capelgrove.

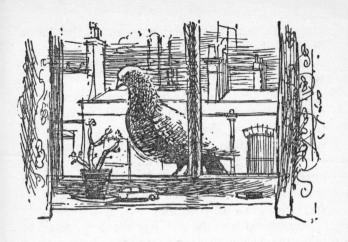

CHAPTER I

EARLY ON A BIRTHDAY

THE tapping on the window woke him. He was fast asleep, and then wide awake because of the tapping. Perhaps the pigeon always began as early in the morning as this, for it was certainly always tapping when the boys woke. But that was usually much later, with full daylight and with the smell of breakfast-cooking coming from downstairs.

Cold, scentless, dim was the early morning, and Paul and Frankie still lay sleeping. But Ben had woken at once, and at once he could not stay in bed a moment longer. He got out and went to the window. 'Pij,' he said softly through the glass; but the pigeon knew that this was not the boy who gave the food, and moved doubtfully off to the edge of the window-sill. The sill was always white with pigeon-droppings, so that Ben's mother – who did not know of the daily feeding – said that the bird was an obstinate creature that did not know when it was not wanted; but it did.

The sky was a dirty pinky-yellow where dawn over London fought with the tired light of thousands of street lamps. The birds were awake – pigeons, sparrows, starlings; but nobody was in the street. It lay empty for Ben; and he could not wait a moment later in bed – in the bedroom – in the house. With action he must fill the space between now and breakfast time, when the post came.

He dressed quickly and left the bedroom. The other two were still sleeping, and the pigeon had resumed its tapping. He crept out on to the landing. His parents were still asleep: his father snoring, his mother silent. As soon as Mrs Blewitt woke, she would begin a little rattle of cups, saucers, teaspoons, tea-caddy, teapot, and electric kettle. When the tea was made, she shook her husband awake. And when his snores had ceased to buzz through the house, you knew that the Blewitt family had really started its day.

Ben passed his parents' door, and then his sisters' – more warily. May was talking to Dilys. May was still half asleep, and Dilys three-quarters, but that did not matter in their kind of conversation. May, the eldest of the family, was going to marry Charlie Forrester early next year, and Dilys, very close to her in age, was going to be her bridesmaid. So they talked of weddings, and wedding-presents, and setting up house with a three-piece suite and curtains with pelmets and a washing-machine.... 'And a wedding like a newspaper photograph, with a bridesmaid and a page,' said May, going back to her favourite beginning. Ben was tiptoeing so carefully – so slowly, that he had to eavesdrop. They spoke of the prettiness of a page-boy to carry the bridal train; and they wondered if Frankie, being really still only a little boy – although not really pretty any longer, and he might need some careful persuading to the idea. . . .

Frankie? Ben's eyebrows went up; but it was none of his business, this morning of all mornings. He tiptoed on, down the stairs and out of the house. He closed the front door behind him with care, and then said quite loudly, 'It's my birthday.' The pigeon came to the edge of its sill for a moment, to look down at him, nonplussed. 'Ah,' said Ben, looking up towards it, 'you just wait and see.'

He said no more, even to Paul's pigeon, even in this empty street, and even so near to the time of his birthday post. His grandfather Fitch had promised him – well, as good as promised him – a dog for his birthday. That was some time ago, when Ben had been on a visit to his grandparents. Grandpa had been watching him play with their dog, Young Tilly, and had suddenly said, 'What about a dog of your own, boy – for your birthday, say, when that comes round?' He had spoken from behind his gnarled hand, because Granny was there, and she missed little. She disapproved of dogs, even of Till. So Ben had only breathed his 'Yes' to his grandfather, and Mr Fitch had nodded in reply. But surely that had been enough.

Grandpa would have to tell Granny in the end, of course, to get her agreement; and then he would have to get hold of just the right kind of dog. There might be delay, for there would be need of delicacy and discretion. All this Ben had understood, and he did not alarm himself that his dog was not mentioned in the weekly letters to his mother. Grandpa wrote the letters at Granny's dictation. She would have written them herself, but she had arthritis and could not use a pen properly. So Grandpa wrote for her, very slowly and crabbedly. Granny told him what to say, first of all about the weather and then about the rest of the family. Old Mr and Mrs Fitch had six surviving children, besides Mrs Blewitt, and all grown up and married and with children of their own. By the time Granny had finished with news of them, there was no room for talk about dogs. Moreover, Grandpa hated writing and by the end of each letter his fingers were cramped and exhausted with the effort of holding and subduing the pen. All this Ben told himself reassuringly, having faith that his grandfather would neither forget a promise nor break it.

For months now, Ben had been thinking of dogs. As long as you hadn't been given any one kind of dog, you had a choice of the whole lot. Ben had not bothered to be reasonable in his imagining. He had had Alsatians, Great Danes, mastiffs, bloodhounds, borzois. . . . He had picked and chosen the biggest and best from the dog-books in the Public Library.

This morning Ben was making for the River – some way from his home, but worth the walk. Looking over the parapet, you had the only really extensive view possible in this part of London, and that was

the kind of view you needed when you were thinking of a really big dog.

He turned out of his side-street into another and
then into a main road. There was very little traffic
yet, and he made the street-crossings easily, with
only a brisk, almost absent-minded look in both
directions. Already his mind was leaving London in
the early morning for Dartmoor at night. Over that
wild, nocturnal waste the hound of the Baskervilles
was silhouetted against a full moon low in the sky.
The dog's spectral eyes dwelt upon the figure of Sherlock Holmes. . . .

But a boy couldn't *do* much with a bloodhound,
unless there were criminals loose. Not a bloodhound
then, this morning. The road along which Ben was
trotting rounded a bend and came within sight of the
bridge over the River. This was the point at which
the Blewitt family still sometimes revived the old,
old joke about Ben's littleness. If he grew to be six
foot high, Ben sometimes thought, they would still
make that joke. For from the other side of the bridge
towered up Big Ben.

Ben Blewitt was still thinking of his dog. An Irish
wolfhound perhaps – but they looked so unkempt
and terribly sad in the photographs in the dog-books.
If he were dealing with wolves, he would really
prefer a borzoi. . . .

The traffic crossing the bridge into central London
had been very slightly increasing all the time, and
the number of pedestrians. Ben was outpaced by a
man in a bowler hat and dark suit, carrying a briefcase. He had walked from Tooting and was going to
his office in the City, where he liked to be at his desk

by half past eight in the morning. He did this every morning – he was not a married man.

He passed Ben on the bridge, and went on to his work; but Ben stayed in the middle. He laid his elbows along the parapet and gazed over that amazing length and width of water, here in the heart of London. The only buildings to interrupt the expanse were the bridges, and they put only their feet into the water as they strode across.

This was what he had come for. The expanse of the River reminded him conveniently of the enormous expanses of Russia, the home of the borzoi. At school Ben learnt about Russia – what Russians choose to eat for breakfast and what agricultural implements and crops they use on which soils; he wasn't very much interested. His father read about Russia in the newspaper, and thumped the table as he read. Paul and Frankie read about Russian space-travel. But Ben's Russia was different from all this. For one thing, his country was always under deep and dazzling snow. The land was a level and endless white, with here and there a dark forest where wolves crouched in the day-time, to come out at night, howling and ravening. For Ben, it was day-time in Russia. Sleighs had been driven out into the snow, and left. Each sleigh was covered with a white woollen blanket to match the snow. Beneath the blanket – but wait: already men on horseback were beating the near-by forest. Wolves came out. They were rushing past the sleighs. Men concealed in the sleighs threw back the blankets and, at the same time, unleashed their coupled borzoi dogs. Magnificent, magnificent beasts! They leapt forward after the wolves.

The wolves were fast, but the borzois had greyhound bodies, their whole bodies were thin, delicately made, streamlined for speed. The wolves were fierce, but the borzois were brave and strong. They caught up with the wolves: one borzoi on each side of a wolf caught it and held it until the huntsman came up with his dagger –

At this point Ben always stopped, because, although you couldn't have wolves, he wasn't so keen on killing them either. Anyway, from the far side of the bridge the moon-face of Big Ben suddenly spoke to him and said half past seven. The wolf-hunt with borzois had taken a long time. Ben Blewitt turned back from the River to go home to breakfast.

He broke into a run as he realized that the morning post would have arrived.

CHAPTER 2

A DOG BEHIND GLASS

THE stream of traffic was much thicker as Ben hurried homewards. He rushed up to his usual crossing at the traffic-lights, and a policeman said warningly, 'Now then, sonny, not so fast,' thinking he might recklessly try to cross at once. But Ben waited for the red traffic-light as usual. However urgent your business, you simply had to, in London. A cat which did not know about this scudded across the road without waiting. 'Oh!' said Ben, and closed his eyes because he could not bear to look, and then opened them again at once because, after all, he had to know. The cat looked neither to right nor to left, but suddenly quickened her pace as a car flew towards her. Cat and car sped on paths that must cross. 'She's done for!' said the policeman. The car passed, and there was the cat, safe on the farther pavement. She disappeared at once down some area-steps, and Ben thought that when she reached the bottom she would certainly sit down to get her breath back and to count her nine lives. The policeman was shaking his head.

Ben crossed soberly and safely at the red, and then began running again. When he turned into his home street, he saw that the time was late enough for most of the dustbins to have been put on to the pavement. His father was just trundling the Blewitt dustbin out to be emptied in its turn. This was the day of his father's late work-shift on the Underground.

As Mr Blewitt was going indoors, he saw Ben at the end of the street and waved to him to hurry. Perhaps it was just for breakfast, but perhaps it was for the post. Ben tore along.

The post had come, and it was all for Ben. His father had piled it by his place for breakfast. There were also presents from May and Dilys, Paul and Frankie; and his mother and father had given him a sweater of the kind deep-sea fishermen wear (from his mother, really) and a Sheffield steel jack-knife (from his father). They all watched while, politely, he opened their presents first of all, and thanked them.

He was not worrying that there had been no dog standing by his place at the breakfast-table. He was not so green as to think that postmen delivered dogs.

But there would be a letter – from his grandfather, he supposed – saying when the dog would be brought, by a proper carrier, or where it could be collected from. Ben turned eagerly from his family's presents to his post.

He turned over the letters first, looking for his grandfather's handwriting; but there was nothing. Then he looked at the writing on the two picture-postcards that had come for him – although you would hardly expect anything so important to be left to a postcard. There was nothing. Then he began to have the feeling that something might have gone wrong after all. He remembered, almost against his will, that his grandfather's promise had been only a whisper and a nod, and that not all promises are kept, anyway.

He turned to the parcels, and at once saw his grandfather's handwriting on a small flat one. Then he knew for certain that something was wrong. They would hardly send him an ordinary birthday present as well as one so special as a dog. There was only one explanation: they were sending him an ordinary present *instead of* the dog.

'Open it, Ben,' said his mother; and his father reminded him, 'Use your new knife on the string, boy.' Ben never noticed the sharpness of the Sheffield steel as he cut the string round the parcel and then unfolded the wrapping-paper.

They had sent him a picture instead of a dog.

And then he realized that they *had* sent him a dog, after all. He almost hated them for it. His dog was worked in woollen cross-stitch, and framed and glazed as a little picture. There was a letter which explained: 'Dear Ben, Your grandpa and I send you hearty good wishes for your birthday. We know you would like a dog, so here is one. . . .'

There was more in the letter, but, with a sweep of his hand, Ben pushed aside letter, packing-paper, string, and picture. They fell to the floor, the picture with a sharp sound of breakage. His mother picked it up. 'You've cracked the glass, Ben, and it's a nice little picture – a little old picture that I remember well.'

'I think it's a funny birthday present for Ben, don't you, Paul?' said Frankie; and Paul agreed. May and Dilys both thought it was rather pretty. Mr Blewitt glanced at it and then back to the newspaper he had opened.

Ben said nothing, because he could not. His mother looked at him, and he knew that she knew that, if he hadn't been so old, and a boy, he would be crying. 'Your granny treasured this because it was a present from your Uncle Willy,' said Mrs Blewitt. 'He brought it home as a curio, from his last voyage – the last voyage before he was drowned. So you see, Granny's given you something that was precious to her.'

But what was dead Uncle Willy or a woolwork dog to Ben? He still could not trust himself to speak; and now they were all looking at him, wondering at the silence. Even his father had put the paper down.

'Did you expect a *real* dog?' Frankie asked suddenly.

Everyone else answered for Ben, anyway.

His mother said, 'Of course not. Ben knows per-

fectly well that Granny and Grandpa could never afford to buy him a real dog.'

His father said, 'And, anyway, you can't expect to keep a dog in London nowadays – the traffic's too dangerous.' Ben remembered the cat scuttering from under the wheels of the car that morning, and he hated his father for being in the right. 'It isn't as if we had any garden to let a dog loose in,' went on Mr Blewitt; 'and we're not even near an open space where you could exercise it properly.'

'There's the park,' said Dilys. But Ben knew that park. It was just a large, flat piece of grass in front of a museum. There was a straight, asphalted path diagonally across it, and seats set in islands of asphalt. There was a notice-board by the gate with forty-two by-laws beginning 'No person shall – ' Eight of these said what no person should let a dog do there; and an extra regulation for that park said that dogs must be kept on leads. But you never saw a dog there, anyway.

May was saying, 'What about the River?' She only thought sensibly on her own subject, nowadays. 'Couldn't a dog swim in the River for exercise?'

Then Paul and Frankie and even Dilys laughed at the idea of Ben's exercising the dog he hadn't been given in the only open space, which was the River. They laughed merrily among themselves. Ben's hands, half hidden by the wrapping-paper that his mother had picked up from the floor, clenched into angry fists. Mrs Blewitt, still watching him anxiously, took the letter again to skim through the rest of it. 'They say they hope you won't be disappointed by their present – well, never mind that – and – why,

Ben, just listen! – they ask you to go and stay with
them again as soon as you're able. Isn't that nice?
You always like that. Now, let's see when you might
go. . . . Not next week, but perhaps the week after,
or perhaps even – '

On this subject Ben had to speak. 'I don't want to
go there,' he said. 'I don't ever want to go there
again. I shan't.'

CHAPTER 3

THE UNSPEAKABLES

AT the breakfast-table borzois, bloodhounds, Irish wolf-hounds, and all the rest had vanished together, and Ben returned to loneliness. To be the middle child of a family of five may not be as sociable and warm as that central position sounds. Paul and Frankie were much nearer to each other in age than they were to Ben, and so were May and Dilys. The two youngest and the two eldest made two couples, and in between them came Ben, alone. He had never been much interested in the girls' affairs, anyway. Paul and Frankie followed more sensible pursuits, and Ben sometimes allowed himself to play with them for relaxation. But, really, their games, their plasticine, their igloos made of eggshells and Secco-tined cotton-wool, and all the rest – these were things he had done with. Even their pets seemed childish to him: Paul's pigeon, Frankie's white mouse, their silkworms, and racing beetles stabled in matchboxes. Ben needed a mature, intelligent crea-ture-companion. Nowadays it always came back to the same thing: a dog.

Because Ben seemed somehow on his own, his grandparents Fitch had often had him to stay with them. They lived in the country in a house so small that there was not room for more than one visitor at a time; and, of the five Blewitt children, Ben was usually that one. And Grandpa had a dog – a bitch. She was called Young Tilly only because she was the daughter of Old Tilly; she was really quite elderly herself. But Tilly was still game for anything. She panted at Ben's heels as he wandered along the drift-way that ran by his grandparents' home. He could not say why, but this was what he most looked for-ward to on his visits: a fine day, and going along, but not in a hurry, a stem of grass between his teeth, and the company of a dog that snuffled and panted and padded behind or to one side, or suddenly pounced into the hedgerow, in a flurry of liver-and-white fur, with the shrill bark of 'A rabbit! A rab-bit!' and then came out backwards and turned round and sat down for a moment to get her breath back and admit: 'Or perhaps a mouse.'

All this Ben gave up at that bitter breakfast-table when he said aloud that he would never visit Grand-pa and Granny again. After all, he could not. You could not possibly accept the hospitality of someone who had so betrayed faith. In disappointment and indignation he had said he would never go there again. He would not.

Only, Ben's indignation was flawed by a sentence – if you could call it that – at the end of the hateful birthday letter. It had been added by Grandpa after the signature – that is, after Granny had ceased dictating. There was a spelling-mistake in the sentence, which made it certain that Granny knew nothing of the addition, for she always checked Grandpa's spelling. Under Granny's nose but without her knowledge, Grandpa had managed guiltily, hurriedly, urgently, to write a telegraph-sentence of four words: 'TRULY SORY ABOUT DOG.'

Old Mr Fitch had written as he might have spoken from behind that gnarled hand, furtively: 'Truly sorry about dog.' To say so, in such a way, was almost painful – and Ben did not wish to pity his grandfather now.

Ben first knew of the telegraph-sentence when his mother made him read through the rest of his letter, after his birthday. She had also propped up the woolwork picture on the living-room mantelpiece, trying to make the family admire it. Ben averted his eyes; but his father had taken notice.

'We always used to think,' said Mrs Blewitt, following his gaze, 'that the hand in the picture was the hand that did the embroidery.'

'A woman,' said Dilys, for they were all looking at the picture now, except for Ben.

'A dotty woman,' said Mr Blewitt. 'The dog's all right, I suppose, for a dog in wool, and the hand's

23

all right; but the two of them don't go together for size at all.'

'Perhaps a little girl did the embroidery,' said Mrs Blewitt, apologizing for the lack of skill in proportion.

'A *little* girl!' Mr Blewitt snorted. 'Just look at the size of the hand behind the dog! A giantess, I'd say.'

Mrs Blewitt tried to make Ben feel how lucky he was to own a picture of a dog embroidered by a little giantess. 'I said that it was a foreign curio, Ben! Your Uncle Willy wrote on the back the name of the foreign place where he bought it – Mexico, I think.' She took the picture from the mantelpiece and turned it round: 'Yes: "Bought in Mexico, on his third voyage, by W. Fitch."' Then she hesitated. 'And there was something already written on the back when he bought it.'

'Well, what?' asked Mr Blewitt.

Mrs Blewitt simply passed the picture to him, so that he could see for himself.

'Ah,' said Mr Blewitt, after he had read.

'What does it say?' asked Paul.

'Read for yourself.' So the picture went from Mr Blewitt to Paul, then to May, Dilys, and Frankie. Each looked at what was written there, mumbling over it, but saying nothing. The picture reached Ben last because he had deliberately not interested himself in it. But curiosity made him look to see what none of the others would speak aloud. On the back of the picture, in a handwriting older than Uncle Willy's, were the words:

CHIQUITITO
CHIHUAHUA

24

'It's a double tongue-twister in as foreign a language as could be,' said Mr Blewitt.

Ben still held the picture back to front, staring at the second – and possibly the stranger – of the two strange words. Oddly, in spite of its outlandishness, it looked familiar to him. He thought that he might have seen it in print somewhere, not so long ago. Seen it, not heard it, for he had no more idea than the others how one should pronounce such a word.

'The second word . . .' he said slowly, trying to remember.

'Ah, now!' said Mrs Blewitt. 'The second word was the name of some place in Mexico. I remember Willy showing us on the map.'

On the map – then that must have been where Ben had seen the name printed. Only – only, he hadn't been studying a map of Mexico recently; indeed, he couldn't remember when he had ever looked at one closely enough to notice any names. They weren't even doing Mexico at school.

What did it matter, anyway? He reminded himself that he hated the little picture, as an unforgivable betrayal by his grandfather. Yet, again – 'Truly sory about dog.' He could almost see his grandfather's hand writing that, his fingers clamped round the pen desperately driving it through the curves and angles of the capital letters: 'TRULY – '

'You know, Ben,' said Mrs Blewitt, 'if you went to stay with your granny and grandpa, you could find out all about your little picture. I know Uncle Willy told your granny, and she never forgets anything.'

Ben looked at the picture, but thinking of something else: 'Truly sory – ' He saw his grandfather saying it with furtive but true, unmistakable sorrow. He saw his face behind the curved, gnarled hand – his grandfather's face creased all over with wrinkles, and the skin an old red-brown from his working so long in all weathers, mending the roads for the Castleford County Council. His grandfather had blue eyes, and a browny-white moustache that lengthened out sideways when he smiled. He would smile with anxious apology as he said, from behind his hand: 'Truly sorry about dog.'

'You might do well to take the picture with you, when you visit them,' Mrs Blewitt said, growing bolder from Ben's silence. Ben knew that he ought not to let his mother take for granted that he would do what he had said he was never going to do again. But he continued in silence.

Frankie spoke: 'Ben said on his birthday that he never wanted ever again – '

'How often have I told you not to talk with your mouth full?' Mrs Blewitt said swiftly. Frankie's mouthfuls were large, so he would have to chew some time before speaking. Meanwhile, 'You could go next week, Ben,' his mother pointed out.

Now Paul protested: 'But that's just what Frankie was talking about. He was just going to say that Ben said – '

'Be quiet, Paul. Frankie can speak for himself,' said Mrs Blewitt, 'when he has finished his mouthful – of a size he should never have taken in the first place.'

Paul and Frankie had to be silent, but Frankie was on his last chews and gulps.

Mrs Blewitt clinched the matter with Ben: 'So it's settled you go, with the picture.'

'All right,' said Ben; and Frankie nearly choked.

'But, Ben, you said you'd never go there again!' he cried.

'I can change my mind, can't I?' asked Ben. 'And you've just spat some boiled egg on to your jersey.'

'You go straight into the scullery, Frankie Blewitt, so that I can wash it off at once.' Mrs Blewitt shooed Frankie ahead of her, and said over her shoulder to Ben, 'Write now. Say you'll arrive a week on Saturday, by the afternoon express. Grandpa can meet you at Castleford station after his market-day shopping.'

So, the following week, Ben went. He took one large suitcase, containing his oldest clothes for the country, and bathing-trunks in case the weather grew warm enough for him to bathe in the River Say. The case also held a tin of fudge, two plum cakes, and a meat pie, all home-made by Mrs Blewitt. She always sent what she could, because nowadays Granny could manage so little cooking, and Grandpa had learnt so few recipes. In the middle of the suitcase, packed round with socks and handkerchiefs to protect its glass from further damage, travelled the picture of the woolwork dog.

Mrs Blewitt saw Ben off at Liverpool Street Station. Old Mr Fitch met him at the other end of his journey.

As the train came into Castleford station, Ben saw his grandfather waiting with the crowd on the platform. He was carrying a bulging shopping-bag in one hand, and the other held Young Tilly's lead. She was crouching on the platform behind him, as close to his ankles as she could, and peering between them. She disliked trains, and this one – being an express –

swooped and roared and rattled up in just the way she most hated.

The train, slowing now, passed Mr Fitch and Tilly, and they both caught sight of Ben at the same time. Mr Fitch began to move, but Tilly was quicker. She dashed out from behind his ankles, found herself over-bold in her nearness to the still moving train, and dashed round to the back of Mr Fitch's trousers again; then she came out as before, but more cautiously. Her movements brought the lead in a complete turn round Mr Fitch's legs. By the time the train had stopped and Ben was getting out, Tilly had lashed old Mr Fitch's legs to the platform and, at the end of a shortened lead, was trying to choke herself and bark at the same time.

Old Mr Fitch could take no step forward, and his hands were fully occupied. But Ben, approaching, saw his browny-white moustache lengthening. 'Ah, boy!' he said. His eyes looked bluer than ever, because he was wearing his best blue suit, which he usually wore only for chapel on Sundays. With a shock Ben suddenly knew that he must be wearing it for *him*.

There was a muddle of leaping dog and lead and suitcase and shopping-bag, as they greeted each other, and then they disentangled everything. They were going to leave the station. Fumbling in his pocket for his platform ticket, not looking at Ben, Mr Fitch said, 'She put her foot down about the dog, you know. But I was truly sorry.'

'I know,' said Ben. 'You told me so.' With his free hand he took one of the handles of the heavy market-bag, and helped his grandfather carry the burden out of the station to the bus.

CHAPTER 4

TO LITTLE BARLEY AND BEYOND

THE country buses started from a special place in Castleford, a place not frequented by town buses; and, on market-day, the passengers were nearly all people like Grandpa Fitch, doing their weekly shopping. A bus crew usually knew its whole load of passengers by sight, even by name.

'Fine day, Grandpa,' said the driver of the Yellow Salden bus, who was leaning against his vehicle, smoking. He knew that old Mr Fitch lived half-way to Salden, by the driftway beyond Little Barley.

'It is, Bob,' said Grandpa. 'Got my grandson with me.'

'Wouldn't know you apart,' said the driver, and winked at Ben.

They got on to the bus. It was a single-decker, so there was no bother about taking Tilly upstairs. She crouched under Grandpa's knees, and on top of them he carried all his shopping and Ben's suitcase, up-ended. Ben himself had given his seat up almost at once to a woman with shopping and a baby.

When the bus was quite full and the driver had swung up into his seat, the conductress called down the crowded gangway: 'Anyone *not* going beyond the Barleys?' There was a hush among the passengers, for this was rather like asking whether anyone in a party had not been invited. 'I – ' said a hesitant voice, and everyone turned round or craned forward to see who. A lady with a suitcase and no shopping said, 'I – well, I was going just to Great Barley. The timetable said this bus went to Great Barley.'

'*Through* Great Barley, without stopping,' said the conductress. 'Full and five standing, on a market-day, we don't reckon to set down or pick up until after the Barleys. There's other buses to do that.'

The lady was civilly helped off the Salden bus and directed to a Great Barley one. Then the Salden conductress asked her question again, and a third time just to be certain. Each time there was an unbroken hush. Then she rapped on the driver's window and they set off – the five miles from Castleford to Great Barley, and straight through Great Barley, and bouncing over the two bridges into Little Barley, and through that, and well ahead of time, and everyone looking forward to early teas.

Beyond Little Barley the bus entered real country-side, with shaggy elms at the far limits of fields and meadows on either side of the bus route. A house stood quite by itself at the side of a field-track.

'The driftway!' cried the conductress, in case

Grandpa, from behind his luggage, had not seen where they were. But he was already struggling out of his seat, with Tilly and Ben pressing close behind him.

The bus stopped for the first time since Castleford traffic-lights. There was someone waiting to get on, anyway: young Mrs Perkins, who was the Fitches' next-door neighbour.

'I popped in twice to see her,' said Mrs Perkins to Grandpa, as he came down the bus steps. 'She wouldn't let me lay your tea, though. Said she could manage. Last I saw of her was going upstairs to watch for the bus from the bedroom window.'

'Thank you, my dear,' said Grandpa. He and Ben and Tilly and the baggage had got off; Mrs Perkins got on. The driver leaned from his window and said something he had been thinking out ever since his remark to Grandpa Fitch in Castleford: 'All three so alike that I can't tell which of you is the dog!'

'That's Bob Moss!' said Grandpa, as the bus drove off. The driver was laughing so much that you could see the spasms of it in the wobbling of the bus along the road. Then Mr Moss remembered his responsibilities: the bus straightened its course, and dwindled into the distance.

Mr Fitch let Tilly off her lead, and she went ahead of them up the driftway. A little way along it there stood what looked like one house – really, two semi-detached, brick-built cottages that some farmer had put there for his labourers, long before people had thought of building houses where they might easily be connected with sewers and water-pipes, electricity and gas. In one half of this double house lived young

Mrs Perkins and her husband; in the other half, the Fitches. The front of the house looked over the road and its infrequent traffic. The back looked up the driftway – a rutted track that ambled between fields and meadows, skirted a wood, crossed the river by a special bridge of its own, and came out again at last – with an air of having achieved nothing and not caring, anyway – into another country road just like the one it had started from.

Evidently Mrs Fitch had seen the bus, for she was coming down the stairs as Grandpa and Ben came through the front door. The front door opened straight into the living-room, into which the stairway also descended. Ben had a rear view of his grandmother in a black dress with little purple flower-sprigs on it. She was climbing down the stairs backwards and very slowly, because of stiffness in the knees. As soon as she heard the front door open, she called, 'Don't let that dog bring all the driftway in on its paws!' Tilly stopped on the threshold, sighed, and sat down. Mrs Fitch reached the last stair-tread: 'I've laid the tea, as you see, in spite of what's-her-name Perkins thinking I'm not up to it any more.' She reached floor level and turned to face them: she was a little old woman, thin, and yet knobbly with her affliction; but like some tool of iron, much used and worn and even twisted, but still undestroyed and still knowing its use.

'Well, Ben!'

Ben went forward and kissed her, a little timidly.

All Granny Fitch's grandchildren felt a particular respect for her; so did her sons-in-law and daughters-in-law, and even her own children; even Grandpa

Fitch felt it. He and Granny had been married for nearly fifty years, and they had brought up eight children – not in this tiny house, of course, but in another not very much larger. Grandpa had always worked on the roads, for the County Council, which was a steady job, but not well-paid. On the birth of their first child, Mrs Fitch had discussed the future with Mr Fitch, and he had taken the Pledge – for economy, not for principle. So he gave up his beer, and he gave up his pipe at the same time, and he had always given all his weekly wages into his wife's hands. Mrs Fitch had gone out to do morning cleaning in Little Barley as soon as the eldest Fitch child had been old enough to begin looking after the youngest; and she had managed. People in the Barleys remarked that the Fitch children were cheaply fed, but well-fed; cheaply dressed, but warmly in winter and decently in summer. They had all gone to the village school, where they worked hard – their mother had seen to that. One of them, by means of scholarships, had reached a university; two had gone to Castleford Technical School. One of these had taken a job in London, where she had met and married a young fellow with a good job, working on the Underground Railway. This was Lily Fitch, who became Mrs Bill Blewitt, and the mother of Ben.

In the struggle of bringing up the children, Granny Fitch – for she always took the family decisions – had never accepted charity. Not much was ever offered, anyway, in her experience. You could not call scholarships charity: they were worked for – earned. Now Granny and Grandpa were old, and

Grandpa had retired from road-work. They lived on their pension, and that was just enough. They still took no charity, even from their children. They were independent, Granny said; they always would be, unless anyone wanted to make a silly splash with expensive brass-handled coffins, when the time came.

In spite of her arthritis, Granny got about where-ever she wanted in the little garden or indoors. This afternoon she had laid the tea-table for Ben's coming, so that Grandpa had only to brew the tea, while Ben made the toast.

Over the tea-table Granny questioned Grandpa – what he had bought in Castleford market, how much he had paid, whom he had met, what they had said. Then she questioned Ben. She wanted to know how he was getting on at school, and Paul, and Frankie. She wanted to know about Dilys's deciding to change her job, and about May's getting married – and, of course, all about May's Charlie Forrester, whom Granny had met only once: was he really sober? was he steady? was he hardworking? was he helpful about the house? Grandpa, unobserved, took an extra spoonful of sugar in his tea, while Ben answered briefly, carefully, accurately, saying he didn't know if he didn't know, for all this was what Granny liked.

After tea old Mr Fitch usually read to his wife, whose eyesight had dimmed from much plain sewing when all the little Fitches had had to be so cheaply dressed. Granny had the choice of Grandpa's reading from the Bible, the Chapel Magazine, or any recent family letters. Grandpa read as haltingly as he wrote, so he gladly gave up his task to Ben this evening. There were two letters to be read: the first was from one of Ben's aunts who had settled in Essex, and the other was from an uncle in Canada. As Ben read, Granny would occasionally stop him to call, 'Do you hear, Joe?' and Grandpa would come out of the scullery, where he was washing up the tea-things. Then his wife would repeat to him the news of the letter, in the very words of the letter, for Granny had a remarkable memory for things both near and long ago. Each time, Tilly – from her position just outside the open front door – would whine a little, hoping that this meant the end of the reading. Every time she did so, Ben whispered 'Tilly . . .' in a steadying voice that promised her his company later.

When he had finished reading the Canadian letter, Granny said, 'Would you like the stamp?'

'Well . . .' said Ben, not liking to seem ungrateful. 'I mean, thank you . . . But, as a matter of fact, I have – well, really, I have those Canadian stamps, so if you don't mind – '

'Answer what you mean, boy,' said Granny, and the end of her knobbed forefinger came down like a poker-end on the table, so that Grandpa in the scullery jumped, and Tilly, who had been crawling forward until her nose rested on the threshold, winced back.

'No, thank you, Granny,' said Ben.

'Not interested in stamps now?'

'No.'

'But in dogs?'

'Yes,' said Ben, quickly and truthfully because he had to, but unwillingly.

'Disappointed you didn't have a live dog on your birthday?' The clash and splash of washing up stopped in the scullery. Ben was silent too. 'Answer,' said his grandmother.

'Yes,' said Ben.

Again, a silence. Then Granny: 'What possessed Joe to promise such a thing. . . . Do you know how many grandchildren we have?'

'Twenty-one.'

'Supposing your grandpa and I began giving them all a dog each – twenty-one dogs. . . .'

Grandpa appeared in the doorway of the scullery. 'Not one each. One to a family.'

'Seven dogs, then,' said Granny.

'One's in Canada.'

'Six, then.'

Grandpa went back into the scullery, having reduced the number of dogs as much as was in his power. Ben could see that, even so, there were far too many dogs. He couldn't have had one. He began to tell his grandmother that, anyway, you couldn't really have a dog in London. But Mrs Fitch was continuing her own line of thought: 'And I hope Lily'd have more sense, too. A dog eats bones that would make good soup, leaves mud on the lino, and hairs on the carpet. Yet men and children – oh! they must have a dog! It beats me why. Look at that foolish Till!' Young Tilly knew her name, but knew the tone in which it was spoken; she groaned hopelessly. 'We have her,' said Granny, 'as we had her mother, because she's said to keep down the rats and catch rabbits for the pot. But there never have been rats here, and there aren't rabbits any more; and, anyway, she's too old and fat to catch anything except a bit of bacon rind sneaked down on to the floor.'

36

Grandpa, with the tea-cloth in his hand, came right out of the scullery, and spoke with fire: 'There aren't any rats because she keeps them down all the time; and it's not her fault if there aren't rabbits any more. And stout, not fat.' He went back into the scullery before Granny could reply.

'Well,' said Mrs Fitch, 'that is something your grandpa and I shall not agree about. Ben, will you put the letters away for me, please? With the others, in the top drawer in the chest in my bedroom, on their right piles.'

Ben had done this before. He went upstairs to the deep drawer that held all the letters from Granny's children. They were divided into eight piles, one for each son or daughter. He recognized his mother's handwriting on one pile. One pile was much smaller than the others, because it had not been added to for many years; the postmarks were all foreign, as the stamps would have been, of course, except that they had been cut out long ago for grandchildren who were collectors. These were the letters written by Uncle Willy, who had been drowned before he had had time to marry and set up a family – Uncle Willy, who had brought the woolwork dog from the place with the unpronounceable name in Mexico.

Ben put the two latest letters into the drawer and shut it, with a sigh for the dog he had been cheated of. Somebody sighed in sympathy behind him. He turned. There was Tilly. She was never allowed upstairs, and one would have thought that she could never have conceived the bold possibility of a dog's going up there. But, as she waited on the threshold downstairs for Ben's coming, she had seen the hedge

37

shadows lengthening along the driftway, and had smelt the end of the day coming. She could not bear that she and Ben should miss it altogether. Grandpa had come out of the scullery and Granny had then engaged herself in a one-sided conversation on the worthlessness of dogs. Taking advantage of this, Tilly had slid into the house and upstairs, to find Ben.

Ben took her great weight into his arms and staggered downstairs, to where a window opened on to the back garden. He dropped the dog through the window and went down to his grandparents.

'I've put the letters away. Can I go out now?'

'Yes, be back before dusk,' said Granny. 'I expect you'll want to take that dog.'

'She's gone from the door,' said Grandpa, looking. 'But no doubt you'll find her outside.'

'I'll find her,' said Ben. He stepped outside, into the early evening sunshine and the smell and sight of flowers and grass and trees with clean country air above them up to a blue sky. He dropped his eyes from the blue and saw Tilly's face round the corner of the house. She advanced no further, but jerked her head in the direction of the driftway. 'Come *on*,' her gesture said.

Ben picked a stem of grass growing beside the porch, set it between his teeth, and followed her.

CHAPTER 5

LIFE WITH TILLY

IT wasn't that Ben wanted to live in the country –
oh, no! The country was well enough for holidays
and visits, but Ben was a Londoner, like his father.
Mr Blewitt was an Underground worker, and, as the
only English Underground was in London, Mr Blewitt
could no more live out of London than a fish could
live out of water. Besides, he liked London; so did
Ben.

Ben liked to rattle down moving staircases to plat-
forms where subterranean winds wafted the coming
of the trains; he liked to burrow along below London.
Above ground, he liked to sail high on the tops of
London buses, in the currents of traffic. He liked the
feel of paving-stones hard beneath his feet, the
streaming splendour of a wet night with all the
lamps and lights shining and reflected, the smell of
London. After all, London – a house in a row in a

back-street just south of the River – was his home; and he had been called – so his father said – after Big Ben.

But he would have liked to have had a dog as well.

That was why Ben particularly enjoyed his country-visits to his grandparents. During a stay, Tilly became his. This was her own doing, and was done with delicacy, for she became his companion without ceasing to acknowledge Grandpa as her master.

Grandpa gave Tilly's care over to Ben. He made her dinner – kept an eye open for all rinds of bacon, for bones, and other left-overs including gravy, added dog-biscuit and a little water, and stewed it all up in Tilly's old enamel bowl on the kitchen-range. He combed out her spaniel curls, dusted her for fleas, gave her a condition powder – did everything. He shielded her from Mrs Fitch, who knew perfectly well that there was a dog about the place, and yet never allowed herself to become reconciled to the fact of it. Ben picked up Tilly's hairs whenever he saw them indoors, rubbed her feet on the doormat before he let her inside, and walked between her and his grandmother when they entered together. Young Tilly herself knew how to evade notice. In spite of her bulk – 'a back made to carry a tea-tray,' Grandpa said – she could move so lightly that there was not so much as a click of her toe-nails on the linoleum.

Tilly was with Ben, whatever he was doing. On the first days of his visit, he spent most of his time about the house and garden, helping Grandpa. He kindled the fire in the range, fetched the milk from the milk-box at the end of the driftway, pumped the water, dug the potatoes, fed the fowls, and gathered the eggs. Always Tilly was with him. They spent one whole afternoon with Grandpa, helping to knock up a new hen-coop for a hen with a brood of very late chickens. The chicks ran over Tilly's outstretched paws as she dozed in the sun to the beat of Ben's hammer on the nails.

On other days they were more adventurous. Granny directed Grandpa to pack a lunch of sandwiches for Ben, and he went out after breakfast until nearly tea-time – with Tilly.

They went down the driftway. Once – in spite of everyone's saying there weren't any more, nowadays – they started a rabbit. Tilly threw herself into the chase, ears streaming behind her, until the rabbit began really to run. Then, intelligently, Tilly stopped.

Once, in a copse, they started a squirrel; and Tilly would not believe she had no possible chance of catching it. She thought it must fall.

Once they found an old rubber ball in a ditch: Tilly found it and Ben threw it for her, and they only lost it hours later, in a bed of nettles.

The weather became hot, and they bathed. Just before reaching the driftway bridge over the Say, they would strike off across marshland to the river. Tilly led the way, for bathing was her passion. The marsh grasses and reeds grew much taller than she was, so that every so often she reared herself up on her hind legs to see where she was going. She dropped down again to steer a more exact course, each time resuming movement with greater eagerness. As they neared the river, Tilly could smell it.

Her pace quickened so that she took the last few yards at a low run, whining. She would never jump in, but entered the water still at a run, and only began swimming when she felt her body beginning to sink.

Tilly swam round and round, whining, while Ben undressed by a willow-tree. He did not bother to put on bathing-trunks, for there was never anyone about. He dived in and swam, and Tilly threshed the water round him.

There was never anyone about – until the last day of Ben's visit. That day, the weather was stiflingly hot, and Ben and Young Tilly bathed in the morning to keep cool. Afterwards, they lay under the willow-tree where, even in its shade, the heat dried fur and skin. They shared the lunch between them – hard-boiled eggs and thick cheese sandwiches, and a bottle of lemonade as an extra for Ben. That made the day seem even heavier and drowsier. They slept.

So not even Tilly was awake when the canoe appeared for the first time, coming out from under the driftway bridge. There were two boys and a little girl in it. Between the knees of the older, red-haired boy, who sat in the stern, was a dog: an upstanding-looking mongrel, mostly terrier perhaps. He glanced towards the bank where Ben and Tilly lay, but they were hidden by the grasses, asleep. No wind blew a scent from them. The canoe passed and went out of sight.

The boy and the dog slept on. Breezes began to blow the leaves of the willow-tree, so that their silvery-green undersides showed light against a darkened sky. Great black clouds crept overhead.

Except for the abrupt, shivering little breezes, the air was hot, still, heavy before the storm. Then a single raindrop splashed on Ben's bare shoulder. He woke, and his movement woke Tilly.

The oncoming storm tried its strength out with a few more big drops, and Ben began hurriedly to collect his clothes to dress. Tilly was shivering and whining round him, getting in his way. Then she fell silent, turning towards the river, alert. Ben looked where she was looking, and at once dropped down behind the screen of grasses. The canoe they had missed before was coming back. Seeing the dog in it, Ben put his fingers through Tilly's collar. She had stiffened, but was willing to remain still and quiet.

The canoe was hurrying to get home before the rain. The two boys were paddling with all their might, and – to leave the stern-man quite free – the dog had been sent forward into the bows. There he sat, in front of the little girl, looking ahead over the water and from side to side at the banks. This time, on one of his side glances, the dog saw or smelt Till. There was no doubt of it, and Ben felt Tilly, under his hand, quiver responsively. The dog stood up now to look better at the bank, and the boat rocked as he moved.

'What is it, Toby?' called the boy at the stern; and, from the way he spoke, Ben knew he must be the master of the dog. With a pang he knew it: the boy was not much older than he, he did not look much richer – even the canoe was old and shabby – but he lived in the country, where you could exercise a dog. So he had a dog.

The other boy in the canoe cried that they must

not stop for anything Toby had seen on the bank – it was already beginning to rain quite heavily. The canoe sped on. As it went, the dog in the bows turned sideways and finally right round in order to continue looking at the place on the bank where Tilly was. Then the canoe disappeared under the bridge; and the rain was really coming down.

Then Tilly seemed to go mad. She raced up and down the bank, barking, and then flounced into the water, and swam round furiously, barking and snapping at the raindrops as though they were a new kind of fly. Ben had not meant to bathe again, but now, seeing Till in the poppling water, he could not resist. He dived in and swam under her, which always agitated her. He came up in a shallow, and stood with the raindrops fountaining in the water round him and beating on his head and shoulders and rushing down them. 'Tilly! Tilly!' he shouted, for Tilly – now that the canoe had gone far off – was setting off in its pursuit, still barking. She heard Ben and turned, coming back with the same speed as in her going, and with such an impact on Ben's legs when she reached him that they both went down together into the water, their barking and shouting almost drowned in the rushing of water and wind.

Thunder was rolling up, with lightning. They went ashore. Ben pulled on his clothes, and they began to run home. The marshland was becoming a slough; the driftway was becoming a marsh. Black clouds darkened their muddy way; lightning lit it. By the time they reached the refuge of their home-porch, water seemed to be descending from the sky in continuous volume instead of in separate raindrops.

Ben stumbled in through the front door. A pathway of newspapers had been laid from its threshold to the scullery. 'Straight through to a hot bath,' called Mrs Fitch; 'and that dog's too wet and muddy for a decent home.'

'She's not; and she's frightened of lightning,' said Ben. The violence of the storm excused contradiction. He picked up Tilly and carried her along the paper-way into the scullery, his grandmother no longer protesting. In the scullery Grandpa was pouring cans of hot water into a tin bath. He winked when he saw Young Tilly, and fetched a clean sack to rub her down.

Ben had his hot bath, and towelled himself, and Grandpa gave him his dry change of clothes. The rain was streaming in wide rivers down the scullery window. 'We bathed in it, Grandpa,' said Ben, 'as we were going to be caught in it, anyway.' He remembered the hurrying canoe, and described it and its occupants.

'The red-headed one'll be young Codling,' said Grandpa, 'and the others must be Bob Moss's two youngest.'

'And the dog? Does he belong to the red-haired boy?'

'Aye.'

'Tilly was frightened of him.'

'Of young Codling?'

'No, of his dog.'

'She's a sly one,' said Grandpa emphatically, closing one eye. 'That Toby fathered her puppies some two years back. But she's too old for such tricks now.'

46

Ben sighed. Young Tilly's mother, Old Tilly, had been old when she had had her last litter of puppies, of which Young Tilly had been one; but Young Tilly was now even older than Old Tilly had been then.

The storm continued, and during tea there was a particularly violent outburst. Young Mrs Perkins, sheltering under a raincoat, dashed in from next door to ask, 'You all right?' She said excitedly that this was the worst storm her husband could remember. Granny was saying that the importance of that remark depended upon how far back a person could remember, and that depended upon his age, which might be nothing to speak of. But Mrs Perkins was already dashing home again.

Up to now, Tilly had been hiding under the furniture; now she made a rush to get out through the door after Mrs Perkins. On the very threshold she darted back from a flash of lightning that, branched like a tree, seemed to hang in the sky, ghastly, for seconds. She yelped and fled back again to the shelter of Grandpa's chair. She squeezed under it so far that she stuck, and the old man had to get up to release her.

'Fat, and a coward,' said Granny.

Everyone knew that Tilly was – well, timid, yet she wanted to go out, even in this thunderstorm. She spent all that evening crawling towards the front door, and then dashing back in terror. For the storm continued with lightning, thunder, and floods of rain.

CHAPTER 6

PROMISES AND RAINBOWS

'THIS is the weather for Genesis,' Granny had said at last. 'Try chapter six.'

So Ben began to read aloud the Bible story of the great Deluge of rain, the Flood, and Noah and his Ark. For, though afternoon had passed into evening, the wind still rushed at the driftway cottages, the thunder rolled, the lightning flashed, the rain fell in torrents.

Some years ago, when Mrs Fitch had still been active enough to walk to Little Barley chapel on a Sunday, she used to read daily Bible-passages according to the chapel's printed scheme of Scripture-readings. Then arthritis stopped her attending chapel, and – away from it – she threw over the printed scheme and set Grandpa to read the Bible aloud to her from beginning to end, starting him again at the beginning as soon as he came to the end. But, at each time through, Granny became a little more choosy. The Gospels she always heard in their entirety; but the Epistles of Saint Paul were made shorter and shorter each time Grandpa reached them. Granny liked most of the stories of the Old Testament, but occasionally showed impatience with the leading Character: 'That Jehovah – that Jahwa – that Jah!' she said. 'Could have done with a bit more Christian charity sometimes!'

On the evening of the storm, Grandpa handed over to Ben in the midst of the Psalms.

' "Judge me, O Lord," ' read Ben; ' "for I have walked in mine integrity – " '

Granny sniffed. 'These goody-goodies! Try him a bit farther on, Ben.'

' "I have not sat with vain persons," ' read Ben. ' "neither will I go with dissemblers. I have hated the congregation of evil doers; and will not sit with the wicked – " '

Mrs Fitch said, 'What a very lucky man! Most of us have to sit where we can, and be thankful to get a seat at all, and put up with it without grumbling.'

Ben found himself thinking of the squash on the Yellow Salden bus. He considered, and then said that perhaps the Psalmist hadn't meant –

'Don't say it!' Granny interrupted. 'That's what they used to say at chapel. If there was something that seemed foolish or downright wicked in a Bible-reading, they'd say, "Oh, but of course, Sister Fitch, it doesn't really mean that at all." But if it was something that they fancied anyway, they'd say, "Why, but of course, Sister Fitch, it means just what it says." I know 'em!'

Grandpa opened his mouth to defend the chapel, but shut it again. Ben said, 'Shall I go on?'

'No' – for Granny was ruffled; and then she had said, 'This is the weather for Genesis, anyway. Try chapter six.'

Grandpa composed himself with relief to this change; but Granny was still on the alert as Ben read.

'Wait a minute, Ben! How old did you say?'

Ben repeated: ' "And Noah was six hundred years old when the flood of waters was upon the earth." '

'Six hundred years old – well, I never!' Granny said ironically. 'But go on, Ben.'

' "And Noah went in, and his sons, and his wife, and his sons' wives with him, into the ark, because of the waters of the flood. Of clean beasts, and of beasts that are not clean – " '

'I see you, Young Tilly!' Granny said suddenly. 'Creeping over the lino again on your filthy paws!' A storm-gust shook the house, and at that – rather than at old Mrs Fitch's words – Tilly fled back to shelter again. 'Go on, Ben.'

' "Of clean beasts, and of beasts that are not clean, and of fowls – " '

'Joe, are you sure you shut all the chicks in?'

'Aye.'

'Go on, Ben.'

' " – of fowls, and of everything that creepeth upon the earth, there went in two and two unto Noah into the ark, the male and the female, as God had commanded Noah. And it came to pass after seven days, that the waters of the flood were upon the earth. In the six hundredth year of Noah's life – " '

Granny said something under her breath which sounded surprisingly like 'Sez you!'

' " – in the second month, the seventeenth day of the month, the same day were all the fountains of the great deep broken up, and the windows of heaven were opened – " '

'Joe!' cried Mrs Fitch. 'The skylight window – you forgot it!'

'No,' said Grandpa. 'I remembered.'

Ben went on with the story to the very end, to the rainbow that God set in the sky after the Deluge: ' "I do set my bow in the cloud, and it shall be for a token of a covenant between me and the earth. And it shall come to pass, when I bring a cloud over the earth, that the bow shall be seen in the cloud: and I will remember my covenant, which is between me and you and every living creature of all flesh; and the waters shall no more become a flood to destroy all flesh." '

' "Every living creature of all flesh," ' Granny repeated. 'That's to say, all beasts clean and – ' She looked thoughtfully at Tilly, ' – unclean.'

'She's not an *unclean* beast,' said Ben; 'she just gets dirty sometimes. So do I.'

'You don't have mud hanging from the ends of your ears, regularly,' Granny said. She mused. 'Fancy taking all that trouble over them: unclean beasts, useless beasts, beasts that eat up the bones for good soup. . . .' She marvelled, without irreverence, at God's infinite mercy to those two, dog and bitch, who had boarded the Ark so that, long afterwards, there might be Tilly and Toby and all other dogs on the earth today. So her mind came into the present. 'And you really expected one of those on your birthday, Ben?'

'It was only – only that I thought Grandpa had promised. . . .'

Ben's voice died away. Grandpa was looking at the floor between his feet; Granny was looking at Ben. She said: 'And a promise is a promise, as a covenant is a covenant: both to be kept. But, if you're not God Almighty, there's times when a promise can't be kept.' She looked at Grandpa: 'Times when a promise should never have been made, for that very reason.' Now she was looking neither at Ben nor at Grandpa, as she concluded: 'Even so, a promise that can't be kept should never be wriggled out of. It should never be kept twistily. That was wrong.'

Granny in the wrong: that was where she had put herself. There was an appalled silence.

Ben dared not change the subject of conversation too obviously, but he said at last: 'You know, that woolwork dog that you sent instead of the real one – I meant to ask you something about it.' Perhaps he really had meant to do so, but he had been putting his question off from day to day, and here was the last day of his visit. Now, however, he was glad to go upstairs, get the picture from the suitcase where he had left it, and bring it down to Granny.

He handed it to his grandmother back to front, hoping that she would not find the crack in the glass. He pointed to the inscription on the back. 'I don't know what the foreign words mean, or at least I don't know what the first one means.'

Granny had taken the picture into her hands, but without needing to look at it. 'I remember,' she said. 'Two words. Willy said them and explained them.' She paused, and then began, 'Chi –,' as though she were going to say 'chicken'. She paused again, and then said slowly and clearly: 'Chi-ki-tee-toe.'

'Oh,' said Ben. 'I see: Chi-ki-tee-toe – Chiquitito.'

'Chi-wah-wah.'

'Chi-wah-wah – Chihuahua,' Ben repeated. 'Chi-quitito – Chihuahua.'

'According to Willy,' Granny said, 'Chiquitito is a Spanish word – they speak Spanish in Mexico, where the picture comes from. In Spanish, Chico means small; Chiquito means very small; Chiquitito means very, very small. This is the picture of a dog that was called Chiquitito because it was so very, very small.'

Ben looked at the picture – for only the second time, really, since it had come into his possession; the first time had been on his birthday morning. You could see only one side of the dog, of course: it's nose pointing to the left, its tail to the right; it was done in pinky-brown wool, with a black jet bead for an eye. But this was the representation of what had been a real, flesh-and-blood dog – a dog called Chiqui-tito. 'Chiquitito,' said Ben, as he might have said 'Tilly', or 'Toby'.

'And Chihuahua is the name of the city in Mexico where the dog lived,' said Granny.

'I know.'

'Name and address,' Grandpa said. 'As you might say: Tilly, Little Barley; or Tilly, the Driftway.'

Granny frowned. 'There's more to it than that. The dog belongs to a breed that only comes from this

53

city of Chihuahua, so the breed is called after the city.'

Now Ben remembered where he had seen the word 'Chihuahua'! Not on any map, but in one of the dog-books in the Public Library. He had been looking for borzois and other big dogs, but now he remembered having noticed something about the other extreme for size – the smallest breed of dog in the world: and the name of the breed had been Chihuahua. So this Chiquitito had been a very, very small dog of the smallest breed in the world. No wonder the hand in the picture looked so large: it looked large against a dog so very, very, very small. 'The hand really could be a little girl's,' said Ben.

'That's what Willy thought: the hand of the little girl who owned the dog and embroidered its picture.'

Again Ben felt a pang at the thought of someone his own age, or even younger, who had owned a dog. She had lived in Mexico. He had only the roughest idea of that country as wild and mountainous, with jungly forests and erupting volcanoes. But he was sure that there was plenty of open space there, and that the city of Chihuahua would not be the size of London, or with London's dangerous traffic. So the little girl in Mexico had had a dog, while he had not.

'I wonder what she was like – she and her dog.' For he envied her – the girl of whom all you could say was that she had had a right arm and some kind of white dress with long sleeves and ribbons at the wrist – and a dog called Chiquitito.

'I doubt she's gone long ago,' Granny said. 'And her dog. As Willy's gone. . . . People and creatures go, and very often their things live after 'em. But even things must go in their own good time.' She handed the picture back to Ben. 'They got worn out, broken, destroyed altogether.' Ben was glad that she had not noticed the crack in the glass. 'And then what's left?'

There was no answer from Ben or his grandfather, but the melancholy wind round the house seemed to say, 'Nothing. . . . nothing. . . .'

They went to bed early that night, because Ben was catching the first bus to Castleford station the next morning. He could not get to sleep at first, the wind so lamented, the rain so wept at his bedroom window. Then it seemed as if he had been asleep only a little while when he woke with a start. His grandmother, in her nightgown, was standing by his bed. 'Look through the window!' she said. It was daylight, but very early. There were clouds still in the sky, but shifting and vanishing; and the rain had almost stopped. 'Look, and you'll see how He keeps His promise – keeps it twice over!' And Ben saw that the early morning sun, shining on rainclouds and rain, had made a double rainbow.

CHAPTER 7

AN END –

THE morning of Ben's going was fine, with the still – almost exhausted – serenity after a long, wild storm. Blue sky was reflected in the deep puddles along the driftway as Ben and old Mr Fitch went to catch the bus.

They nearly missed it. To begin with, Tilly, who was supposed to be going with them and who would have been put on her lead in another moment, left them. She simply turned up the driftway, towards the river, as they turned down it, towards the road. Grandpa and Ben wasted some time shouting after her. She moved fast, and kept her head and her tail down; but she would not admit by any hesitation or backward glance that she heard her name being called. She was deaf, because she was off on her own this morning.

They gave Young Tilly up, and went on. And then, just as they reached the road, Grandpa said, 'But did you remember to take Willy's little picture off the mantelpiece this morning?'

Ben had left it there the night before, and now he had forgotten it. He was not sure that he really wanted it, but there was no time to stand working things out in his mind. He turned and ran back to the cottage. He startled his grandmother with a second good-bye, snatched up the picture, and was running back along the driftway as the Yellow Salden bus came in sight.

They caught the bus by the skin of their teeth. Ben was carrying Uncle Willy's picture stuffed in his pocket.

In the station at Castleford, the London train was already in, but with some time to wait before it left. Grandpa would not go before that, so Ben leant out of the carriage window to talk to him. There seemed nothing to talk about in such a short time and at a railway station. They found themselves speaking of subjects they would have preferred to leave alone, and saying things that they had not quite intended.

'Tilly didn't know you were off for good this morning,' said Grandpa. 'She'll look for you later to-day. She'll miss you.'

'I'll miss her,' Ben said.

'Pity you can't take her to London for a bit.'

'She'd hate London,' said Ben. 'Nowhere for a dog to go, near us. Even the River's too dirty and dangerous to swim in.'

'Ah!' said Grandpa, and looked at the station

clock: minutes still to go. 'When you thought we should send you a dog, did you think of the spaniel kind, like her?'

'No,' said Ben. He also looked at the clock. 'As a matter of fact – well, do you know borzois?'

'What! Those tall, thin dogs with long noses and curly hair? *Those?*'

'Only one. Or an Irish wolfhound.'

'A *wolfhound?*'

'Or a mastiff.'

'A – ' Grandpa's voice failed him; he looked dazed. 'But they're all such big dogs. And grand, somehow. And – and – ' He tried to elaborate his first idea: 'And – well, you've got to admit it: *so big.*'

'I wasn't exactly expecting one like that. I was just thinking of it.'

'You couldn't keep such a *big* dog – not in London,' Grandpa said.

'I couldn't keep even a small dog.'

'Perhaps, now,' Grandpa said, 'a really *small* dog – '

The porters were slamming the doors at last; the train was whistling; the guard had taken his green flag from under his arm.

'Not the smallest,' said Ben; and hoped that his grandfather would accept that as final.

'But surely, boy – '

'Not even the smallest dog of the smallest breed.'

'No?'

'Not even a dog so small – so small – ' Ben was frowning, screwing up his eyes, trying to think how he could convince an obstinately hopeful old man. The train was beginning to move. Grandpa was beginning to trot beside it, waiting for Ben to finish his sentence, as though it would be of some help.

'*Not even a dog so small you can only see it with your eyes shut,*' Ben said.

'What?' shouted Grandpa; but it was now too late to talk even in shouts. Ben's absurd remark, the unpremeditated expression of his own despair, went unheard except by Ben himself. The thought, like a letter unposted – unpostable – remained with him.

Ben waved a last good-bye from the window, and then sat down. Something in his pocket knocked against the arm-rest, and he remembered that this must be the picture. He looked up at his suitcase on the rack. It had been difficult enough to get it up there; it would be a nuisance to get it down, just to put the picture inside. Even so, he might have done that, except for the other two people in the compartment: the young man with the illustrated magazines would probably not mind; but there was a much older man reading a sheaf of papers he had brought out of his briefcase. He looked as if he would be against any disturbance, any interruption.

Because he had been thinking of it, Ben quietly took out Uncle Willy's picture and, shielding it with one hand, looked at it. This was the third time he had looked at it.

Still looking at the dog, Chiquitito, he recalled his recent conversation. He could not have the smallest dog of the smallest breed in the world. Not even a dog so small that – if you could imagine such a thing – you could only see it with your eyes shut. No dog.

The feeling of his birthday morning – an absolute

misery of disappointed longing – swept over him again. He put the little picture down on the seat beside him, leaned his head back, and closed his eyes, overwhelmed.

He had been staring at the woolwork dog, and now, with his eyes shut, he still saw it, as if it were standing on the carriage-seat opposite. Such visions often appear against shut eyelids, when the open-eyed vision has been particularly intent. Such visions quickly fade; but this did not. The image of the dog remained, exactly as in the picture: a pinky-fawn dog with pointed ears, and pop-eyed.

Only – only, the pinky-fawn was not done in wool, and the eye was not a jet bead. This dog was real. First of all, it just stood. Then it stretched itself – first, its forelegs together; then, each hind leg with a separate stretch and shake. Then the dog turned its head to look at Ben, so that Ben saw its other eye and the whole of the other side of its face, which the picture had never shown. But this was not the picture of a dog; it was a real dog – a particular dog.

'Chiquitito,' Ben said; and the dog cocked its head.

Ben had spoken aloud. At the sound of his own voice, he opened his eyes in a fright. Where the dog had been standing, the young man sat looking at him in surprise; the elderly businessman was also looking – and frowning. Ben felt himself blush. He forgot everything but the need not to seem odd, not to be noticed, questioned.

He turned to look out of the window. He kept his eyes wide open and blinked as briefly and infrequently as possible. He felt two gazes upon him.

After a while the young man spoke to him, offering to lend him one of his magazines. Ben devoted himself deeply to this, until the train was drawing into London.

Now, of course, Ben had to get his suitcase down. The young man, gathering his own things together, helped him. There was some confusion, and the young man's magazines and several other objects fell to the floor. He picked up all his possessions hurriedly, in order to be ready to leave the train as it slowed up to the platform at Liverpool Street. And Ben, looking through the carriage window, caught sight of his mother on the platform – and there was Frankie, too – and Paul! He began to feel the impatience and excitement of homecoming; his mind suddenly filled with it; other thoughts, even the most important, were pushed into the waiting-rooms of his brain. As the young man sprang to the platform, Ben was at his heels. He heaved his suitcase out, and ran.

The elderly businessman was the last to leave the carriage. He put his papers back into his briefcase in an orderly way, re-furled his umbrella, moved over to the mirror for a glance at his tie, and – crunch! The heel of his shoe had trampled something on the floor that should not have been there, and part of which was glass, from the sound of it. This time the woolwork picture suffered more than a crack to its glass. The whole glass was smashed and ground – with dirt from the floor – into the representation of whatever it had been – you could hardly tell now. The frame, too, was utterly broken.

The man looked down in irritation as well as in

dismay. He really could not be held responsible. The picture must have belonged to one of the other two passengers, but they were both lost in the streaming crowds by now. He would make himself late if he concerned himself with the further fate of this – this – well, the thing was only a wreck now, anyway. He was going to leave it; and, because he did not even want to think of it, he pushed the thing a little way under one of the seats with his foot. There, a not quite emptied ice-cream carton dribbled over it, completing the destruction of what had once been a picture.

You could hardly blame the cleaner, who came later to sweep out the carriages, for thinking that this was just a bit of old rubbish, dangerous because of the broken glass. The cleaner put it with all the other rubbish to be burnt; and it was.

So the little woolwork picture had gone at last – in its own good time, as Mrs Fitch would have said. During its existence it had given pleasure to a number of people, which is mainly what things are for. It had been lovingly worked by the little girl who lived in the city of Chihuahua and who owned the Chihuahua called Chiquitito. Willy Fitch had found it in a curio shop in a Mexican port – and how it got there from so far inland remains a mystery – and it had pleased him, so that he bought it to take back to his mother as a present. The gift had pleased Mrs Fitch, partly because it came from her son, no doubt; and, much later, she had given it to her grandson. It was true that to Ben himself the woolwork picture had brought bitter disappointment. Now the possibility of its ever having an effect of

any kind upon any human being again seemed gone.
For the picture itself was gone – broken and utterly
destroyed.

As old Mrs Fitch would have said, What's left? It
seemed, nothing.

CHAPTER 8

– AND A BEGINNING

BEN did not go straight home from Liverpool Street
Station. This was the last day of the boys' summer
holidays, when Mrs Blewitt always gave them a treat.
That was why she had brought Frankie and Paul to
meet Ben. They all went straight to have baked beans
on toast in the station Help-Yourself that overlooks
the comings and goings of the trains. There they discussed what they should do with their afternoon.
They all – including Ben – suggested and argued; but
it was Paul's turn to decide, and he chose the Tower
of London – partly because of the ravens.

Ben enjoyed the Tower without foreboding. He
said to himself, 'And I'll have time to think afterwards. . . .'

After the Tower, Mrs Blewitt took them to a tea-shop, because she said she had to wash that dank old air out of her throat and voice at once. Then, talking, they went home; and there was Charlie Forrester helping May to fry sausages, and they were both very excited because Charlie really thought he'd found somewhere for them to live when they were married. Charlie worked for a building firm that specialized in the conversion of old houses into flats, and his firm had got him the offer of a flat in a house they were beginning to work on in North London. Cheap, too, for the size – it would be a larger flat than they wanted. But if Dilys would really come and share the flat and share the expense – and Dilys was nodding and laughing – and get her new job in North London. . . . Mrs Blewitt listened, watching the sausages bursting but not liking to interrupt, and anyway thinking sadly that North London was a long way from South London. But, as Charlie said, the air was good because that part of London was high – 'and within reach of Hampstead Heath, Mrs B.!'

So, above the spitting of the fat in the frying-pan, Charlie and May and Dilys were telling about the flat in North London, and Frankie and Paul were telling about the Tower, and Ben was just thinking he'd take his suitcase upstairs to unpack quietly, by himself, in the bedroom, when – he remembered. He hadn't put it into the suitcase, after all. He hadn't – he touched his pocket, but knew he hadn't – put it back into his pocket. He must have left the little picture in the railway compartment.

He set down his case and made for the door. But he met his father coming in from work: 'Here!

You're not going out, Ben, just when we're all ready to sit down to a hot meal!' And his mother heard, and made him come back. And his father wanted to hear all about his stay with his grandparents, as well as about the flat Charlie had found, and about the Tower of London.

He did not tell them why he had been going out. Secretly he determined to go back to Liverpool Street Station the next day, after school. This evening it would probably have been no use, anyway – too early for lost property to have been brought in. But he would go tomorrow to get the picture back; he must have it. He must.

He had lost the picture, and so he was afraid that he had somehow lost a dog – a dog that answered to the name of Chiquitito.

That evening, as usual, Frankie went to bed first. Then Paul, ten minutes later – just so long because he was older; but no longer, because the two of them always had things to talk about. But the excitement of the day had tired them, and they were both asleep by the time Ben came. He undressed slowly and unhappily, thinking of his loss. He turned off the light and got into bed, but then lay, unhopeful of sleep, with his hands behind his head, staring at the ceiling-shadows cast by the street-lamps outside.

But Ben, too, was tired with a long, full day, and wearied out with loss and, above all, the old longing. Even before he was ready to sleep, his eyelids fell over his eyes.

He saw nothing; and then he saw a point – something so small that it had neither length nor breadth. But the point was coming towards him, taking on size as it came. He saw what it must be. 'Chiquitito!' he called softly. The dog was racing towards him, appearing ever larger as it came nearer; and yet, when it reached him, it was still very, very small. He realized how small when he stretched out his hand to it: his hand looked like a giant's against such a tiny dog.

The dog curvetted round him, knowing its name, knowing its master. Then it bounded away, expecting to be followed. So they set off together through strange and wonderfully changing countryside. For by now Ben was really entering sleep and his dreams.

This was the beginning of their companionship.

CHAPTER 9

WOLVES DIE BY HUNDREDS

BEN never fully understood the coming of the Chihuahua; and at first he feared the possibility of its going from him as inexplicably. He did not trust his own need and the dog's responsive devotion.

He thought that material connexion was necessary – the connexion of some*thing*.

He went again and again to Liverpool Street Station to ask for his picture. He was frightened when, on his third successive visit, they told him with finality that the picture had still not been brought in : it must be accounted lost for good. Yet, when he closed his eyes on the succeeding nights, knowing that he would never see the picture again, he still saw his Chihuahua.

He thought that knowledge was necessary to give him power over it. He had worried at first that he did not know exactly what Chihuahuas were like, and liked to do. He began to frequent the Public Library again. He exhausted the resources of the Junior Library and – with the librarian's permission – consulted specialist works in the main Library. Moving from dog-book to dog-book, he was gradually collecting what little information is easily available about the lesser foreign breeds.

The dog Chiquitito was companionably interested in Ben's researches and – on the whole – most responsive to suggestion. 'The Chihuahua is very active, alert, intelligent, and affectionate,' said one book. That very night, the dog's actions became as swift as pinky-fawn lightning; its ears cocked in alertness so constant that their muscles must have ached; and intelligence and affection henceforth marked its conduct to an exceptional degree.

Fawn, it seemed, was only one of the colours in which a Chihuahua might appear. 'Colours are varied: white, biscuit, cream, light and dark fawns, lemon, peach, apricot, sable, blue, chocolate, and black.' Ben, reading the list, was overwhelmed by the richness, and – Non-Fiction was such a quiet part of the Public Library – shut his eyes; and there was Chiquitito in blue fur – a soft, smoky blue that was just believable. With shut eyes Ben watched the blue Chihuahua turn slowly round to show the true blueness of every part except its black collar, black markings, black nose, and bead-black eyes. It seemed to fancy itself.

When at last Ben re-opened his eyes, he found the librarian staring at him. Hurriedly he went back to his looking and reading. But the librarian still observed him. She did not like a boy of that age hanging about in the main Library, even if he had special permission and even if he did stick to the Poultry, Dogs, and Bee-keeping shelves. Now he was reading in another book; and now – look; he had gone a greeny-white in the face. The librarian went over to him at once.

'It says they were considered edible,' said Ben. 'What's "edible"?'

'Eatable,' said the librarian. 'But you feel ill, don't you?'

'I thought it meant that,' said Ben. 'Yes, I do feel rather sick. But I only *feel* sick: I shan't be.'

The librarian, hoping that he was right, made him sit down in a chair, behind which she opened a window. The boy's complexion returned to normal, and he said he would go home. He wanted to take the book out.

The librarian held out her stamp over the date-slip, and then came out with what was in her mind: 'You know, boys of your age should be borrowing books from the Junior Library, not from here.'

'But I told you,' said Ben: 'the books on my subject in the other library are so babyish.'

The librarian looked at the title of the book he wanted to borrow. 'Dogs – there's an excellent book which must be in the Junior Library: *Ten Common Breeds of Dog in Britain and their Care.*'

'I've looked,' said Ben. 'It was no good – truly.'

The librarian stamped *Dogs of the World* for him, but held on to the volume for a moment as she asked, 'And why are you so interested in this subject of yours? Have you a dog of your own, or are you going to get one?'

Ben hesitated, and then said carefully: 'Yes, I have a dog; and no, I'm not going to get one.'

'If you have a dog already,' the librarian pointed out, 'of course you're not going to get one. One dog must be difficult enough to look after properly, in London.'

'It's a small dog,' Ben explained. 'So small that – ' He shut his eyes as he spoke, and held them shut for several seconds, so that the librarian wondered if the child were feeling ill again. But then he opened his eyes to finish what he was saying, rather lamely: 'Well, it's *small*.'

The librarian, watching him go out with the book under his arm, still felt uneasy. She was sure there was someshing wrong somewhere, even if she could not put her finger upon it. She would feel happier, anyway, when he went back to the Junior Library, where he belonged.

That night, in bed, Ben read a little more about the Chihuahua in ancient Mexico. Then he turned out the light, and shut his eyes as usual.

He drifted into sleep, and then into nightmare. Paul and Frankie slept through his screaming, but his mother came. She roused him. Like a much younger child he clung to her, sobbing: 'People with sort of toasting-forks were chasing us, to catch us and cook us and eat us. And they'd fattened us up first.'

Mrs Blewitt tried to soothe Ben by bringing him to a sense of present reality. 'But look, here I am; and here you are, safe in bed; and there are Paul and Frankie, still asleep. No one's chasing us all to eat us.'

'I wasn't with you and Paul and Frankie,' said Ben. 'And they did fatten them to eat them – the book said so.'

'A nightmare about cannibals,' said Mrs Blewitt over her shoulder to Mr Blewitt, who had followed to see what was the matter.

'Not cannibals,' Ben said. 'They used to eat – to eat – ' He wanted no one to know his secrets, but his mother was close and he had been so afraid. 'Well, they used to eat Chi – Chi – '

'To eat chickens?'

'No. Chi – Chi – '

'Cheese?'

He told the truth, but not all of it: 'They used to eat – dogs.'

Mr Blewitt said under his breath, 'Dogs!' Mrs Blewitt frowned at him. She made Ben lie down again, gave him an aspirin, and told him not to dream any more.

Back in their own bedroom, Mrs Blewitt said, 'I told you what it must mean, Bill – his bringing home all those library books about dogs. And now this nightmare. He's still hankering to have a dog.'

Mr Blewitt groaned. He sometimes felt that his five children and their affairs were almost too much for him: May's wedding-plans, and Dilys wanting to leave home with her, too, and now Ben's dog.... Mr Blewitt loved his children, of course, but it was really a great relief, nowadays, to go off to work – to slip down the Underground, where there were hundreds of thousands of people on the move, but none of his business so long as they had their tickets and kept clear of the doors. If some of them wanted dogs and could not have them, that was strictly their affair, not his.

'He just can't have a dog in London,' Mr Blewitt said, out of all patience. 'I'll tell him so, now and for the last time.' He was starting back towards the boys' bedroom.

'No, Bill,' said Mrs Blewitt, 'Not now; and I'll tell him myself – when there's a right time for it.'

The time did not come the next day, for Ben was at school in the morning and afternoon, and called at the Public Library on the way home; and, when he got home, his mother was just setting out with May and Dilys to meet Charlie Forrester and see the flat.

Ben spent the evening reading his latest book from the Library.

'They are small – ', he read of the Chihuahua: well, yes, very, very small, especially some : ' – pet dogs – ', well, perhaps, although 'pet' sounded rather womanish ' – and very timid.' Very *timid*? Ben felt shocked and incredulous. Timid – now, you might call Young Tilly timid – although Grandpa said she was really just prudent; but then, you took Tilly as you found her – you had to. The dog Chiquitito was different – not subject to imperfection.

Unwillingly he remembered that, the night before, the Chihuahua and he had both fled before the ancient and hungry Mexicans. He admitted that he himself had been terrified; but the Chihuahua – had not its accompanying him been an act of affection – of close loyalty – rather than of timidity? Was his dog really a coward? Only the evidence of his own eyes would convince him of that.

That night, when he closed his eyes, he saw a land-

73

scape even before he saw the dog in it. The scene
appeared familiar and then he remembered: Russia.
The whole landscape was white with snow, except
for the dark woods where the wolves hid themselves.
There were the sleighs covered with white woollen
blankets, and men beating the woods. The wolves
came out – they were much larger than Ben had ever
imagined them before, huge, with gnashing teeth;
and there were dozens of them – one whole pack at
least. From the dark, distant woods they came rushing towards the sleighs, and in their very path stood
Ben.

Then he realized that the dog Chiquitito stood beside him. This time it was black in colour – Ben had
never before seen such an absolute, such a resolute
black. The dog looked up at him. Very *timid*? The
Chihuahua's pop eyes seemed almost to start from
its head in indignation; and at once it set off, with the
greatest activity. It raced across the snow to meet
the oncoming wolf-packs; it was like a swift moving bead of jet against the snow. It reached the wolf-
leader, and the black point rose to the grey mass.
There was a dreadful howling, and red blood, and the
wolf-leader lay dead, and the black point moved on.
The Chihuahua was only a hundredth part of the size
of any wolf, and the wolves were at least a hundred
times as many; but it opposed them with activity and
intelligence and, above all, with incredible daring.
The dog was more like David against Goliath, more
like Sir Richard Grenville at Flores, than any ordinary Chihuahua against several packs of wolves. Ben
watched; the borzoi dogs came out from under their
white woollen blankets to watch in amazement and

deep respect. When every wolf of every pack lay dead in its own blood on the snowy plain, the dog Chiquitito trotted back. One ear was slightly torn.

Ben said to him, before them all: 'Not in the least timid – never. On the contrary, bold and resolute. Very, very brave.' The huntsmen by the sleighs, who had not even troubled to take out their hunting knives to finish the wolves off, seemed to understand, for they clapped. The dog Chiquitito modestly lowered its eyes and, under Ben's very gaze, its whole body blushed – turned from the original resolute black through a pinky-grey to a deep peach. Then that colour slowly ebbed and muddied until the dog was its usual fawn.

And so, the next day, Ben took the dog-book back to the Public Library and said that he did not want any more books on that subject, anyway. The librarian was relieved.

And that evening, when his mother took Ben aside to begin her little talk ('You know, Ben, you had a nightmare because of all this reading about dogs'), Ben said: 'I've given up dog-books, this very day. One of them turned out to be such rubbish.'

'But, all the same,' his mother persisted, 'you're still thinking about a dog.' Ben did not deny this. 'You're still wanting to have a dog.'

'No!' said Ben. 'No, truly! I'm not wanting a dog any more, because I've *got* – '

'Yes?'

Ben changed his mind about what he was going to say. 'I've got over it.'

CHAPTER 10

LONDON EXPLOITS

MRS BLEWITT could hardly believe that Ben no
longer wanted a dog. In her experience, he did not
give ideas up easily; besides, if he were like Paul or
Frankie, he needed an animal of some kind. Well,
within reason, he could have any small one that
wasn't a dog.

'How would you like a white mouse, like
Frankie's?' Mrs Blewitt asked.

'No, thank you. I don't want a white mouse.'

'Well, then – ' Mrs Blewitt swallowed hard: 'well,
then, a white rat?'

'No, thank you,' said Ben. 'I don't want anything
at all. I just want people to leave me alone. Please.'

He really meant what he said: to be left alone, in

peace and quiet, so that he could shut his eyes, and see. For, by now, night-time visions were not enough for him. He saw the dog Chiquitito as soon as he closed his eyes in bed, and they were together when he fell asleep, entering his dreams together. But, when he woke in the morning, a whole day stretched before him, busy and almost unbearably dogless.

You might have thought that week-ends and half-holidays would have provided Ben with his opportunity, but not in a family such as the Blewitts. Ben's mother did not like his staying indoors if the weather were fine; and, if it were wet, too many other people seemed to stay indoors.

So Ben reflected, as he slipped up to his bedroom one wet Saturday afternoon. He had left his father downstairs watching football on television; May and Dilys were cutting out dress patterns; Mrs Blewitt was advising her daughters and making a batch of buns for tea; Paul had disappeared, and Frankie –

When Ben reached the bedroom, there was Frankie. He was sitting cross-legged and straight-backed on his bed: this meant that he was exercising his white mouse. The mouse ran round and round his body, between his vest and his skin, above the tightened belt. In her ignorance of this Mrs Blewitt always marvelled that Frankie's vests soiled so quickly – had such a *trampled* look.

At least there was no Paul in the bedroom, although Paul's pigeon loitered on the window-sill, peering in.

But Frankie was going to talk. 'I suppose it's because you're older than I am that you can have one. . . . A white *rat*! And Mother always used to say that the very idea made her feel sick!' Mrs Blewitt's offer to Ben had gradually become known. Such a piece of information seeps through a family to any interested members, rather as water seeps through a porous pot.

'But I don't want a rat.' Ben climbed on to his bed and composed himself as if for a nap.

'If you take the rat,' said Frankie, 'I'll trade for it: some really good marbles – '

'No,' said Ben.

' – and I've a shoe-box full of bus tickets. And another of milk-bottle tops.'

'No.'

'You're a grabber,' Frankie said coldly. 'But, all right, you can have it: my penny flattened on the railway line.'

'No,' said Ben. 'I told you: I'm not having the rat. I don't want it. I just want to be left alone. I just want peace and quiet to shut my eyes.'

There was a very short silence. Then Frankie said, 'This is our room just as much as yours, and I can talk in it as much as I like; and you look just silly lying there with your eyes shut.'

'Go away.'

Frankie went on grumbling about his rights, which distracted Ben. Then he fell abruptly and absolutely silent, which was distracting in a different way. Ben opened his eyes and jerked his head up suddenly. Sure enough, he caught Frankie at it – sticking out his tongue, wriggling his hands behind his ears, all at Ben, in the most insulting manner.

'I've told you to go away, Frankie.'

'This is our room as well as yours. Some day it'll be only ours, and then you won't be allowed to come in at all without our permission.' This was a reference to the re-allotting of bedrooms that would follow May's marriage and Dilys's leaving home with her. The girls' bedroom would be left empty. Ben, as the eldest of the remaining children, was to move into it, by himself. He looked forward to the time: then at least he would be allowed to shut his eyes when he wanted.

'And until then we just kindly let you share this room with us,' said Frankie.

'Go away, I say!'

'A third part of it, exactly – to look silly in, with your eyes shut!'

Frankie was goading Ben; Ben was becoming enraged. It was all more unbearable than Frankie knew. Ben was not allowed even a dog so small that you could only see it with your eyes shut, because he was not allowed to shut his eyes.

At least he was bigger and stronger than Frankie. He became tyrannical. 'Get off that bed and go away – now!'

Frankie said, 'You're just a big bully.' But he *was* smaller and weaker, and he had the responsibility of the white mouse. He got off the bed – carefully, because of the mouse – and went away.

Ben felt only depressed by his unpleasant triumph. He was at last alone, however. He shut his eyes: the dog Chiquitito sat at the end of the bed. . . .

Suddenly Ben was sure in his bones that he was still being watched. He opened his eyes a slit. There seemed no one. The pigeon was staring through the glass – but not at him. Ben opened his eyes altogether to follow the direction of the bird's gaze: below

79

Paul's bed lay Paul. He had been going through his stamp-album, but now he was watching Ben with curiosity.

'Spying on me!' Ben shouted with violence.

Paul rolled out of reach of his clawing hand, and said: 'I wasn't! There was nothing to spy on, anyway. You were just lying there with your eyes shut and a funny look on your face.' But he scrambled out of reach of Ben's fury, and fled. Ben locked the bedroom door after him, although he knew that he had not the least right to do such a thing. He shooed the pigeon off the window-sill. Then, with a sigh, he composed himself upon the bed once more to shut his eyes and see the dog Chiquitito in real peace. . . .

Almost at once Paul came back, having fetched Frankie. They rattled the doorknob and then chanted alternating strophes of abuse through the keyhole. Frankie ended by shouting, 'You're not fit to have a white mouse, let alone a white rat!' Their father came upstairs to see what the noise was, and made Ben unlock the door. Then his mother called them all for tea. That was that.

So, as Ben was clearly never going to see enough of his dog in the privacy of his own home, he began to seeks its companionship outside. He discovered the true privacy of being in a crowd of strangers.

In a Tube train, for instance, Ben could sit with his eyes shut for the whole journey, and if anyone noticed, no one commented. He felt especially safe if he could allow himself to be caught by the rush-hour, and on the Inner Circle Tube. The other passengers, sitting or strap-hanging or simply wedged upright by the pressure of the crowd, endured their journey with their eyes shut – you see them so, travelling home at the end of any working-day in London. Like them, Ben kept his eyes shut, but he was not tired. And when the others got out at their various stations, he stayed on, going round and round on the Inner Circle – it was fortunate that Mr Blewitt never knew of it – and always with his eyes shut. No one ever saw what he was seeing: a fawn-coloured dog of incredible minuteness.

If Ben were sitting, he saw the dog on his knee. If he stood, he looked down with his shut eyes and saw it at his feet. The dog was always with him, only dashing ahead or lingering behind in order to play tricks of agility and daring. When Ben finally left the Tube train, for instance, the Chihuahua would play that dangerous game of being last through the closing doors. While Ben rode up the Up escalator with his eyes shut, the Chihuahua chose to run up the Down one, and always arrived at the top first. Only a Chihuahua called Chiquitito could have achieved that – and in defiance of the regulation that wisely says that dogs must be carried on escalators. This dog exulted before its master in deeds which would have been foolhardy – in the end, disastrous – for any other creature. On all these occasions the dog's coat was black, as it had been for the encounter with the thousand wolves.

On buses, the Chihuahua sprang on or off when the vehicle was moving, as a matter of course. (Ben trembled, even while he marvelled.) But its greatest pleasure was when Ben secured the front seat on the top deck, and they went swaying over London to-gether. Ben had always loved that; and all the things that Ben liked doing in London, the dog Chiquitito liked too.

Ben would walk to the bridge over the River, rest his elbows on the parapet, and shut his eyes. There was the dog Chiquitito poised on the parapet beside him. The parapet was far enough above the water to have alarmed a dog such as Tilly, but not this much smaller dog. Without hesitation, it would launch itself into the void, and, in falling, its tininess became even tinier, until it reached the water, submerged, and came up again, to sport in the water round unseeing crews and passengers on river-craft.

Then Ben whistled softly and briefly. At once the swimmer turned to the bank with arrow-swiftness, reached a jetty, leaped up the steps, ran under a locked gate (any other dog would have had at least to squeeze through), and disappeared from view. A moment later the dog trotted back on to the bridge, to where Ben waited.

Once Ben used to wonder what a Mexican Chihuahua thought of the greasy, filthy London Thames after the wild, free rivers of its native country. But nothing of the smell, dirt, noise, traffic, and other roaring dangers of London daunted the Chihuahua. It seemed to take London for granted. It never even cocked an ear when Big Ben boomed the hour.

One day Ben noticed a small silver plate on the dog's collar: an address-plate. Here he read the name of the dog and the name of its home city, as on the back of the lost picture. But the name of the home-city had changed:

CHIQUITITO

LONDON

CHAPTER II

A CHRISTMAS EVE TO REMEMBER

BEN BLEWITT was just an ordinary boy with an unsurprising character and abilities – except for his ability to see a dog too small to be there. Unlike the Chihuahua, he had never been a daredevil; he was inclined to be rather slow and cautious. Perhaps for that very reason he took a particular delight in the dog's feats.

And still he had to have more and more of his dog's company. In school, now, he would often sit with a studious-seeming hand shielding his shut eyes, watching the dog Chiquitito as it leapt from desk-top to desk-top in a kind of wild, impertinent sport.

He heard only absent-mindedly the voices of the

other pupils and of the master. His attention was entirely upon his Chihuahua. Look! the creature was almost flying through the air now, in its daredevil leaps – and under the teacher's very nose, too!

'What have I been saying, Blewitt?'

Ben opened his eyes, and did not know. He never knew the answers to questions in class nowadays. Angry schoolmasters reprimanded him and punished him for inattention. Still he persisted in watching his Chihuahua whenever he could. He had never been a brilliant boy in school; now he seemed a stupid one. He knew it, without being able to care. He supposed that his termly report would not be a good one, perhaps not even passable. His father would be severe; his mother would grieve. Still he must watch his Chihuahua.

'Blewitt – Blewitt, I say! Open your eyes – or is there something wrong with them?' And by now the question was not sarcastic. Word went privately from the form master right up to the Head, and then went privately right down again to Mrs Blewitt, who was asked to call upon the headmaster one afternoon. The Head said that he did not wish to worry Mrs Blewitt unduly. Her son's odd behaviour recently might be due to no more than faulty eyesight, possibly to be corrected by the wearing of glasses. The Head's suggestion of an immediate and thorough testing of the boy's eyes, merely as a precaution, should not alarm Mrs Blewitt.

At once Mrs Blewitt was alarmed, and more than alarmed. She felt some foreboding that no oculist could dispel; but she took Ben to have his eyes tested.

The oculist's conclusion was that Ben had excellent eyesight; he could read even the tiniest test-lettering. Outside again, Ben said to his mother, 'I told you that I could see even the smallest things. As a matter of fact, I know I can see things so small that other people can't see them at all. There's nothing wrong with my eyes.'

'Then why do you sit with them shut so often? I've caught you at it at home; they say you do it at school. You're not short of sleep.'

'My eyes are tired.'

'The oculist is positive that they're not.'

'They're not tired *by* seeing things,' Ben said carefully. 'They're tired *of* seeing things – the same old things – great hulking things, far too big – big, dull, ordinary things that just behave in the same dull old way –'

'If you mean your teachers and the other boys, you are speaking very rudely indeed!'

Ben sighed. 'I didn't mean to. I was really thinking of what my eyes would rather see, that's all.'

'But, Ben dear, just tell me *why* –'

'I've told you.'

It was Mrs Blewitt's turn to sigh. She gave up; but from now on, secretly and fearfully, she watched Ben.

The dog Chiquitito was becoming a continuous presence for Ben. When the boy's eyes were shut, the dog was there, visibly; and when his eyes were open, the dog still seemed present – invisibly. Ben felt it there – knew it was there, now loyally and alertly beside him, now with its active and bold spirit speeding it to engage in some new and extraordinary exploit. Always the dog was either before

Ben's eyes or in his mind. His mother, watching him
when he did not know he was being watched, saw
him with eyes open but vacant – abstracted and ab-
sorbed, she supposed, in some inward vision. She told
herself that the boy slept well, ate well, and admitted
to no worries; but she was uneasy.

Meanwhile, autumn was settling into winter, with
fog.

In the country, the fog was white. Old Mr and Mrs
Fitch watched it rise from the ploughed fields round
the house and thicken from the direction of the
river. Grandpa watched the solid Tilly fade and
vanish into it, when she slipped off on one of her
private expeditions down the driftway; and she
would come back with the hairs of her coat beaded
with moisture. Grandpa himself went out as little as
he could; but the damp seemed to seep indoors to
find him, so that he began to complain of aches in
the back. Old Mrs Fitch said that his back must be
ironed with a hottish iron over brown-paper. She
could not do it herself, nowadays, but Mrs Perkins
came in from next door and – under Mrs Fitch's
direction – gave him this relief.

Then the two of them settled by the fire again, and
Tilly was allowed to lie on the rug between them,
where she groaned and twitched in her sleep, dreaming of summer and of other dogs, no doubt. And the
soft whiteness of the fog drifted up to the window,
pressed against the glass, and looked in on them.

In London, the fog that came up from the River
was whitish, too; but later, another fog began. No
one could say where it was coming from, but everyone could taste its tang in the air, and feel the oppres-

sion of its descent. The sky seemed to thicken, and at the same time to come lower – so low and heavy, it looked as if it would soon need propping up with poles. And then, at last, one day when all indoor lights were on by three o'clock in the afternoon, the sky fell and lay upon London in a greasy, grey-yellow pea-souper of a London fog.

People were saying that soon you really might as well walk in London with your eyes shut. Ben tried it, going slowly, of course, along the pavements of streets he knew well. The Chihuahua, now lemon-yellow in colour – perhaps for better visibility – went slightly ahead. It semed to know the streets as well as Ben did, going not too fast, but with an unerring sense of direction. Ben followed with absolute trust; he gave himself into the Chihuahua's care.

All landmarks and familiarities melted into fog. Pedestrians fumbling their way home overtook even-slower-moving vehicles; as the fog thickened, they would come up abruptly against cars abandoned half on the pavement. By that time, the buses, having reached the safety of their garages, refused to venture out again.

The streets filled with fog and emptied of traffic and people. Nobody in London went out unless he had to – except for Ben. In the evening he slipped from the house to roam the streets with the dog Chiquitito. Fog enclosed them in a world of their own. They owned it, and they owned each other. For, if Ben were the Chihuahua's master, the dog itself possessed Ben's eyes and thoughts, directed his actions.

At last the fog cleared away into sparkling cold

weather in time for the very beginning of the Christ-
mas rush. The Blewitts began to get ready for their
Christmas. May was knitting hard to finish a pullover
for Charlie; Mrs Blewitt was gathering things for a
Christmas hamper to go to Granny and Grandpa;
Christmas cards and parcels had to be posted early to
Mrs Blewitt's brother in Canada; and soon all the
Blewitts were busy making or buying presents for
aunts, uncles, cousins, and for each other.

All except for Ben. Usually, at Christmas, he
would join with May and Dilys or with Paul and
Frankie in giving presents. This year, May and Dilys
thought he must be joining with Paul and Frankie;
and Paul and Frankie thought he must be joining
with May and Dilys. He was doing neither, nor was
he preparing to give presents on his own. Ben had
regretted the passing of the fog, and he simply could
not be bothered with the coming of Christmas. He
cared for another thing.

This year, Mr Blewitt said, their family Christmas
must be rather quieter than usual – certainly less expensive – because of May's wedding so soon afterwards. Plans for the wedding were already mixing
with preparations for Christmas. May had come out
into the open with her ambition for a page-boy at her
wedding. There was a terrible scene when Frankie,
who had been making multicoloured paper-chains
and paying no attention, realized that they wanted
him. Paul, knowing that he himself was too large for
the part, laughed so much that he fell over on to the
heap of paper-chains, to Frankie's double fury. Dilys
stood by May; Mr Blewitt stood by Frankie. Mrs
Blewitt seemed to waver between the two sides but

finally came down on Frankie's by reminding them all of a little cousin who might act in Frankie's place. The boy was only five, hardly old enough to object or even to realize into what he was being led, and Mrs Blewitt was sure his mother would agree. She fetched a recent photograph of the child. May and Dilys said that he looked sweet; Mr Blewitt said that with those curls he would be useful as either page or bridesmaid. Paul stopped laughing at Frankie, and they both went back to the paper-chains.

To all this Ben was as if deaf and blind; none of it – Christmas or wedding – concerned him.

This was the last Christmas for the Blewitts as just one family – before May Blewitt became Mrs Charlie Forrester. So Mr Blewitt had decided on a special family treat: he would take everyone up to the West End to see the decorations and lights and the shops and to have tea. He would take them on Christmas Eve itself – he had that day off instead of Boxing Day.

This was just the kind of interruption to his thoughts and visions that fretted and wearied Ben. He did not want to go with the others, and he said so to his mother. But Mrs Blewitt was determined that her husband should have the pleasure of seeing the whole family enjoying his treat. Ben was not ill; he had nothing else to do (no one knew of those un-bought, unmade Christmas presents); he *must* come; he *must* enjoy himself.

The West End on the afternoon of Christmas Eve was as Ben had known it would be: people – people – people; and lights – chains of twinklers and illumina-tions of fantastic design slung to and fro across the

main streets. And people – people – people; and shop-
windows in which objects glittered frostily or shone
with coloured lights or turned and turned for the
ceaseless attraction of the passing people – people –
people. So many people pressing and passing that Ben
lost his sense of a Chihuahua with him; and yet he
never dared to close his eyes to look for it, since so
many people were always telling him to keep them
particularly wide open. As he blundered unwillingly
along, strangers said, 'Look where you're going,
sonny!'; and his father said, 'Look sharp and keep
with us, boy!'; and the rest of the family told each
other and him, over and over again, 'Look!', or 'Just
look there!', or 'You must just look at that!'

When at last they queued up for their tea, Ben
hoped to be able to take a quick glance at his Chihuahua; but he found his mother looking at him, and
he dared not shut his eyes. When they sat down to
tea, she was opposite to him, and he felt her eyes still
upon him with a subdued anxiety. He must wait for
some later opportunity.

On the bus on the way home the whole Blewitt
family secured the two seats just inside the door,
facing each other. They sat three a side, with Frankie
on his father's knee, and laughed and talked across
the gangway. Only Ben sat silent, and Mrs Blewitt
watched him, and he knew that she watched him.
His eyes ached with the effort of keeping open when
they wanted to shut – to *see*. He was tormented by
the longing to see his dog, that must be on the bus
with him at this minute. Surely it was. As the bus
passed Big Ben and then over the bridge, the dog
must recognize a favourite scene. While Mr Blewitt

was still ringing the bell for their Request Stop, the dog – with all the daring of a Chihuahua – would be leaping off the platform of the moving bus. Now it must be waiting for them on the pavement. Now it must be trotting ahead of them as the family began to walk the rest of their way home. Now it must have stopped for them to catch up at the traffic-lights, where they had to cross the road.

The lights were changing to green, and the traffic was beginning to move forward. The Blewitts, know-ing that they must wait, bunched together, talking again of the afternoon. 'Mother!' said Frankie. 'Did you see the toy fire-engine – but did you see it? Did you?' He pulled impatiently at her sleeve, because she was looking over his head, watching Ben.

Ben stood a little apart from the rest of his family, with his back to them. He was facing squarely on to the road, so that only passing drivers might see that at last he was closing his eyes.

He was sure that the Chihuahua was at his feet. He turned his shut eyes downwards and – with over-whelming joy and relief – saw it. The dog's colour was black. The intrepid creature looked up at him for an instant, then sprang forward to cross the road among the streaming traffic; and Ben followed it.

A moment can last – or seem to last – a long time; and two moments must last twice as long. For the first moment Ben was simply following his dog Chi-quitito. The roar of the moving traffic – broken now by the sharper sound of brakes – was nothing to him. Only, there was a woman's voice screaming his name, 'Ben!' It was his mother's calling him back – oh! but it was surely too late – to safety. The syllable of her scream pierced to Ben's tranced mind and heart. It opened his eyes.

In the second moment he thought that, with open eyes – eyes that see the things that all eyes see – he actually saw the dog Chiquitito. He saw the Chiquitito that had been his companion now for so many weeks; he also saw the Chiquitito that had been worked in wool long ago by the nameless little girl in the white dress; and he also saw no dog – that is, the no-dog into which the other two vanished like one flame blown out, into nothingness. And the last dog he was master of: no-dog. He had no dog.

In that same, second moment, a car with screeching brakes hit Ben a glancing blow that flung him forward towards a van whose driver was also stamping on his brake and wrenching at his wheel. As the vehicles came to a standstill, Ben fell to the road between them.

The boy lay unconscious, bleeding, one leg unnaturally twisted. Mrs Blewitt was not allowed to take him into her arms, as she tried to do, lest he had some internal injury which movement might make worse. A policeman came. An ambulance came. The men very carefully loaded Ben Blewitt on to their stretcher and put him inside. His parents went with him to the hospital.

The other Blewitts went home under May's care. Frankie and Paul were sobbing, and Dilys comforted them, but she was crying too. They left the crowd of spectators staring at Ben's blood on the road, and a policeman taking down names and addresses and other information from drivers and other witnesses. The driver of the car that had hit Ben was a grey-haired woman. She could not answer the policeman's questions for crying into her handkerchief and repeating over and over again: 'But he walked straight into the road with his eyes shut – *with his eyes shut*!'

And the van driver supported her evidence. 'He was walking like a sleepwalker – or like a blind man – a blind man being led – you know, a blind man following a guide-dog.'

CHAPTER 12

MR FITCH SPELLS ALOUD

BEN had a broken leg, three broken ribs, a broken
collarbone, and concussion. The hospital thought
that there were no internal injuries; the bones should
mend well, especially at Ben's age; but the concussion was severe.

He was a long time recovering consciousness. During that time his mind wandered in a kind of no-
man's-land between waking and dreaming. Through
this land he went in search of his dog. All the places
he had ever known or read of or heard of or even
dreamed of mixed together, and mixed with the dog
he sought. At one time he was with Young Tilly on
the driftway bridge over the River Say, and she
would not dive even from that little height into the
river because she was afraid. She ran away, howling,
and there was a shadow over the bridge. Ben thought

95

it was cast by a storm-cloud, until, looking up, he saw a Mexican volcano that he had never noticed before, towering up at the other end of the driftway. Tilly had gone, but there were three other dogs, and he seemed to hear Granny Fitch's voice saying, 'A promise kept three times over!' For the three dogs were all his. One was the dog embroidered in wool by the little girl with the ribboned white sleeve: Ben could see that – strictly as in the picture – the dog had only one side to its woolwork body and only one eye, of a black bead. The second dog was the dog so small that you could only see it with your eyes shut, and it was black. The third was no-dog.

Then, always, something terrible began to happen. The volcano would begin to erupt; and, instead of running away from it, the dogs – led by the coal-black Chihuahua – ran towards it, and Ben ran after them. He gained on them – he almost had them. But then the first two dogs vanished, leaving only no-dog: Ben had no dog. He began to scream, and when he listened to his voice he recognized his mother's, screaming 'Ben!', as she called him back to safety.

Or perhaps the three dogs led him towards fierce hungry men with toasting-forks; and, of the three dogs, all vanished but no-dog: Ben had no dog. Then he began to scream, and it was his mother screaming and calling him back: 'Ben!'

Or perhaps the three dogs sped across a snowy plain towards a thousand packs of wolves, and suddenly two dogs vanished, leaving no-dog: Ben had no dog. And the calling back began again, 'Ben!'

Over and over again the woolwork dog vanished and the black-coated Chihuahua vanished and Ben found that he had no dog, and heard his mother calling his name. But gradually the visions and terrors became – not less confused, for they always remained that – but less continuous. They dimmed, too, as firelight does in a room into which sunshine enters.

His mother said 'Ben' instead of calling it. She spoke it quietly and very carefully, as though trying to wake him without startling him. Ben opened his eyes, and there she was, in her hat and coat, sitting by his bed in the hospital. She saw at once that his eyes were open and looking at her, and she put out her fingers to touch his cheek so that he should know that she was quite real, and that he was getting better. Then Ben closed his eyes again for a while.

Christmas Day was over without Ben's ever having known it. The Blewitt family had hardly noticed it at all, anyway, because of his lying unconscious in hospital. Drearily, too, they had decided that May's wedding must be put off, and Charlie Forrester, with May crying on his shoulder, said that he understood and that it was no use people getting married when they felt so miserable.

But then the hospital promised that Ben would fully recover, even if his recovery took some time; and a postponement of the wedding would really be very awkward, for all the guests had been invited and the arrangements made. Granny Fitch, for example, was sending Grandpa up to London – an expedition he had not made for many, many years. And the mother of the curly haired little cousin had already written that he was beginning to ask for his hair to be cut short like other boys' and she did not know how much longer she could manage to keep him looking as a page-boy should. Taking everything into consideration, Mrs Blewitt thought that May should have her wedding at the proper time, even if Ben could not be there; and Mr Blewitt muttered that, in some ways, Ben was a lucky boy to be in hospital.

May smiled again, and Charlie looked relieved; and Ben, when he was asked, said that he did not mind. So the wedding would take place on the day fixed, after all.

The only difference to Ben was in his being visited. Since he first went into hospital, his mother had never failed to come daily. But now she warned him that the house would be full of guests on May's wedding-day and that she really could not be sure of managing to slip away. She promised that someone else of the family would come in the afternoon, and she would try to come in the evening, if she possibly could.

A day without a visitor at all would have been very dull. There were only two other occupants of Ben's small ward: a boy who had to lie on his back and spoke very little, and a child – a baby, really – who stared silently at Ben through the bars of his cot. There was a window, but from Ben's bed one had a view only of sky. On the day of the wedding the sky was a wintry blue – the New Year had been cold but fine, so far.

The morning passed, and then the early afternoon, and at last Ben's visitor came. Somehow he had not expected Grandpa to be the one. Old Mr Fitch was wearing not only his blue suit but a blue hat as well, in honour of his grand-daughter's wedding. He took his hat off as he sidled into the ward. He managed with difficulty as he was also carrying a bunch of very short-stemmed snowdrops and a large Oxo tin tied with string.

'Well, boy!' Grandpa whispered. He tiptoed up to Ben's bed and put the snowdrops on the bedtable. 'Just a few – the first – from up the driftway. Picked 'em myself early this very morning.' He put the Oxo tin with them and tapped it. 'Six. Your granny says you're to tell the nurses not to mix 'em up with shop ones for the other patients, and they're to boil them a good five minutes, being new laid. You like a runny yolk and hard white.'

Grandpa then sat down on the visitor's chair, put his hat under it, and his hands on his knees, so that he was comfortable. Then he looked round at the boy in the bed, the boy in the cot, and at all the ward.

'What was the wedding like?' Ben asked. Grandpa turned back to him and remembered that Mrs Blewitt had told him to entertain Ben by describing the wedding-party. He went through the guests – Forresters and Blewitts and Fitches. The Fitch relations had outnumbered the other two put together – Bill Blewitt was an orphan with only one sister, anyway. Then Grandpa went on to the food and the drink.

Ben listened languidly. He stared as he listened, wondering at the oddity of his grandfather being here, in the middle of London, instead of in Castleford, or Little Barley, or at the driftway. Sometimes Grandpa paused to look round him, as if similarly surprised, even alarmed. When a nurse came in, he got up in a fright, nearly knocking his chair over, and treading on his hat. She smiled at him, made him sit down again, and began attending to her cot-patient.

To put his grandfather at ease, Ben asked, 'How's Young Tilly – and Granny?'

'Your Granny's as well as can be, and Tilly – ' Grandpa's moustache widened into a smile. Then he glanced at the nurse, who was now putting Ben's snowdrops into water. He dropped his eyes; he coughed artificially.

'How's Tilly?' repeated Ben.

'Poor bitch,' said Grandpa, without raising his eyes. 'She's not so well.'

His words and manner were so evasive that Ben knew something was up. Suddenly he remembered Tilly vividly – saw her, in his mind's eye: liver-and-white, curly haired, fat, frolicsome, and – although she was called Young Tilly – getting old. Old for a dog, that is; but Ben did not know exactly how old, and he did not know at what age a dog such as Tilly might be expected to die. 'Is she – is she very ill?'

'Not ill at all, exactly.' Grandpa glanced round at the smart young nurse, who impressed and frightened him, and then looked directly at Ben. He curved his hand round his mouth to speak a private message. As Mr Fitch wrote with such difficulty, he always supposed that others would be as easily confused as himself by the spelling of words. 'She's going to pea-you-pea,' he confided.

'P – U – P?' Ben repeated, not understanding for a moment; but the nurse, pausing at the foot of the

bed, exclaimed, 'Pup – have puppies! Now, isn't that nice! What breed will they be?'

Grandpa was flustered, but answered, 'The bitch is mostly spaniel, ma'am, but what her puppies will be like, we daren't say.' He turned to Ben: 'You remember that Toby you saw in the Codlings' canoe once? He's likely the father, as the time before, and he's mostly terrier.'

'Spaniel–terrier puppies – how very nice!'

'Puppies!' Ben said wonderingly.

'Aye, and us all thinking that sly bitch was past having puppies ever again! When they're born, you must come and see them, Ben.'

'There, Ben!' said the nurse. 'Whatever could be nicer?' She went out to fetch something.

'Puppies....' said Ben. Not dogs you could see only with your eyes shut; not dogs you could see only one side of, because they were worked in wool; not no-dogs. Real dogs, these – little flesh and blood and fur dogs – Tilly's puppies. He could not help saying, sadly, 'I wish...'

His grandfather picked up his hat and looked intently inside it, but seemed not to find there any suggestion of what he should say. He turned the hat round several times, and at last remarked, 'Your dad was saying this very day, over a piece of wedding-cake, that he thought you'd given up this idea of a dog in London. He said it was just impossible for you to have a dog where you live.'

'That's true,' said Ben. 'Just impossible to have a dog – even the smallest dog – impossible to have any size of dog at all.' And because he was remembering the one size of dog – the wonderful dog – that he had mistakenly thought it would be possible to have, and because he was still weak from illness, a tear went slowly down each cheek.

His grandfather saw the tears and looked away. 'You must come and see those puppies before they grow so big that we have to get rid of them. Your granny won't have 'em about the place longer than she can help.'

Ben tried to rally himself. He asked, 'Doesn't she like Tilly's having puppies?'

'Like? There's not much she can do about it. Your gran's a woman to reckon with; but, then, Tilly's female too. She's been a match for your granny this time.' Grandpa laughed at the joke of it; but Ben did not feel like laughing, and the nurse, coming in again, said he looked tired now. Grandpa took the hint and stood up, gripping his hat. 'Your granny said I was most particularly to hope you were better and give her love and say you're to come and stay as soon as you can, because country air is what you'll need.'

'There!' said the nurse.

'Thank you,' said Ben. His grandfather went, the nurse showing him the way out. And Ben turned his face into the pillow and – observed only by the little boy through the cot-bars – wept for a dog he could never have. That evening, when his mother slipped in for a few minutes with a piece of May's wedding-cake, Ben told her of Granny Fitch's invitation to stay, but not about Tilly's puppies.

For some time after the wedding, Ben had to stay in hospital. But he began to have more visitors, and not all from his family. The elderly woman whose car had knocked him down could hardly be counted even an acquaintance. Ben knew that he should apologize to her for the accident, admitting that it had all been his fault; and he did so. She began saying something about his walking into the road with his eyes shut, but then burst into tears. Ben tried to comfort her, but she continued to cry into her handkerchief. She left him a box of chocolates.

Then a policeman came. He sat with his helmet off, by Ben's bed, talking in a hushed voice. When Ben said that he was sorry and that the accident had been his fault, the policeman gently said, 'Yes.' He left Ben with a copy of the Highway Code – although nowhere in that is there any warning against trying to cross the road with your eyes shut.

Sooner or later, Ben knew, his mother would question him about his strange action on that terrible Christmas Eve. She would have connected his behaviour then with other behaviour, reported from school or observed by herself. In her anxiety she would press him for an explanation. He wanted to explain, but knew that he must not: his accident and May's wedding had been enough trouble to the family without reviving his old longing for a dog. And, unless he began by speaking of that, he could never explain.

At last, the question : 'Ben, dear, I want you to tell me something. On Christmas Eve, why were you trying to cross the road with your eyes shut?' He fobbed his mother off with some half-truth about aching eyes on that afternoon. 'But, no, Ben tell me. . . .' He could not, because he must not.

However, when she cried a little, in a kind of despair, he went so far as to tell her one thing clearly : it would never happen again. He promised. With this simple but absolute assurance Mrs Blewitt had to allow herself to be satisfied.

Never again would Ben close his eyes to see a dog too small to be there: that dog had vanished at the traffic-lights on Christmas Eve, just as the woolwork dog had vanished one day on British Railways. Those two dogs gone, he was left with a third – no-dog: Ben had no dog.

CHAPTER 13

A TRIP FOR BEN'S BONES

MRS BLEWITT had been taken with the idea of
Ben's going to his grandparents as soon as he was
well enough. The hospital had suggested their convalescent home by the sea, but that sounded un-
homely and bleak to Mrs Blewitt, especially at this
time of year. And Ben wanted to go to the country,
he said.

To begin with, Ben would need to have breakfast
in bed and other attentions which old Mr and Mrs
Fitch could not be expected to undertake. So, first of
all, he would come to his home from hospital. Mrs
Blewitt began to get ready for him the bedroom that
had belonged to May and Dilys.

Mrs Blewitt was glad to be busy and particularly
glad to welcome Ben home at this time. She missed

May and Dilys more than she had ever foreseen in the excitement of the preparations for the wedding, the wedding itself, and the good-byes afterwards. Now there was no one to talk to about the affairs that particularly interest women and girls. Soon after the wedding, at tea-time, Mrs Blewitt had been about to speak of the Spring Sales, when she stopped herself with a cry: 'What's the use! With a houseful of men!' Mr Blewitt, Paul, and Frankie gazed at her dumbly, helplessly; and May and Dilys, in North London, were so far away.

Ben's return only made one more man in the house, but at least he was a convalescent – someone she could fuss over. In the morning, when Mr Blewitt had gone to work and the younger boys had gone to school, Mrs Blewitt would slip upstairs to Ben's bedroom and talk with him before starting her housework; and Ben was glad of company, after all, in that large, new room all his own. He had no particular use for solitude nowadays.

Mrs Blewitt would bring Grandpa's letters upstairs to read aloud the bits that concerned Ben's coming visit. The last letter had a postscript: Mrs Blewitt studied it, baffled. 'I really can't think what it means, Ben, except that it's a message of some kind to you.'

'Let me see.' Ben read, in hurrying capitals: 'TELL BEN T PUPED (9).' He felt an emotion which he at once controlled. 'It must mean that Tilly has pupped – had nine puppies.'

'Well!' said Mrs Blewitt. 'Fancy! What a surprise!' She thought a moment, and then looked at Ben anxiously, but his face was expressionless.

'Do you think – ' he began slowly, and his mother

at once dreaded that he would want the impossible – to have one of the puppies in London. 'Do you think that I ought to tell Granny about losing the picture, when I go to stay?'

'What picture?' His mother had ceased to think of the woolwork picture soon after she had heard of its loss. She had never connected the picture with any dog that Ben might even impossibly hope to have.

'The picture of the little girl's dog called – called Chiquitito.'

'Oh, that!' Mrs Blewitt considered carefully. 'I don't think you really need to tell Granny, because after all the picture was given to you for your own – it was yours when you lost it. And telling Granny may make her sad, because the picture was a present to her from Uncle Willy. But, on the other hand, she's quite likely to ask you about the picture some time, and then, of course, you'd have to tell her. So, on the whole – yes, if I were you, I think I'd tell her before she asks.'

'I didn't think of all those reasons, but I did somehow think that I should have to tell her.' Ben sighed.

'Don't let Granny guess that the picture was never any good to you.'

'I won't.'

The day came for Ben's journey into the country. His mother was coming with him to Castleford on a day excursion ticket, partly to see that his bones travelled safely, and partly because she always tried to manage one of her day trips to her parents between Christmas and Easter. Besides, she had a great deal to talk over with her mother.

The train reached Castleford in a fine February

drizzle. Old Mr Fitch was waiting on the platform, with some shopping as usual, without Young Tilly, but with a large umbrella instead.

'We shan't need that, Pa,' Mrs Blewitt said, after kissing him, 'because we're going by taxi.'

'By taxi!' cried Grandpa. 'Why, whatever will your ma say!'

'Just this once, because of Ben's leg and ribs and collarbone. Bill gave me the money for it.' Mrs Blewitt insisted. In the splendour of a taxi, the three of them drove from Castleford to Little Barley and beyond and bumped cautiously up the driftway to the Fitches' front door.

They were, of course, much earlier than they would have been if they had waited to take the bus, and Granny Fitch was not expecting them. She was still in her wrap-round overall dress, and had been having a little sit-down in front of the fire. She had fallen asleep.

'Ma!' Mrs Blewitt called from the front door; and Mrs Fitch woke with a start and in some confusion of mind, so that – simply and solely, without time for thought – she saw her daughter. 'Lil!' she cried, and Lily Blewitt ran forward into her open arms. Ben hung back in the doorway, watching, feeling forgotten and odd for a moment, as he saw his own mother become the child of *her* mother.

Then Mrs Fitch held her daughter from her, adjusted her spectacles, and peered sharply at the large-faced clock. 'But you certainly didn't come by the bus.'

'We hired a car,' Mrs Blewitt said.

'*Hired a* – Joe!'

'It was Lily would do it,' Grandpa said hastily.

'But the expense!'

'Bill paid for it, Ma.'

'I don't care who paid for it,' said Granny; 'and you probably tipped the driver.'

'Bill gave me the money for that, too. It was all because of Ben, you know, Ma.'

'Ah, Ben. . . .' Granny shifted her attention to Ben, who now came forward to be kissed. Then Granny, forgetting the taxi at least for the time being, bade Grandpa come in, and not let all the warmth out of the open door, and put the umbrella into the scullery, open if it were wet, furled if it were dry – which it was, but Grandpa was given no chance of saying so.

Grandpa did as he was told. As he went, he took from the corner of the kitchen-range a chipped enamel bowl from which rose a faint, warm, gravy smell. He saw Ben watching, and winked at him. Ben quietly left his mother and grandmother talking together and followed Grandpa into the scullery.

'Where are they? Where is she?'

Grandpa put the umbrella away, ran a little cold water into the dog-stew to cool it, set it on the floor, and answered: 'The puppies are in the old sty down the garden, but Till's just outside now, if I know her.'

He opened the back-door, and there was Young Tilly waiting in the shelter of the porch. She came in with a preoccupied air – no more than an unsurprised wag of the tail even to Ben – and made straight for her dinner. She ate quickly, in large mouthfuls.

'She needs to eat well, with those nine greedy pups,' said Grandpa.

When she had finished, Tilly sat down, looked at Ben, moved her tail again, lay down, and seemed to go to sleep.

Ben was disappointed and a little shocked: 'Shouldn't she go back to them again, at once?' he asked.

'They're all right by themselves for a bit, and she knows it,' said Grandpa. 'She's a good mother, but she's not one of these young, fond ones. She feels a bit old for pups, I daresay, and she wearies of them. Then she stays here.'

'Shall we go and look at Tilly's puppies?' said Ben half to Tilly herself. She only opened one eye at her name, and did not respond. Grandpa, too, said that they had better postpone going until the rain had eased off a bit. Besides, Granny was calling to them both, asking whether they expected to have their dinners carried to them in the scullery.

Mrs Blewitt, with Grandpa's help, got the dinner, while Ben was made to rest on the sofa. Granny, after leaving full directions, went upstairs slowly but determinedly to change into the black silk dress which she had planned to wear for this visit.

They had hot-pot for dinner, followed by pancakes made by Mrs Blewitt. They were old Mr Fitch's favourite, but he could not manage the tossing. Then they had cups of tea and slices of home-made cake that Mrs Blewitt had brought with her. And then the table was cleared and Mrs Blewitt spread out the wedding-photographs.

Granny pored over them: the bride and bridesmaid and page and bridegroom – 'I only hope he wears well' – and the guests. Grandpa took pleasure in pointing out any representations of himself – especially one which showed him wearing his hat. 'It wasn't wasted, then,' Granny commented.

'And this – ' Mrs Blewitt ended up with a snapshot photograph. 'This is the house they're living in – May and Charlie, and Dilys, too, of course. They have a flat on this floor.'

Granny looked. 'Well, I suppose that's how people have to live in London.'

'But they're lucky, Ma; and I'm as pleased as they are about it, of course, except that – well, if only they weren't so far away!'

'That's what comes to you, when children grow up,' Granny said.

'And it isn't just that I miss them: they're still so young – it's Dilys I think of most, of course. They live in a nice place, really they do – hilly, so it's lovely air, for London; but it's all among strangers, and so far from us. . . .'

Granny was listening closely, nodding. Mrs Blewitt said, 'Really, I've been thinking – ' Then she glanced at Ben, who was also listening. She looked out of the window. 'It's stopped raining, Ben. Wouldn't you like a little stroll outside?'

Ben jumped up and looked expectantly at his grandfather. But first of all Grandpa had been looking at photographs, and now he seemed to be forgetfully settling down to a nap. Ben reminded him: 'Couldn't we go down the garden for a bit?'

'Ah?' said Grandpa, drowsily.

'Joe, Lil and I want to talk, so you'll take the boy now and show him those dratted puppies.'

And Grandpa and Ben went.

CHAPTER 14

PIG-STY IN THE RAIN

THEY went to see Tilly's puppies. She did not want them to go; but, if they were going, she knew that her duty was to go too, and to go ahead. She went briskly but with a waddle, being incommoded by the swinging heaviness of the milk for her puppies.

The sty had once belonged to some pigs, but was now perfectly clean, with plenty of fresh straw on the concrete floor and a special lamp suspended low from one corner of the roof to give a gentle heat. Beneath this the puppies had all crawled and crowded together, and lay sleeping, a large, thick, sleek blob of multiple puppy-life.

Grandpa and Ben stooped under the corrugated iron roof of the sty and sat down on upturned buckets padded with folded sacking. Tilly had gone in front of them, but now she stood a little to one side and behind, very quietly. 'She's not keen on their knowing she's here at all,' said Grandpa. 'She knows they'll be squeaking and pushing after her milk, once they do know. And they're none of 'em starving.'

Grandpa plunged his fingers into the heap of puppies and brought one out at random. He dropped it into Ben's cupped hands. It just filled them – as a full grown Chihuahua might have done, Ben thought. 'Chiquitito!' he said softly.

Ben felt perfect happiness. He shifted the puppy into one hand – which it slightly overflowed – in order to be able to stroke it with the back of the forefinger of his other hand. Then he put it down and gently picked up another. The puppies varied in size, but all were sleek-coated and fat. Their colours varied, too: liver-and-white, like Tilly herself, black and white, or mostly black, or mostly brown. One was as brown as if a gravy tureen had just been emptied over him; another was all-over brown, too, but lighter.

Tilly watched Ben handling her puppies, but she did not seem to mind. If he held a puppy out to her, she began licking it with thoroughness. This was her habit with any puppy that came within easy reach – although she was so unsystematic that she might spring-clean the same one several times running and leave others untouched.

When Ben had held each puppy in turn, he wanted to see Tilly with them all. 'Come on, then, old girl!' Grandpa coaxed; but Tilly groaned, wagged her tail, and would not budge from her distance. At last, with Grandpa always pushing her gently from behind, she reluctantly got up and waded forward into her little sea of puppies. At once it broke round her in eager, ruthless welcome. Puppies cried and snorted and pushed and trod each other down in a soft, squashy stampede to reach her teats. Tilly gave herself up and subsided among them. She licked some convenient ones, but otherwise paid no attention – as they paid no attention to her lickings. Over the pulsing bodies of nine hard-sucking pups, she looked at Grandpa and Ben, patiently, mildly, and she yawned.

'Well, there you are, boy,' Grandpa said, as though the interest were exhausted. It was, for him. He said he was going back to the house, before the hard rim of the bucket ended by giving him sciatica, and anyway it was beginning to rain again.

Ben stayed on, alone, to watch. He liked being in the sty with the rain sounding on the iron roof just above his head, and the dim, warm light from the lamp, and the smell of straw and puppies. He liked being alone with Till and her feeding puppies. Sometimes he could be of help. He brought home a puppy that had strayed or been pushed beyond Tilly's tail and was whimpering for lost food. He righted another puppy that – still sucking – had somehow got turned upside down. He unburied another – always sucking – that had been quite trampled under and out of sight by the others.

He could bear to leave them only when he had to – when his mother called from the house for tea. He stood up to go, and at once Young Tilly heaved herself up and began to walk carefully away from her motherhood. Most of the puppies, satiated with milk, had already given up sucking in favour of sleep. The few remaining fell from their mother like over-ripe pears – which by now they rather resembled in shape. Almost without complaint they crawled back with the others into the puppy-heap under the warmth of the lamp.

Ben went in to tea with Tilly at his heels. Granny did not notice the dog because she was looking at the boy. She and his mother had both stopped speaking and were considering him in a way that made him know they had been talking of him. 'He certainly looks as if he could do with better air all the time,' Granny said, as if concluding some discussion. The remark was senseless to Ben, and he forgot it at once. His mind and all his sensations were dazed, drugged, utterly overwhelmed by puppies. But the remark had been of importance, and helped towards important decisions of which Ben knew nothing until later.

After tea, Mrs Blewitt caught the bus back to Castleford and then the train back to London. That night, after Paul and Frankie had gone to bed, she said: 'I had a good long talk with Ma this afternoon, Bill, about things.'

'Things?' Mr Blewitt was listening to his wife but watching the television screen.

'You know, our being so far away from Dilys and May and her Charlie, and this house being really bigger than we need since they've gone – '

'Is it?'

'Yes,' Mrs Blewitt said firmly. 'Oh, and other things! Anyway, I've had half an idea in my head, and I told Ma this afternoon. She thought it was a good idea.' Mrs Blewitt began to explain.

Soon there was no doubt that Mr Blewitt was listening, with increasing amazement. He leaned forward, switched off the television set, and turned to face his wife.

'But, Lil, have you taken leave of your senses! First a street-accident, and then a wedding, and then – then *this*! You take after your ma for energy, Lil, and that's a fact! Are we never to be allowed any peace and quiet?'

Mrs Blewitt soothed him. This was only an idea; there was no need to take any decision yet. (Mr Blewitt leaned forward to the television-switch.) But the idea had many advantages. (Mr Blewitt sank back again with a groan.) She had seen those clearly this afternoon when she had talked things over with Ma. 'As Ma said, look what good it would do Ben, for one! He'd have better air – we all should!'

'I suppose it all comes down to this,' said Mr Blewitt. 'You and your ma have made a plan. So it's as good as decided.' Poor Mr Blewitt! He hated changes and moves.

CHAPTER 15

TO HAVE AND NOT TO HAVE

BEN was breathing a great deal of the sleepy puppy-air of the Fitches' pig-sty, for he visited the puppies several times a day; and he was feeling better and better.

During his stay, the puppies began to be weaned. Grandpa started by persuading them to drink cow's milk from a dish as well as – soon, instead of – Tilly's milk. None of the puppies was interested in cow's milk at first, and Ben's job was to accustom them to the idea. He planted them round the rim of the milk-dish, brought them back to it when they wandered away, lifted them out of it when they began paddling across, and gently pushed their muzzles into it. Gradually, in a muddled way, they gained a taste for the new drink, first by licking it off the coats of those who had fallen in, at last by lapping from the dish.

When they began to feed as fast-growing puppies, they made more mess in their straw, and Ben took on the job of cleaning the sty out regularly and laying fresh straw.

In their daily company, handling them often, Ben came to know each puppy well. He gave them their names, which Grandpa – who hadn't thought of names until Ben came – adopted. Two were Punch and Judy, because they resembled the Codlings' Toby in colouring; two others, coloured liver-and-white, were called Mat and Tilda, after Tilly (whose real name was Matilda); then there was Midnight, all black; and Cloudy, who could not make up his mind whether to be black or white or even a proper grey; and Spot – whose name needed no explanation once you saw him; and Gravy, an all-over dark brown.

That was eight, and now Ben's invention began to fail. About the ninth puppy there was nothing distinctive, unless perhaps he was the smallest – but he might grow out of that. His colour was like Gravy's only lighter. Ben, searching his mind for an apt name, stared at the puppy: 'He's brown . . .'

'A very handy name, too ' Grandpa said heartily. 'I like Brown.' And so – with Ben's acceptance of his grandfather's mistake – the ninth puppy was named Brown. Once he was called that, you could only wonder that he might ever have been called anything else.

Old Mrs Fitch had never seen the puppies – didn't want to, she said. She grumbled, too, at Ben's spending so much time with them – 'cooped up in a pigsty – what would his mother say?'

Ben heard from his mother regularly. In one letter

Mrs Blewitt reported a Sunday visit that the family had paid to May and Charlie and Dilys in their new home. She had thoroughly enjoyed a proper talk with her two daughters, and had come to the final conclusion that their district was the best in all London to live in. For one thing, it was so far from the river-fogs and damps of the Blewitts' part of South London. The air of North London was so pure, she wrote; but there! Ben was breathing fresh country air for the present, anyway. When old Mrs Fitch had had that read to her, she began sending Ben for afternoon walks along the driftway.

The driftway, smitten by winter, was cold, lifeless. It was hard to think of Grandpa finding even half a dozen early snowdrops there; he had known where to look. There seemed nothing now. Last year's grass lay rotting and tangled round the feet of melancholy, broken-armed skeletons of what might once have been cow-parsley, meadowsweet, teasel. The hedges were without leaves, so that Ben could see through them to the cold, raw earth of ploughed fields; and winds blew over the fields and draughtily through the hedges.

Ben trudged along because he had to, and Tilly – when she would come at all – followed spiritlessly, her head drooping. She did not fuss over her puppies, but her thoughts must always be with them.

They never went further than the driftway bridge over the Say. The river, swollen with winter waters, was fast-moving and dangerous-looking, and grey and cold. No one would want to bathe in that. The willow-tree beside which Ben had undressed was a bleak landmark in a desolate marsh.

Leaning over the handrail of the bridge, Ben felt a melancholy creeping over him, fixing him to this spot. There was, of course, no Mexican volcano in sight; but here he felt truly, as he had felt in his nightmares, that he had no dog. He had lost the woolwork dog; he had lost the visionary dog. He might tend and fondle Tilly's puppies but none of them was his. He named them for other owners; not one of them was his Chiquitito. He had no dog.

At last, Tilly, who had been sitting beside him on the cold, damp concrete of the bridge, got up and began plodding back the way they had come, unwilling to keep him company any longer. Ben turned and followed her. Dusk came by the end of the afternoon, and, as they neared home, they often saw the lit windows of the Yellow Salden bus as it passed along the main road. Ben could see the passengers inside looking out over the lonely, wintry landscape, glad that they were not there.

Then Ben, not even having the heart to call at the pig-sty on the way, went drearily in to tea. After tea he always read to his grandmother, his grandfather listening too. Then, bed.

Ben had been waiting for a good time, preferably when his grandmother was alone, to tell her of the loss of the woolwork picture. He chose a Sunday evening after his walk and after old Mr Fitch had gone off to the chapel-service in Little Barley. Ben was left to keep his grandmother company. He had been reading the Bible aloud; he broke off, and went on again at once: 'You know Uncle Willy's picture. . . .'

He paused, waiting; but his grandmother, who had

been listening with her eyes shut, did not open them now. Ben wondered whether she thought that this was all part of the Book of Jeremiah, or whether she had fallen asleep – but that was unlikely. Just as he was preparing to repeat what he had said, she opened her eyes. 'What happened to Willy's picture?'

'I lost it.' He told her when and where.

She said nothing.

'I'm sorry,' Ben said. 'I know it was a present to you from Uncle Willy.'

'And then a present to you, but you didn't take to it.'

'It wasn't exactly that, but – '

'You wanted a real dog.'

'Yes.'

'You still do.'

It was Ben's turn to be silent.

'That Joe should never have promised you a dog.'

'Please!' said Ben. 'It doesn't make any difference now, truly.'

'A promise was broken.'

Another silence. Ben wondered if he should go on reading aloud, but his grandmother did not ask him to do so. She had shut her eyes again. Perhaps she was really asleep this time.

Ben closed the Bible and put it aside. He glanced at the clock. Grandpa would be home soon, and then it would be time for bed. Always, before bed, he tried to slip out for a last look at the puppies. He was pretty sure that Grandpa guessed where he went, but not Granny. He glanced at her now and decided that she really was asleep. He tiptoed into the scullery and out through the back door.

He never hurried in saying good night to the puppies. He held each one separately, bending his face over it, saying its name: 'Midnight. . . . Tilda. . . . Cloudy. . . . Brown. . . .'

He became aware of some difference behind him, where the entrance to the pig-sty was. The flow of air from the outside was blocked by some body – a silent presence – in the doorway. For a moment Ben was frightened – too frightened to move or to show his awareness in any way. His grandfather would have hailed him, 'Well, boy!' at once – he always did; and the only other person it could rightfully be was his grandmother, but she never stirred out of doors in this weather, and in the dark, too.

But, looking out of the corner of his eye, Ben could see – just within the light from the lamp – a pair of black buttoned shoes and grey cotton stockings above them: this was his grandmother.

She was standing at the entrance of the sty – probably stooping to watch him. He did not know why she watched, and could only suppose that she would be angry with him for being here yet again, and so late. He waited for her to speak, and in the meantime went on fondling the puppies, pretending not to know that she was there.

But she did not speak. After a while there was a little squeaking sound from her shoes, which meant that she had turned away from the sty to go back to the house. Ben gave her plenty of time, because she would hobble so slowly, and it was dark. Then he followed. When he got indoors, she was sitting in her chair by the fire, with her eyes shut, as though she had never moved from it. Only, she was breathing a little heavily, and there was mud on the toe of one shoe.

Ben, not seeking trouble, sat down quietly, but then did not know what to do. He looked at his grandmother again, and found her eyes open and fixed upon him.

'Shall I go on reading, Granny?'

'To the end of the chapter, please.' He began to look for the place again. 'Ben, you were promised a dog. The promise ought to have been kept – kept properly. We ought to have done that. So, now, one of those puppies is yours by right.'

'Mine – oh!' For a moment Ben was dazzled by the amazing thought that he owned one of Tilly's puppies. Which? – for they would let him choose. He was indeed dazzled, for his mind's eye followed a rapid sequence of colours: liver-and-white, black and white, cloudy grey, dark brown, light brown – He stopped there because the puppy called Brown was the one nearest to Chiquitito-coloured. He would choose Chiquitito-Brown for his own, and together – he and this second Chiquitito, as small and as brave as the first – together they would roam London –

Then he remembered: if he were offered all the dogs in the world, he could not accept one. He could not keep a dog in London, where there was nowhere to exercise it, nowhere for it to run free.

His grandmother had been watching him – watching the expression on his face change from one moment to the next, with the change of his thought

'Yes, but – ' Ben said heavily.

'Yes,' said his grandmother. 'That's how things are,

and I'm sorry for it.' As she hated to wrap her meaning in politeness or irony or anything but its own truth, Ben knew that she was truly sorry. 'And now, boy, go on reading from the Book of the Prophet Jeremiah.'

CHAPTER 16

A VIEW FROM A HILL-TOP

HE was Ben's, then; and not Ben's.

He was not an extraordinary puppy as yet, and he was much darker than the true Chiquitito-fawn. Nevertheless, Ben hung over him, loving him, learning him, murmuring the name that should have been his: 'Chiquitito . . .'

Ben was there when Chiquitito-Brown barked for the first time. Standing four-square and alone, the puppy's body suffered a spasm of muscular contraction which released itself when he opened his jaws. The open mouth was just about the size to take the bulk of, say, a finger-end. From this aperture issued – small, faint, but unmistakeable – a bark. Then Chiquitito-Brown closed his mouth and looked

126

round, quivering back in alarm at the sound he had heard.

For the puppy, more like his mother than his heroic namesake, was not brave. That would have to come later, Ben reassured himself; and in the meantime – 'You're really Chiquitito,' Ben told him again and again, trying to teach him his new name and the new nature that went with it. At least the puppy was still very, very small.

Grandpa, of course, did not know of the renaming; but he guessed, from Ben's favouritism, which would have been the boy's choice among all the puppies. On the last day of Ben's visit, he asked: 'And what shall I do with Brown, since you can't take him back to London with you?'

'What will you do with the others?'

'Offer them round to the family – your uncles and aunties,' Grandpa said. 'And those pups that aren't taken that way – we shall sell 'em off if we can, give 'em away if we can't.'

'Then you'll have to do the same with him.' Ben held Chiquitito-Brown squirming between his hands for the last time. He put his face against the puppy's head, breathed his good-bye.

And, on the evening after Ben's departure, Grandpa squared up to the table and wrote round to the families offering a gift of a puppy to each. He did not bother to ask the family so far away in Canada, of course, nor the Blewitts themselves.

After some time he began to get the replies. Ben, at home again in London, heard that an uncle who had settled in the Fens, the other side of Castleford, would take one puppy – Midnight; and another –

Gravy – was going to the aunt who had married a man in Essex.

Ben laid down the letter which had brought this news, and thought: two puppies gone – that left seven to be disposed of, Chiquitito-Brown being one.

Ben, quite well again now, was back at school, thus altogether resuming normal life. He was never seen with his eyes shut in the daytime; he was never found in strange abstractions of thought. He was a perfectly ordinary boy again – only, perhaps, a little dispirited. But his mother was satisfied that the change to North London would work wonders in Ben, and in them all. For the Blewitt family were going to move house: Mrs Blewitt's idea had really been a plan, as her husband had grasped, and now it had been decided upon and would be carried out.

'But I've to be within reach of my job, mind that,' said Mr Blewitt. Mrs Blewitt pointed out that, for someone with Mr Blewitt's kind of Underground job, there wasn't much to choose between living towards the southern end of the Northern Line, as they did at present, and living towards the northern end of the same Line, as they would be doing.

'Yes,' said Mr Blewitt. Then he closed his eyes: 'But the upheaval – leaving somewhere where we were settled in so well.' Mrs Blewitt pointed out that the departure of May and Dilys had already unsettled them: the house had become too big for them. (Perhaps, if the Blewitts had not been so used to squeezing seven in, five would not have seemed too few in the space. Or perhaps they would not have seemed too few if Mrs Blewitt had not been thinking of the comfort of living nearer to her daughters.)

And besides, Mrs Blewitt went on, the *air* –

'I've heard enough about the flavour of that air,' her husband said with finality. 'If we go, we go. That's all there is to it, Lil.'

'We go,' Mrs Blewitt said happily, as though all problems were settled now. So the rest of the family were told. Frankie – who took after his mother, everyone said – was delighted at the thought of the excitement of removal. Paul only worried about his pigeon: he did not yet realize that birds can be as cordial in North London as in South. Ben said nothing, thought nothing, felt nothing – didn't care.

His keenest interest, but sombre, was in the news that Grandpa sent in his letter-postscripts. Old Mr Fitch was now getting rid of the rest of Tilly's puppies, one by one, in the Little Barley neighbourhood. Jem Perfect of Little Barley was taking one – Punch; and Constable Platt another – Judy. That left five, Chiquitito-Brown among them.

'It's only a question of time,' said Mrs Blewitt. 'If anyone can hear of the right kind of house or flat for us, it will be Charlie Forrester. He's on the spot; he's in the know. We only have to be patient.' She glowed with hope.

Another weekly letter came from the Fitches. 'Here you are, Ben,' said Mrs Blewitt, 'there's a message for you again.'

The postscript read:

TELL B MRS P TOKE TILDA

That meant that the Perkinses from next door had taken the puppy called Tilda. It would be nice for Young Tilly to have her own daughter living next

129

door. And that left four puppies, Chiquitito-Brown still among them. Ben suddenly realized that his grandfather must be keeping his – Ben's – puppy to the end : he intended to give him away the last of all. But, in the end, he would have to give him.

The Blewitts were going to look at a family-sized flat that Charlie Forrester had found for them in North London. It was a house-conversion job, he said, and wouldn't be ready for some time; but it might suit them. There was even a back-garden, or yard, nearly fifteen foot square. As the only viewing day was Sunday, all the family went.

There seemed nothing special about the district – just streets leading into streets leading into streets – or about the house itself -- just like all the other houses in all the other streets : Ben himself could not even dislike the street or the house, outside or in.

His mother was disappointed at it. 'Only two medium sized bedrooms, and a little box of a room where Ben would sleep.'

'I thought his present bedroom was too big,' said Mr Blewitt.

'But this is poky.'

'It would just take Ben's bed and leave him room to get into it, anyway,' said May, who had come with her Charlie. She was taking them all back to their flat for tea afterwards.

'Well, what do *you* think, Ben?' Mrs Blewitt asked.

'I don't mind,' said Ben. He was indifferent; and Paul and Frankie were bored – they were scuffling in empty rooms, irritating their father, whose nerves were on edge. He sent all three out of the house.

They wandered together from one street to the
next and so came to a road that was less of a side-
street than the others. The two younger boys pricked
their ears at the whirring and rattling sound of roller-
skates, and took that direction. Ben did not care for
the sport, but he followed the others – as the eldest,
he was always supposed to be partly in charge.

Boys and even a few girls were roller-skating in
zigzags down a wide, asphalted footway that sloped
to the road, with a system of protective barriers
across at that end. Paul and Frankie recognized this
as ideal skating ground, fast but safe. They settled
down to watch. Soon, Ben knew, they would try to
borrow someone's skates for a turn, and they might
succeed. Anyway, they would be occupied for some
time.

Ben went on, chiefly because he did not care for all
the company and noise. He climbed the sloping way,
crossed a railway bridge, and came out by a low
brick building. It was probably a sports pavilion, for
it looked out over a grassed space, part of which was
a football ground. To one side there was a children's
playground with a paddling pool and easy swings.
Asphalted paths skirted the whole open space, which
sloped steadily still upwards to a sky-line with trees.

Ben left the asphalt and struck directly up over
the grass towards the highest point in sight. As he
climbed he became aware of how high he must be
getting. He took the last few yards of the ascent
walking backwards to see the view in the direction
from which he had come – southwards, right over
London.

He thought that he had never seen a further, wider

view of London; and, indeed, there is hardly a better one. The extremity of the distance was misted over, but Ben could quite easily distinguish the towers of Westminster and even Big Ben itself. The buildings of London advanced from a misty horizon right to the edge of the grassy space he had just traversed. The houses stopped only at the railway-line. He could see the bridge he had crossed; and now he saw a spot of scarlet moving over it. That would be Frankie in his red jersey, and the spot of blue following him would be Paul. He could see them hesitate, quest-ingly, and then the red and blue moved swiftly in a bee-line to the children's playground. Well, that would certainly keep them busy and safe until May's tea-time.

Ben had reached his summit facing backwards – southwards, and he had looked only at that view. Now he turned to see the view in the opposite direc-tion.

There were buildings, yes, some way to the right and to the left, for this was still within the sprawl of London; but, between, there were more trees, more grass – a winding expanse.

So – it went on.

Ben stared, immobile, silent. People strolled by him, people sat on benches near him, no one ap-peared aware of the importance to Ben Blewitt of what he now saw. Even if the place were no bigger than it seemed on this first entry, it was already big enough for his purposes. *And it went on.* He had a premonition – a conviction – of great green spaces opening before him, inviting him. He felt it in his bones – the bones of his legs that now, almost as in a

dream, began to carry him forward into the view. Asphalted paths, sports pavilions, and all the rest were left behind as he left the high slopes of Parliament Hill for the wilder, hillocky expanses of Hampstead Heath.

CHAPTER 17

THE REAL QUESTION

OF course, being a Londoner, he had heard of Hampstead Heath, and several times recently Charlie, May, or Dilys had mentioned its nearness to their part of North London; but Ben had paid no particular attention. He had even been on the Heath once, years before, when he was very little. Mr and Mrs Blewitt had taken their three eldest children (Paul and Frankie were not yet born) to the August Bank Holiday Fair, held on part of the Heath. There had been merry-gorounds and coconut shies and crowds through which May and Dilys had dragged him, each holding one of his hands. That was really all he remembered.

This time there was no fair, no dense crowds of people : he was on his own on the open Heath.

For a while he would follow a path, never asphalted

or gravelled, never ruled straight to any plan. The ways across Hampstead Heath are mostly tracks that go where Londoners' feet have made them go, muddy in winter, dusty and scuffed in summer. Then he would cut across grass and through bushes to reach some point of vantage: there were no notices prohibiting it. The grass on Hampstead Heath is tough, tousled, wild, free – green and springy at the time of year when Ben trod it; later, brown and trampled and tired, longing for the repose of winter, whose damps also rot away the litter left by careless people. The trees and bushes on the Heath seem to grow where they themselves have chosen, and in irregular shapes comfortable to themselves. Ben liked them like that.

There are slippery slopes and potholes, which the wary avoid, for fear of twisting an ankle; but Ben was agile. There are marshy places in hollows, with no notices warning people that they may get their feet wet. Ben got his feet wet, and did not care.

He wandered up and down, round and round, farther and farther. He came to the slow, wide dip of heathland beyond which Kenwood House presents its bland front. He stared, and then turned away, and on. Wherever he went he saw people – plenty of people on such a fine afternoon; but the Heath is never overcrowded. The sun was hot for the time of year, and some people were even lying on the grass: elderly men on spread-out waterproofs, Sunday newspapers over their faces; young lovers in their embraces, careless of rheumatism from damp grass or dazzle from the sun. A mother sat knitting while her baby practised walking. A boy flew a kite. Children at play called to each other over wide spaces. And Ben saw

dogs – dogs that ran freely, barking without correc-
tion. You were not even sure to whom any particular
dog belonged until a distant shout recalled him.

Ben roved on, by a stretch of water and men fishing
in it and a public house beyond. Then he climbed a
slope up to a road and traffic – traffic that moved on
all sides of a pond where fathers and children sailed
boats. Beyond this a flagstaff and flag reared itself up;
and beyond again was more grass, with bushes, sloping away to more tree-tops. So the Heath still went on.

But Ben paused. From the feel of his legs, he knew
that he had come a long way, and he knew that the
time was late from the feel of his stomach, which
was empty for May's tea. Besides, he had seen enough
already; the place was big enough – vast and wild.
And it still went on.

He turned round, set off impetuously back, realized
that he did not know the way after all his indirect
wonderings, and then saw the keeper – the first he
had seen since entering upon the Heath. He must be
some kind of park-keeper, from his brown uniform
and the metal badge on the front of his hat. He had
just strolled up one of the paths and was now standing a moment, watching the people or nothing in
particular.

In the ordinary course of things, Ben would not
have asked his way of a park-keeper. He did not like
them. But now he wanted to lead up to a more important – a vital question which only a park-keeper
could answer with authority.

He edged up to him : 'Please!'

'Yes?'

'Please, could you tell me the way to get back?'

Ben described the railway bridge, the sports pavilion and playground, the grassy hill –

'You want Parliament Hill,' said the keeper, and pointed his direction out to him.

Ben thanked him, set off slowly, came back, and said: 'Please!'

'What is it now?'

But Ben lacked the courage for the real question. He invented a substitute: 'I wanted to know what flag it is up there – please.'

'It's our flag – the London County Council house-flag.'

'Oh. Why is it flying today?'

'We fly it every day, unless we fly the Union Jack instead. Anything else you want to know?'

Yes, indeed, if only he dared ask; but – 'No, thank you – no – at least, that is – what do you fly the Union Jack for, then?'

'Special occasions: anniversary of the accession of the Queen; Queen's birthday; Queen's wedding-day; birthday of Queen Elizabeth the Queen Mother; opening of Parliament –' He was slowing up in his list, eyeing Ben.

'Thank you very much,' said Ben.

Now or never: if he hesitated again, the keeper would decide that he was thinking up questions just to be impertinent. He would ask Ben why he didn't go home, now that he knew the direction. He would send him packing, with the really important question unasked, unanswered.

So, for the third time, and very quickly this time: 'Please!'

'Now, look here –'

'Please – *please*: can anyone take a dog on the Heath and just let him run free? Are there no rules saying that dogs mustn't do things?'

The park-keeper looked horrified. 'No rules – no by-laws? Of course there are by-laws! We can't have dogs getting out of control on the Heath.' As the keeper spoke, two dogs – one in pursuit of the other – tore up the path on which he was standing. He stepped slightly aside to let them pass, never removing his gaze from Ben.

'But how exactly must they not get out of control?' Ben asked.

'Biting people, mainly.'

Well, that was quite a reasonable rule: Ben began to feel cheerful.

'Mind you, there's one pretty severe regulation for some dogs. Have you a dog?'

It was the same difficult question that the librarian had once asked – difficult, now, in a different way. 'I *own* a dog,' said Ben; 'but I haven't got it.'

'What kind?'

Ben thought of Chiquitito-Brown, and of his parentage. 'It's difficult to say. You see –'

'Is it greyhound breed?'

Ben thought of Tilly and then of Toby; either of them might have some greyhound-blood coursing secretly in their veins, but on the whole – 'No, not greyhound.'

'Your dog's lucky. On Hampstead Heath greyhounds must wear muzzles.'

'And other breeds of dogs, and just mongrels?'

'Needn't. Provided they're kept under reasonable control, of course, as I've said.'

The same two dogs as before tore past again in the same pursuit, except that one was gaining on the other.

'And no leads?' asked Ben.

'No. I've told you: provided they're kept under control.'

A few yards from where Ben and the keeper stood, one of the two dogs had caught the other up, and they were now rolling and growling in a play-fight. Such an incident was beneath the keeper's notice. He said to Ben: 'Just remember, always under proper control on this Heath. And now cut along home the way I told you to go.'

Ben went running, light as air from the joy he felt.

He was very late for tea, of course. Everyone had finished, except for Paul and Frankie, who were being held back from the remains saved for Ben. Everybody was cross with him: Paul and Frankie for his having come back at all, the others for his being so late. He explained that he had been walking around and forgotten the time.

They resumed conversation, and, when he had a moment free from eating cold, butter-soggy toast, Ben asked about the flat seen that afternoon: had they decided to take it?

'Well....' said Mrs Blewitt.

In short, they hadn't decided. May and Dilys said it was a good flat, not expensive, especially for those parts; and Charlie said that if they didn't take it, someone else soon would; and Mr Blewitt said that they might as well move there, if they had to move at all. But Mrs Blewitt was full of doubts. The place was poky, for one thing.

'I didn't see anything wrong with it,' said Ben. 'You said that little room was poky, but I didn't think so. I'd like to sleep there: I like it: I like the house: I like where it is.' He wanted them to know; he wanted to do all that lay within his poor means: *'I'd like to live there.'*

'My!' said May; and Charlie said, 'You'll soon have a voice as loud and clear as Big Ben's!'

Everyone laughed at that; and Ben was glad that he had not spoken of wanting to live within reach of the Heath. They might have laughed at that, too. His family were not unsympathetic; but they would not see the overwhelming importance of living near the Heath. Paul and Frankie might have a glimmering of understanding; but not his mother and father. His mother wanted a flat or house comfortable for the family and easy to run; his father wanted somewhere handy for his job. Of course, they would enjoy going on the Heath occasionally – on fine Sunday afternoons for a family stroll, for instance. But Ben would be on the Heath every morning before breakfast, every evening after school, every weekend, every day of the holidays. The Heath was a necessity to Ben – to Ben and his dog, the second and no less wonderful Chiquitito, Tilly's puppy.

But nothing at all was decided yet.

There was only one more thing Ben could do to help forward his hopes. That evening, at home, he wrote a postcard to his grandfather: 'Please keep my puppy for me. Will write more later.' He posted the card on Monday morning; it would arrive with the Fitches on Tuesday.

On Tuesday Mrs Blewitt received a letter written

by her father, with a long message for Ben. No less than three of Tilly's remaining puppies had been disposed of: Judy, to the caretaker of the chapel in Little Barley; Cloudy to Mrs Perkins's mother in Yellow Salden; and Mat to a friend of Bob Moss's in Castleford.

That left only one puppy: Chiquitito-Brown.

'Chiquitito!' Ben whispered to himself, catching his breath at the narrowness of the shave; but he knew that he had been in time. His card must have crossed Grandpa's letter in the post. Grandpa would be warned by now.

That Tuesday morning old Mr Fitch read Ben's postcard aloud to his wife. Neither of them questioned keeping the puppy: it was Ben's. 'As long as he takes it away some day,' said Granny. 'That's all.'

'Well,' said Grandpa, 'it sounds to me as if he hopes to keep a dog in London, after all.' The idea gripped him: he smiled; his fingers tapped a cheerful beat on the postcard; he was brimming with optimism and happiness for Ben.

'All I hope is that he's not due for any disappointment,' said Mrs Fitch.

CHAPTER 18

'BRING MRZZL FOR JURNEY'

WHEN Ben had been much younger – and Frankie probably still did this; perhaps even Paul – he used to hold his breath when he wanted something badly. He held it, for instance, when they were passing a plate of cakes round and there was only one of his favourite kind.

Now, when he wanted something more than he had ever wanted anything else in all his life, he felt as if he were holding his breath for days on end – for weeks.

His parents could still not make up their minds to take the flat they had seen that Sunday. It was not exactly what Mrs Blewitt had hoped for, she said. On the other hand, she had to admit that other flats were usually more expensive, or less convenient, or farther from May and Dilys. She admitted all that; and the admitting made her incline increasingly – but still hesitantly – towards taking the flat. Slowly, slowly she was veering round to it.

Ben listened to his parents' discussions. He saw the way that things were going; but he could not be sure that they were going that way fast enough. For Charlie Forrester had said that if the Blewitts did not take that particular flat, then somebody else would, soon enough. The Blewitts would lose their chance, through indecision and delay.

So Ben held his breath. He would not allow himself to show emotion – almost, to feel it. He determined not to count upon having a dog; he would not hope for a dog – even think of a dog. Yet, equally, he could not think of anything else properly at all. The dog that he chased absolutely from his thoughts in the daytime stole back at night, into his dreams: Tilly's tiny, pale brown puppy, who was also the minute – the minimal, fawn-coloured, intrepid, and altogether extraordinary Chihuahua named Chiquitito. Ben called him by that name as, in his dreams, they roamed Hampstead Heath together.

Even when Mrs Blewitt came to her decision, and, after all, the flat had not been snapped up yet by anyone else, so the Blewitts could have it – even then, Ben hardly dared breathe freely. So much might still go wrong.

But when the date of house-removal was actually fixed, and Mrs Blewitt was altering the curtains to fit the new windows, Ben said: 'By the way, I could have a dog when we're living there, couldn't I?'

Mrs Blewitt stopped whirring the sewing-machine.
'Ben!'

'Really, I could!' Ben explained what his mother
had never realized – the closeness of the new home
to the Heath. He could exercise a dog properly,
easily, regularly; he himself would see to its feeding
and washing; he would see that it did not bring mud
into the house or leave hairs there – Ben over-rode all
objections to a dog even before they could be made.

'But, Ben!' said his mother. 'If you *can* have a
dog, I want you to. In spite of your granny's scold-
ing, we always had a dog when we were children. A
family of children should have a dog, if possible.'
Ben suddenly leaned over the sewing-machine and
kissed his mother. 'Mind you! You must talk to your
father, of course.'

And she went back to her whirring.

When Mr Blewitt came in, he saw the justice of
Ben's case: there was no reason why Ben should not
keep a dog in the part of London they were moving
to. But where would Ben get his dog, and how much
– on top of all the expenses of house-removal –
would it cost?

'Nothing,' said Ben, 'because Grandpa and Granny
have been keeping one of Tilly's puppies for me, just
in case. They'll give it to me as soon as I ask for it,
for a birthday present.'

'Your birthday's some way ahead yet.'

'Well, really, it would be for my last birthday.'

'And, although the dog will belong to Ben,' Mrs
Blewitt said, 'all the family will enjoy it.'

'As we all enjoyed Frankie's white mouse when it
last got loose – you especially, Lil.'

'Oh, no!' Ben said eagerly. 'It won't be like having a white mouse – truly.'

'I daresay not. Bigger, for one thing.' But, in spite of his sardonic speech, Mr Blewitt accepted the idea, as his wife had done; and Paul and Frankie eagerly welcomed it.

'What is your dog like?' Frankie asked. They had not seen any of Tilly's puppies.

'Very, very small.'

'When you last saw it, Ben,' said Mrs Blewitt. 'Remember that puppies grow fast.' But Ben paid no attention.

'Go on, Ben,' said Paul. 'What colour is it?'

'Brown – a lightish brown.' He hesitated, then said boldly: 'Well, really, a pinky-fawn.' That was the colour it must be – Chiquitito-coloured.

'Go on.'

'And it's very bold and brave.'

Mr Blewitt asked what Ben was going to call his dog. Again he hesitated (but not because he had not made up his mind), and at once the others began making suggestions: Rover, Plucky, Wagger –

'No,' said Ben. 'None of those. He's got his own name already.'

'Well, what?'

He knew that they would object, so he began, 'Well, Grandpa has been calling him Brown –'

'Sensible,' said Mr Blewitt.

'But his real name is Chiquitito.'

A hush fell. 'Chicky *what*?' asked Mr Blewitt. He did not remember – none of them did – that this had been the name on the back of the woolwork picture.

' – Tito,' said Ben. 'Chiquitito.'

146

'You can't call him that, Ben,' said Mr Blewitt. He meant that the thing was – not forbidden, of course – just impossible. 'His name is Brown.'

'Chiquitito,' said Ben.

Then they all pointed out to Ben what an un-handy, absurd, unthinkable name that was for a dog. They argued with him and laughed at him. He stuck by what he had said. In the end they gave up without giving way, and they forgot the dog for the time being. After all, it had been decided that Ben should not fetch his dog until after the house-removal.

The Blewitts moved house. When all the bumping and muddle and dust and crossness were over, and they were really settled into the new flat, Ben – with his parents' agreement – wrote to his grandfather and grandmother. He arranged to go down for the day to fetch his dog.

Ben travelled down to Castleford alone, on a day-excursion ticket. He took a carrier-bag of home-made cooking from his mother, and his father had bought him a dog's lead and a leather collar with a silver name-and-address plate on it. His grandfather had asked him to bring the lead and the collar, and he had also written at the end of his last letter: BRING MRZZL FOR JURNEY. This was a British Railways regulation for dogs; and Ben had bought the muzzle out of his own money, and been proud to do so.

'For a very small dog,' he had said.

'Bad-tempered?' the shopman had asked sympathetically.

'No. Just fierce when provoked.'

Now, carrying all these things, he stepped out of the train at Castleford; and there were his grandfather and Young Tilly waiting for him. No other dog; but his grandfather said at once: 'He's waiting at home for you.'

Nothing now – surely nothing – could go wrong.

Even the weather was perfect, and the hawthorn was already out along the driftway hedges as they walked up from where the Castleford bus had dropped them. The Fitches' little half-house was sunning itself, with the front door stopped open. Granny was sitting on a chair outside, very slowly shelling peas into a colander that glinted like silver in the sunshine.

'Well!' she said, as they came up; and almost at once a dog began barking. Ben saw him come bounding out from behind the back of the house, barking jollily. He saw that he was large – almost as large as Tilly herself – and coloured a chestnut brown.

The dog saw Ben. He stopped. He stared at Ben; and Ben was already staring at him.

'He's not used to strangers up the driftway,' Grandpa said softly. 'He never sees 'em. He's a bit nervous – timid. Call him, Ben.' Then, after a pause: 'He's your dog: why don't you call him to you?'

Ben said: 'He's so big, and brown – I didn't expect it.'

'Call him.'

Ben wetted his lips, glanced sideways at his grandfather, and called: 'Chiquitito!' His tongue tripped over the syllables: the name turned out to be terribly difficult to call aloud.

The dog had taken a step or two backwards. Ben called again. The dog turned round altogether and fled round the corner of the house, out of sight.

'*What* did you call him?' asked Grandpa.

But Granny knew. 'Why do you call him after Willy's dog?'

Not after Willy's dog, but Ben's dog – the dog so small you could only see it with your eyes shut: the minute, fawn-coloured, brave Chiquitito. 'Because he's going to be Chiquitito – he *is* Chiquitito.'

'He's Brown,' said Grandpa. 'You can't change a dog's name like that – it only confuses him. Besides,' – he used Ben's own emphasis – 'he *is* Brown. You can't change that any more than you can change his nature. Call him again, boy – call him Brown.'

But Ben's mouth had closed in a line of deep obstinacy.

CHAPTER 19

BROWN

CHIQUITITO-BROWN was playing with his liver-and-white sister, Tilda from next door. They chased and pounced and barked in the Fitches' little front garden. Tilly, their mother, lay in the sun on the front doorstep, her forepaws crossed, watching. Whenever one of the young dogs flounced too near her, she grumbled in her throat.

'They get on her nerves nowadays,' said Grandpa, '– puppies of that size and spirit. They know she'll stand no nonsense from them, but sometimes they over-excite each other and then they forget. Then Till gives a nip or two, to remind 'em. She'll do much better when there's only one to manage – when Brown's gone.'

Ben and his grandparents had finished their dinner,

150

and soon it would be time for Ben to take the afternoon bus back to Castleford. His grandfather was not accompanying him, but – of course – Chiquitito-Brown was. So far Ben had not spoken to his dog again, and had not even touched him. Gloomily, from the shadow of indoors, he had watched him playing in the sunlight with Tilda.

Now Grandpa called Chiquitito-Brown to him, and held him while he directed Ben to fasten the collar round the dog's neck. This was the first time that Chiquitito-Brown had felt a collar, and he hated it.

'You'll have to scratch his name and address on the plate as soon as you get home,' Grandpa said. 'Or you could do it here and now. It wouldn't take long for a boy with schooling to scratch "Brown – " '

'No,' said Ben; 'not here and now.'

Then Grandpa held the dog by the collar, while Ben clipped on the lead; and Chiquitito-Brown hated that too. He felt himself in captivity, and feared his captor – a stranger, whose voice and hands were without friendliness.

Ben, having said his good-byes, set off for the bus, but Chiquitito-Brown would go with him only by being dragged in a half-sitting position at the end of the lead. Tilly watched, unmoved; Tilda, in astonishment.

Grandpa called after them: 'Pick him up, boy, and carry him.' Ben muttered, but picked him up. The dog was heavy to carry, and he struggled; but Ben held him firmly, grimly. So they went down the driftway.

Granny shaded her eyes, looking after them.

'People get their heart's desire,' she said, 'and then they have to begin to learn how to live with it.'

The weather had been perfect in London, too: office-girls, blooming in coloured cotton dresses and white sandals, had eaten their mid-day sandwiches on park benches in the sun; City business men had ventured out for the whole day without umbrellas.

After her morning's housework, Mrs Blewitt had washed all the loose-covers, and pegged them out in the little back garden in the sun. Frankie and Paul had helped. Then it was dinner-time; and after that the two boys went out on to the Heath.

'Be sure you're back in good time for tea,' Mrs Blewitt told them. 'Remember, Ben will be bringing his dog; everyone will be here to see it.' Mr Blewitt would be back for tea, and May and Charlie and Dilys were calling in.

'We'll be back,' said Paul.

'We'll come back by the Tube-station,' said Frankie. 'We might meet him.'

They nearly did. Ben, coming out of the Tube-station with the brown dog under his arm, saw the two of them peering into a sweet-shop window – they had been dawdling and window-gazing for nearly half an hour. He knew, as soon as he saw them, that he did not want to meet them; not with this dog.

He slipped quickly round a street-corner, out of sight. Then he set the dog on the pavement, with the dry remark, 'We can both walk now.' But where? He did not want to go home – not with this dog.

The brown dog dragged reluctantly at the end of

the lead as Ben went up the asphalted way to Parliament Hill. On the top, Ben stopped and unfastened the lead. He felt a bitter relief that he was free of the dog now. He gave it a push: 'Go away then, you! Go!'

The brown dog, nameless because no longer named, moved away a little and then sat down. Ben tried to shoo him, but he simply moved out of reach and sat down again. Then Ben set off angrily over the Heath; the brown dog got up and followed him at a little distance. He knew by now that Ben did not want him, and so he did not really want Ben; but Ben was all he had. So the two of them went across the Heath, together but not in companionship.

Ben walked steadily, but he had neither destination nor purpose. He walked away the worst of his anger, and also what was left of the afternoon. There had been a good many people on the Heath when he first came, but now they were going home. It was late for their teas, or even time for their suppers.

He topped a rise and saw the landmark of the flagstaff by the pond. It was flying the Union Jack, and he remembered what the keeper had said: that the Union Jack was flown only to celebrate special days. Perhaps this was a royal birthday; but, seeing the flag, Ben was reminded that this was to have been a day of celebration for him. This was the wonderful day when he got his dog. As he gazed, the flag of joy began to descend. A keeper was lowering it: he detached it altogether, furled it, and carried it off; and that was that. Ben turned abruptly back over the Heath.

The flag on Hampstead Heath – Union Jack or

L.C.C. house-flag – is run down at sunset. The people who had not been drawn home to teas and suppers were now leaving the Heath because of chilliness and the fall of evening. Only Ben wandered farther and farther over the Heath; and the brown dog still followed him, but at a greater distance now, more laggingly.

There was solitude, stillness of evening, dusk that was turning the distant trees from green to black. . . . Ben slowed his pace; he sat down on a slope commanding a wide expanse. He was alone on the Heath now, except for the brown dog. The dog had sat down in the middle distance and was gazing at Ben.

Ben knew that, if he called the dog by the name he was used to, he would surely come; but Ben did not call him. And if he never called him, in time the dog would get up and wander away. He would be lost on Hampstead Heath – a nameless, ownerless, brown puppy-dog for some policeman to take in charge at last.

Did Ben care? He remembered his shame on the bus, when the brown dog sat trembling on his knee and the conductress had said, 'He needs a bit of cuddling; he's scared to death.' He remembered taking the dog into the guard's-van of the train at Castleford: he had been about to put on the muzzle, according to regulations, when he guard had said, 'Don't you bother with that. The animal looks more afraid of being bitten than likely to bite.' Ben had been humiliated; for the whole journey he sat at a distance, on a crate of chickens, his face turned away from the dog. Their arrival at Liverpool Street Station, the escalators, the Tube train – all of London that this dog first encountered terrified him. Ben had had to carry that heavy, trembling weight everywhere. He did so without tenderness or pity. He felt a disappointment that was cruel to him and made him cruel.

No Chiquitito ... Ben let his head fall forward upon his knees and wept for that minute, intrepid, fawn-coloured dog that he could not have. Other people had the dogs they wanted : the Codling boy and the Russian huntsmen and people he had seen on the Heath this very afternoon – and, long ago, in Mexico, the little girl in the white dress with long, white, ribboned sleeves.

But Ben – no Chiquitito. . . .

He shut his eyes tight, but he could see no invisible dog nowadays. He opened his eyes, and for a moment he could see no visible dog either. So the brown dog had gone at last. Then, as Ben's eyes accustomed themselves to the failing light, he could pick him out after all, by his movement : the dog had got up; he was moving away; he was slipping out of sight.

Then, suddenly, when Ben could hardly see, he saw clearly. He saw clearly that you couldn't have impossible things, however much you wanted them. He saw that if you didn't have the possible things, then you had nothing. At the same time Ben remembered other things about the brown dog besides its unChiquitito-like size and colour and timidity. He remembered the warmth of the dog's body against his own, as he had carried him; and the movement of his body as he breathed; and the tickle of his curly hair; and the way the dog had pressed up to him for protection and had followed him even in hopelessness.

The brown dog had gone farther off now, losing himself in dusk. Ben could not see him any longer. He stood up; he peered over the Heath. No. . . .

Suddenly knowing what he had lost – *whom* he had lost, Ben shouted, 'Brown!'

He heard the dog's answering barks, even before he could see him. The dog was galloping towards him out of the dusk, but Ben went on calling: 'Brown-BrownBrownBrown!'

Brown dashed up to him, barking so shrilly that Ben had to crouch down and, with the dog's tongue slapping all over his face, put his arms round him and said steadyingly, 'It's all right, Brown! Quiet, quiet! I'm here!'

Then Ben stood up again, and Brown remained by his side, leaning against his leg, panting, loving him; and lovingly Ben said, 'It's late, Brown. Let's go home.'

Other Puffins by Philippa Pearce

TOM'S MIDNIGHT GARDEN

Tom knew he was going to be bored and lonely in his aunt and uncle's home near the fens. And at first he was: until he made the strange and wonderful discovery that was too fantastic for anyone else to believe.

THE SHADOW-CAGE AND OTHER TALES
OF THE SUPERNATURAL

A collection of ten superb tales of the supernatural. Philippa Pearce takes the ordinary elements and objects of everyday life and invests them with powers that are overwhelming, threatening, and always disturbing.

WHAT THE NEIGHBOURS DID
AND OTHER STORIES

Eight beautifully told stories of blackberrying, a boy's stolen outing with his grandfather, and the tree the boys never *meant* to fell.

MINNOW ON THE SAY

'You rotten thief!' shouted Adam, 'That's my canoe!' Not a hopeful start for a friendship, you might think, but David and Adam did become friends and were inseparable for the whole of that summer. A summer made unforgettable with the *Minnow*, the river Say, their treasure hunt and the awareness that their special friendship might soon be interrupted.

THE BATTLE OF BUBBLE AND SQUEAK

Sid and Peggy and Amy adore the two gerbils, Bubble and Squeak, but their mother detests them. A ding-dong family battle results, and it's very uncertain which side has the more ammunition. Delightful illustrations by Alan Baker.

THE ELM STREET LOT

The gang of children who meet on Elm Street are always in on the action, whether it's tracking down a lost hamster or going on safari across the roof-tops.

THE WAY TO SATTIN SHORE

There is a mystery about Kate's family, but her family either knows nothing or will tell nothing. Her two elder brothers, her grandmother, her new friend Anna and her missing father all have a part to play in Kate's search to fit the jigsaw pieces of past and present to find a new picture for the future.

LION AT SCHOOL AND OTHER STORIES

A growling lion spends a morning at school and frightens the school bully; a little boy saves a mouse's life; and the magic Great Sharp Scissors cause havoc – just some of the surprises in store in this charming collection of nine lively tales.

WHO'S AFRAID? AND OTHER STRANGE STORIES

Ten marvellously varied stories make up this superb collection.

WOOF!
Allan Ahlberg

Eric is a perfectly ordinary boy. Perfectly ordinary, that is, until the night when, safely tucked up in bed, he slowly turns into a dog! Fritz Wegner's drawings illustrate this funny and exciting story superbly.

VERA PRATT AND THE FALSE MOUSTACHES
Brough Girling

There were times when Wally Pratt wished his mum was more ordinary and not the fanatic mechanic she was, but when he and his friends find themselves caught up in a real 'cops and robbers' affair, he is more than glad to have his mum, Vera, to help them.

SADDLEBOTTOM
Dick King-Smith

Hilarious adventures of a Wessex Saddleback pig whose white saddle is in the wrong place, to the chagrin of his mother.

A TASTE OF BLACKBERRIES
Doris Buchanan Smith

The moving story about a young boy who has to come to terms with the tragic death of his best friend and the guilty feeling that he could somehow have saved him.

Mossop's Last Chance

Michael Morpurgo
and
Shoo Rayner

Collins

Look out for more *Jets* from Collins

For Anna

First published by A & C Black Ltd in 1983
Published by Collins in 1988
20
Collins is an imprint of HarperCollins*Publishers*Ltd,
77–85 Fulham Palace Road, Hammersmith, London W6 8JB

ISBN 0 00 673008 6

Text © 1988 Michael Morpurgo
Illustrations © 1988 Shoo Rayner

The author and the illustrator assert the moral right to
be identified as the author and the illustrator of the work.
A CIP record for this title is available from the British Library.
Printed and bound in Great Britain by
Caledonian International Book Manufacturing Ltd, Glasgow

Chapter One

There was once a family of all sorts
of animals that lived in the
farmyard behind the tumble-down
barn on Mudpuddle Farm.

At first light every morning
Frederick, the flame-feathered
cockerel, lifted his eyes to the sun and
crowed and crowed, until the light
came on at old Farmer Rafferty's
bedroom window.

One... by one... the animals crept out... into the dawn... and stretched... and yawned and scratched themselves;

but no one ever spoke a word, not until after breakfast.

SSSHHH!

Mossop was a tired old farm cat who spent most of his day curled up asleep on the seat of Farmer Rafferty's tractor. Mossop paid no attention to Frederick – he got up when he pleased.

GUMLOP XL5

Farmer Rafferty was usually a kind man with smiling eyes, but like Mossop he was old and tired, and he ached in his bones in the wet weather. His animals were his only friends and his only family.

7

So, Frederick woke him up every morning.

Penelope and her speckled friends laid their eggs for him.

Auntie Grace and Primrose let
down their milk for him.

Upside and Down kept the pond
clear of weeds.

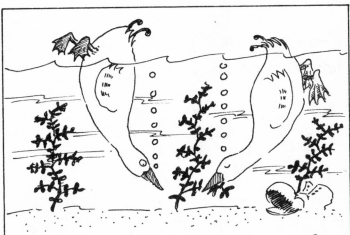

Captain carried him all around the farm to check the sheep.

Jigger, the almost-always-sensible
sheepdog, rounded up the sheep.

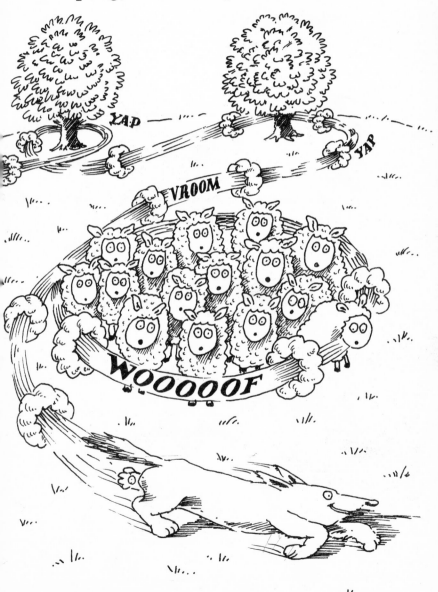

And Mossop was
supposed to catch
mice and rats.

Chapter Two

Farmer Rafferty always liked to sing as he worked. He sang in a crusty, croaky kind of voice.

-la-la- tiddley-um-pom pom-tiddley-um-pom pom-with a hey and a ho and a tiddle-iddle-po and-a- bing-bang-

That morning though, as old
Farmer Rafferty went into the
tumble-down barn to fetch corn
from the corn bin, he suddenly
stopped singing.

Oh!

The animals crowded into the barn
to find out what was the matter.
They found Farmer Rafferty
standing by the corn bin holding a
mouse up by its tail.

Have we or have we not
got a cat on this farm?'
said Farmer Rafferty
in the nasty,
raspy voice
he kept for
special occasions.

'We have,' said
Auntie Grace, the
dreamy-eyed
brown cow.

'She's right,' said
her friend Primrose,
who always agreed
with her.
'We have, and
he's asleep on
the tractor seat.'

'Having a catnap,'
sniggered Upside
or Down – no one
could ever tell
which was which.

'Having his beauty sleep,'
mumbled Egbert,
the greedy, grumbly
goat who ate anything
and everything.
'Not that it'll help
him much.'

'Fetch him,' ordered old
Farmer Rafferty.
'Fetch that Mossop
here. I have a thing
or two to say to him.'

But at that very same moment
Mossop wandered into the barn,
yawning hugely.

Chapter Three

Mossop knew, and everyone knew,
that Farmer Rafferty always meant
what he said. So the whole day long
Mossop hunted

through the hay barns,

in amongst the barley sacks

and along the rafters.

But it was
no use, his
heart wasn't
in it.

He hadn't caught a mouse for a long
time now –

he was too old,

too blind,

too slow,
and he knew it.
Everyone knew it.

That evening, tired and miserable,
Mossop made his way back to his
sleeping seat on the tractor.

'How many did you catch, Mossop?' asked Peggoty who lay surrounded by her piglets on top of the steaming dung heap.

Peggoty was a practical sort of a pig. She could add up – which was more than any of the others could.

'Catch anything, old son?' said
Jigger. Mossop shook his head.
'You've only got to say the word and
I'll give you a hand. Nothing would
give me greater pleasure.'

Captain's right, but thanks anyway Jigger. I'm too old.

Only got one eye and he doesn't work like he should.

And I'm slow as an old carthorse- begging your pardon, Captain. Anyway my claws are scarcely sharp enough to scratch myself.

As for my teeth- I've only got a few of them left and they're not much good anymore.

And all the animals – except one –
gathered round the tractor because
everyone loved Mossop.

But Albertine the goose sat on her
island in the middle of the pond,
and thought deep goosey thoughts.

Everyone agreed with Diana the silly sheep, which made her very happy.

'If Mossop can't see well enough,
then he should wear glasses,'
Auntie Grace said. 'That's what
Mr Rafferty does when he's reading.
He sees a lot better that way.'

But somehow that didn't seem to be
a good idea after all.

'If Mossop's claws aren't sharp
enough, we could sharpen them up
on Mr Rafferty's axe grinder,' said
Peggotty. 'Mr Rafferty's axe always
cuts better after it's been sharpened
doesn't it?'

But Mossop didn't think that
sounded much fun either.

I've got it!

clever clogs

Jigger said.
'Mossop could have false teeth like
Farmer Rafferty. After all, old
Farmer Rafferty always eats a lot
better when he's got them in. He
keeps them on the kitchen window
sill. I've seen them.'

So they all went off to look at
Farmer Rafferty's teeth.

34

But in the end they decided it
wouldn't be fair on Mr Rafferty to
take his false teeth, and anyway
they were far too big for Mossop.

We must think harder. There's always a way round everything. We must think.

And so they thought.

Even Egbert the goat
tried to think, but he
found that a bit
difficult, so he ate a
paper sack instead.

Everyone thought . . . except Mossop,
who was far too tired to do
anything but sleep.

Chapter Four

Out on the island in the middle of her pond Albertine sat all by herself and thought deep, secret, goosey thoughts.

She rose to her feet, flapped her
great white wings and honked until
everyone gathered at the water's
edge in high excitement.

When Captain had calmed them down, she spoke, and everyone listened. They knew that Albertine was a very clever goose.

Within minutes every mouse and every rat on the farm had gathered in the tumble-down barn.

Not going out with that Bill any more are you?
Course not, e's a rat.
Never knew there were so many of us.
What are we here for?
Yes, that's what I'd like to know.

Captain called the meeting to order, but the mice and rats all threatened to leave because Jigger was licking his lips.

Captain told Peggoty to sit on the dog's tail, just in case.

Albertine rose to speak.

Mice, rats and rodents all,
welcome.

And she told them her master plan.
They listened hard – except for one
little mouse who was playing chase
in the corner with Pintsize,
the tiniest piglet.

'How many of you are there?' asked Albertine politely, when she had finished.

'A hundred and twenty-five, Guv'nor, including the little 'uns,'
said the spokesrat, after proper consultations with the spokesmouse.

But Peggoty the practical pig knew better.

A hundred and twenty-six to be precise.

If you say so, Porker.

'Never mind. That will be quite enough for what I have in mind,' said Albertine, smiling.

Chapter Five

Mossop woke from his comfortable dreams on the tractor seat and saw the sun sinking through the trees. He knew the time had come for him to leave. Sadly he said goodbye to all his old friends.

Everyone was there to see him off
except for Upside and Down who
never missed their tea, not for
anything.

There were tears in Mossop's eyes as
he crawled under the farmyard gate
for the last time.

MUDPUDDLE FARM

la-la-doobie-doobie-ho-ho-jingle-langa-dingle-dangle-la-la-la-la-la

'Of course he won't,' said Captain.
'He's happy again now. You can
hear him singing.'

ie·doo· yum-tum-doobie·dah· doh·ray·me·fah·so·la·te·do·tiddle·um·pom·pom·

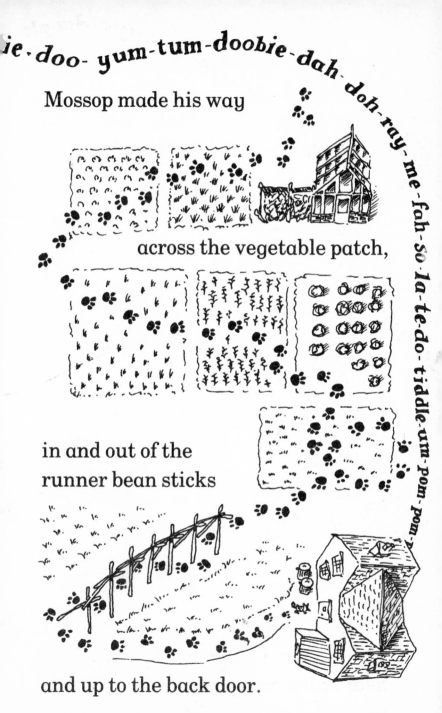

Mossop made his way

across the vegetable patch,

in and out of the
runner bean sticks

and up to the back door.

He pushed the door open...

and padded down the hallway...

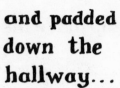

to the kitchen...

Where old Farmer Rafferty was sitting with his feet warming in the oven.

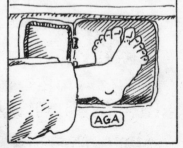

'Excuse me Mr. Rafferty, but
Captain says you wanted to see me
before I went,' said Mossop. 'I haven't
got any excuses Mr Rafferty.
I tried my best but I'm just not the
cat I was. It's age, Mr Rafferty,
old age. Well, I'll be on my way now.
Goodbye Mr Rafferty.

He took Mossop to the front
doorstep, and there in front of his eyes,
were row upon row of mice and rats.

They went right up to the goldfish
pond and round and back again.

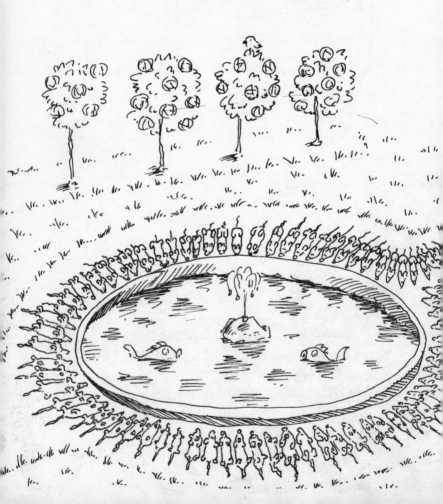

Mossop just stared and stared. He couldn't believe what he was seeing. Farmer Rafferty hung his old war medal around his neck.

Farmer Rafferty went back inside the house shaking his head and muttering to himself.

Then one by one they stole off into the darkness until they were all gone.

And in return, we keep our old Mossop that everyone loves and who's so old and slow he could hardly catch a cold.
Only one thing to say, no other cat beside me ever had better friends, and that's a solemn fact.

And he smiled as only cats can, yawned hugely, tucked his paws neatly under his medal, closed his eyes and slept.

The night came down, the moon came up, and everyone slept on Mudpuddle Farm.